Sam and Lollie sat at opposite ends of the boat, each trying to out-glare the other. Lollie felt she was winning.

Sam lolled against the bow, his arms hooked over the rim. He rubbed his dark, stubbly jaw. "Why the hell are you so mad?"

Lollie stuck her nose up and looked away. "Because I saved you!"

"So?"

She slowly turned back around. "So? So? Your backside isn't throbbing from riding one of those horned cows. You didn't have your hand crushed by some love-struck native girl. You didn't have mud flung at you and natives yelling at you."

"Are you through?" He hadn't moved, hadn't flinched, just sat there, grinning.

"No! I hate you, Sam. I really do."

"Then why did you save me?" He looked as if he were really enjoying this, which made her even madder.

"Because I thought *you* needed saving for a change!"

"I suppose I did. Come closer, Lollipop." He put his hand behind her head and pulled her up until she was just a kiss away . . .

_____

"Jill Barnett is a storyteller extraordinaire."

—Kathe Robin, *Romantic Times*

Books by Jill Barnett

The Heart's Haven
Surrender a Dream
Just a Kiss Away

Published by POCKET BOOKS

Just a Kiss Away

JILL BARNETT

POCKET BOOKS

New York   London   Toronto   Sydney   Tokyo   Singapore

An *Original* Publication of POCKET BOOKS

POCKET BOOKS, a division of Simon & Schuster Inc.
1230 Avenue of the Americas, New York, NY 10020

ISBN: 0-671-72342-1

First Pocket Books printing November 1991

10 9 8 7 6 5 4 3 2 1

POCKET and colophon are registered trademarks of
Simon & Schuster Inc.

Cover art by Melissa Gallo

Printed in the U.S.A.

To Jan Barnett and Kelly Barnett Walker,
Sam's for you.

Just a Kiss Away

1

Luzon Island, Cavite Province,
July 1896

The machete just missed his head.

And Sam Forester needed his mercenary head, preferably still attached to his body. He spun around. A guerrilla soldier stood a foot away with the long curved knife held high, ready to strike again. Sam punched him. A familiar crunch rang from his callused knuckles to his wrist. He shook the soreness from his hand and stared down at the soldier. The man wouldn't get up soon.

Sam picked up the machete and a moment later whacked a path of escape through the dense jungle bamboo. Where the growth allowed, he ran. Damp, pointed leaves of oleander scratched his face. Cut bamboo crunched under his feet. Wet, furry vines slapped at his shoulders and head. He raised the machete and sliced through a low, smothering ceiling of jade vine. All the while he could hear the others chasing him.

He burst into a clearing—no jungle to tangle him up, to hold him back. He pushed harder for the chance to gain a little ground. Running, running, pulse throbbing in his ears, he looked up. It was still dark. A virid canopy of giant banyans blocked out the afternoon sun. Ahead all he saw was a wall of green—the never-ending sea of tree-palm fronds and another dark wooden forest of island bamboo.

Mist steamed up from the humid ground as if the earth had cracked open over the seas of hell. A sweet, almost sickening smell hung like fog in the heavy air. The smell grew stronger, the leaves around him thicker. He ripped at them, driving on, harder and harder, tearing through a dense, twisted prison of sweet jungle jasmine. The rough, woody vines caught on his shoulder, scratched his arms and hands. They seemed to suddenly wrap around him like long grasping fingers, determined to slow him down, hold him, or trip him. But he couldn't trip. His escape depended on it. One fall and they'd have him. The guerrilla soldiers were that close. Though now he couldn't hear them over the pounding of his heart, he could still sense them, could feel them. They were hot on his heels.

Then he heard them right behind him, crashing through the underbrush. They panted. They swore. They stuck to him as if they were his own shadow, ever present. He heard the crack of their machetes—long, deadly, curved steel blades that splintered a path in the tall bamboo. With each chop, each hack of metal against splitting wood, the frenzied sound of pursuit ran an icy path of fear through Sam's bones.

Sweat streamed down his tanned face, under the black leather eye patch he'd worn for eight years, over the hewn angles of his life-weathered face, and trickled down through the dark shadow of a three-day beard. His perspiration mixed with the sweltering beads of humid, thick, steamy air that cloaked everything on this heaven-and-hell island.

His vision blurred from the wet air . . . or from the sweat; he wasn't sure which. He sped on, stumbling once when he couldn't see anything but a dark wet blur. He swabbed his good eye with a torn sleeve. His heart drummed in his ears. It was a beat to run by.

A new fragrance filled the air. The smell of risk.

A sudden blood rush sent him running faster, pounding

through the jungle. The bitter metallic taste of danger was so palpable, so real, that it swelled in his dry mouth with the same urgency of sexual impulse. His brink-driven breaths increased, faster, faster, until they burned in his chest like hot acid. His legs churned. His ridged thighs contracted. Mud suddenly swallowed his feet. He couldn't move.

Damn! He pulled forward, determined not to let dirt and water stop him. He fought on, dragging and slogging his legs forward. His boots felt like lead. The mud got deeper. It sucked at his thighs. His calves ached. The muscles in his forearms tightened. He trudged on and on. Now the mud was only ankle-deep. He broke free, still ahead of the men who chased him, and soon he had gained ground once again.

He ran. They pursued. It was a game in which he wavered on the edge, maybe even the edge of death. He was in his element. He tested the fates. He challenged the odds. And he gambled with his life, because the thrill was keener and so much more intense when the price of failure was so dear.

A white, wicked smile cut like lightning across his hard jaw.

Sam Forester lived for this.

Binondo District, Manila, 4:00 P.M.

The house stood tall, impressive by its sheer height. Prized white coral rock formed the walls around the city estate, walls that blocked out the strange foreign mix of cultures on the island, walls which also ensured that the area within was the way the owner wanted it—private, protected, and perfect.

There were two iron gates, one in front and one in back, embellished with an intricately carved grapevine motif, the exact same design used in the high transom windows of the house. Layer after glossy layer of thick black paint coated

3

the gates and the small iron grilles that crowned the many windows of the house. Not one spot of the ever-prevalent island rust marred the home of Ambassador LaRue, of the Belvedere, South Carolina, LaRues, owners of Hickory House, Calhoun Industries, and Beechtree Farms.

Within those precious coral rock walls there was no bustle, just a courtyard paved in rich burnt-red imported tiles identical to those that shingled the steep pointed roof of the house. No breeze fanned the dark glossy leaves of the crape myrtle trees that stood like proud sentries in that still courtyard. But beads of humidity spotted and sparkled from the thick climbing vines of Chinese honeysuckle that draped just like South Carolinian wisteria from the wrought-iron balconies of the second story.

A fragrance swelled through the courtyard, the rich, sweet smell of the tropics. Breaking the silence, a distant tapping drifted down from an open corner window in the second story. The tapping was slow, yet for some odd reason had the sound of impatience. It faded for a moment, then grew, faded, then grew, repeating over and over until it stopped with the suddenness of a gunshot.

Eulalie Grace LaRue plopped into a chair and rested her chin on a tight fist. She frowned at the tall clock ticking away its eternal minutes. It read four o'clock. She switched fists. That took up two more seconds. She sighed—a delicate, all encompassing southern sound, honed to perfection over the years by the genteel alumnae of Madame Devereaux's Ladies' Conservatory, Belvedere, South Carolina. That took up four whole seconds.

She glanced at the clock again, wondering how three hours could seem like years. But it had been years, she reminded herself, seventeen long years since her father left Hickory House, the ancestral home of the LaRues of South Carolina, for his foreign post somewhere in Europe.

Her mother, a descendant of John Calhoun, had died in childbirth when Eulalie was two, so her father had left her in the care of her five older brothers and a few trusted family servants. She could still remember how, days after

4

he'd left for his foreign post, she had asked her eldest brother, Jeffrey, where the place called Andorra was. He'd taken her hand and led her down the curved mahogany staircase to the giant dark oak doors of the room Eulalie had been forbidden to enter—one of the many things forbidden her because she was female. At the time, her five-year-old mind had dubbed her father's study "the forbidden room," but over the years there were so many "forbiddens" she had run out of terms.

On that particular day when her brother first opened the doors, she had balked, standing in the doorway twisting the blue velvet ribbons that held back her blond hair. He'd reassured her that it was all right for her to come into the room as long as one of her five brothers was with her. She could still remember the sense of awe with which she had tentatively followed Jeffrey into that huge, dark, wood-paneled room.

The room had seemed stuffy and tight and she'd felt a flush of heat that made her stomach tighten. She'd taken a few deep breaths and hardly had a chance to take in her surroundings before her brother led her to the tall globe that stood next to a massive desk. He spun the globe, an action that'd made her even dizzier until he stopped it, and showed her a small pink spot on the map. He told her that was where her father was.

She could remember staring at the small pink dot for the longest time. Then she'd asked if their father would be okay and when he would come home. Jeffrey had just looked at her for a long moment, then told her what a pretty little LaRue lady she was, with her big blue eyes and silky blond hair, just like their mother, and that little girls, especially the LaRues, needn't worry about such things. At that exact moment, Eulalie had been struck with the stomach ague, and she'd upchucked on the desk.

Jeffrey never answered her question.

And in the subsequent years, the question had still been evaded. Yet whenever a letter from her father had come, Jeffrey had always brought her into the study—first making sure she was well—to see the colored dots on that globe: from Andorra to Spain to Hejaz to Persia to Siam and, most recently, to the Spanish colony of the Philippine Islands. Somewhere around the age of fifteen, Eulalie had stopped asking when her father would come home, but she'd never stopped hoping.

All that hope and prayer came to fruition three months ago, when another letter had come to Hickory House. She had been arguing with her brother Jedidiah about whether she should be allowed to take the carriage to a special tea without a brother in tow—a request she knew was fruitless but was nonetheless worth the effort since it killed the boredom of that afternoon—when Jeffrey had called a family meeting. Jedidiah had immediately scowled at her and asked what the hell'd she done now.

Offended by his attitude, yet no less anxious to hear what Jeffrey had to say, she'd used every bit of Madame Devereaux's training and stuck her nose high in the air, grabbed her skirts in hand, and walked right past her scowling brother with all the ladylike grace of an organ hymn, for about five feet. . . . Then she'd hit a sour note. She'd tripped on the silk fringe of the Aubusson carpet and had reached out to grab the nearest thing—the mahogany smoking stand. They both went crashing down, along with her brothers' imported cigars and fifty-year-old French brandy.

Eulalie chewed a nail and frowned at the memory. It had taken three days to convince her brothers, especially Jed, that she could travel to the Philippines as her father's latest letter had requested. She could still remember the joy she'd felt when Jeffrey read the letter. Her father wanted her to come to the Philippines as soon as possible.

All five brothers had started arguing about it. Jeffrey said he still felt she was too young, but then, he'd always thought of her that way because he was fifteen years older than she. Harlan said she was too fragile, Leland claimed she was too naive, and Harrison said she was too helpless, but Jeffrey read on, and all those fears were put to rest, because her father had arranged for her to travel with a family, the Philpotts, Methodists who were on their way to save the heathens of the lower Philippine island of Mindanao.

Eulalie had been so excited. The excitement died the minute Jed had opened his mouth. Although eight years her senior, he was the most vocal of her brothers. He'd claimed that wherever she was, an accident would happen. Immediately five sets of blue male eyes had turned to the empty spot where the smoking stand had once stood. Then they'd all looked at her.

She'd claimed he'd never forgiven her for falling into that old dry well when she was three and he was the only one small and thin enough to be lowered down to save her. She'd said it wasn't fair to blame her for something that happened when she was three. For three days they argued, mostly Eulalie and Jed. He had rambled on, likening her to the opening of Pandora's box. He'd spouted off a parcel of things that could happen to her and made her sound like the plague. She'd argued she wasn't a jinx, as he'd said. Everyone knew there was no such thing. His only answer had been that he had the scars to prove it. So by Saturday night she was reduced to tears, deep sobs that swelled from her disappointed depths like the sea in a storm. She cried all night.

But God must have been on her side because it was the sermon on Sunday that freed a puffy-eyed Eulalie from Jed's claim. Pastor Tutwhyler picked that exact morning to talk about how superstitions were the devil's foolery, and a true Christian would never succumb to such ideas. She could have run from the LaRues' front pew and kissed the man the moment he'd started preaching. After the service she'd heard Mrs. Tutwhyler talking about how the Reverend was inspired by Belvedere's newest establishment, a palm reader from New Orleans. But Eulalie didn't care what inspired it. The sermon had done the trick.

And now, three months later, she was here, sitting in a bedroom of her father's home in Manila, waiting as she had for all those years. She'd arrived a day earlier than expected and her father was in Quezon Province, supposedly returning by noon today.

A knock sounded at the door and Eulalie looked up. Josefina, her father's housekeeper, entered, a piece of paper in her hand. "I'm sorry, missy, but your father's been delayed."

Her stomach dropped, and the air in the room seemed suddenly stuffy. She wanted to cry, but she didn't. She sagged back in the chair, disappointment making her shoulders droop far more than Madame Devereaux would have ever allowed. She took a deep breath, gave the ticking clock one last look, and did what she'd been forced to do for so many years. She waited.

The jungle thickened. The machete couldn't cut through fast enough. The bushes blocked Sam in. He dropped to the ground and crawled under the wood ferns, dragging himself over the hard exposed roots and clammy earth. Lizards shot past him. Several bamboo beetles over two inches long crept over from the thick humus that covered the jungle ground. Twigs and damp leaves caught on his hair, pulled at his eye-patch string. He stopped to unhook it, breaking off the green twig that had snagged it. A milk white sticky sap dripped from the broken vine. Sam rolled, dodging the liquid. It was a leper plant whose sap could eat an acid path through human skin in less than two minutes.

One deep relieved breath and he crawled farther. The vines and jungle seemed an endless trap. The sound of hacking still echoed from behind him. They hadn't reached the thick stuff. That knowledge sent him on, crawling over the damp ground, completely entrapped by twisted jungle cover. Sweat still eked from every pore in his body. It was sweat from the humidity and sweat from his nerves.

A slick black vampire snake with a bite more torturous and deadly than a stake through the heart slithered among the vines near his head. He lay still as stone. The sound of hacking knives and splitting bamboo broke from behind him. Without taking a breath, he watched the small reptile's glassy green stare. Luckily, the snake's thick-lidded eyes were turned away from him. Its jet-colored triangular scales undulated as it slid in a sinuous motion up, over, and through the tangled roots.

From behind him, the hacking stopped. So did Sam's heart. The men had reached the dense thicket of jungle. His heart took up the beat again, growing louder and louder. Between the snake and the soldiers, Sam was trapped.

The narrow street swelled with people—Spanish, Chinese, and native—a common island sight, unlike the frilly pink parasol that was the exact color of the Calhoun azaleas. It twirled like a brilliant silk top above the dark natives who milled in the busy street. The parasol paused, letting a Filipino family pass by. The woman turned and chided her daughter along. The daughter, a lovely girl of about thirteen, giggled and, in their native language, said something to her parents. The man and woman laughed, joined hands with the smiling daughter, and disappeared into the crowd.

Beneath the shade of that absurd little pink parasol, Eulalie turned quickly away, her stomach somewhere around her throat. It didn't do any good to wish for something that could never be, but she couldn't help feeling a little lonelier and a little sadder.

She picked nervously at her high lace collar, now little more than a damp bit of scratchy linen that had flopped over her mama's wedding cameo. She tried to block out the image of the family while rearranging the collar. Her fingers hit the cameo, paused, and unconsciously ran over the delicate carved contours of the brooch. She attempted to smile, but failed, swiping in agitation at her damp hair instead. She looked heavenward, at the sun, as if seeking the strength she needed to ignore her desire for the loving parents she'd never had. A long moment passed before she moved her parasol a bit closer to her head, an attempt to block out the heat of that withering tropical sun.

Her expression pensive, she gave a small sigh for what could never be, and she walked through the Intramuros, where the old walled sections still protected the inner city of Manila. She went out one of four dark gray-stone arches and into the outlying northern streets, heading for the marketplace. Josefina said the Tondo market was a busy, teeming place where she could bide some of her time until her father returned from the interior that night. She had been so nervous and anxious that she'd spent the morning pacing and watching the tall clock in the salon. Finally she'd chewed one nail to the quick before she decided that the housekeeper was right.

Parasol twirling, she stepped up on a primitive walkway and continued along, her small, squat heels tapping a hollow sound like a bamboo marimba, only slower, for a lady never hurried. Instead, she glided, just as Madame Devereaux inbred in her girls, imagining the yards of skirts as sails, moving around her in a slow undulating rhythm, like a wave hitting the shore. A true lady could feel the correct tide of rhythm as naturally as a native felt the beat of a drum.

Her French kid shoes—the new ones with the darling square toes in shiny black creaseless patent leather—crunched on a bed of slick stones inlaid in the middle of the dirt walkway. She'd heard tell that the stones were there to pave the dip where tropical rainwater and mud collected nine months out of the year.

She stepped on a stone and sank ankle-deep into mud. She jerked her foot out of the mud hole and hobbled over to the adobe building across from her. She closed her parasol and leaned it against some stacked baskets lined up like tin soldiers along the walkway. Hankie in hand, she cleaned her shoes and then stared at the ruined hankie. It wasn't worth saving, so she tossed it into a spittoon and turned to retrieve her parasol. In one quick motion, she popped it open and turned, never seeing the baskets teeter and fall, one by one, like dominoes down the walkway.

Off she went in the opposite direction of her father's

house, nestled in Binondo. The streets were filled with wagons, carts, and crowded horse-drawn trolleys emblazoned with the name Compañia de Tranvías. Josefina had told her about the trolleys and how her father felt about them.

A fatal disease called surra ran rampant, sucking every bit of life from the native horses. The trolley company didn't care, choosing instead to run the poor animals until they literally dropped dead in the streets. Sympathy for the horses and anger at the company's cruel practice kept her father from using the trolleys.

As she rounded the corner just a few blocks from her new home, she saw why he refused to ride them. Horses—ponies really, no bigger than three-month-old calves—struggled to haul a loaded trolley through the street in front of her. She'd never seen horses look so poorly.

She just stood there, stunned, immobile, trying to come to terms with something so pitiful and foreign to her. The horses at Hickory House and Beechtree Farms were her brother Harrison's prized possessions and treated as much. They were almost part of the family. These animals were as thin as the skinny lizards called geckos that scurried all over the island. She'd never been exposed to animals so feeble and sick. The sight turned her stomach. Nothing, not the hot sun or the crowds, would make her set foot on one of those vehicles.

Before she'd ever seen the trolleys she'd make the decision to walk, since that was what her daddy did, and she was eager to please him. Now, as she watched the horses struggle to pull the loaded cars she felt ashamed that her first reason for walking was selfish, only to please the father she so needed to please. Because of her own worrying she hadn't thought about the animals.

But it was hard for her to understand something she'd never seen. Diseased animals were surely not something she could ever remember seeing. Not in Belvedere, at Hickory House, at Beechtree Farms, or at Calhoun Industries, not at any of the homes of the families with whom they mixed socially. And if there were any, her brothers would have shielded her from the sight.

The LaRue men protected her. She was the last living female in the LaRue family, a respected, honored southern name as old as the hickory trees that lined the long drive of the family estate. Her mother had been a Calhoun, another name that was practically an institution in the state of South Carolina, a place where blood lines determined social acceptance.

Her mother had also been a true lady, cherished and coddled and loved by all the LaRue men. But she had died when Eulalie was so young that the only image she had of her mother was from the picture over the salon mantel and the descriptions by her brothers and the others who'd worshiped and adored her. Like her mother, she'd been sheltered from anything her five brothers deemed the least bit dangerous or unsavory or unrespectable. Other than Madame Devereaux's—a school she'd been expected to attend, where she'd been escorted to and from that bastion of female propriety in the family carriage—church, and an occasional soiree, she had always been attended by at least two of her five brothers.

Thus she hadn't mixed much, hadn't seen much but her well-guarded little world, where everything ran its smooth and normal course, where her name gave her acceptance and opened the magic doors of society, where ladies behaved as such and were in turn cherished and protected by their menfolk.

All except one man, the man whose name she bore, her father. The one man who hadn't been around to cherish Eulalie was her father. He was the reason she was here, and he was the reason she was so nervous and unsure, wondering how one went about meeting the father she hadn't seen in seventeen years, wondering what his impression would be. When he finally returned tonight that meeting would take place, and more than anything she wanted it to be perfect.

* * *

His heart pounded louder and louder, booming like cannon blasts through his head. The snake slithered on. Sam exhaled for the first time in almost two minutes. He was free again, almost. He had to get to the river. He moved on, dragging his body through the brush. He could feel the thorn vines scratching through his shirt. A deep mulch of leaves blanketed the ground, and soon the vines grew sparser. He crawled farther, until wet, loamy dirt as black as a moonless sky covered the ground.

An instant later he was free again. He shot upright and ran on. Birds burst like buckshot from a giant banyan tree. Their dark shadows filled what little sky bled through the jungle overhang. Feathers rained down. Unknown animals screeched and rustled off.

Suddenly he was surrounded by a sea of color—red frangipani, yellow hibiscus, and purple orchids. The sweet smell of tropical blossoms swelled in the air and over his dry tongue and throat. He was in a floral jungle, layer after thick layer of flowering plants. He tore through it. The perfume faded.

Then it was there. Water. He could smell the river. Humidity and dankness swelled around him, signs that the river was nearby. The taste of silty water filled the air. The hum of Spanish and native dialect faded behind him in the distance, replaced by the rush of fast-moving water.

If he could reach the river, he might make it. The Pasig River led to Tondo, outside Manila. The crowded market streets were his only chance of losing the men who chased him. They were Aguinaldo's guerrillas, and they wanted him. He had information on a gun shipment that the Spanish, Aguinaldo, and Sam's commander, Andrés Bonifacio, all wanted. If anyone but Bonifacio caught him, he was as good as dead.

Eulalie moseyed around the corner and there it was. The Tondo marketplace. A bustling, noisy hub of activity where everything seemed to scurry so fast it almost made a lady dizzy. Primitive wagons and gray weathered carts stood in clusters with their gates down, while rainbows of merchandise spilled out into the cobbled square. Everywhere there were merchants hawking their wares.

Drawn by her exotic surroundings, she wormed her way through the marketplace, mesmerized by the colors—a myriad of glistening Chinese silk moires and downy velvets in royal purples, rich dark reds, ocean-deep blues, and glowing saffron yellows piled in teetering stacks of thick and thin bolts that towered above the small Chinese merchants. She moved farther into the crowd, where a cartful of giant tubelike rolls of wool and silk rugs blocked her path to those wonderful silks. She paused, looking around, seeing only native heads and colorful baskets surrounding her.

As she stepped back to find a new path, something caught her eye. She stopped and stared. The Filipino women walked around the circumference of the marketplace with baskets of merchandise atop their heads. Although it wasn't a new sight to her—the washerwomen back home carried their baskets the same way—these baskets were twice as big, and the women were so small they were almost half-size. The tall baskets held heaps of golden papayas mixed with green and pink mangoes, and some right strange orangish melons that were foreign to her.

Rising from her right was the strong odor of the sea, and she turned toward it. A few carts stood catawampus to her, and they were smothered in a whole mess of dead fish. The fish sellers poured buckets of ocean water over the catch, trying to keep them fresh in the intense island heat of the afternoon. Every time they doused the fish, the odor subsided for a short time. But soon the smell returned and sent her moving away through the crowd and away from its stench.

The excitement and freedom of the frenetic atmosphere of the Tondo marketplace captured Eulalie just like those snared fish. Fate set the line, destiny the hook, and she was lured by her fascination with the crowd, completely unaware of the deep, raging waters toward which she swam, and of how this one afternoon would take her small sheltered, protected, socially prominent and lonely little life and shoot it all to hell.

2

Sam wasn't dead yet, but he felt as if he were in hell. He was damned tired, soaking wet, and his lungs burned as if he'd inhaled fire. Still running, he ducked beneath a low banyan, jumped a knot of exposed roots, and thundered on. He'd have given a month's mercenary wages for the soothing sear of whiskey down his throat instead of the ragged scorch of exertion. If he could lose them, he'd head straight for the nearest bottle of imported malt whiskey. He could almost taste the Old Crow right now. The image spurred him on.

His machete whacked a path along the river edge, severing the thick bamboo. He could hear them behind him. They had gained on him, were closing in. Their voices were clearer. He could make out some words, Spanish and Tagalog. He cursed under his breath. He wasn't as young and quick as he used to be. A bolo sailed past him, stabbing into another banyan trunk with a sharp, deadly twang.

He got younger real fast.

Ten minutes later he hit the outskirts of Manila. Five minutes after that Sam ran down an alleyway. The bastards were still on his tail. He raced into the marketplace, glancing left, then right. He heard shouts and turned. The men split up. They would cut him off. He made for the crowd and wove his way through. He was tall, too tall. The soldiers stood a short distance away, pointing at him. Three more closed in. Sam turned, hopped a wagon shaft and shoved a stack of rugs at the closest soldier. One was buried; one fell. He spun and punched the other, then was off again, making his way across the marketplace until he hit its crowded center.

Sam dropped under a wagon and lay there watching. Boots caked black with jungle mud shuffled by as one soldier shoved his way past the wagon. Soon another, then another, until he was sure they had scoured the area. Slowly he started to snake his way out from under the wagon, belly-crawling to the wagon's edge. He'd roll out and disappear into the crowd. Tactics decided, ready to move, he edged his right hand out from beneath the wagon.

A small, square-toed woman's dress shoe crunched down on his hand. Sam bit back a yell. His free hand shot out and gripped the woman's foot, wrenching the squat little bone-crushing heel out of the back of his drinking hand.

He grunted in relief; she screeched. He released her ankle and crawled quickly back under the wagon. The shoes shuffled backward before they were swept up with the crowd. He examined his hand. There was a deep gouge between this thumb and forefinger. It hurt like hell.

More boots stomped past the wagon, dragging his attention from his hand. Sam lay still. They passed, and he slowly edged out from under the back of the wagon. It was clear. Only native Filipinos milled about.

Stooping, Sam worked his way through the crowd, ducking when a soldier was near. He moved along, frequently turning his head to the right to check his blind side. He made it as far as the fish vendor. Turning, he looked to the right, then quickly turned left.

A daggerlike object surrounded by a pink blurr flashed toward his good eye. He reeled back. Christ! he thought, instinctively straightening, he'd almost lost his other eye. He stood there staring at the pink parasol bobbing its way through the crowd.

He had straightened to his full height—a big mistake.

A soldier burst from the crowd, coming at him, bolo knife raised. Sam spun left. He spotted the fish vendor with his saltwater pail raised. Sam ripped it from the man's hands and heaved it, pail and all, at the soldier. Then he ran, overturning two carts to ensure his getaway. Stooping, he plunged into the excited marketplace once again and disappeared into the crowd.

Eulalie could have sworn someone grabbed her ankle. She'd scoured the ground, but couldn't see a thing, having been swept along by the moving crowd. One thing she'd learned today was what the word "crowded" really meant. She wasn't used to hordes of people, and while the crowd did frighten her, it also excited her. The marketplace was a new experience, so different from her calm, peacefully protected life in Belvedere.

The strangest things happened here. That thing with her foot and then, just a few minutes later, she'd been trying to get away from another horrid-smelling fish cart and suddenly there was all this foreign hollering. When she'd turned around, everyone was looking at a man with a water bucket stuck on his fool head. Like the foot-grabbing, she'd paid it no mind and moseyed past an overturned cart.

Only a few feet away was exactly what she sought. A long wagon displayed fans of every vibrant color and pattern. Lining one side of the wagon were some huge baskets, so she stepped around them and made her way to the business side of the wagon.

She just couldn't decide which one would be best for tonight. There was a darling leaf green silk fan with some birds hand-painted on it. It was more colorful than a new patchwork quilt. Then there was a pale blue one with a wharf scene, ships and all, on it. She held the two fans in her gloved hands and tried to choose. Then the vendor, an old woman with bright eyes and a gummy smile, stuck out the perfect one.

It was deep purple with a bright pink floral design that looked to be the exact color of her parasol—Calhoun pink. She laid down the other fans and snapped her parasol closed. Then she compared the colors. It was a perfect match. To free her hands, she poked her parasol into the dirt, but it wouldn't stick, so she gripped the parasol handle tightly and raised it higher. . . .

Thwack! she jabbed it into the soft mound of dirt near the wagon.

It was the oddest thing. She could have sworn she heard some muffled swearing. She stopped fumbling with her purse and looked up. It couldn't have been the woman. The voice had been a man's. She looked behind her, but didn't see anyone.

Shrugging it off as market noise and an active imagination, she pulled some coins from her purse, paid the woman, grabbed her closed parasol, and, fan in hand, sailed through the marketplace, figuring she could find a few more doodads before she had to make her way home.

Sam's leg hurt like hell. He let go of it, tore the bandanna off his damp neck, and wrapped it around his aching calf. He couldn't bloody believe it when that pink umbrella had stabbed his leg. He'd been snaking along from wagon to wagon, working his way across the marketplace. He must have moved his leg too close to the edge because the next thing he knew, a sharp pain sliced through his calf. It had been all he could do not to yell. Instead, he'd sucked in a chestful of air, held it, and exhaled every curse he'd ever heard and a few he'd made up.

He finished tying the knot, hoping the pressure of the bandage would ease the ache in his leg. He turned and glared at the spot where the umbrella assassin stood, but she was gone. Her lucky day, he thought, unsure of what he would have done but knowing full well what he'd have liked to do. But he'd never murdered a woman . . . yet.

Sam continued moving from wagon to wagon, pausing when the soldiers stomped by. They were determined fellas, he'd have to give them credit for that. Aguinaldo must want those guns real bad.

The wagons formed a T about ten yards away. The market vendors turned their wagons only at the corners of the market square. If his calculations were right, he should be nearing the northeast corner of the marketplace, which was close to a maze of adobe-walled alleys in which he could make good his escape. Aguinaldo's men couldn't find him there; of that Sam was sure. If he could reach those alleys, he'd be home free.

He belly-crawled a few more feet. His leg throbbed and he paused. Only a little farther, he thought. Just a little farther. He sucked in a deep breath and crawled on until he was barely five feet from where the wagons ended. Close, he was so close.

Then he saw the shoes—ladies' high-button black shoes with bone-crushing heels. The pink parasol with its spear-like tip hung alongside the woman's frilly skirts, and Sam turned away, intending to move on. A fan plunked to the ground right next to his head. He looked over. The upside-down blond head of a woman stared at him in horror, her hand just touching the dropped fan.

"Oh, my Gawd!" Her head flew up out of sight.

Aw, crap. There was an eternal pause, and Sam waited for her scream, knowing he'd have to make a run for it.

The scream never came.

The crazy woman bent down again, her whiskey-blond hair hanging to the ground as she peered at him. Only this time she held that damn umbrella like a sword, the sharp point aimed right at him.

"Are you some kind of pirate?" she asked in the thickest southern drawl he'd ever heard.

She was going to get him killed. Slowly he edged closer to her.

"Well, answer me, sir. Are you?" she repeated, obviously a little irritated, jabbing her parasol to punctuate each word.

Sam held a finger to his lips, indicating she should be quiet. She appeared thoughtful and didn't seem to notice that he'd repositioned his legs, ready to move in an instant.

"Did you grab my foot?" Her face filled with suspicion, and then she shook the parasol at him as if she were ready to give him a piece of her mind, something Sam was sure she couldn't afford.

"Well, did you?"

That did it. He grabbed the parasol, jerked it back, and shot to his knees. His other arm snaked out and clamped around her waist, pulling her under with him. Now she screamed. His mouth covered hers to silence her, and he rolled farther under the wagon, pinning her squirming body beneath him. She kept yelling against his mouth, which was damned uncomfortable, not to mention loud. He released the parasol and replaced his mouth with a hard hand. She moved her hand around, trying to grab the closed parasol, but he ripped it from beneath her pinned body and jammed it across her throat.

"Shut up!" he gritted.

She did. Her eyes grew big as silver pesos, almost swallowing her small flushed face. He looked away and up as two pairs of boots ran by the wagon. Tension shot through him, and every muscle in his body stiffened. Unconsciously, he pressed down harder with his body. Her small, deadly foot scraped against his throbbing leg. He scowled at her. She lay still as a doldrum sea but her eyes darted a look at the ground outside the wagon.

He followed her gaze to where the soldiers' boots stood right next to the wagon. The men talked, and he listened, trying to hear their plans. She mumbled something against his hand, and he pressed harder on her mouth.

"Not a sound," he threatened in a deadly whisper, "and I won't kill you."

Her gaze shot back to the ground. Then he saw it. Her fan lay there right next to a soldier's foot. If the man bent down to pick it up, he'd see them.

Sam looked back at her, waiting. She stared at his eye patch. He wanted to laugh. One thing about losing his eye was that women always reacted to the patch, some with revulsion, some with curiosity, which was how this blonde looked at him—both curious and afraid. That was fine with him. If she was afraid, she'd keep her mouth shut, and that was all he cared about at the moment.

The guerrillas talked on. He listened. They knew he was here somewhere, hiding, so they planned to split up and comb the whole marketplace, going from wagon to wagon and looking underneath. He had to get out. Now. He looked behind him at the trail of wagons, then at the corner ahead. There were no wagons, but the open space was filled with people. Beyond that and on the left was a big adobe church; on the right stood a ring of brick warehouses. Between them was the maze of walled alleys—his objective.

He took a deep breath and pulled his machete out, holding it barely two inches above the woman's face. Her breath stopped. He could feel her terror. "Not one sound or I'll use this. Understand?"

She nodded, blue eyes wide.

He pulled the parasol off her neck and placed the knife there, whispering, "I'm going to take my hand away. If you make one sound, I'll slit your sweet throat."

Slowly he pulled his hand from her mouth. At the same time he let the cool steel of the machete blade rest against her flushed neck. She didn't make a sound. He bit back a winner's smile and continued to pin her with a lethal gaze. He hooked the parasol to his belt, a preventive action. He'd had enough close calls with it and didn't want to chance that she would try to use it as a weapon. He moved his left leg toward the huge baskets that lined the back of the wagon. With his foot he managed to shove one aside enough to crawl through.

"Very slowly we're going to get up and crawl out that space. Got it?"

She glanced at the opening and then turned her frightened eyes back on his face. She swallowed hard, then nodded.

He slowly lifted his body off hers, sure to keep his knees on either side of her thighs so she couldn't roll out the opposite side. "Turn over."

Her shoulders jerked at his command.

"Turn over!" he gritted again, pressing on the knife to

21

intimidate her before lifting it enough so she could turn without slitting her own throat.

She rolled onto her stomach.

He kept the knife at the back of her neck and sat on his haunches. His calf throbbed from the pressure. "Get on your knees."

She didn't budge.

"I said get . . . on . . . your . . . knees. Now!"

"The knife . . ." she whispered, indicating the reason she couldn't move.

In one slick movement his arm was under her ribs, and he jerked her up against his chest, repositioning the knife against her white, pulsing throat. Her head pressed back against his shoulder, her back against his ribs, her bottom against his groin.

For a long, hot moment he held her that way. He could smell her scent—gardenias, musk, and female fear. His breath grew shallow. He looked down at her. Her skin was pale; she was too frightened to be flushed. She didn't flinch at his look. She just stared. It was then that he noticed her eyes. They were an odd crystal blue, the color of alpine ice. Her breath, as shallow as his own, whispered past her full, dry lips. His gaze roved over her small chin, down her white neck, strained with her thin blue veins exposed from the position of her head. He watched her pulse beat rapidly in her neck. His own pulse increased, pounding as it had in the jungle.

Two pairs of soldiers' boots thudded by. Sam jerked his gaze away, and after a moment he nodded at the opening. "Move."

They edged out the opening. Sam kept one arm around her, and with his other hand he held the knife in its threatening position. Daylight glared in his eye, momentarily blinding him. He pulled her against him to make sure she couldn't get away. He felt one of the oversize baskets against his own back, and so while his vision adjusted he got ready. Vision cleared, he looked around, seeing only the crowd.

"Now!" he said, jerking her up with him and taking off in a stooped run for the alley.

Suddenly the woman was like a lead weight.

"Run!" he ordered, watching, stunned, as she dug in those cursed heels and just stood there, shaking her head. Her eyes had a glazed look of pure fear. Sam had seen that look before, on dying men.

He dragged her a few more feet before she pulled back on his arm, bringing them both to a dead stop.

He had to jerk the knife away to keep from cutting her fool throat. The close call stunned him. At that same instant two guerrillas came at him, one from the left and one from his back. Sam fought like the devil himself, punching, kicking, and head-butting.

An arm locked around his neck, jerking him backward while the soldier's arm tightened on his windpipe. He reached behind him and gripped the man's head. His lucky day, no helmet. He bent his head forward, then slammed it back as hard as he could, cracking his opponent in the forehead. He shook his own head to clear it and spun around, fists raised, ready. The soldier staggered back, dazed. Sam punched him out with an upper cut that would have done John L. Sullivan proud.

The other one got up, came at him again. Sam's fist slammed into the neck of the soldier, and he fell to the dirt right next to his sprawled friend. Wiping the blood from his own busted lip, Sam turned. Five other soldiers closed in from behind the woman. She, on the other hand, looked as if she was going to throw up.

To hell with that, he thought, and took off toward the alley. He closed the distance, ignoring the crowd, pushing and shoving, until he was there. The eaves of the adobe cast the entrance to the alley in shadow. He rounded the corner, knowing he was finally safe.

And then he heard her scream—the world could have heard that woman scream.

Common sense told him to run even faster, far, far away. His conscience stopped him dead in his tracks. His calf throbbed, his hand hurt, and both pains should have warned him.

She was trouble.

The trouble screamed again, loud enough to crack a wall, high enough to shatter glass. He grimaced. He couldn't leave her. She might be trouble, but she was also *in* trouble because she'd been seen with him.

He moved back in the shadows and took a look. Two soldiers held her while another placed a deadly bolo to her chest. She had no color in her face. Yeah, she was in trouble, and though he'd threatened her in the same way, he wouldn't have used the knife on her.

These men would.

3

She was gonna throw up.

But there wasn't time. One moment she stood there with foreign soldiers yelling at her and a knife at her chest, and the next moment a huge hard arm clamped around her waist, lifted her, and slammed her horizontally onto a hard male hip. Instinctively she tried to wiggle free, but the iron grip of her captor kept her pinned to him with an arm as unyielding as a tree trunk. She knew the feel of that arm. The one-eyed man with the knife had come back.

Her stomach lurched as he flung her around. He spun on one leg, the other hiked up to kick one of those gawdawful mean soldiers who kept threatening her. She gulped deep breaths of air. Grunts and moans and the hard slap of pounding fist against flesh echoed around them, but she couldn't see anything except the blurred flying images of uniformed human figures hitting the ground.

He stopped turning long enough for her to focus her eyes. A soldier flew past her line of vision. She started to scream but the man spun around again, kicking out at the next soldier. With each of his neck-whipping spins, she flopped around. Her hair reeled outward and her stomach upward. She wanted to scream, but her open mouth had the breath sucked from it and her skirt took up enough air to show the whole island her lacy ruffled drawers.

Her limbs dangled like limp chicken necks. The lady in her locked her ankles, trying to salvage some scrap of dignity, and seeking some sense of equilibrium, she grabbed the man's thigh. She discovered something. She had been wrong about his arm. His *leg* was the tree trunk.

Around she went again, and he squeezed tighter, pushing the air from her lungs. Her head swam; her vision blurred. She shook her head to clear it.

"Hold still, dammit!"

She squirmed, trying to get free, and his knife handle pressed into her ribs.

"I said hold the hell still! I've got you!" He kicked out at one of the fighting soldiers, and the ground suddenly rose. She slammed a hand over her mouth. She was gonna die, or vomit.

She didn't do either.

The man took off at a full run with her still clamped under his arm and now bouncing on his hard hip. Her corseted ribs ached from each jarring stride, but it didn't matter because just as this madman said, he had her again. She wondered why, and what he was gonna do with her. From what she'd seen of him under the wagon, she'd have bet the farm he'd killed before.

Think! Look at him, she told herself, remembering a novel she'd once read. The heroine had looked her killer in the eye, and the villain hadn't been able to go through with the killing. That one look had saved the woman's life. At this point she'd try anything. She wiggled around, trying to look at him. A black eye patch and one dark brown bloodshot eye glared back. He never once broke stride.

She shut her eyes tightly. She didn't want to be his next victim.

At that thought cold fear crept over her. She felt a scream building, slowly at first. Whenever she was truly frightened, whenever she had no control of over what was happening, she screamed. She'd screamed in the well, and she'd lived to tell about it. She hadn't screamed with him before because he had held a knife at her throat and warned her not to. It hadn't been easy, as scared as she was, but the thought of him slicing through her screaming throat had been enough to keep her quiet. She didn't want her last sound on this earth to be a gurgle.

She made up for it now and screamed for all she was worth.

He swore, then hiked her up higher on his hip, grunted, and clamped his hand over her mouth. Not once did he stop jogging along.

She kept screaming, hoping someone would hear her calls for help, but even to her own ears the sound was muffled behind his sweaty hand. He whipped around a series of dark, musty corners, and finally he stopped.

"Looks like it's safe now," he informed her, hardly winded. "You need to learn when to shut up. They could have followed the trail of your mouth." With that, he flung her upright and set her on the ground with all the finesse of a pile driver. Her wobbly legs buckled, and she raised a gloved hand to her eyes to try to block out the bright flashing spots. She couldn't have screamed now for anything. She was too swimmy-headed.

"Don't faint there, sister. I've lugged you around enough already, and my arm's getting tired." With that mannerless pronouncement, he grabbed the back of her neck and rammed her head down to her knees. Her corset stays almost cut her in half.

"Breathe!" he ordered, keeping her head jammed down.

The stays were like a vise. She gasped to get air.

"Good," he said, adding as he released her head. "I guess you can obey orders."

In the slowest, most ladylike way possible, she straightened and stared at her killer. He was so tall that she had to crane her neck to look up at him. His hair hung to his shoulders and was thick and straight and as black as his sinister eye patch. Despite all his cuts and bruises, he had the devil's face, with sharp angles and chiseled ridges, and he was in desperate need of a shave.

His muscular tanned neck showed from the open collar of a dirty and torn khaki shirt that was so damp it stuck to his massive body, which was, in size, the very spit of a strongman she'd once seen on a P. T. Barnum poster. The width of his shoulders and the sheer breadth of his chest were enough to dwarf her. Halfway down that Herculean chest several buttons were missing from his shirt, showing a slick, steel-rippled plane of stomach muscles. From his wide brown leather belt hung three knotted loops that held a variety of evil-looking knives, including the one he'd pressed to her throat. Her gaze trailed slowly down to the tip of longest blade. Just below it a faded yellow bandanna stained dark with blood twisted around his upper calf.

"Pass muster?" he said in a tone that scraped right down her spine. His voice was American—common Yankee, to be exact.

"Pardon me?" She looked up.

He wore a nasty white grin that was pure Yankee arrogance.

"Never mind. Let's get out of here before they pick up our trail again." His hand gripped her wrist and jerked her along behind him as he rushed down the dark alley.

She tried to pull her hand out of his grip, but he held fast. He overpowered her by sheer strength, so she had no choice but to stumble along behind him. Her mouth, however, was not so passive.

"Why are you doing this?" she called out to his back.

"Because those men would have hurt you." He jerked her around another series of corners.

"You threatened to cut my throat," she reminded him.

"Yeah, but I was just trying to save my skin."

Before she could respond, he dragged her over a cobbled street, and it was all she could do to keep on her feet.

"Sir! Sir! Please stop!"

He jerked to a stop, had the gall to drop his shoulders as if he were frustrated, and turned slowly around, his look all irritation. "Now what?"

"If you weren't about to kill me, why are you kidnapping me?"

"Kidnapping you?" He scowled. "I'm not kidnapping you. I'm saving your sweet neck!"

He wasn't gonna kill her or kidnap her. She sighed with relief. Then his words registered. "Save me from what?"

"Those soldiers would have used you to get to me."

"But I don't even know you."

"Right, but they don't know that, and they wouldn't believe you if you told them. They would just figure you were lying, question you over and over until they'd finally get fed up and get rid of you." He took her arm and started to move. "Now let's go."

"Where?"

"Back inside the city. Then I can get you to whatever hotel you belong in and out of my hair."

She stiffened at his rudeness, then dug in her heels to try to stop their motion, but he dragged her three feet before finally stopping. She drew herself up and told him, "But I'm not staying in a hotel."

He spit out a vile oath, and then very slowly, as if speaking to a foreigner, he asked, "Where are you staying?"

"The Binondo District."

"Okay." He nodded, taking in a long breath for patience. "That's in the opposite direction."

She agreed, but he wasn't looking at her because he appeared to be counting under his breath. Her brother Jed acted like that, except he was a southern gentleman.

The Yankee madman clamped on to her arm and took

off again, running so fast that he all but dragged her over an even rougher stone walk.

"Would you please slow down!"

He ignored her and dragged her on. Her heel caught on the jutting edge of a stone and broke. "My shoe!"

He hauled her a few more feet, then thankfully stopped and turned around. She hopped on one foot while she tried to ram the heel back in place. "My heel's broken."

He glanced at his hand for a brief moment, then said, "Disarmed, huh?"

She frowned. What an odd thing to say . . . but then, everyone knew that Yankees didn't think like normal people. She decided to try to make him understand. "Sir, you don't seem to understand—"

At that instant he picked her up in his arms.

"Put me down!"

He ignored her and headed south.

"Pay me some mind!"

"I didn't know you had one."

She fumed, but remembered a lady didn't show her anger. It was beneath her. She did what she'd been taught. She didn't speak to him.

Five minutes later she realized that was exactly what he wanted, and she gave up on acting like a genteel lady. She'd tell him off.

"You've broken my shoe," she complained, breaking the silence.

He ignored her.

"My new fan's gone."

More silence, and he whipped around another corner so fast her head spun. It took a moment for her to try again.

Remembering her drafty drawers, she added, "My dignity's been completely shattered."

"Good," he finally said. "Then you won't mind this."

He threw her over his shoulder, clamping his tree arm across the backs of her thighs just as she screeched. With each jog, his hard shoulder now jabbed her corset into her ribs. It kept her from finding the breath to yell. She stared

29

in a dizzying blurr at his hard back, her only view, and she almost gave up, until she remembered one more thing.

She managed one deep breath and raised her head away from his broad back. "I've lost my parasol!"

He never broke stride, just continued down the street, muttering some fool thing that sounded like "There *is* a God."

Eulalie had twenty-seven bruises. She counted every one while she bathed. Her arm had marks from that man's tight fingers; her wrist and shoulder ached from being pulled like taffy all over Manila. She sank lower into the tepid soapy water, hoping it would soothe her. Instead, her ribs cried out. She'd forgotten about them, briefly. Earlier, she'd been absolutely sure that every fool one of her corset stays had left permanent indentations on her rib cage.

Josefina had said the bath would help, and it did. But she couldn't help but remember the housekeeper's face when the Yankee toted her home. He had charged like a bull through the wrought-iron gates, across the tiled court-yard, and up the stone steps, which accounted for some of her bruises. Then, instead of knocking like most humans, he'd kicked on the heavy doors until poor, stunned Josefina pulled them open.

"You're home," he'd said and whacked her on the derri-ere. "All safe and sound." Then he deposited her in front of a stunned Josefina. "And you're out of my hair," he rudely added before he spun around and was out the gates before Eulalie could do more than see straight.

The little housekeeper had said there were more and more of his type living here since the Spanish relaxed the trade laws. She said she shouldn't have let Eulalie go off by herself, which prickled. It was just like being at home with her brothers. Now Josefina would probably start watching over her.

She rose from the tin tub, dried off, and put on her pink ruffled lace dressing gown. Then hairbrush in hand, she brushed her long hair, letting it spill freely down her back to dry. Josefina had brought her a plate of sliced mango, bread, and cheese to tide her over until dinner. The meal was to be delayed until her father's return.

Picking up the tray, she sat in a high-backed caned chair and placed the tray in her lap. The silence hit her. It was so quiet. She heard no sounds from the street because the house sat on the back of the property. Her nervousness grew. With five older brothers there was always noise at home. Hickory House was not a quiet place. She tapped her foot on the floor to give the room some sound.

With knife and fork, she cut the fruit and delicately placed a piece of it in her mouth. Very slowly and carefully she chewed, making sure her lips never parted. She swallowed, then looked around the empty room.

At home she always had polite dinner conversation with one of her brothers. It was a lady's tool to kill the time between bites, assuring herself that she wouldn't overeat. But there was no one to talk to. She took another bite, chewed and swallowed again. The food hit her nervous stomach like a cannonball. She set the tray aside and paced the room, wondering what her father was like.

Finally bored into action, she went downstairs to his study. She paused outside the double doors, a little nervous, a little excited, a little scared. One deep breath and she went inside, closing the door behind her. She leaned back, the door handle still in her hand, and she took in the room. It was dark, the only catches of light being those that filtered through huge shutters on the wall of windows opposite her. As her eyes adjusted to the dimness she could see well enough to cross the room and open the sliding wood shutters. Light flooded the room, and she turned, hoping the place would give her some insight to her father.

But the room was not much different from the study at Hickory House. Carved wood bookcases lined two walls, and there were the requisite oxblood leather chairs, the large, flat-topped desk, and a huge but faded carved rug. All the masculine objects and ornaments were there, from the large brass-bordered gun case to the misty odor of tobacco. Nothing special. Nothing that said, "I'm your daddy." Nothing that helped her. In fact, as she looked around, the excitement and anticipation that had driven her for weeks suddenly faded like the rich colors in that rug.

She walked over to the desk, hitched her hip on one corner, and looked at the globe, remembering how many times as she was growing up she'd looked at the pale colored splotches that represented her father's new posts. As she got older, she'd looked up the countries in Collier's, trying to imagine her father amid the colorful images described in the encyclopedia. But her image of him held no vivid color; it was little more than a sepia-toned figure in a photograph, like the one she kept near her bed at home. She had vague bits of remembrances of him, but seventeen years had dimmed those memories.

At times, alone up in her rooms at Hickory House, she'd imagined what her life would have been like if her daddy had been there and if her mama hadn't died. She knew it would have been different, and she wasn't sure if her fantasies came from a deep yearning for something she'd never had or from boredom with what she did have.

Her brothers loved her in their own way; she knew that, and that they cared for her. They took their duty seriously, so much so that there were times when she felt smothered and chained. As a child she'd dreamed of a mother's gentle hand and soft words. Someone who smelled like gardenias and would hold her against a soft neck to make the childhood hurts go away.

As a sensitive young girl on the verge of womanhood, with no confidence, she'd dreamed of a mother's wisdom and experience. Someone she could emulate. Someone who knew how she felt when her brothers placed all those tags on her. They didn't understand that it hurt to be thought of as too young, too fragile, and naive. It hurt to be thought of as a jinx and most of all as helpless, and she'd wanted someone who could make that hurt go away, or at least understand why it hurt her.

But most recently, as a young woman, she'd dreamed of

having a mother's listening ear. Someone who'd really listen to her, who'd stand up for her against her brothers' notions. Someone who would tell her about love and men and marriage, and someone to whom she could tell her deepest secrets and all those insecurities she hid. For as much as she tried to fight it, as much as she wanted to be otherwise, she knew she truly was afraid to be on her own. Things did seem to happen to her when she was alone, like today.

Her purpose had been to go out and buy a fan. Instead she'd come home fanless, and she'd lost her parasol, broken a shoe, not to mention almost getting her throat cut and being kidnapped. She just wasn't very capable, and deep down inside she worried that maybe because she was inept, it was difficult for people to find something in her to love.

She wondered, as always, if maybe she would have been different if she'd had at least one real parent. Her mother had died, so she couldn't be there, but Eulalie tried desperately to be the exact image of what her mother had been, a lady. She wasn't very good at that, either.

But her father hadn't died. He had chosen not to be there, and though she had tried to be like her mother, hoping that might bring him home, he'd never come. He'd written to her from all the faraway places, just as he had written to her brothers. But it just wasn't the same. Her father had been there when her brothers were growing up. He hadn't been there for her. And all her life she'd wondered why.

She glanced around her father's study. Seeing no answers there, she closed the shutters and crossed the room. Then she turned for one last glance at the study, shoulders down, a vacant, unsure feeling wedged in her chest, and she walked out of the room, more alone and more vulnerable than she had been in a long time.

The note had arrived two hours ago. He was coming home. Eulalie paced the reddish plank flooring of her room for what must have been the hundredth time. She stopped and smoothed out the imaginary wrinkles on her dress. Though she'd worn it when she waited earlier, Josefina had pressed all of the wrinkles from the gown. It was pink—Calhoun pink, the color her mother had worn in the huge portrait that hung in its place of reverence above the drawing room fireplace.

Eulalie had studied the dress in the painting; she knew every flowing line, every glimmer of shot silk, every scrap of imported white lace. She'd had the best dressmaker in Charleston copy the gown for her and had taken an hour to get her hair just so. Small pearl earrings hung from her ears. Lovely little French kid slippers with Louis XV heels graced her feet, and the hem of her whispering gown allowed for the little pink and red beaded shoe rosettes to peek out as she glided across the room.

She grabbed her skirts and lifted them so she could get another glimpse of her slippers. She wiggled her toes inside the shoes and watched the beads catch the lamplight in the room. The rosettes twinkled back at her like winks from the stars.

A loud clatter rang up from the courtyard. She dropped the skirts in a flurry of lace flounces and ran to the shuttered windows, but she could barely see a thing through the narrow wooden slats. She tried to slide the shuttered doors open, but they jammed. All she could see through the small opening was the center of the massive courtyard. Between the dark of night and the carved post rails of the long verandah outside her room, she couldn't make out a fool thing.

Her heart pounded drumlike in her chest, and she ran to the large oval mirror that hung over her lingerie chest. She stared at her image, looking for flaws. She had to look perfect. This first impression was just too important.

But something was wrong. She frowned at her reflection, trying to figure out what was missing. *The cameo.* She'd forgotten her mother's cameo. Some more noise clattered up from below, and she rummaged through her jewelry case until she found the cameo. Quickly she pulled it off its wrinkled blue silk ribbon and threaded it through a brand-new piece of pearly white velvet ribbon. Holding it to her neck she took in her image again. Now everything was perfect. She bent her head slightly forward so she could tie the ribbon loosely at the back of her neck. Then she looked up at the reflection.

The dark native face of a soldier appeared over her left shoulder. She opened her mouth to scream, but he placed the cold barrel of a gun at her head.

And Eulalie LaRue, of the Belvedere LaRues, owners of Hickory House, Calhoun Industries, and Beechtree Farms, did the most ladylike thing she'd ever done. She fainted.

4

The splintered door of the crude hut flew open. Yellow morning light as bright as the Chicago fire flooded the doorway, momentarily blinding the bound prisoner hunched in a dank corner of the grass hut. Aguinaldo's men entered, a long, thick bamboo pole slung over their shoulders. Hanging from the pole was a lump of rough burlap that wiggled and snorted and squealed like a stockyard hog.

With a solid thud the men dumped the bundle on the ground, then pulled out the pole and crossed the room, slamming and bolting the door in their wake. The bundle didn't move for the longest time, as if being dropped had knocked it senseless. It regained its life swiftly, with more kicks and blows than a slum street fight. The bundle rolled, and the burlap peeled away, leaving that pink flower of the South sprawled in the middle of the now dim hut.

Sam groaned. He was wrong. It had been senseless to begin with.

He shook his head and stared at his hands, bound almost prayerlike. Praying wouldn't help. She was here, following him like that proverbial black cloud. Her muttering brought his gaze up again. She looked ridiculous—a mumbling bundle of pink and white lace that tried to wiggle into a better position. He took a deep, cleansing breath, half in irritation and half in resignation. God had a sense of humor, but he wondered why he seemed to be the brunt of it lately.

He watched her maneuver, a pink flurry of scoots and shifts, into a sitting position, not an easy task with her bound hands and feet, and made worse by her miles of frilly female clothes. They rustled louder than native oaks in a gale wind. But her mouth was the clincher. She talked under her breath the whole time. He had a hunch that he'd experienced his last quiet moment, but then suddenly both the rustling and her muttering stopped cold.

"Oh, my Gawd . . ."

Sam looked at her stunned face and silently waited, counting, one . . . two . . .

"What's going on here?"

Three seconds. "I suppose you could call it a revolution." He rested his elbows on his bent knees, his bound hands dangling between, and he watched her face flash with every little thought: doubt, belief, fear, then worry. She looked around the hut as if she expected someone else to be there.

Her voice barely above a whisper, she asked, "What're they gonna do with us?"

Sam shrugged, choosing not to tell her they'd probably not live out the week, if they were lucky.

"Why do they want me?"

"They wah-ahnt you because they think you're involved with me. Remember the marketplace?"

Her full lips tightened into a thin line. She didn't like him mimicking her drawl. He stored that knowledge for use later. She shifted her legs to one side, trying to get comfortable with all her frills. She looked him straight in the eye and as sweet as sugar asked, "Why would they ever think that you and I would be associated?"

He just stared at her, didn't move, didn't blink. The little snob. He should have left her in the marketplace. He kept staring, trying to intimidate a little fear into her, or at least make her think about what she'd said. She still awaited his answer, a pure innocent look on her face.

He shook his head and laughed to himself. Finally he said in a wry tone, "I guess they don't know you're not my type."

"Well, I should say so." Her expression said she'd be about as likely to hitch her hooks into him as she would be to eat one of those three-inch-long cockroaches that had run around the edges of the hut last night.

Leaning back farther into the corner, he watched her a moment. He could almost read her thoughts on her face.

Ah, he thought, the lamp just lit. It had dawned on her what he'd said. She recovered nicely, once again making eye contact as she spoke. "You mean you're not my type of beau. I understand."

When he didn't say anything, she rambled on, "I'm from South Carolina. A LaRue of the Belvedere LaRues—you know, Hickory House, Calhoun Industries; my mother was a Calhoun, you see—and Beechtree Farms."

She pronounced the last word as far-ahms. She drawled on, reciting her pedigree like some prized filly. He'd met enough of her type in his thirty-odd years. Virginal little blue bloods with nothing between their fancy pearl earrings but air. Ladies—that breed of women who could barely think past their next party.

Christ, but this one could talk. Now she'd gotten back about as far as the Revolutionary War—some great-great-grandparent on her father's side who had signed the Declaration of Independence.

Hell, Sam didn't even know who his father was. He could still remember asking his mother once where he'd come from. His uncle had said to his stepfather—both of them drunk and laughing—that Sam had come from a long line his mother listened to. He'd been confused at the time, but a few years later he'd learned what his uncle meant.

Growing up in a Chicago slum made a kid's innocence a short-lived thing. The area he'd been born in was only a few blocks away from the Union Stockyards. They'd lived in a rat-infested one-room flat on the fifth floor of a crumbling old brick building where the stairs were rickety and half the railings broken away. Some of the tenants—a gin-sotted woman and a couple of kids—had been killed falling from the open top landings. He could still remember the screams echoing a spine-raking, seemingly endless dirge up the stairwell only to finally cease with a dull thud and dead silence.

Inside the apartment the windows were cracked and loose. Noxious, hot summer fumes of a nearby sweat factory seeped through the gaps, as did the ridged, brittle cold of the Chicago winters. At age seven, Sam had finagled a job at that factory, working twelve-hour night shifts shoveling coal in the heavy burn furnace just so he wouldn't be cold anymore. His few dollars a week supplied them with bread, and some milk for his two half sisters.

Sam didn't have a long pedigree, but he knew how to stay alive. He knew how to get what he wanted, and his years on the streets had taught him to outthink and outfight the most practiced, the most shrewd, and the most calculating minds.

And in the last ten years he'd been getting paid for those skills, and paid well, by whatever faction needed him. He'd been in the Philippines for five months, hired by Bonifacio to train his men in guerrilla strategy and to use the Hotchkiss breech-loading rifles and, more importantly, those coveted Sims-Dudley dynamite guns that were due from his arms source any day.

He glanced at his fellow prisoner. She was still at it, going on about rh-ice and indee-go on her mother's side. Right now he wished he had one of those dynamite guns. He'd cram it in her mouth.

She finally made eye contact. There was a moment of blessed silence, a very brief moment.

"Don't you think so?" she asked, referring to some dumb thing she'd been chattering about.

He leaned back against the corner, his motion crackling the dry grass of the walls. He paused before he spoke, making sure he had her complete attention. "When you were growing up on your farms, did you ride around in one of those fancy black carriages—the kind with all that shiny brass and a team of horses whose pedigree was as perfect as your own?"

He had her. Confusion lit her soft southern-sweet features, and she nodded.

"I thought so." He paused. "When we were kids we used to play a game." He met her wide stare. "You know what that was?"

She shook her head.

"Whoever could hit those fancy carriages with the most broken tenement brick won."

Her face paled.

"You know what the prize was?"

Clearly shocked, she slowly shook her blond head.

"If you were young—say, five or so—you got the best spot to pick pockets. As I remember, it was near Sixty-fourth Avenue, and there was a dark alley right next to it, a great place to ditch the copper. Now, if you were about eight, well, then, you got first crack at stealing the bread off of Grissman's bakery wagon while the others bullied old man Grissman away from the wagon doors by heaving garbage and street muck at him. The children who were older than that . . . well, there weren't many 'children' left who were older than that. You grew up fast on Quincy Street. If you wanted to survive."

She just stared at him, as if the life he described could never have existed in her sheltered, pampered little world. He'd finally found something that shut her up. So he closed one eye, feigning sleep. The sound of her gown rustling made him crack his eye open a bit to look at her. She still

39

stared at him, a wealth of emotion in her expression. He looked down and missed the look of pity that crossed her face.

He stared at his bound hands and resisted the urge to shake his head in disgust. She was worse than most. The real world didn't exist for her. The pale skin, her open mouth, and her appalled eyes said as much. That look told Sam what he'd always suspected. Those people in their carriages never bothered to look at the slums. There was no place in their perfect little worlds for the poor and the ugly, no mars in their finish, no flaws in their diamonds. If the world around them wasn't perfect, then they'd wall it off and surround themselves with one that was. And they would never let that wall down. The ugly might get in.

Finally quiet, she began to fiddle with some sparkly thing on her shoe.

Ah, sweet peace. He bit back a satisfied smile and watched her try to come to grips with her situation. Her pensive gaze went to the old, moldy woven mats on the floor. Her nose wrinkled in disgust. She looked toward the opposite corner, where an ancient water bucket, its bands rusted a burnt brown, sat with an equally rusty tin ladle. Sam had tasted the water inside. He doubted she would. Just the murky color would send her running. He wondered how long it would take this pink flower of the South to wilt without water.

Her gaze went up to the high-pointed ceiling of the hut, where bamboo rods crisscrossed as support for the long, dry savannah grass that formed the primitive roof. It was a haven for bugs, those huge, abundant bugs that lived in the tropics. He doubted she knew that, or cared, the bugs not being part of her ancestry.

Now she stared in dismay at the locked door. Her shoulders sagged in defeat, and she sighed a huge, lung-windy sigh that could only have been missed by a deaf man, or a dead one. Its lack of subtlety was so ludicrous and it struck him so funny that he had real trouble holding back a smile.

He turned away, knowing his face showed his amusement. He'd always prided himself on his ability to hide his thoughts and emotions. Seldom had he found anyone or anything who could weaken that skill. In his profession he couldn't afford to.

She had managed to do it twice in one day. He wrote it off to lack of food and sleep.

Now she chewed on a fingernail, her attention still held by the locked door. Maybe she was catching on; maybe she even had enough sense, after all, to realize the seriousness of her situation. Yet experience told him otherwise. Ladies had no common sense, especially little pampered pink belles who deigned to glide down from their pedestals long enough to wreak havoc on the real world—the tough one he lived and fought in, the life that kept his mind sharp just in order for him to exist.

No, he thought, with a shake of his head, she didn't have a clue to that world. She survived on the world of her past, her precious bloodline. He survived on a line of blood, too, a line of spilled blood that trailed behind him longer than her precious pedigree.

He also knew that trail wouldn't end, not today or tomorrow. On that last thought, he drifted off, knowing his body needed sleep to watch and wait, for timing was essential to his escape.

He'd been asleep for a while. She had no fingernails left. It had taken her a while to chew them down to the quick. Madame Devereaux would have taken one look at her hands and plastered hot pepper oil on them. She could almost feel it burn her lips. She squirmed, looking around the dark hut. The ground was damp and musty and hard, the air stuffy, and she was right scared.

She ventured a glance—her third in as many minutes—at the Yankee. He was so still. She'd never seen anyone sleep so quietly. All of her brothers snored louder than hurricane winds, Jeffrey, the eldest, being the stormiest of the bunch. When she was about five, he'd had to change bedrooms. At the time his room had been right below the nursery, and his nightly snoring had given her hourly night-mares. Finally her other brothers had made him change rooms, claiming that her screaming was keeping up the whole county.

Since her brothers snored, she'd assumed all men did, figuring all that hot, arrogant air had to go somewhere. Based on her brief and frustrating encounters with the rude Yankee, she'd have thought he could snore the roof down. She glanced up, staring for a long moment at the high roof. She could have sworn something moved in the thick grass. She squinted to see better, but when she saw nothing she figured it was just a slight breeze ruffling the grass roof.

She turned back to her fellow prisoner. Not a sound from him. He was so still it was almost eerie. Not even his breathing was detectable. There was no rise and fall of his chest; even his postion remained unchanged. He sat against a corner, knees drawn up, mud-encrusted boots flat on the ground, khaki-covered arms across his bent, grass-stained knees, his bound hands hanging between them as still as a dead man's. But the strangest thing was the tension that spread from him throughout the small hut. She had the feeling that even in sleep his muscles didn't relax. Like a cornered cougar ready to pounce, the man slept as if wait-ing. She wondered if he'd learned to do that as a child.

The picture he'd painted with his blunt words remained in her mind. It wasn't easy to imagine what his childhood had been like. She glanced up at him. He was still asleep. She couldn't imagine having to steal to live, spending a child's playtime picking pockets and running from the police.

At Hickory House the nursery was half a floor wide, with a hand-painted rocking horse, imported German and French dolls, complete with trousseaux, and bright spinning tops as big as leather balls. Hundreds of her brothers' iron sol-diers lined painted shelves also filled with books and puz-zles. One whole corner contained stacks of wooden blocks, a huge tin of pickup sticks, and the precious bags of color-ful glass marbles her brothers never allowed her to touch.

She remembered the times when, as a child, she'd been bored with it all and complained she had nothing to play with.

As a child this man had played with broken pieces of brick. Glancing at his eye patch she wondered if that was how he had lost his eye. She felt a sudden urge to take every toy in that nursery to the poor section of Chicago.

Footsteps clumped around the outside of the hut. An instant later the sound of a wooden bolt rasped against the door. It opened, spilling daylight over her. She looked at the Yankee. He hadn't moved an inch, but he was awake. She could feel it, and when she looked at his eye, it was wide open, staring back.

"Well, well, what have we here?"

Her head jerked back around. A man stood in the doorway, his features undiscernible with the glaring daylight behind him. He had a stocky build and wasn't overly tall, but he towered above the two soldiers standing just inside the hut. Both held long, deadly sharp knives like the one the Yankee had held against her throat.

Very slowly the man stepped inside. His skin was dark, his hair slick and black, the same color of his eyes, which were looking right into her. She willed away the goose pimples she got from his penetrating stare, but she didn't avert her eyes. Fear made her continue to stare at this man, at his wide face, pitted cheeks, and broad nose, which suddenly cracked to reveal uneven teeth and a smile too sly to be friendly. It reminded her of the way Jedidiah's nasty hunting hounds bared their teeth. She suddenly felt as if she were seven, treed by a pack of dogs and back in that giant oak. She made eye contact again, afraid not to watch him. And she could tell he knew it, too. He was, after all, as they said at home, in the catbird seat.

He walked straight toward Eulalie, never taking his black eyes off her. He stopped only a foot in front of her, and she had to crane her neck back to continue to meet his eyes. He broke eye contact first, raking down her body instead. Then he slowly walked around eyeing her the way her brother Harrison eyed a prime piece of horseflesh.

She was scared and knew her shaking hands gave her fear away. He finished his inspection, stopping for an obvious moment to stare at her clasped hands. She willed them to stop. They shook more. He held out his palm. The soldier on his right slapped his long knife in the man's hand, then returned to his position guarding the door.

Those black eyes met hers, and he placed the deadly tip of the cold knife against the throbbing pulse in her neck.

"Where are the guns?" He still smiled.

"Leave her alone, Luna." Those words were the first the Yankee had spoken, an order to Luna, the man who held a knife to her throat. She didn't speak, just waited.

Luna let his eyes run over her before he turned to the corner. "Nice, very nice, amigo." He raised the knife tip to her lips. "Too bad."

She tried not to shake.

He moved the tip of the blade to the top of her gown and sliced through the imported lace ruffle. She gasped, partly from fear and surprise but also because of what he'd done to her special dress.

"I have my orders, amigo. Aguinaldo needs those guns at any price, even at the expense of this one." Luna kept the knife point at her heart and stared at the bound Yankee, who no longer appeared ready to pounce. Instead he leaned against the wall as casually as if he were waiting for a ride, as if the knife this madman held against her heart couldn't kill her, as if she were expendable. She began to wonder who was the real madman.

Well, if the Yankee wasn't going to save her, she would save herself. "I don't know anything about any guns, and I don't know him. I'm a LaRue of the Belvedere, South Carolina, LaRues and an American citizen."

Luna's face showed his surprise, then something akin to calculation. "LaRue—as in Ambassador LaRue?"

"You know my father?" she said, relieved to know that her father's influence would save her.

The Yankee swore such a foul word that Eulalie couldn't get enough air to gasp.

Luna pulled back the knife. "Ambassador LaRue's daughter." He turned to the Yankee and began to laugh. "You didn't know, did you?"

There was no response, only the sound of Luna's laughter. She didn't think it was funny, but then, she didn't really care because this man knew her father and soon she'd be out of this awful place.

Luna pulled the knife away from her chest and made a gallant little bow. "Forgive me, Señorita LaRue."

This was all a mistake. She smiled and sighed with relief.

A moment later the Yankee swore again.

Luna still smiled. "No more knives." He handed the knife to the guard. "Now if you will excuse me. I have some . . . some messages to send." He turned and crossed to the door, pausing to look at the Yankee. Luna laughed again as he stepped outside, closing the door behind him. Yet even with the door shut his laughter could be heard.

She stared at the closed door, hoping and praying that her father would be at home when Luna's note arrived.

5

"He forgot to untie my hands," said little Miss LaRue, daughter of one of the most influential Americans on the islands, and the perfect bait for Aguinaldo's junta.

"Colonel Luna doesn't forget anything," Sam told her, knowing the colonel's reputation as Aguinaldo's henchman, handling any and all of the dirty work involved in suppressing any rebel factions, especially those that tried to

supplant their power. Sam's commander, Andrés Bonifacio, led the most prominent of those other factions.

"Well, of course he forgot." She gave him a look that
said he was the dumb one.

"How do you figure that?"

"He knows my daddy, so the colonel is obviously gonna
send him a note about me. He said he had messages to
send."

"He'll send him a note, all right."

She gave him a puzzled look. "This was all some kind
of mistake." She stared in dismay at her bound hands and
tugged at them futilely, then added, "You heard him
laughing."

"He was laughing because you gave him exactly what
he needed."

"Oh?" She jerked at the ropes. "What was that?"

"A hostage."

"Me? A hostage? Now, that's just plain silly." She tried
to wave a hand of dismissal but the ropes made it impossible. She frowned at them in obvious annoyance.

Sam shrugged and watched while she struggled to get up.
Her skirts rustled, and she braced her bound hands on the
ground. She rearranged her legs until she was on her knees,
pink-covered frilly bottom up. She pushed herself into a
standing position, wobbling a bit when her hem caught on
her foot.

This was some show.

"There," she mumbled and hobbled over to the door,
teetering on the squat heels of her fancy shoes. She raised
her hands and knocked on the door. It swung open. One
of the guards stood with his bolo knife pointed right at her.
She looked at the knife with surprise and said, "Oh, good."
She held up her hands. "Would you cut these off, please?
Colonel Luna must have forgotten before—"

The door slammed in her face. Her back stiffened in
surprise, and she muttered, "Well, I like that."

Sam shook his head as he laughed. She was so green.

"I don't think that's the least bit funny!" She glared at

him, then raised her hands again and pounded on the door for a good minute. It flew open again. This time both soldiers had their knives drawn.

"That was very rude. I want you to cut these off right now, you hear?" She held out her hands.

One of the soldiers said something to the other, and they both turned and smiled at her.

Sam groaned. The soldiers looked like Cheshire cats with a cornered mouse.

"Turn!" one of them ordered, grabbing her by both shoulders and spinning her sideways.

She raised her chin and gave Sam a smug smile.

He just watched and waited.

"Hands out!" The soldier kept his hold on her shoulders.

She stuck her hands out and turned to the soldier who held the bolo knife. She smiled. "Go right ahead."

He raised the knife up in the air at arm's length, then slowly he lowered it, letting the blade rest for a full minute on her wrists, like an executioner about to behead his victim.

Sam mentally counted, one . . . two . . . three . . .

"Oh, my Gawd!"

Four seconds, he thought. She was slowing down. He revised that thought when she jerked her hands back faster than he could pick a pocket. Hmmm. He didn't think she could move that fast.

The soldiers laughed and pointed at her, having a great sadistic time at her expense.

Green. She was so green she made the jungle look pale.

She turned her horrified face toward him. "Did you see that? They were gonna cut off my hands!" She turned around as the soldiers stepped outside and said, "I don't think that's the least bit funny. I want to see Col—"

They slammed the door again, but their laughter carried back inside.

"Still think this is just a little waiting party, Miss Lah-Roo?"

She faced him, her face as naive as her next words. "You heard him. He as much as said he wouldn't hurt me."

"Only a fool would believe that."

She was quiet for a moment, then said, "You told me the same thing."

"Yeah. Well, I meant it."

Her nose went up a bit. "It escapes me, sir, why I should believe you and not the colonel."

"Because I'm telling you the truth."

"How am I supposed to know that?"

"You don't."

"That's the point I'm tryin' to make here, Mr. . . . What is your name?"

"Sam Forester."

"Mr. Forester—" She stopped speaking, staring at him as if he'd grown horns. "Do you know anything about some kind of guns?"

"No . . ." He gasped in mock horror. "Me?"

She tried to cross her arms but couldn't. "You don't have to be rude, you know."

"Why the hell do you think we're in this mess?"

"I don't know. I'm askin' you!"

"Well, don't ask. Your ignorance could save that sweet white neck of yours."

She frowned. "That's what those soldiers wanted in the marketplace. They kept asking me something about a forest of guns." She looked at him. "It was Forester's guns, wasn't it?"

One . . . two . . .

"They think I know about your guns!"

"Five seconds. Will wonders never cease?"

"Well, you don't have to be so smart-mouthed about it!"

"One of us has to have something smart come out of his mouth."

"You, Mr. Forester, have no manners, and I find you right rude!" With that pronouncement she proceeded to pound on the door and tell the soldiers that she wanted to see Colonel Luna "right here and now!"

Fifteen minutes later she was still at it. Her repeated pounding on the door matched the pounding ache inside his head. He wanted to pound her.

His only consolation was that her voice was getting more and more hoarse, and as he rubbed the bridge of his nose and closed his eye, he sincerely hoped her hands were just as sore as his ears.

Eulalie didn't know her hands could ache so or that anyone could be so mean-spirited, ignoring her like those guards did. She could hear them talking through the door. They thought it was funny. To them she was a joke, and that sort of treatment was foreign to her—at least until she'd met the Yankee. Her gaze went to his corner. He hadn't said a word, just ignored her, like the guards. Even with all the noise she'd been making he acted as if she wasn't there. But she was here, in this dirty, silent hut, and she hated it. She sighed and gave up trying to get the guards to fetch the colonel. She walked into the center of the hut and sat down, staring at the grass walls and listening to . . . nothing. It was too quiet.

She took a deep breath and broke the frightening silence. "So your Christian name is Sam?"

He nodded slightly, shifting against the wall.

"Is that short for Samuel?"

"Yeah." He pinned her with his bloodshot brown eye.

"I see." She nodded, searching for something else to say to fill the void. "You're from the North. Chicago, right?"

He grunted something she was sure was an affirmative. It looked like she was gonna have to carry this conversation.

"I already told you where I'm from."

He mumbled something that sounded like "a hundred times." She ingored him and went on, "My full name is Eulalie Grace LaRue. My grandmother, on my father's side, was a Eulalie, and so was her grandmother and a great-great-aunt on the French side of our family. They were all Eulalies. Now, the name Grace was my mama's idea. At least that's what my brother Jeffrey told me. He's the oldest? Well, he said, 'Eulalie is an old family name, but Grace . . . well, that's just a name our mama loved. So she named you Eulalie Grace.' " She paused for a breath and to give him time to soak in the whole story. "So I'm Eulalie Grace."

He had a blank look on his face, and that bloodshot eye appeared a little glazed. She blamed that on the bad light in the hut.

"I suppose," she went on, still trying to carry the conversation, "that given our circumstances and the fact that this is our second meeting, we can address each other by our Christian names."

He still didn't say anything, just picked up a tin cup that sat beside him and stared into it.

"So I'll call you Samuel and—"

"No!"

His shout startled her.

"No one calls me Samuel," he said through gritted teeth.

"Oh. All right. I'll call you Sam, and you can use the name my friends and family use."

He raised the cup to his mouth and drank.

"They call me Lollie." She smiled.

He spit a good three feet, then choked and coughed. She started to crawl toward him to give him a pat on the back, but he finally got his wind back. He looked at her strangely, and with his mouth twisted into a suppressed grin he asked, "Your name is Lollie LaRue?"

She nodded, frowning at his tone.

"I don't think I've ever caught your act."

"Pardon me?" She didn't understand what he meant, but something in his grin said he was making fun of her.

He laughed and laughed. It wasn't very nice or well mannered. She surely didn't see anything odd about her name. It was a fine old southern French name. Back home, Eulalies were always called Lollie; everyone knew that. And no southerner would ever laugh at someone's name. It was rude to make fun of something someone couldn't change.

But this man didn't care, because then he said something

he really thought was funny. Something about her buying
fans in the marketplace to use in an act. She didn't understand, but it hurt that he was obviously laughing at her. A
little angry, she turned her back, partly to keep from watching him laugh at her expense, but mostly to keep him from
seeing she was hurt by it.

The hut was quiet. Too quiet. It drove her crazy. She
didn't like the silence, because it scared her. She looked
over at the Yankee in the corner. He was asleep again.
They hadn't spoken since she'd turned her back on him,
and the only sounds had been an occasional shout or noise
from outside. Inside there was no sound, which made her
situation all that much harder to deal with.

No one to talk to. Time passed in glacial increments. Out
of nervousness she began to hum "Dixie," unconsciously
choosing to fill the chilling silence. She'd just hit the "land
of cotton" verse when she thought she heard a deep, pain-
filled moan coming from Sam's corner.

She stopped humming and looked at him, wondering for
the first time if maybe he had groaned because he was
wounded. Craning her neck she watched him silently. His
shoulders moved a bit, as if he'd gotten relief from whatever pained him. She didn't see much in the way of
wounds, except that brown, bloody area where the bandanna was tied around his calf. Maybe that injury was more
serious than it looked.

He'd managed to tote her home without breaking stride,
and never once had he limped or appeared the least bit
pained. Maybe something else hurt him. Maybe he had a
headache. She got headaches in the middle of summer
whenever it was particularly hot and sticky. A nap always
helped her, so she figured she ought to leave him alone, let
him sleep, even though she had a thousand questions she
wanted answered to put her mind at rest. And she needed
to talk; the urge was just festering inside her.

Humming helped and it shouldn't bother his sleep.
Maybe a lullaby would be a good compromise. She slowly

began to hum her personal favorite, not even realizing when instinctively she began to sing the lyrics:

"Hush, little baby, don't say a word.
Papa's gonna buy you a mockingbird.
If that mockingbird don't sing,
Papa's gonna buy you a diamond ring.
If that diamond ring don't—"

"Do me a favor. Pretend you're that mockingbird and shut up." One angry, bloodshot brown eye glared at her.

"I was just tryin' to help."

"Help what? Bring down the walls of the hut with your screeching?"

She inhaled a deep indignant breath. "I do not screech. I'll have you know that I sang contralto in the choral group at Madame Devereaux's." Wanting to stand up for herself but uncomfortable with what she considered bragging, she looked down at her lap and smoothed some wrinkles from her skirt, then added, "According to the music instructor, my voice was very clear and resonant."

He barked with laughter. "For a dying alley cat."

"Obviously you know nothing about voice." She tried to look down at him, but she couldn't get her chin up that high. He was being rude on purpose, and even his awful upbringing was no excuse for purposely hurting someone. She sensed that this man wanted to hurt people, and any pity she'd felt for him was fast disappearing.

"I know about knives and bullets, torture and pain, and your voice, Miss Lah-Roo, is a pain in my ears."

"Well, that's just too bad, now, isn't it. I'm gonna sing if I feel like it. This is for your ears." She began to sing "Carolina" in full tremolo.

He stood and moved toward her as if to shut her up himself. She was just debating giving in for the sake of her welfare when the lock rasped again and the door flew open.

The soldiers came in, frowning.

She stopped singing. They stopped frowning, but their

knives were still poised, just as before. Behind them came another man carrying two wooden bowls filled with steamy rice and some kind of fragrant sauce. Her stomach growled, very unladylike. She hadn't eaten since yesterday afternoon, and that had been the mango and bread she'd had before her bath.

She hadn't really thought about food, out of habit, for one of Madame Devereaux's rules was that a lady never let hunger get the best of her. Never. She'd learned at a young age that a true lady, like her mother, ate lightly, delicately, and never, ever let her hunger be known. Yet sometimes, on rare occasions, her stomach would protest, doing all that embarrassing gurgling as if it were cheering the food's arrival. She pressed her hand to her stomach as if that gesture could quiet the growling.

The little man handed a bowl to her. Food of any kind would have smelled good. Her mouth began to water as she stared at the bowl. The rice was brown, covered in a clear sauce with chunks of meat, and though the whole thing looked a little pasty, the smell was tempting.

Walking over to the corner, the server gave the other dish to Sam, who sat back against the hut wall again. She looked up, properly waiting for him to be served, and for their utensils to arrive.

He didn't wait. Stunned, she watched him wolf down his food. He actually used his fingers to scoop up the rice. Her mouth fell open.

The door began to close and she realized the server was leaving. "Stop! Wait! Please."

She grabbed the door and almost spilled her food. He turned back toward her. She smiled politely. "I would like some silverware, please."

Sam choked, coughing as if he was about to die. She wasn't that lucky, though. His manners were atrocious, so it didn't surprise her one bit that he'd choked. It was probably from cramming a handful of food in his mouth before he'd had a chance to swallow. The man used his fingers like shovels. It was disgusting.

The server still stood there, blankly staring at her.

"Silverware." She raised her voice, hoping to make him better understand her.

He shrugged.

Sam coughed.

"A fork, knife—oh, I don't suppose you'd give me that. Well, at least a spoon, please," she repeated, louder, miming the action of eating with silverware. Odd noises came from Sam's corner, but she ignored them and kept gesturing. The man frowned, still not understanding.

She pretended to stick a fork into the bowl, then made exaggerated sawing gestures as if she were cutting meat.

He watched her intently, then grinned. *"Cuchillos!"* And he pantomined eating.

"Yes!" She returned his smile. "Yes, I'd like some coocheehoes, please."

The man nodded, then went out and closed the door. The sound of a throat clearing echoed from Sam's corner. She looked at him. "Are you gonna be all right?"

His face looked a little red, and moisture glistened in his crinkled eye. The man should really be more careful. Good manners might save him from choking to death. She decided he needed an etiquette lesson.

"Mr. Forester . . . Sam. Where I come from it's considered rude to eat before everyone is ready, especially before a lady."

He shoveled some more food inside and then talked around it. "Is that so?" He chewed some more and finally had the grace to swallow. "Where I come from, you eat what you can, as fast as you can, or someone else will eat it for you."

His words instantly reminded her of his background— poor and hungry. Surely he didn't think she would steal his food. Before she could suggest that he didn't have to worry, the door opened again and the little man came in holding out a small spoon.

"Thank you kindly." She smiled and accepted the spoon, waiting until the man left before eating. The sounds of

Sam's noisy eating smacked from the corner. With those eating habits, Madame Devereaux would have made him miss three meals to learn proper abstinence. She started to dip her spoon into the rice, but her mind flashed with the image of children playing with broken bricks instead of blocks, hungry children who had to steal bread to eat.

Sam had already learned about abstinence. She wondered what it was like to be really hungry, not because you had to be ladylike but because you had no food. Suddenly all the food she'd wasted over the years came to mind, along with a strong dose of guilt. She paused and glanced at him. He continued to eat as if it were his last meal.

She set the bowl down and struggled to get into a standing position. Concentrating on keeping her balance, she bent down and picked up her meal, straightening very carefully so she wouldn't spill the rice. She balanced the bowl in both hands and shuffled across the room until she stood barely a foot away from him.

He looked up at her, suspicion on his hard-bitten face.

She held out the bowl. He looked at it, but didn't budge.

"Here," she offered with a smile, "you can have mine."

For one brief instant, confusion and something akin to embarrassment flashed across his face, but quickly melded into a hateful red look of male anger.

She backed up a step, wary of his reaction.

"Keep your damn food, Miss LaRue, and your misplaced pity. I don't want either of them." He looked as if he wanted to hit her.

She was afraid he might just do it, too, so she shuffled back over to her spot near the door, a little hurt by his reaction. She was only trying to be nice. After plopping back down on the hard floor, she stared at the bowl of food, not understanding his anger. Where she came from a person accepted a gift graciously. He didn't. Her eyes burned, and she swallowed hard around the dry knot of wounded feelings that had lodged in her tight throat.

Hesitantly she scooped a small spoonful from the bowl

and delicately placed it in her mouth. She put the spoon back in the bowl, intending to savor the flavor of the food.

It had none. She stared at the strange food. Her appetite was gone. He didn't want her food, but now neither did she. She looked around the primitive dank hut, at the rusty old splintered water pail and the green moldy mats. Nothing was familiar.

There was nothing she knew here, nothing familiar, nothing to hold on to. And that scared her to death. More than anything, she just wanted to go home to Belvedere and her overprotective brothers. Right now, she'd have given anything for that protection, and for a shoulder to lean on.

6

"Ransom? Oh, my Gawd!"

Two seconds . . . not too bad. Sam watched Lollie gape at the colonel, stunned into silence—a rarity—by the news that she was to be ransomed to her father for twenty thousand U.S. dollars—Aguinaldo's own gun money.

"The details are being negotiated now. The exchange will take place in a few days, if your father cooperates." Luna walked slowly around her, letting what he didn't say hang like impending doom in the air.

Sam didn't even have to count this time. He could tell by her expression that she knew exactly where she stood. Her light blue eyes flashed with doubt, then worry, then absolute despair. Even he felt sorry for her, his sympathy aided by the fact that she was being quiet, for a change.

He regretted that thought real fast.

She looked at him, then up at Luna, and she let loose with the noisiest bawling scream he'd ever heard. The hysterical high-pitched scream-crying was loud enough to bring down the wailing wall. And she didn't stop.

The cool Colonel Luna's mouth hung open. The two guards had their hands pressed over their ears and clear expressions of pain on their contorted faces. The colonel began to dig through his pockets.

Sam's fingers itched. His ears rang. It had been a long time since he'd felt the need to choke the living daylights out of something. Her screams raked an irritating path down his spine. Every muscle in his body tensed. Her face was a vivid purple, her fists white, and her voice . . . God, her voice howled through the hut, almost echoing from the high rafters. The only sound he could compare it to was imaginary—thousands of sick, baying wolves on the floor of the Grand Canyon. Something sprinkled down on his head, shoulders, and arms. It was dry grass. Two cockroaches crackled to the ground next to him, and geckos scurried like rain down the grass walls.

Lollie LaRue was bringing down the rafters.

Luna rammed a gag into her mouth. Immediately Sam's tense neck and shoulder muscles slackened. He took a long, relieved breath. She jerked the gag out and started again.

"Where's the gag?" Luna and his guards searched the ground.

She was sitting on it. Sam had seen her ram it under her skirts, which meant she knew exactly what she was doing. God, she could scream. He could feel the racket ring in his teeth. If he hadn't hated Luna so much, he would have gone over and gotten the damn gag himself, just to shut her up. He'd suffered through worse torture, but on a scale of one to ten, this was a good eight—ten being the loss of an eye, and one being the bite of a whip.

Luna gave up the search and moved toward her. Sam stiffened, instinct telling him what was coming. Her face was still purple, her eyes were squeezed tightly shut, and her scream had dropped a gravelly octave. Luna stood at her side, his face a picture of anger and frustration. Then, as he raised his fist, his look changed to one of sick delight.

"If you damage the goods, you won't get paid," Sam said, his voice inflected with boredom he was far from feeling. Luna meant to batter her into silence. Sam could see it on the man's face. He knew that look.

Luna stopped, obviously struggling to keep from following through with his swing. Slowly he lowered his hand, still knotted in a tight fist.

"Leave her," Luna shouted to his guards before he spun on his bootheel and left, his guards following like shadows. The door slammed shut.

"You can stop now. They've gone."

Her scream tapered off, and her damp icy blue eyes popped open.

"Quite effective," he complimented her. "Use it often?"

She stared at him for the longest time. He didn't break their stare, and finally she admitted in a hoarse voice, "Only when my wits fail me."

"That often, huh?"

"You know, Samuel—"

"Sam, not Samuel." He paused. "*Nobody* calls me Samuel."

"Oh, all right, then. You know, Sam, you have to take fault for this." Her voice rasped defensively.

"You're probably right, but casting the blame won't save us now."

"Well, my daddy will pay the ransom. He'll pay it, you'll see. He'll save me," she said almost too quickly. Her voice was firm, contradicting the doubt that showed in her ice-colored eyes. She stared over her shoulder for the longest time, an unseeing look in those same light eyes.

If he'd ever met a woman who needed saving, it was this one.

"I never doubted it for a minute," he said. Her eyes snapped back to lock her gaze with his. Curiosity piqued, he tried to read her expression. It was wistful, as if she'd lost something precious. She averted those eyes, her fingers nervously twisting that sparkly thing on her shoe again.

What was this? he thought. Her actions belied her words. They implied that she was unsure about her rescue, despite her tone. She'd tried to sound sure, but her eyes said she wasn't. He wondered who this poor little rich girl needed to convince, him or herself. He didn't comment, though, just warned her. "Don't try a stunt like that again. Luna won't let you get away with it. He'd have no problem sending you back dead, and he will if that ransom isn't paid."

Her face turned grayer than Lake Michigan in winter.

It was a little easier to feel sorry for her when she wasn't screaming. He didn't need any more hysterics, so he figured he'd be better off if he lied to her. At least then they could get through whatever time was left. The more time they had, the more chance there was for escape.

"Look, I'm sure your father will come up with the money. In a few days you'll be back home. You can go back to Belleview—"

"Belvedere," she corrected distractedly, continuing to twist her shoe thing.

"Okay, Belvedere. Back to your Peachtree Farm—"

"*Beech*tree Farms." She sniffed a bit and rubbed a white finger across her uppity little nose.

"Yeah, whatever. Then you'll be back at that Hick House."

She gave him a perturbed look and stated rather loudly, "*Hick*ory House."

"Hick or hickory, what's the difference? They're both in the South. Besides, you'll be the hell home, all right?" What a pain. He wondered why he even tried. Who gave a rat's ass about any of those homes of hers, especially since she'd play hell ever seeing any of them again.

She squirmed around for a minute or so and finally pulled the gag out from under her butt. She stared at it for a second, raised her head, and looked around the room. She scooted over to the water bucket.

Ah. The flower was going to get a drink. Maybe she was

human after all. A gecko scurried out of a dark corner and up his leg. Sam flicked it off. Annoying little buggers. The sound of sloshing water captured his attention, and he looked up.

She was washing with their drinking water.

"What the hell are you doing?" he shouted, shooting upright so he could hobble over there.

She dipped the rag into the water, wrung it out with a couple of dainty twists, and casually washed her face and neck.

He towered over her, glaring down, unable to believe she could be that stupid.

She rubbed the damp rag over her eyes, then opened them, wiping under her hair and around the back of her neck. The whole time she purred like a creamery kitten.

"I'm washing," she answered with an innocent look, acting as if it was the most natural thing in the world to do with the only water they had. She bent her head down, letting her bourbon-blond hair fall over her face while she ran the cloth over her neck. Through a curtain of hair she added, "I was feeling right sticky."

He jerked the rag from her hands.

She whipped her head up, her hair falling down her back, and gasped, "What did you do that for?"

"Because, Miss Lollipop LaRue, you're bathing with our drinking water." He glared down at her.

"Surely not." She frowned at the bucket.

He swore.

Now she leaned over the bucket, letting the murky water spill through her hands. She looked up at him, her face filled with disbelief. "But this water is . . . brown."

"Brown or not, that's all there is to drink."

She sat there, shuddering. Her expression said she'd sooner die than drink that water.

He stumbled back to his corner and heard her knocking on the door. The guards didn't open it. She banged louder. "Hey, y'all? Y'all! We need some more water!"

Still nothing. She glanced at him, then at the bucket. Her shoulders drooped. She sighed, stood there for a forlorn minute, and then slowly hobbled back over to the far corner. She slid to the floor, her head bent and her shoulders wilting like the conquered. She fidgeted with the rag, folding it this way and that. Every so often she'd sigh, not the lung-windy, dramatic expelsion of air she'd blasted out earlier. These were sighs of defeat. One thing neither of them could afford to do was give up.

"Hey there, Miss Lah-Roo."

Her head shot up.

"Sing for me will you? I sleep better to the sound of a good cat fight."

Her blue eyes iced with anger. Good, he thought. She still had some fight in her. His respect for her went up a notch, which didn't really mean much, since it was so low to begin with.

Her nose went up, and she rammed her shoulders back like a Prussian soldier. "I wouldn't sing at your funeral."

God, what it took for him not to laugh. He'd have to give her credit for one thing: she wasn't boring. In fact her presence broke the monotony. It was like dangling a string before a cat; he could play with her, and that kept his mind sharp.

She still glared at him. He could see her striving to make him shrivel. Her look dared him to respond. So he didn't. He feigned nonchalance with a shrug of his shoulders and concentrated on listening to the sounds around the hut, as he'd been doing since the first hour of his capture. High above this single corner was a window. Through it he could get a good idea of what was happening in the encampment—when the guards changed, the number of men, and the sounds of wagons. The angle of daylight, the depth of shadows, and the smell of meals all gave him clues to the time of day and the camp's routine.

He'd lean his head back against the wall, close his eye and concentrate, picturing the camp as the sounds came

through the window. It was the only way he could de ᵔr-
mine the best time of day to make his escape.

"Oh, my Gawd! Get it off me! Get it off!" Eulalie sat
up, grabbing at her hair and shaking her head like a lathered
horse.

She could feel the giant beetle's legs scurrying over her
scalp.

"Hold still, dammit!" Sam bent over her and jerked her
head close to his chest with two hard handfuls of hair.

"Ouch! Oh, get it, pleeeeease!" Her nose smashed
against his shirt pocket, which felt like it was iron-backed.
One of his fists tightened, pulling her hair tighter and burning her scalp. Smarting tears filled her eyes. "Oooooh!"
She sucked in a panicked breath. She could still feel the
bug moving as his fingers picked through her tangled hair.

He swore a couple of times. Then she felt him grab the
bug and rip it and part of her hair out.

"Aaaaaaaak!" Her hands shot over her throbbing head.

"Oh, shut up! It's out now." Disgust filled his voice, and
he heaved the squirming, hair-tangled bug across the room.
It hit the floor with a loud crackle.

She just sat there shivering while chills raced up her
arms. She still felt as if bugs were crawling all over her.
"Noah should have squished those things."

He sat back on his heels and gave her a one-eyed stare.
"They're harmless."

"I don't care. I hate bugs. The only things I hate more
than bugs are spiders."

He continued to watch her, only now he had an odd
smile on his face. It was not reassuring.

"Are there spiders here, too?" She looked back and
forth across the hut, waiting for the army of spiders to
come running toward her. Suddenly she could feel all
kinds of creepy things around her. Her heart wedged in
her throat.

"If there are, we'll all know it. I'm sure they heard you
in Belleview."

"Belvedere," she corrected.

"That's right," he said, his tone amused. "Belvedere, that bastion of the Lah-Roos. Don't they have bugs there? Oh, I forgot. Don't answer that," he said, holding up his rough hands. "They wouldn't allow any, since the bugs didn't sign the Declaration of Independence."

"That's unfair, not to mention rude. I—"

The sudden rasp of the lock stopped their bickering. They both turned toward the opening door. Light from a kerosene lantern flooded the room, momentarily blinding her. Then the colonel stood in the doorway. One guard held the lantern and the door while two others held a knife and a long rifle poised for use.

Lollie glanced at Sam. He was eyeing the rifle.

The heat of Luna's weaselly stare drew her attention. He raked his gaze over her.

She held her breath.

"They've agreed to the ransom. The exchange will take place in two days. We'll go by boat to Colorido Bay."

She stopped in mid-sigh. He'd said they were going by boat. Her stomach lurched at the thought, remembering the voyage over here and how she'd spent the entire time in bed or on the floor of the marine water closet, sicker than she'd ever been in her entire life. Other than the steward who'd brought fresh water, towels, and oranges, the only person Lollie had seen on the whole voyage was Mamie Philpott, the Methodist, who'd stood outside the water closet singing evangelical hymns. "Rock of Ages" had been the worst. The woman had sung it every time the ship lurched.

But seasickness would be worth it to get out of here, worth it to finally see her daddy. He *was* gonna save her. She smiled and looked up. Colonel Luna had that look again, and her smile faded. He walked toward her, never breaking his stare. She could feel Sam tense. Luna stood in front of her and reached out, running his finger down her cheek and under her chin. He tilted her face up. She wanted to close her eyes, but forced them open. The tension in the hut almost crackled.

"Too bad." Luna said, finally breaking eye contact. He turned on a bootheel, eyeing Sam, who suddenly looked as laggard as an old hound dog. "Care to change sides, amigo? Both Aguinaldo and your Bonifacio want the same thing—independence."

Sam smiled at him, and she knew instantly that she never wanted to be the recipient of that smile. It was predatory; it was calculating; it was lethal.

"It's not the goal I question, Luna. Aguinaldo or Bonifacio, it makes no difference to me." His words just hung there.

Luna's expression changed, and some of his threatening air disappeared. "Ah, a wise choice. A man like myself—"

"Hardly a wise choice." Sam cut him off, suddenly looking like a spider with a fly. "It's not Aguinaldo's goal I question. It's his choice of officers I find . . . lacking."

Luna's face flamed purple. His eyes narrowed. "Take him," he ordered, then walked outside.

"No!" Lollie screamed, grabbing onto one of the guards. He shook her off. She fell back, her bound feet making her lose her balance. She scrambled upright. "Please. He's an American citizen!"

The guards ignored her and yanked Sam through the door. Before it shut she caught one last glimpse of Sam's face. It was perfectly blank.

7

Sam stood just inside the hut, his gaze locked on the opposite wall. It took every ounce of will to keep his burning shoulders back. He didn't breathe, just concentrated on that blurred wall and waited for the guards to slam the door. It took them an agonizing century.

A gasp sounded from somewhere on his left. "What have they all done to you?"

He didn't answer her. He knew that if he opened his mouth to speak nothing would come out but the groans he tried so hard to suppress.

The door shut, the hut darkened, and Sam's knees gave way.

He laid face down on the ground, his ribs bruised and aching from being kicked, his left leg numb with pain from the times Luna's boot had missed his ribs. His hands and fingers were so swollen from torture that the binding around his wrists felt like a vise.

For the life of him he couldn't move a bare inch. He was tired, so tired, and yet he fought the urge to sleep. He needed to know he still had control of his body. Complete control. It was an exercise of will. One he couldn't afford to neglect. Too many times in the past his control had kept him alive.

Somewhere to the left he could hear her shuffling across the hut. She stood there for a long moment. Then he felt her tentative touch on his upper arm. He turned his head slightly and winced from a jab of pain.

He wanted to open his eye but it took too damn much

effort. He had none left after the hours of beating. But Luna still knew nothing. Sam hadn't revealed his real source for purchasing the dynamite guns or the rifles. He'd given Luna a phony name of an arms supplier that would take at least three days to check out. By then Sam intended to be long gone. If, he thought, he could ever move again.

Christ, but his jaw hurt . . . felt like he'd done ten rounds with the Boston Strong Boy.

After a few long seconds, her fingers brushed the curtain of black hair out of his face, grazing his jaw in the process.

"Sweet Jesus." A moan escaped his split lips, and she patted them gently with a damp rag.

"You poor man."

It sounded as if she was crying. That was all he needed, a hysterical Lollie LaRue.

He swallowed, a monumental effort, then licked his lips. "I told you before. I don't need your pity. Keep it."

He heard her suck in a breath, and her hands jerked back as if singed. He waited for her to scurry back to her corner to lick her own wounds. He didn't feel her move. She muttered something, and he listened closely, unable to make out the words. Then he felt that rag again, wiping his face even after he'd tried to spurn her help.

He was so tired, everything ached, so he stopped fighting the lure of pain-free oblivion offered by sleep. The rag patted the gash in his forehead, and he winced. Then her muted mumbling pierced his fog of pain. He couldn't smile, but he wanted to. Sleep was coming, heavier and heavier, and yet his last conscious thought was of her words. They weren't words of defeat or panic or sorrow. They were fighting words. Sweet little lady Lollie LaRue had just called him a damn Yankee.

"Will you stop that goddamn mumbling!"

Lollie looked up at Sam, who scowled at her from his bruised and swollen face. She smiled sweetly then began to hum "Dixie."

He took a deep breath and immediately winced. Her humming tapered off. He was hurting, and he looked a mess, but she wouldn't be foolish enough to try to do something for him when he was awake and moving. And she wasn't about to let him know she felt sorry for him. He'd just throw her help back in her face, like he'd tried to do last night. She had more gumption than to let a battered man lie there bleeding. It wasn't Christian.

The entire night he'd slept in the middle of the hut, never moving. She'd wondered if he'd died. After that she'd spent the longest time watching his back to see if he was still breathing. Every so often she could detect the ever so slight rise and fall of his back. She'd torn off a huge hunk of her petticoat and tried to put it under his head. He'd been asleep and awakened throwing a sharp two-handed right cross that missed her face by only a scant inch. She'd kept her distance after that.

Sometime after dawn had cast its pink-gold light into the hut, he'd crawled back to his corner. She'd watched him struggle and started to help but he'd scowled at the wad of petticoat, cut her to the quick with his sharp, snide remarks about it being too late for charity work. He told her to get back up on her pedestal and leave him the hell alone. Then he'd given her a look so venomous she didn't dare touch him. Once in his corner he hadn't made another sound.

Meanwhile she'd almost gone out of her mind. Another beetle, a three-inch monster, had fallen from the roof. It had missed her by a couple of feet, but that hadn't made her feel any better. She tried to talk herself out of her fear. She had no one to talk to but herself. He'd groused at her to "try something new and be quiet."

She gave him a tentative glance. The bruises on his jaw were almost as dark as his eye patch, but more purple than black. His lower lip had swelled to the size of a pout, and a bloody gash dissected it. A matching gash scabbed over one of his devil's cheekbones and across his forehead.

She'd never seen a beaten man before and could have lived the rest of her life without ever seeing one again. Colonel Luna had done this, and it scared her silly. She wanted to get as far away from that madman as she could, but there was another day of imprisonment left.

Sam swore, loud and raunchy.

It took every bit of her pride not to ask him why.

Shifting, he tried to pull at his boot. His hands slipped and he swore again. She turned away, until she could feel the heat of his stare, assessing her like he always did.

"I need some help."

That was the last thing she had expected to hear, Sam Forester asking for help. But he had.

She moved over near him and waited expectantly.

He gestured to his left boot. This was the first time she'd gotten a good look at his hands. His fingers and hands were swollen and tinged blue. But the battered condition of his fingernails was what made her breath catch. The nails were black, as if they'd been slammed or hammered until they bled.

Chills hit her as she remembered the pain of having her fingers slammed in a door when she was ten years old. She could still feel them throb as if it were yesterday. Her nails had turned purple, too, but nothing like Sam's. She felt so all-fired helpless. Her chest tightened, and she fought the urge to cry. She understood why he'd been so hateful.

It was pride. Sam had pride. He'd been beaten enough and didn't need her to bruise that pride, too.

"Pull off my boot." He stretched out his legs, lifting them off the ground so she could grip the heel of the left boot.

With her bound hands and his bound feet it was hard to get a good grip. Her hands slipped over and over.

"Jesus Christ!"

She ignored him and tugged on the heel again. The heavy rope around the boot made removing it difficult. It didn't budge, no matter how hard she pulled.

"Looks like it's going to take divine intervention for you to manage to take off that boot." He scowled at her.

"Is that why you were yelling? Praying for help?"

"Hardly. Ouch! Can't you do anything?"

"That's unfair. I can surely take off a boot. It's just—"

"I can tell. You're doing such a good job of it."

Tiring of his sarcasm and determined to prove she could do something as simple as removing his boot, she grabbed it, locking her bound hands around the heel and hugging it to her chest. Leaning forward just a smidgen, she glared at him, took one deep breath, and threw her whole body backward.

The boot came off with a pop. Lollie's back hit the hard ground, and she saw stars.

He groaned a laugh.

She struggled to sit up and tried to give him a look that would fry an egg. He laughed harder, wincing in between. If he weren't such a beaten, sorry sight, she'd have thrown the boot at him. Instead she stuck her nose up and ignored him.

"Reach inside and feel around. There should be a long ridge next to the seam."

She stuck her hands inside the warm boot and found the bump. Surprised, she looked up at him and slowly drew out a lethal-looking dagger.

"Cut the ropes." He held up his hands. "They're cutting off my circulation."

She sliced through one knot of rope and he loosened it enough to pull his hands free. He sagged back against the corner, rubbing his hands over and over. She stared at the dagger, thinking, then looked up at him. His lips moved, as if he were counting.

"Do you mean to tell me you've had this knife all the time?"

"Amazing, only four seconds," he muttered, then took the knife from her hands. His grip slackened and the dagger fell to the ground. "Damn."

She couldn't believe it. They'd been shuffling around this ungodly, primitive black hole of a hut for days, and all that time he could have cut their bonds. "We could have escaped with this knife."

"I wasn't ready," he answered then gave her a look of arrogant disbelief. "We?"

"Of course we could have. You could have cut us loose and used the knife on the guards."

"This knife on a hundred guerrilla soldiers? Hardly." He gave her a long look then said, "My, my . . . bloodthirsty little lady, aren't you?"

"Well, I didn't mean kill them, exactly . . ."

"What did you mean?" He gave her a smirk that said he knew what she'd meant whether she did or not.

"Well . . ." She paused to think, then commented, "Since when have you gotten a conscience, Mr. Forester? Besides, you used a knife on me, remember?"

"Hmm, three seconds. How could I forget? That's the reason we're in this mess."

"Surely you're not blaming me?" She pointed to her chest, stunned that he'd reason that this was her fault. All she'd done was make the foolish mistake of going to that marketplace alone. And why was he always talking about time, seconds in particular? She looked at his battered face and commented, "That beatin' must have licked you senseless."

He gave her a wry look and said, "Funny, I thought the same about you."

He was making fun of her again, but she didn't get it, which frustrated the blazes out of her. She started to scoot away.

"Wait!"

She turned and gave him her own "now what" look.

"I can't get enough of a grip to cut the rope from my feet. You'll have to do it."

Her first thought was to refuse to help him, but his beaten face, obnoxious look and all, and his swollen hands stopped her from being ungracious. The memory of him standing so proudly inside the hut, beaten to a pulp and waiting until the guards had left, made her pick up the knife.

She gripped the handle in her hands and tried to saw on the rope that wound and twisted around his ankles. The

rope was thick as a fist and knotted over and over so that
even with his boot off it still bound him tightly.

"What's taking so long? Just cut the damn thing." He
peered over her while she worked to try to sever the
twisted rope.

"It's so thick," she complained, trying over and over to
cut through. Deciding her angle was wrong, she re-situated
herself and tried to apply more pressure. Gritting her teeth,
she shut her eyes and sawed really fast, finally giving the
knife one big sawing push.

The rope snapped and the knife sank into something soft.

He yelled that foul word again.

Her eyes flew open. His swollen hand held his leg above
the ankle. Blood seeped through his fingers.

"Oh, my Gawd!" She fumbled to her knees. "I'm sorry!
I'm so sorry!" Lifting the hem of her skirt, she tried to
dab at the wound.

"Get . . . away," he gritted.

"Please," she pleaded, feeling so bad. It was an accident, but the fact remained that she'd cut his leg, and he
was already hurt. She could feel tears of humiliation well
up in her eyes, and she choked them back, only able to
whisper, "I'm so sorry."

The sound of approaching footsteps came from just outside the tent. She gaped at the door, waiting for it to open
and for Sam to be caught unbound.

"Slide these ropes back on. Quickly!" he said quietly.

She turned, seeing that he'd already rewrapped his ankles
and stuck his foot half into his boot.

"Hurry, dammit!"

She fumbled with the pieces of rope, her nervous fingers
abnormally awkward.

"Come on, Lollipop, get the lead the out." He pushed
his wrists at her.

"Hold still!" she whispered in agitation, finally getting a
loose knot of ropes on his wrist.

The door opened and she spun around too fast. It took
a moment for her to focus.

The little man came in with their rice and a bucket of fresh water. She sighed with relief, afraid that Luna would find Sam out. After setting the bucket in the nearest corner, the server handed her a bowl of rice. He grinned as he held out a spoon. She started to smile back, but Sam poked her in the back with the hard toe of his boot.

She jerked up and turned around frowning. Her angry gaze met his. He pointedly looked down. She followed his gaze. The ropes around his hands had come undone.

The server sidestepped, starting to hand Sam his dish. If Sam lifted his hands the ropes were so loose they'd fall to the ground.

"I'll take it." She scooted in front of Sam and reached for the other bowl. The man paused. She gave him a full smile.

He blinked, shook his head, then slowly held out the bowl.

Lollie took it, not breathing until the man had crossed the hut. He closed the door behind him and the sound of the bolt rasped through the door. She released a huge sigh then turned around, smiling proudly because she'd done something right. In her mind it made up a little for wounding him.

Still smiling, she held out the bowl, pride glowing on her face.

A huge black beetle landed in the bowl with a dull plop.

She screamed and threw the bowl away, hugging her bound hands to her chest and rocking with horror.

After a minute she looked up at Sam.

Her face twisted into a grimace of dread. She sat back on her heels, figuring a little distance between them was necessary for her safety.

The bowl sat atop his head like a papal cap. Globs of rice oozed from the bowl, sliding down his face and dangling from his clenched jaw. The only sound in the hut was the plop of rice hitting his chest and crossed arms.

He looked . . . upset. His neck was purple, like her brother Jed's, only worse. In fact, she was certain his flared nostrils could have blown dragonlike smoke, except that the rice on his nose would have blocked it.

She opened her mouth to say something. Anything.

"Not . . . one . . . word." He swiped the rice off his good eye with an obviously tensed hand. It occurred to her that he wanted to punch something.

Her mouth clamped shut. She scooted back again, still wary.

Without warning the black beetle scurried between them. She squealed, stiffening and squeezing her eyes shut.

One slow deep breath and she opened them.

Sam's boot squished the beetle into the hard dirt. Revulsion on her face, she looked up. He glared at her and continued to grind the bug much harder than necessary. From his face she could tell he wished it was her under his boot.

Caution made her move away from him, which was difficult with her hands and feet still bound. She frowned at her hands, then glanced at the dagger next to his leg. After a thoughtful moment she said, "Would you—"

"No!" he roared.

She jumped.

His shoulders moved, his purple neck tensed. The cat was back, ready to pounce.

Fighting the urge to protect her throat, she scooted back across the room fast enough to give Madame Devereaux a goiter. Then she sat in the dark corner, feeling the way Eve must have felt after foolishly eating that apple.

Although the rice really was an accident, just like the slip of the knife, she wanted to apologize, but he wasn't a forgiving man, so she chose to just keep quiet, a monumental effort when she wanted so badly to speak and be forgiven.

"So long, Lollipop."

The exchange was on. Sam watched the guards cut the ropes that bound her feet. She looked up, her light eyes tentative and frightened.

"Good-bye, Mr. Forester," she whispered, her eyes downcast.

They hadn't spoken during the last day. Since she'd dumped the rice on him she'd stayed in her corner, he in his. All her snobbery was gone, replaced by a meek blond shell. He liked her better with a little spunk in her; as hard as it was to admit, her quietness seemed unnatural. He glanced at her again. An odd sense of guilt, something he hadn't felt since he'd understood his uncle's joke, swept through him.

With the exchange taking place today, he could afford to ease the girl's fear. After all, he reasoned, she'd be out of his hair, and he'd be long gone by the time Luna returned. He had to be. Death at the colonel's hands would be his only other option.

She stood so regally, yet her shoulders and demeanor screamed defeat. It touched the warrior within him.

"You'll be back in Manila by tomorrow," he assured her.

She gave him a weak smile, and her eyes misted.

"Go home. Go back to Belleview."

She sniffed. "Belvedere."

He grinned in spite of his sore jaw and split lip. "All right, Belvedere."

She looked him in the eye, an apology searching for forgiveness.

"Forget it, Lollipop. It was an accident." He gave her a quick nod of his head, a mock salute of sorts. Her face lit with a blinding smile just before they led her away.

Sam stared at the closed door. He kept his severed ropes in place and listened to the sounds of them walking away from the hut. After a few minutes of waiting, he glanced up, figuring by the sounds that it was midmorning. Not long afterward he heard the guards change—the sound he'd been waiting for. The camp would be disrupted for only about ten minutes. Then Luna and the escort would be gone and the guards would watch him even more closely, not wanting to risk the loss of their prisoner while their commander was gone. If that happened, heads would roll.

But that wasn't Sam's problem; escaping was. He shook off the ropes and pulled his dagger from inside the top of his boot. He sawed a U-shaped opening large enough to crawl through in the corner of the hut, and slowly pushed open the cut section. As it opened, he bent so he could see outside.

There were five other huts in view, which meant five huts could clearly see the back of this one. That was a problem and a hindrance to his escape. But it was also a challenge. Suddenly his bruised body didn't ache so much. His fingers were able to move freely; his expression came to life. Sam needed this.

The area in back of the hut was clear. Ignoring his bruised ribs and sore hands, he crawled through the opening. Crouched, he quickly replaced the section of grass wall so the hole was undetectable. He crept along the back of the hut, pausing when he reached the corner.

An alert guard stood by the door. He'd play hell getting by that one. The man had that zealous-guard stance. To Sam's right was a wide open space, then another hut. Laughter echoed from inside along with the smell of food. It was the mess hut. *Damn. The busiest place in a camp.* Quickly he moved back to the other corner. The coast was clear. He rounded it and moved along that side of the hut. A thick copse of banyan trees stood about fifty yards away to the south, protected by two rows of looped barbed wire. He heard footsteps. They came from in back of the hut.

Sam took off at a full run, jumped the wire, once, then twice. His feet hit the ground, jarring his aching ribs so hard that he lost his wind. The second he felt the cool shadow of the trees he dove for the ground, gasping for air and rolling into the damp, yard-high guinea grass that grew beneath. He lay as still as stone, his ribs aching like the very devil and his breath coming in shallow pants, which he fought to keep silent.

The men stopped about ten yards away. The fetid scent

of the oozing wet ground hit his nose. He waited. They moved on. Slowly he got to his knees, moving in a crouch toward the riverbank that bordered the encampment. Time was running out. His mental clock ticked. Soon they'd discover he was gone.

Reaching the bank, he belly-slid down into a blanket of deep green lotus pads that floated on the murky river water. He made his way along the mangroves lining the bank, moving beneath the thick acrid-smelling branches that hid him from view. The racket of a steam pump chugged and clattered in the air.

He stopped. A boat was close by. The river narrowed and turned; the mangroves stopped. Someone had cleared this section of the bank. Sam moved away from the bank, out to a thick stand of water bamboo—a new source of cover. His head was the only part of him above water, and it was obscured by the thick swamp reeds.

Here the width of the river almost doubled, forming an inlet where a long, gray-weathered wooden dock stood on bundled bamboo piers tinged green with river slime. A faded green and white river trawler sat on the north side of the pier, and fatigue-clad soldiers milled about the dock and decks, some on guard and others readying the boat to cast off. White steam spit a cloud into the already wet air, and the clunk, chug, and clatter of the steam engine drowned out any conversation Sam might have overheard.

Fully loaded, the boat had a conglomeration of splintered wooden crates and gray, rust-banded barrels along the port side. Once black, but now half red with the ever-prevalent rust of the tropics, the steam engine rose from the middle of the ancient river trawler. Next to the rusty boiler, a palm frond canopy served as a roof for the small pilot wheel.

Huddled around the open bow of the boat like birds to bread crumbs stood a group of armed rebels. They soon parted to give Sam a glimpse of Colonel Luna standing over his precious pink cargo—the Lollipop. She sat on a narrow bench on the foredeck next to a mooring winch. From her frantic gestures and Luna's impatient tapping of his bolo knife against his boot, Sam gathered they were having some kind of argument.

He glanced past the dock to a large clearing, where five more armed guards stood watching the river. From their perch high above the riverbank, they could watch the whole inlet, assuring Luna and the boat of protection and ruining Sam's chance of making his way downstream.

The movements on the dock told Sam that the boat was about to cast off. The engine geared into a constant chugging, and the dockmen bent over the cleats, uncoiling the lines that held the trawler. Sam had to think fast.

There was no time to find a log or driftwood branch to hide him from the armed patrol. The boat backed up slowly, building up steam. Sam inhaled long, slow breaths that filled his lungs with oxygen and put a purgatory of pressure on his battered ribs. One last breath and he dove deep, hoping to make it to the boat before it could reverse engines and head downstream.

He swam underwater, pulling with all his strength, thankful that some anonymous male ancestor had given him the gift of a big frame and a strong upper body. At this moment, he called on every bit of power and strength in that torso. His lungs burned from holding an eternal breath. The vibrations of the engine drew him in the right direction, closer and closer until he could feel the water around him ripple.

As fast as a rifle shot the sound died. Then metal scraped metal and the engine clunked. There was nothing but silence. His lungs burned, his ribs ached, his numb legs kicked on and one arm pulled, then the other, dragging the drawing weight of his clothed body through the water with a stubborn determination earned in the Chicago slums.

Come on . . . come on, swim, you bruised bastard, swim.

A clank echoed through the water less than two feet from him. Water suddenly rushed around him with a push of current. Then with a loud, squealing scrape of metal the engine kicked in.

Sam surfaced just in time to grip a portside tow handle

by the trawler's rudder, a good five feet from the propeller blade. His hands ached, but he held fast, fighting the wake as the boat headed downstream.

She'd like to died, but hung her head over the right side of the boat and vomited instead. From somewhere on her left, the colonel swore in Spanish. She stared at the blurred river water and concentrated on breathing. Then it dawned on her that swearwords sounded exactly alike in any language. It was the disgusted male tone that gave them away.

She'd tried to tell the man that she couldn't take the boat ride well. He didn't believe her. She gagged some more. Bet he does now, she thought, remembering how they'd cut the ropes from her bound hands so she could hold onto the rail while she hung her head over the side. The boat floated along, rocking slightly from side to side, side to side. . . .

Her head swam, chills raced up her back and over her arms, and her stomach lurched in counterpoint to the boat. She finally sat up, raising one limp hand to her damp forehead. The men stared at her in horror.

"Could I have a wet rag, please?" She lolled back against the rail. Her whole body felt like peach jelly.

The colonel ordered a soldier to find something, then turned his back on her. She wiped away the tears that streamed down her hot cheeks. Her eyes always teared when she threw up. The boat moved as they met a swifter current, and she swallowed air and leaned back over the side, ready to get sick again.

Concentration came to her rescue and she managed to control her weak stomach. Soon she could feel someone's stare. She pushed up from the rail, opened her eyes, and turned ever so slowly. The soldier had returned and held out a damp piece of cloth. She plastered it over her clammy forehead and collapsed back on the hard bench, moaning as her stomach protested those fast movements. The boat swayed again and again. She flipped the cloth over to stop her queasy chills. Moans slipped past her lips with each motion of the boat. She couldn't stop them, besides which moaning made her feel better.

Each second spent on the water was an hour, each minute seemed like a day. Her stomach lurched again, sending her upright with her head over the side. And as she hung there, the wet rag gripped like a missal in her hand, she prayed that they would get to that bay, and soon.

Sam gripped the tow handle of the rebel trawler and kicked at the wake. They were headed for Colorido Bay, where the exchange would take place. Once near the bay, Sam could let go of the boat and swim to shore where he'd have to cut through four days' worth of jungle to get to Bonifacio's camp. The boat ride would shave almost two days off his journey back. It had been a stroke of luck, being able to let the trawler haul him downstream.

Occasionally, over the steam engine's sputter, he could hear the rebel soldiers talking from the deck high above him. He was safe, chest high in the water and hidden from the deck view by the breadth of the trawler's stern. The steam engine sputtered, and Sam lay back in the water, letting it lap at his sore muscles.

Something popped, then whistled.

By instinct Sam ducked. If there was one thing he knew as well as his own name it was the popping sound of gunfire.

He turned toward the north bank, where a group of Spanish soldiers fired on the rebels. It was an ambush.

Gripping the tow handle, he watched for a safe place to let go and make his way toward the bank. The rebels returned the gunfire, but men dropped from the deck into the water like clay pigeons. Four barrels splashed near him along with one of the wounded rebels.

He let go of the boat and treaded water, using a barrel for cover. Slowly he guided the barrel toward shore. A few minutes later he reached the bamboo reed and managed to crawl up the bank where he hid in a cluster of fire bushes.

The boat chugged along. Then a round of bullets hit the

engine, sounding like target practice on tin cans. The engine sputtered and died. There were still six rebels on the deck, Luna being one of them, and they returned the Spanish fire. Sam watched a moment, then caught a pink flash crawling between some bullet-riddled crates. He swore. First she scurried left. A bullet slammed into the crate next to her, sending her scuttling back to the far crate with all the stealth of a blind pig.

Lollie LaRue was going to get herself shot.

Sam shook his wet head in disgust. All the woman had to do was stay there. The Spanish wouldn't keep her once they found out she was Luna's prisoner. The Spanish watched their relationship with the United States; they didn't need any more diplomatic trouble. The situation between the two nations was already too close to exploding into trouble.

Now if Eulalie, an American, were found with him, also an American and a mercenary, that would be another story. The Spanish had been beating through the jungles, weeding out as many guerrillas and mercenaries as they could, and they knew of his reputation and who hired him.

A scream pierced the air. He knew that sound only too well and turned toward it. The pink twit cannonballed into the water, arms reaching for the nearest barrel. She missed it.

Sam groaned.

She sank like granite.

Without a thought, Sam slid back into the river. He pushed the barrel across and dove, looking for her in the murky brown mud of the river. He swam deep, dodging Mauser bullets from the Spanish rifles. They'd seen her. He amended that: they'd heard her. The king of Spain had probably heard her.

And her mouth was what saved her now.

A dull gurgle sounded from his right. He turned and saw her. Blue eyes open and frantic, her mouth open and screaming. He grabbed her hair and yanked her toward the surface, heading straight for a barrel. He'd never known a person could scream underwater. They broke the surface, and she coughed and gasped. He tried to cover her mouth to quiet her. She took in her air and turned around, linking her arm around his neck and holding on for all she was worth.

"Thank you, thank you," she mumbled around a cough.

They made it to the bank, and Sam crawled out first, then dragged Lollie up and into the bushes. She kept moaning and groaning. Too loud.

"Shut up or you're going to get us killed.

She did clam up, but too late. A Mauser bullet whizzed over his head, lodging in a nearby tree with a dull thud. Her mouth hung open, and her eyes grew wide.

Sam knew that look. He lunged at her. Three more bullets whizzed past them.

Naturally she screamed.

8

Lollie couldn't talk around the gag. But she tried, until she realized that he would just continue to ignore her. All he did was tighten his grip on her wrist and drag her through the jungle even faster.

She glanced behind her. There was no one there. Surely they were safe now, although they hadn't been earlier.

Just after she'd screamed at the gunshots that had whizzed past them, a Spanish soldier had come charging out of a stand of trees. He'd headed straight for Sam. She had cowered in the bushes, frozen with fear. She hated guns.

Sam had saved them, though, knocking the soldier out,

then dragging him into the bushes. He'd taken the man's rifle, pistol, knife, pack, and canteen before he pulled her a few yards away, forcing her to the ground with a knee in her back. For a brief instant she questioned whether he'd saved her only to turn around and kill her. But that made no sense at all. The next thing she knew, he'd gagged her with a piece of her own wet petticoat.

She'd tried over and over to pull the gag off, but it was knotted too tight, the damp cloth making it nigh on impossible to loosen. And she only had one hand. Sam had a death grip on the other.

He hauled her through a patch of sharp bamboo, never once slowing down, and she knew if she did, as she'd tried to earlier, he'd just jerk her even harder through the thickest spots of jungle growth or mud. With the suddenness of a jackrabbit, he changed directions, veering sharply to the left. A few minutes later he pulled her up some mossy rocks to a hidden ledge. He pinned her face down with a massive arm and hard leg. Her throat ached and burned from exertion.

"One noise, one sound out of you, and we're dead," he whispered in her ear.

At those words her desire to talk disappeared. They lay there, face down, his heartbeat pounding like thunder against her back. The vibration felt so strong and loud she said a brief silent prayer that the Spanish wouldn't hear it.

Her own heart beat at the same speed. His breath, hotter and damper than the air around them, brushed her ear. The sensation sent a rush of odd chills through her. This place was hot, humid, dank, not a place for gooseflesh. Again his breath hit her ear, and again she felt the chills. She shivered. His breath stopped. She could feel his gaze on the back of her head as sure as if she were staring at him instead of at the brown-gray stone of the ledge. The heat from that look chased away those odd chills. But the moment passed and soon they both breathed normally again, as normally as two people could when they were an instant away from death.

Sweat seeped from her skin, mingling with the odor of murky river water and the gamy scent of their bodies, male and female, too long unwashed. But dulling that musk was the odd smell of the jungle—the tinge of strong wet earth, a hint of exotic flowers, and green. In the deep jungle, even the green of the plants smelled. Oddly enough, it smelled clean.

A sound caught her attention. She listened closely, holding her breath. Knives splintered bamboo. She stiffened. Leaves and bushes rustled. His body pressed down. A dull squish of boots slogged in the mud. The soldiers were so close she could hear them whisper, and it scared her held breath right past her gag. They stood right below the ledge, so close she'd have sworn they were taking aim.

Her lungs screamed for air, so she fought hard to breathe slowly, sure that they could hear her very breath.

There was a shout.

Lollie closed her eyes tightly, fighting the urge to scream, waiting for the bullet.

Forced human silence weighted the air.

They both stopped breathing.

The screech of a bird high in the trees cracked the quiet. Whispering seeped into the air. Leaves crackled, plants rustled, both signaling the frantic sound of men running—away.

She sagged with relief, letting her forehead fall on her hands. She breathed again. So did Sam. They lay there for the longest time, not moving, only breathing, and still listening for the absolute silence that proved the soldiers were gone.

But each second brought her attention away from sound. She was aware now of Sam's weight, the hard muscles that held her still, aware that the dampness of their clothes was no shield against his solid muscle and her softness. Their bodies were as hot as steam from a vat. She swallowed, yearning to move her head—an intense need she could barely control. For some inexplicable reason she wanted to see Sam's face, see his look.

Then his weight shifted and he knelt next to her. His hands closed over her shoulders, and he pulled her to her knees before him. Her wish was granted. His gaze met hers. After wishing for this barely a minute before, it was the strangest thing. She couldn't see clearly. His features were blurred. She averted her eyes, only then realizing there were tears spilling from them. They were tears of fear, a result of the danger she'd just experienced and the fear of some odd link to this hard man.

His hand touched her head, streaking a trail of fire across her clammy skin, then sliding through her wet hair, the pads of his fingers burning every inch they touched. She waited, shaking inside from a mixture of emotions she'd never before felt. His hands stopped at the knot of the gag. He untied it and it fell unnoticed to her lap.

She sucked in a sharp breath at the sudden touch of air on the chafed corners of her mouth. They burned. Closing her eyes, she willed away the soreness, finally opened them when she felt a soothing cool touch dab at one burning corner of her mouth.

"Press this against it." He doused the gag with fresh water from the canteen and handed it to her. He recapped the canteen.

She continued to stare at him, trying to understand what she felt. After a confusing moment she gave up.

He hooked the canteen back on his belt, adjusted the rifle strap over the shoulder, then looked up. "Let's go."

With that command, he jumped down from the ledge and held his hands up to help her. She glanced at the rag, wondering what to do with it.

"Come on, let's go!"

She sat down on the ledge and barely got situated before his large hands gripped her waist and lifted her off the rock. She braced her hands on his shoulders, the gag still clutched in one tight fist. He set her on the ground, gently for a change, and glanced at the rag. The devil grinned.

She could tell exactly what he was thinking. He thought gagging her was funny. She wanted to throw the thing at him, but didn't. She intended to keep it, so he couldn't use it on her again. She wasn't about to give him the satisfaction of gagging her. She wouldn't scream. At least she'd try not to.

"We'll go west," he told her, readjusting his pack.

She moved on until his swearing stopped her.

"I said *west*." He grabbed her arm and jerked in another direction.

She looked up at the sun but couldn't see it for the dense growth. "That was west," she argued.

"South."

"I thought it was west."

"That's what I get for asking you to think," he mumbled.

"Look." She stopped and rammed her hands onto her hips. "You told me to go west. I went in the direction I thought was west. If you have a problem with that, then just point next time."

His gaze locked on her right hand; the gag was still clutched in her fist. She quickly crammed the wet rag down the front of her gown. His gaze locked on her chest. She crossed her arms and stared back until he finally shrugged and moved past her. She watched him for a minute, deciding if she even wanted to follow him. She looked around her at the dense dark jungle with its odd sounds and rustlings. Something crackled from her left. A trilling sound echoed from overhead. She looked up. A black and red snake slithered on a branch above her head.

She ran to catch up with Sam, looking over her shoulder and above her every step of the way. She finally managed to get about five feet behind him.

"Get the lead out!" he shouted over his shoulder, holding back a thick palm frond and gesturing to her to precede him. She did, and he let go of the branch. It whacked her in the backside.

She stopped. He walked right past her, and she scowled at his back, then scurried along, her heels catching on an occasional ground vine. He moved fast and was well ahead of her again. She thought she heard something. "Sam!" She scurried to catch up with him. "Sam!"

He stopped. "What?"

"Did you hear that?"

"Hear what?"

"That rattling sound."

"Yeah. I thought it was your head." He turned and started walking again.

She heard it again and looked up. A huge frog with a bright red-orange head looked down at her, blew out its cheeks, rattled, and flew to another tree. *A flying frog?* She ran to catch up with Sam again.

Finally, after long minutes of silence, she asked, "Where are we all going?" She stumbled, grabbed a branch, and almost fell.

"Back to the river."

She worked her hand free of the sticky leaves. "Why?"

He hacked at a thick bush and grunted something that sounded like "Because I'm a damn fool."

"I didn't hear you," she said, out of breath from running to catch up with him. In desperation, she grabbed hold of his belt, figuring it was the only way she'd be able to keep up.

"Where are we going?" she repeated.

He stopped, and she slammed into his back, losing her grip on the belt. Slowly he turned, scowling down at her with his devil's eyes. "To get you back to your *daddy.*"

"Oh." She brightened, hope making her stand a little straighter.

"And out of my hair." He turned and stomped on.

"Keep down and keep quiet." Sam soundlessly worked his way through the thick bushes. Wincing, he stopped, then shook his head with disgust. She moved along behind him, stirring more leaves and branches than a herd of wild boar. He turned and watched her, unable to believe she could make that much noise with her mouth shut.

Hunched over, she tried to put that stupid little shoe

back on. When she finally did, she turned and stuck her arms through the bushes as if trying to swim her way out.

Her skirt caught on a branch. She mumbled something. Sam crossed his arms and leaned against the stringy trunk of a monkeypod tree. She turned and fidgeted with her dress for a few seconds. The whole bush shook. Then she grabbed the dress into two tight fists and pulled. The sound of rending fabric filled the air just before she crashed into the base of the bush. He expected a scream or at least a cry, but she didn't utter a single sound.

Sam looked closer, shaking his head when he saw her lips move.

With a shake of her skirts, she ducked and tried to work her way through the thick fire bushes. Now her hair was caught. She scowled at the branches, reached up, and twisted hard, breaking them from the trunk of the bush. They flopped like collapsed antlers down the side of her empty blond head.

Swimming through the bushes, she made it about two feet farther. Then a branch scraped her arm. She sucked in a sizzling breath of pain that sounded like a doused campfire. Sam pushed away from the tree and closed the short distance between them. He grabbed her and hauled her out of the bushes.

He set her down and looked at her, suddenly struck with the picture of her reaction if she were to get a good look at herself. Her hair was still wet, a tangled mess that hung past her shoulders, the fire bush branches still drooping from her head. Dirt smudges streaked her pale cheeks like war paint and the damp gag flopped out of the top of her dress like a limp flag of surrender. Scrapes crisscrossed her pale forearms like scratches on pearls, and her formal pink dress looked as if it had spent two years at the bottom of a ragman's cart.

Lollie LaRue was a mess.

She was also a problem, one that could get them both killed. He couldn't abandon her in the middle of the jungle, and he needed to keep her safe. Yet he had to get to the river, and he had a hunch, based on past experience, that taking her with him would ensure their capture, something neither of them could afford now. It didn't take a genius to realize that just seeing them together would be proof enough for the Spanish. They wouldn't give her a chance to explain. She was with him, and she would be condemned. But he doubted she'd believe him, or take the news too well. He'd have to string her along.

"Do you think you could do something?" he asked, resorting to his string-with-the-kitten maneuver.

Her eyes lit and her stance perked up. She nodded. He almost felt sorry for her . . . almost.

"Okay," he said, leaning down as if to tell her a state secret. "I want you to stay here while I check out the river."

She looked around at the thick, dark jungle that surrounded them, her face unsure. "Wouldn't it be better if I stayed with you?"

"No." Sam hid his smile and looked serious. "It's much better if you stay here. I need you to protect the flank. It's an important job."

Slowly she nodded, still staring into the thick jungle. He turned to leave, knowing from experience that this was the safest place for her. He needed to see if the boat or any of the soldiers, Spanish or rebel, were still on the river.

"Shouldn't I have a knife or a gun or something?"

Not if I want to live through the day, he thought, but responded, "Ever fired a gun?"

She nodded. "Once." The tone of her voice told him all he needed to know.

"That bad, huh?"

"I shot out the leaded-glass window in Jeffrey's study."

"Ah, the oldest brother. The one who told you about your name."

"Oh, you remembered." Her face lit up.

How could I forget when you went on about it for ten minutes? He didn't say that, but nodded instead.

Her smile disappeared. "But Jeffrey wasn't there at the time."

"Lucky for him."

She winced, then admitted, "My brother Jedidiah was, though."

Her expression was so serious that Sam wouldn't let himself smile. He did, however, feel a sudden odd kinship with that brother of hers.

"After breaking the window the bullet hit the gas lamp over the desk. Jed was working at the time."

Sam waited for the rest.

She looked up at him. "Ten stitches and he didn't come around until supper time."

"I'll keep the gun. You won't need it." Sam turned on his heel and started toward the river. He needed to get away before she figured out what he'd done.

"How long will you be gone?"

He stopped and turned back. She was scared, sitting there hugging her knees and giving him that big-eyed stare. Then she tried to smile. She failed and looked down at her knees instead.

"I won't be long."

She nodded and kept looking at the thick jungle as if she expected it to choke her. What really hit him was the way she tried to hide her fear. She sighed, resigned. No arguments, no tears, no screaming or begging, just a wee spark of courage. He almost relented and let her come with him. Common sense stopped him. She was safer here. "Just remember, don't leave this spot. It's too easy to get lost. Stay here."

He was about eight feet into the jungle when he heard her mumble, "How can I protect the flank without a weapon?"

He'd been counting. It had taken her ten seconds to realize that, and by then he was safely away. He moved toward the river, pretty certain that if anyone was still there it would only be someone to guard the boat. Rebels tended to scatter and circle back around if attacked in the jungle, but on that boat Luna and his men had been sitting ducks.

The Spanish were most likely the victors in that skirmish. He'd figured six to eight of them had been tracking Lollie and him. They were probably deep in the jungle by now, still looking for the two of them.

When he neared the river, Sam inched his way toward the bank, making sure he stayed well behind cover. Mind and ears sharp, he scanned the area. The boat was still there, its bowline tied to a tree on the opposite bank. He looked for the guard. There wasn't one. That didn't ring true.

Suspicious, he waited longer, watching for any sign of movement in the brush.

It didn't make sense to leave the boat unguarded. The Spanish as well as the rebels would value the trawler. He buried the rifle under a pile of dead leaves, crawled out of the bushes, and slithered into the water. After taking a few deep breaths behind a cluster of cattails, he dove and then swam underwater to the boat's port side. Slowly and carefully he surfaced, edging around to get a look at the other side.

No guards.

He couldn't be that lucky. The unguarded trawler was a gift. Sam could get the Lollipop and start up the boat. They'd be at the exchange point in Colorido Bay before nightfall. But first he needed to check out the boat. Caution still guarding his movements, he slowly swam toward the nearer bank.

If Lollie had learned a lesson in the last long minutes, it was that the jungle was never silent, and always savage. Birds cawed and screeched, sounding like distant human screams. Moisture permeated the air, forming a thick dew that clung to leaves and vines and dropped like intermittent rain to the black mulch below.

Little light managed to reach the jungle floor, making everything around her smell damp and dead. She eyed the thin blue ribbon of sky that showed above the dark tops of lofty jungle trees—trees so tall and dense that they looked like dark towers to heaven. She felt small and trapped, as if the jungle could swallow her like a single drop of dew.

From the hidden sun, a single beam of light bled through the treetops, falling on her hand like a benediction. She shifted so the bath of sunlight completely covered her. That one thread of light in the jungle darkness reassured her. But that reassurance was short-lived once the insects hummed louder. She knew they nested and crawled everywhere, creepy little bright red and green and yellow creatures, nothing like the small brown locust and worms and beetles back home. She watched a bright green fly with grasshopper legs and a fire red head flit from plant to plant. Despite the carnival colors and its graceful way of gliding through the air, the strange insect only drove home the fact she was so far from everything she knew and loved.

Her hands started to shake. She swallowed, searching for the strength to hold her own with the foreignness of the jungle that caged her. More than anything, she wanted to vent that fear by screaming until she was hoarse. She didn't, because she didn't want to be gagged again, and a part of her needed desperately to prove to Sam Forrester, and to herself, that she wasn't female fluff.

A twig cracked behind her. She froze, not breathing, just listening.

She caught the scent of something. Another quiet footstep sounded . . . closer. The scent grew stronger. It was the odor of human sweat. She closed her eyes. Again a twig snapped. Her eyes shot open; her hand closed tightly around a clod of dank soil, and moisture seeped through her fingers, running over her hands. She took a shallow, slow breath.

Out of the corner of her eye she saw a shadow flicker past. A thin rough cord fell around her neck . . . then jerked, choking her. She threw the dirt, grabbed the cord, and yanked it away from her throat.

Something whizzed past her. She felt its wind. A dull thud sounded. The cord instantly slackened. A Spanish soldier fell next to her, a knife in his chest. A scream of terror pierced the air. It was hers.

Sam stepped from the bushes in front of her, his face a savage mask. He strode toward the soldier and kicked him over onto his back.

"Gawd . . ." Lollie covered her face.

"Come on, let's get out of here." He grabbed her arm and yanked her to her feet, then slipped his knife back into its sheath.

She didn't dare look back, just gulped three deep breaths to still her pounding heart. Then she looked at him. His face was hard, barely human. His mouth, the only crack in his face, was thin, hard, and unyielding, just like his stare. He looked at her with cold power. Then he glanced at the dead man with an ice-edged expression of pitiless anger. Sam Forrester didn't need two eyes. One could be deadly enough.

It seemed as though they'd walked forever, or at least her feet felt like it. His stance was still tight, alert, and ready, but he seemed less intent and had stopped barking orders at her about twenty minutes ago. He only swore when she fell, which she just did.

"Come on." He grabbed her hand and pulled her along with him.

"Are they following us?"

"Doesn't look like it."

"But the man you killed—"

"He might have followed us, but he could have been left behind to clear the rebels from the boat. He's dead. It doesn't matter."

From his tone she could tell the subject was closed.

A few hundred yards more and they emerged onto the riverbank where Sam had brought her after he rescued her before. The boat was moored on the opposite side, and Lollie stopped, assuming they'd now have to cross the river, not that she wanted to set foot on a boat again.

She was wrong. Sam turned downriver.

"Where're we going? That boat's right there."

"We can't take it." He kept on, never breaking stride. "The engine's full of bullet holes. That trawler's dead in the water, which is what you're going to be if you don't move faster."

Lollie hurried behind him, smiling because she wouldn't have to ride in the boat. "Oh, that's good."

He stopped, scowling. "I realize you and I don't see things in the same logical light, but even I can't figure out why you'd be glad to be dead in the water."

Lollie laughed. "Oh, I didn't mean that. I'm glad about the boat."

He stared at her for a silent moment, then rubbed his chin thoughtfully while he nodded his head as if he understood perfectly. All his motions were exaggerated. "Makes perfect sense. Instead of the ease of a two-hour boat ride to get to that bay, you're glad we have to haul butt through miles of jungle and mud."

The scorn-filled look on his face pricked Lollie's pride. The man treated her as if she had no mind and was nothing but a weak snob. She decided to skirt the issue of her seasickness. "I don't like boats."

He muttered something indistinguishable. "Well, Miss Lah-Roo, I hope you like walking as much as you like talking, because that bay is over half a day's walk for a jungle-trained soldier."

He raked her with a long assessing look that started at her head and ended at her toes. He shook his head, and when he looked up at her again she could tell he found her lacking. His tone always implied a lack of respect, and that really hurt.

She couldn't help that she'd been born in privilege and he to poverty. And it seemed unfair of him to dislike her for something she couldn't control. It was as unjust as hating people because of the shape of their nose or the color of their eyes or hair.

Every time she tried to be kind, like offering him her food and trying to help him after the gawdawful beating, he rudely threw the offer back in her face, and she didn't know how to deal with that kind of reaction. It hurt her so much all she could do was run off wounded to her own lonely dark corner, because when she cowered in her corner he wasn't so mean.

She didn't understand him or this confusing, rough, fast world of his. It scared her silly. Not one brother was here, and right now she'd have welcomed even Jed's familiar face. Although he was the hardest on her, Lollie knew he cared about her.

Now all she had was Sam, and to Sam Forrester she was nothing. He didn't understand that she didn't know how to do things here. Everything was so different. She needed desperately to have something familiar, something normal, around her. The only thing close to being familiar was Sam. He was a man, like her brothers, and an American.

He prodded her with the rifle. "Move! That is if you want to see your daddy."

A very rude male American, she amended. Pricked by his attitude, she dug up some good old southern pride, stuck her chin up and took off through the brush on wobbly, heel-sinking steps. Less than five feet into her pride walk she fell face down into a wet, sharp-smelling bush. She struggled to get her footing and managed to wiggle back far enough for him to pull her out.

He didn't. The king of the Chicago slums walked right past her . . . the damned arrogant Yankee.

9

Sam whacked a piece of stringy beef jerky into her outstretched palm. She stared at the hunk of shriveled brown meat as if it were from a cockroach. He sank his teeth into his own piece, twisting his head so he could tear off the bite. Jerky was always tough, but this was the toughest he could remember having, the saltiest, too. She watched him chew, her face stunned, curious, and a little horrified.

"Beef jerky," he explained, gnawing off another salty chunk.

She looked at the food again, then slowly lifted it to her mouth. She bit into it. Her eyes widened. He chewed, watching. She ground her teeth back and forth, trying to separate the bite from the strip, a technique he knew was impossible. She gave a quick, sharp, futile little tug. He hid a grin with another jawful. She pulled again and again, her whole attention now focused on biting off that piece of jerky.

Christ, she was something to watch. With a look of determined concentration, she raised her knees and dug those stupid heels into the soft ground, obviously seeking better leverage. The little southern flower who'd asked so sweetly for silverware now sat against the rough, ridged trunk of a coconut palm, looking dirty, hair-tangled, and forlorn, while she tugged on a piece of dried up old meat like a draft team tugs a wagon—head down and whole body straining with the effort.

Although he tried like hell to hide it, she must have heard

his snort of laughter, because she suddenly looked up at him, her face a bright pink.

He grinned. Her chin went up, and she turned sideways, trying to block his view. She ground down on the meat again, the determination of an army mule registering on her filthy face, and grabbed the strip with both hands, putting her whole body into pulling the meat.

It worked. Her hands slammed into her lap, leaving a wad of jerky in her grimacing mouth. Sam waited for her to chew. She did, with the same enthusiasm she might have used to eat her shoe. Her mouth and jaw strained. Her eyes grew wide, and her lips contorted as her lower jaw ground into the upper, trying to chew the leathery beef.

But more comical than her jaw contortions was the look on her face. She blinked a few times, her eyes watery, and her mouth puckered.

"The salt's good for you." He gnawed off another bite, then waved the beef strip around to emphasize his words. "Keeps you from getting dehydrated in the tropical heat."

Her cheek bulged from the wad. "Mmmah aah haav fumm wahher, poweez?"

He tried not to laugh out loud.

"Huh? I can't undertand you." He understood her, but this was just too good to pass up.

She shifted the wad to the other side of her mouth, frustration on her face and her eyes watering from the salt. "Wahher, poweez!"

Sam waited, trying to look thoughtful.

She pointed at his canteen belt. "Wahher! Wahher!"

"Oh . . . water." He snapped his fingers.

She nodded vigorously.

He stood, unhooked the canteen, and handed it to her.

She grabbed it quicker than a Quincy Street pickpocket. She twisted the cap, but couldn't get it off.

She looked up at him, still standing above her. Her face was desperate. "Uhhpann, poweez . . . harwee!"

It took every bit of his willpower to keep from tormenting her longer. The expression on her face touched some small bit of humanity buried somewhere inside him. He took the canteen from her and unscrewed the cap.

Those ladylike manners of hers forgotten, she grabbed it and took a swig. She chewed briefly, then took a deep breath and swallowed. From the size of the wad, Sam was sure it must have hit her stomach like a mortar weight.

She gasped and took another gulp of water.

"Better eat up there, Lollipop. We need to go on." Sam glanced up at the sky, trying to gauge how much time they had before nightfall. There wasn't much. He'd been wrong about how long it would take them to get there. He'd overestimated her. She was even slower than he'd thought.

"I've had enough, thank you." She handed him the meat and the canteen.

He returned the jerky to the pack and hooked the canteen back on his belt, then turned to give her a hand up. She'd turned around and now picked at her teeth with a fingernail.

"Let's go."

She sat as straight as bamboo, her hand whipping back into her lap. Her face flushed with a guilty look that said he'd caught her doing something wrong.

"I don't mind if you pick your teeth." He hauled her to her feet.

She dusted off her bottom with a few angry strokes. "I wasn't picking my teeth."

"Sure."

"I need a toothbrush," she said, as if that one implement could solve all her problems.

He grabbed her hand and started through the brush, moving faster than they had before. "I'll make sure we stop at the next Marshall Field and buy you one, along with a silver tea set and some of those lah-dee-dah little cups."

She mumbled that she couldn't wait until they got to that bay and away from him.

"I feel exactly the same way," he said over his shoulder, then walked twice as fast as before.

She stumbled. "Can't you slow down?"

"No." He dragged her through a clump of head-high palmilla trees.

She muttered something about obnoxious Yankees who didn't behave like gentlemen.

He let go of the bent palm frond he'd been gallantly holding aside.

It whacked her right in the face. She gasped in outrage, but he ignored it, pulling her with him at a full military run.

The sun sat atop the glowing water in a blazing pink fireball, the brilliant colors of a Pacific sunset—golden orange, burning pink, cool lavender, and deep dark purple—staining into the immanence of a night-black sky. Around the pearlescent waters of the bay were white sand beaches and thick, virid jungle backed by a jagged barricade of mountains bruised purple from the fast-setting sun.

Lollie sagged against a tree, trying to catch her breath and watching Sam pace the white sands. Her lungs burned so from running that she felt as if the hot sun were setting in her raspy throat. Sweat dripped down her face, mosquito bites made her arms itch as if she'd slept in poison oak, and her leg muscles ached like they were bruised. And her poor feet. They felt blistered and raw.

"Can you see the boat?" She sat down and raked her broken fingernails up one itchy arm.

He continued to pace, stopping once to kick at some sand. "It's not here."

"Are you sure?"

He stooped and glared at her, his face only inches away while he pointed toward the calm, empty bay. "Do you see a goddamn boat anywhere out there?"

Her hope dying, she looked down at the sand and mumbled, "I just thought maybe I couldn't see it."

"You can't see it, Miss Lah-Roo, because it's not there. We missed it." He stormed an angry ten-foot path of frustration, talking to himself about what the hell he was going to do with her. From the angry tone of his voice and the purple color of his neck—a color that had nothing to do with the sunset—she could tell that he wouldn't welcome her next question. She wanted to know what they would do next, but for the sake of her own well-being, she wouldn't ask just now. It wasn't the time. So she counted the bites on her arm instead.

He muttered something about being sitting ducks and said they might as well shoot themselves because they were as good as dead. She'd just reached bite number twenty-two when he stopped pacing suddenly, spun around, and took the rifle off his shoulder.

He lifted it up, and she faced the gun barrel. Her breath caught. He was gonna shoot her! He rammed some latch thing back with a deadly click.

She slammed her eyes shut. Her back went ramrod straight, the muscles in her small body as taut as dulcimer strings. She prayed a last prayer for a lifetime of forgiveness, and tried not to scream.

The gun went off; she waited for the bullet.

I didn't feel anything. Oh, my Gawd, I must be dead!

The gun went off again. She sagged against the tree, but still felt nothing. She opened one eye, expecting to see Saint Peter standing at those pearly gates.

All she saw was Sam's broad back. He faced the bay, the rifle aimed straight up, and he fired a third shot, then appeared to scan the horizon for a long moment. She exhaled.

"Damn!" He slammed the rifle butt into the sand and turned around. "We missed them. All that goddamn running and we bloody missed them."

Lollie looked out at the bay, the empty bay, and everything hit her at once. Her father hadn't waited. She didn't mean enough to him for him to wait for her. Or maybe— the thought brought on a stab of pain so sharp she was almost ill—maybe he hadn't come at all.

Her heart settled somewhere in her tight throat. She was alone. Worse than alone, she was with Sam.

Suddenly the tears welled into her eyes. Sobs poured up from deep within her, and she slid bonelessly down the tree trunk, landing on the cool sand in an aching heap. She cried and cried and cried, and though from somewhere far away she could hear Sam swearing, she couldn't stop the sobs.

She was alone, her brothers so far away they probably didn't even know what was happening to her. And her father didn't care about her. All the fears she'd harbored but refused to believe surfaced.

Her father had never come home to his daughter because he didn't care to. She cried, wishing fervently that she had been a boy instead of a girl. Then he'd have come home. Then she wouldn't be here on this awful island, stuck with a man who didn't want the burden of her any more than her father did, and that final, crushing thought was just too much for her.

"Stop it, Lollie! Stop it!" Sam strode toward her. He stood over her, watching her rock and wail. He didn't want to slap her, although he was tempted.

He picked her up. She kicked and cried and squirmed, so he did the only thing he could.

He threw her in the bay.

Ignoring the splash, he turned and walked the few feet to shore and sat in the sand, waiting for her to come ashore wet but calmed down. She didn't, but she was quieter. The wailing stopped, replaced with sputters and coughs. Her arms waved frantically above the water's surface, and she sank like an anchor.

Christ! Sam shot up and waded out to where she'd sunk. The water barely reached his shoulders, but neither did she. He reached down and hauled her off the bottom, bending so he could sling her around his shoulders. Then he waded back to the beach. He laid her on the still warm sand and worked the water out of her. She coughed and hacked until she finally just lay there, breathing normally, but obviously drained completely.

He watched her as she lay there and wondered if this woman was the retribution for every wrong thing he'd done in his hard life. If so, the punishment, in his mind, was much worse than any of the crimes.

She turned over on her back and moaned, flinging an arm across her eyes and just lying there wheezing. Finally she spoke, her tone flat and her voice barely audible. "If you're gonna kill me, just do it now."

Oh, the melodrama. He shook his head, disgusted. "Get up. No one's going to kill you, although you might get me killed if you keep this up."

She lifted her arm a few inches to look at him with red puffy eyes. "You just tried to drown me."

"I doubt you'd drown in less than six feet of water." Sam picked up the rifle and reloaded.

"I can't swim!"

He dropped the cartridges in the sand and glared at her. "What in the hell do you mean you can't swim? Everyone can swim."

"Maybe every *man* can swim, but not me." She sat up. "Where I come from, women don't swim. I never learned, since my brothers didn't consider it safe or proper for a refined lady."

"I didn't think this situation could get any worse," he muttered, bending to pick up the shot. "I was wrong."

"You still tried to drown me." Her voice had a distinct whine to it, something he hadn't noticed before. She had managed to sit up and turn her back to him again. Hugging her knees, she stared out into the dark bay.

"If I'd wanted to drown you, you can bet your sweet southern little butt I'd have been successful. And if you call me a damn Yankee under your breath one more time I just might do it." He struggled into the pack while she still sat there, not moving.

"Get up, we have to get out of here."

"Why?"

"Because of those shots I fired. Your daddy's boat might not have heard them, but someone else might have, and I don't want to stick around here to find out who." He held out his hand to help her up.

She looked at it, then stuck her nose up and watched the bay.

"You want to go swimming again?"

Her head whipped around, her eyes wide, and their gazes locked. After a long tense moment, she looked at his hand still stretched out to her.

"Don't tempt me," he warned.

She took it and stood up, shaking the wet sand from her soaking dress.

It was the second time today she'd been soaked from head to foot. Which reminded him . . . "Tell me something, Miss Lah-Roo, why the hell did you jump off that boat if you couldn't swim?"

She pulled the back of her skirt around so she could get at the rest of the sand. "I was aiming for that barrel."

"That's not what I asked you. Why'd you jump off the boat?"

"I was seasick," she mumbled.

He thought about her answer for a moment, looking for its logic—a futile search. "So you chose to drown instead. Makes perfect sense."

"I told you I was aiming for that barrel!"

"Let me see if I have this right." He leaned on the rifle. "You get seasick."

She nodded, her eyes averted.

"So instead of staying on that trawler with a little upset stomach, you decided to jump through the bullet-ridden air into the middle of the river—despite the fact that you can't swim—hoping you could hang on to a barrel."

"It wasn't a *little* upset stomach, and at the time it made sense."

He snorted.

She turned and looked at him. "It did! Sincerely."

"You can be sincere and still be stupid."

"Why don't you just leave me here, then!" She spun around, crossing her arms like a spoiled little child with the "poor me's."

"Want a cross and some nails?"

"I hate you!"

"Good. Funnel some of that energy into those pampered

little feet of yours and let's go." Sam slung the rifle over his shoulder, turned, and began walking toward the northeast.

Before long he realized she wasn't behind him. Not enough noise—no mumbling, humming, whining—and no sounds of her crashing face down into the nearest bush. He stopped and counted to ten, then twenty. By the time he'd reached a hundred and fifty, he figured he was calm enough to go back.

The spot where he'd left her was deserted—nothing but a depression in the sand. The beach was dark, the moon being only a thin silver sliver in the sky. He scanned the area where sand met jungle, and there he spotted her. She sat against a coconut palm, her knees hugged to her chest and her head resting on them. One small finger picked at her teeth.

He shook his head at the pitiable sight and wondered what the hell he was going to do with her.

She must have sensed his presence because she looked up at him. He walked over to her and stood above her, not saying a word.

"I want to go home," she whined into her knees.

He didn't acknowledge her.

"I want to sleep in a bed. I want to eat real food. I want to take a bath. And most of all, I want to brush this stupid jerky meat out of my teeth!"

"Are you through?"

"I don't know."

Sam waited.

She sat up, her back pressed against the tree but her eyes locked on the bay. "Isn't there any chance they'll come back?"

"No."

"What are you going to do with me?"

He laughed. "I wish I knew."

"Can't you take me home?"

"Forget it."

"Please."

"What do you think I am, some hero in a romance novel?

I said forget it. It's too dangerous, and there's no time. I have to be back at my camp. I've got a job to do. Now get up."

"I want to go home."

"Get—"

"I want to take a bath."

"Up."

"I want to brush my teeth."

"Now!"

Her back went ramrod straight. She turned her head away from him and dug her heels a little deeper into the sand.

"I said now!"

"No."

He dropped the rifle, slid out of the pack, and grabbed her shoulders, then hauled her none too gently up against the tree. With his face barely an inch from her he gritted, "Look, you spoiled little brat. One more whine about those teeth of yours and you won't have any to brush. You *will* get up. You *will* walk. And you *will* keep quiet!"

Her chin shot up. "Not until you tell me where you're taking me!"

"To Bonifacio's camp!" he bellowed.

"Isn't he another one of those guerrilla leaders?"

"Yeah."

"What are you gonna do, sell me to him so he can hold me for ransom, too?"

Sam stared at her, still shaking his fist at her teary, belligerent face. Her words registered. And he'd called her stupid? He was a damn fool.

She'd just given him the solution to his problem. He had no choice but to take her with him anyway. He might as well let Bonifacio hold her for ransom. Andrés needed the money as much as Aguinaldo did. There was no Colonel Luna in Andrés's camp. Sam and Jim Cassidy were serving as officers. They wouldn't let anything happen to her. It was perfect.

He couldn't understand why he hadn't thought of it.

Must be the heat, or that batty woman, because the Chicago street kid in him would never have missed this kind of opportunity. He guessed age affected everyone, and maybe he was getting too old for this.

Well, he'd worry about that after this job was done, until then he had a new plan—to see to her safety. After all, she was a defenseless woman and a fellow American, and now he could make a little money on the side. Bonifacio would give him a bonus—a cut of the ransom. It was perfect.

"What are you staring at?" She eyed him warily.

"Not a thing, Miss Lah-Roo, not a thing." Sam smiled, releasing her shoulders. "Bonifacio and I will make sure you get back to your daddy all safe and sound. Now let's go. The sooner you move the sooner you'll be home." And, Sam thought, whistling as he watched her wobble ahead of him, the sooner I'll get that bonus.

10

"Better eat up."

Lollie stared at the horrid piece of jerky. It was all Sam had given her to eat for the past two days. She had more than her share of the salty, stringy meat permanently wedged between her teeth. She was hungry, but staring at the shriveled brown hunk convinced her she could never be hungry enough to eat one more bite of the awful stuff.

Leaning back against a hard, cool rock, she watched Sam. He chewed, then looked at her, grinning as if this whole thing were just some party, all for him. It was almost as if he relished her misfortune. But no one could be that mean.

She watched him chug down some water before he handed the canteen to her. He eyed her with that one-eyed brown stare as if he were waiting to see what she'd do next. She wanted to ignore him, but she wasn't stupid, no sirree. She knew her body needed water, especially since it wasn't gonna get any food.

She took the canteen and wiped the spout with her petticoat before she took a small mouthful. She swished the water around in her mouth before swallowing.

"I said eat."

"No."

"Planning on starving yourself?" He stood and took the canteen away, picked up the pack and slung it and his precious gun over his shoulder.

"That . . . that jerky sticks in my teeth." She dropped the meat into her lap so she could scratch her arms again.

He held out his hand. "Give it to me."

She handed it to him. Just looking at him standing there, pack in place, rifle slung over his big shoulder, told her he was ready to walk again. The man never rested, hardly slept. He wasn't human.

"I'm tired."

He grunted something indistinguishable.

"I *am* tired," she repeated with a sigh, looking out at the never-ending maze of green jungle. She felt if she had to walk through one more plant she'd just die.

Self-pity in full swing, she talked to the jungle, willing at this point to tell anyone or anything her plight. "I want to take a bath. I want to sleep in a bed, any bed, with real sheets. I want to eat real food and wear clean clothes." She ran her tongue over her teeth frowning, and added, "And I want to br—"

She stopped in mid-word.

He glared at her, waiting for her finish. Silent, she returned his stare.

"And I want you to stop whining, but I doubt I'll get that any more than you'll get your toothbrush. Now let's go." He stood there waiting for her, then said, "When we get to the camp you can have a bath."

"I'm tired of walking." She sagged back and raised a limp hand to her brow, absolutely sure she was gonna get a headache any minute. "Can't we just sit here a spell?"

"No." He extended his hand. "Get up."

Lollie sighed twice, let him help her up, then proceeded to dust the leaves off her fanny. By the time she'd finished and had scratched the bites on her arms, Sam had disappeared into the jungle at what must have been almost a full run. She sighed for strength and stumbled off after him.

Over the last two miserable, horrid days, trailing along behind Sam the Tireless, she'd had nothing to do but walk. Every time she'd tried to sing he threatened to gag her again. She'd tried to talk to him. Sometimes he answered her, sometimes he grunted, and usually he ignored her. She'd had nothing to do but scratch and feel sorry for herself, which wasn't too difficult when she was forced to slog through clinging brown mud and to tramp through jungle that scratched her exposed skin and served as a breeding ground for every creepy critter imaginable.

But the nights were the worst. One night they'd slept on a dirty moss-covered rock ledge with three feet separating them. She'd been on the inside, forced to lie there in the dark, smelling the pungent stink of the moss and listening to the foreign sounds—rustles, hums, twitters, buzzes—and wondering what gawdforsaken creature made those sounds.

The pack made a perfect pillow, so he'd taken it, leaving her to fall asleep on one mosquito-ravaged arm. She'd tried to talk to him. He told her to shut up and go to sleep. She didn't hear another sound from him until he kicked her—well, prodded her—awake the next morning.

The next night there were no rock ledges, so they'd slept against a tree. At least Sam had slept; she hadn't. Which didn't make today any easier to deal with. She was bone tired. Even the mosquitoes knew it, she thought as she whacked those stupid palm fronds and a swarm of mosquitoes out of her face. She'd stumbled over at least a mile of rock beds with jagged black lava that had jabbed into the soles of her shoes and cut her hands when she fell. After that she'd had no trouble shifting the blame for her situation.

Taking a determined step, she intended to tell Sam just how miserable she was. She kept her eyes on his back instead of on the terrain, and her foot slammed into a rock—a slippery rock. She fell. Struggling to her sore knees, she looked up, expecting Sam's help. He hadn't even noticed. She watched his broad, damp, monstrous back move through the jungle ahead of her as if he were just a strolling on a Sunday. She stood up and stormed after him. This was all his fault.

She was miserable, bruised, and so tired, and she needed to take that misery out on someone, or something. After all, she had to tell someone. There was nothing worse than being miserable and having no one to tell about it. She wasn't strong like Joan of Arc or Spartacus.

If Lollie had to play the role of martyr, the world was gonna know it.

Trudging through a deep sticky pool of mud, she glared at Sam's big back, trying to catch up with him so she could give him a piece of her mind. A small rational part of her knew she wasn't being fair, but neither was her situation fair. She was here, stuck with him just like he was stuck with her. And right now fairness wasn't foremost on her mind. Lollie wanted to be home, clean, and riding in a comfortable carriage under the wild oaks instead of plodding like a drudge mule over this humid, sticky island.

The mudhole widened and deepened as they neared its rim. Sam was still a few yards ahead. He reached the far side of the pool first and pushed himself up and out. She stood there, forced by her circumstances to look way up at him.

It was not a good position for griping. She decided it would be more appropriate to discuss this after he helped her out.

He turned to face her. "Give me your hands and dig

108

your feet into the side of the mudhole. From this angle, I need some leverage to help pull you out."

She wiped the filthy hair out of her face and placed her hands in his.

"Can you feel the small outcropping of the rocks on the side?"

She moved her right foot around until she felt the hardness of the rock. She nodded.

"Good. Now tell me when your foot's on it. I'll pull up and you push up at the same time with your foot. Understand?"

"Uh-huh." She stepped on a shallow ridge in the rock. "Okay, pull."

Sam pulled up. She pushed up. Her shoe slipped, and she panicked, feeling the loss of her balance. Naturally, she let go of him and grabbed the side of the hole.

She felt the wind of his body sailing over her.

She heard the splash and winced.

Very slowly she turned around.

His dark head broke the surface, then the intimidating wall of his shoulders. He loomed in front of her like some huge angry monster, mud dripping from his face and head and eye patch. The lethal way he glared at her made her wish the mud had hidden his good eye, too.

If looks could kill, she'd be dead. If eyes could burn fire, she'd be ashes. If she knew what was good for her, she'd be long gone.

"My shoe slipped," she explained, having a feeling that he didn't really want an explanation. He wanted violence.

His hands reached out.

She squeezed her eyes shut, gritting her teeth and waiting.

His large hands closed tightly around her waist, spanning it. He lifted her out of the mudhole, and set her none too gently on the rock rim. The moment he let go, she scooted backward fast.

He was out before she could blink, a muddy giant towering over her. With purpose, he bent down and jerked off her shoes then rammed one of them under his arm. He gripped the other shoe in one hand and grabbed the small, squat Louis XV heel in the other. Then he twisted so hard Lollie could hear it crack.

"What're you doing to my shoes?" She scrambled up, trying to grab them.

"Pretending they're your neck." He wrenched the heel off and tossed it over his shoulder, then did the same to her other shoe. He shoved the mangled shoes in her face.

She looked at them, sniffing back her miserable tears. Her rosettes were gone, she'd lost those somewhere along the trail, and now he'd pulled the heels off, too. It didn't matter that the shoes had been ruined days before. They symbolized her whole wretched state.

"If you start blubbering again I swear to God I'll leave you here." Sam looked as if he could breathe fire.

She sniffed. "I'm hungry. I want to go home. I want a bath."

"I want a muzzle," he muttered.

She looked up at him, wiping the tears from her eyes. "You'd like that, wouldn't you? To muzzle me like some cur." She stared down at her dress. Nothing was pink or white. It was brown from the mud and green from the plant stains. She touched her ratty hair. "I must look like some mongrel dog."

"Yeah, you do, maybe worse." He rolled his eyes as if this were some joke and nudged her shoes with his rifle. "Now put those on, Rover, and let's go for another walk."

She didn't even think. The second he called her Rover she lost the ability to think. She threw the shoes right at his smirking face.

He caught one; the other sailed over his right shoulder.

One look at his face and she knew she'd gone too far.

He dropped the rifle, shrugged out of the pack, and stalked toward her.

She stepped back, holding her hands out. "Don't you touch me!"

He pulled out that huge, sharp knife he called a machete and kept walking toward her.

She screamed and spun around to run. He grabbed her dress, twisted it, and pinned her against a tree trunk. His hard, anger-tight face was barely an inch away from hers. Their stares locked, hers frightened, his angry.

She squeezed her eyes shut, throwing her arms out to the sides in surrender. "Go ahead, kill me! I want to die!"

Nothing happened, but he didn't move, either. Then she felt the very tip of the knife press against her neck.

"You, Miss Lah-Roo, are a big pain in the ass, and I'm putting up with you only because I have no choice. I'm taking you to that camp because I have to. But don't press your luck. If you think you're miserable now, just push me some more and I'll teach you all about misery."

Her eyes shot open.

With one quick slice of the knife, he cut the lace off her dress.

She gasped.

"How would you like to walk through the jungle naked?"

She swallowed.

He grabbed a wad of her skirt in a fist and cut it the way a cook lops off the top of a carrot. He dropped the skirt, and it fell in jagged tatters that barely covered her skinned knees.

After eyeing her from head to foot, he lifted one welt-reddened arm and spoke, his voice deep, calm, and certain. "The mosquitoes will have a feast on all that fine aristo-cratic white skin."

He wouldn't cut off all her clothes, she reasoned.

His face said he would.

He raised the knife again, letting the tip touch the seam between her breasts. "There are palm trees here with leaves so sharp they can cut through your skin faster than a machete."

He pressed the knife a bit closer. She felt the seam threads separate.

"Want to test me?"

111

Scared enough to spit, she shook her head.

"Then put those shoes on, start walking, and shut that damn whiny mouth." He released her, then stood back and bellowed, "Now!"

She'd never moved so fast in her life. She grabbed one shoe and scurried over to the other, lying near a copse of oleander, where she worked her muddy foot into one flat shoe. It was the wrong foot. She slipped her foot out and glanced up.

Machete still in his white-knuckled hand, he took one catlike step toward her. "You have ten seconds. One . . ."

She grabbed a branch and rammed the shoe onto her foot.

"Four . . ."

She tried to work her foot into the other one, keeping a death grip on the oleander branches. She was in such a hurry that the shoe slipped from her hand. Panicked, she bent down, never taking her wary eyes off him.

"Six . . ."

She rammed the shoe on so hard that her toes cracked.

"Eight . . ."

Her heel wouldn't slide in, so she used a finger as a shoehorn. The shoe slid on, just as he pointed the knife at her.

"Ten. Move!"

She did move, and fast.

Lollie plopped down on a rock and hung her pounding head in her hands. Her hair fell over her face in a heavy, dirty blond knot.

It smelled. She smelled. She ached, and she was hungry. A wee part of her still waited to wake up and find out that this was all a bad dream. She looked around her. It wasn't a nightmare. It was real.

Closing her eyes, she buried her palms into her pounding, burning eye sockets. At least there was one good thing: Sam the Tireless had finally given her a rest, telling her not to move while he went to look for Gawd only knew what.

Imagine . . . telling her to stay there as if she would just take off through the wild, primitive, horrid, gawdforsaken jungle as easily as if she daily changed water to wine. She wished she could. A little wine would taste good right now. She licked her lips, wishing for the taste of something besides water.

For the hundredth time she wished she were a man. A man would have known what to do. Her skills would have been in survival instead of etiquette—something that was about as useful here as burning green wood. Boys were raised with freedom that girls weren't given. Boys could ride and shoot and go places alone. They could swim. But girls had to do what was socially correct.

When they grew up things only got worse. Men could eat all they wanted. Women had to take small bites and leave most of the food behind. She wondered who came up with that foolish rule. Probably some hungry man.

Many times she'd watched her brothers eat enough ham to make them snort while she had nibbled politely on two or three small bites. She'd really wanted to eat twice as much as they did, and right here and now she was hungry enough to do it.

She rubbed the bridge of her nose.

Sam thrashed through the brush behind her. She knew it was Sam. She could smell him. She didn't bother to look up. It took too much energy.

"What's the matter now?" he asked, squatting down in front of her.

"I'm just thinking."

"Yeah, the first time's always the worst."

She ignored him. She was too tired, too weak, and too hungry to do anything else.

"Hold out your hand."

Still not looking, she whipped her hand out, expecting to feel the dried leather he'd been giving her to eat. She was right hungry enough now to eat it, or at least to try.

Like pearls from a strand, small, plump, round berries filled her damp palm. She stared at them as if they were flawless jewels. To her stomach they were even more valuable.

"Oh, sweet heaven and Lord above! Food . . . real food! Oh, thank you. Thank you." She popped five into her mouth before she remembered Madame Devereaux's many lectures on manners and excess. She chewed anyway. She was tired of being a lady. Besides, Madame Devereaux was never stuck in a tropical jungle with a one-eyed human locomotive.

The locomotive spoke. "Go easy on those. It's not good for you to eat too many."

They tasted soooooo good. She popped some more in her mouth, and the flavor almost brought tears to her eyes. She rolled the rest of them around in her hand. They were different from any berries she'd ever seen. The skin was as tight and red as that of a hollyberry, but the center tasted as juicy and sweet as the plump spring blueberries from home.

She swallowed, slowly, savoring the flavor, then opened her eyes to meet Sam's stare.

"Better?" he said. Then his gaze left her face and leisurely drifted down her body.

She felt a warm flush of embarrassment, realizing what she must have looked like while eating those berries, so she averted her eyes.

"Time to move on, Lollipop." He stood then, and she could hear him unscrew the canteen cap. "Want some more water?"

"No, thank you. The berries were enough." She licked her moist lips as she moved in behind him. The flavor of the berries still stained them. Only a fool would want to dilute the sweet flavor that remained by drinking water. She wanted to savor their taste for as long as she could.

He hadn't moved, and she could still feel the heat of his gaze. She got up, her dignity still tarnished enough that she couldn't look at him so she made another big to-do over brushing the leaves and wrinkles from her muddy rag of a dress.

She could almost feel his smile as he finally walked past her, heading back into the jungle. It seemed that she was Sam Forester's source of entertainment. A few minutes earlier that would have bothered her, but now, with those luscious berries on her lips and in her shriveled stomach, she didn't mind as much. Let him laugh at her. A LaRue, of the Belvedere LaRues of Hickory House, Calhoun Industries, and Beechtree Farms, was certainly above letting him get to her, especially when she wasn't hungry anymore.

She tramped along behind him, and a few minutes later she was as bored as usual with the same old green surroundings, so she ventured into the realm of conversation with Sam Forrester. "Where'd you get those berries?"

"They grow in the high jungle, which is what we're in now." He stopped and waited for her to reach his side. "See those deep purple orchids?"

She followed his pointing finger to where bushels of lush orchids, thicker than azaleas at Easter, lined the narrow trail.

"The berry vines twine around those plants. If you look closely you'll see the small berries beneath the flowers."

She walked past him and over to one of the plants. She lifted the flower and there, hanging in small clusters, were those delightful berries. She grabbed a few and popped them into her mouth, smiling as she turned back to him.

"Don't eat too many of those," he warned.

She nodded, much more concerned with the incredibly sweet flavor of the berries. They were so good!

He shook his head and moved on. She turned to follow but stopped, turning back to the plant and grabbing a few more handfuls of the berries. Food for the road. Then she hurried to catch up with him, popping berries into her mouth whenever he wasn't looking.

The fruit perked her up, and with renewed spirit she followed him, watching him hack his way through more bamboo. Each firm stroke of his machete sent the bamboo falling to the ground like pickup sticks.

But she wasn't really looking at the knife. She was watching Sam Forester's massive body.

His brawny arm sliced through the air with the power of a guillotine, the blade severing anything in its path. He raised his knife high again, and she watched, noticing how his arm muscles tightened from elbow to wrist so that she could see the outline of his veins, even through the thick black hair on his tanned forearm.

She ate some more fruit—addictive little devils—and her gaze moved to his upper arm, where his shirtsleeve was rolled high. Sam's arm was as big as her thigh, but her thigh was pale and perhaps a little soft. She poked it and felt her finger sink a bit. His arm wasn't soft, though. It was tanned and big and so solid that the muscles showed whenever he moved it.

Strange how she'd never noticed her brothers' muscles. She ate another handful of berries while she pondered that thought. Jeffrey was almost as tall as Sam, but not as brawny. Harlan was long and lean, like Harrison. Leland and Jedidiah were shorter than Sam but almost as broad. She could never remember having any interest in their backs.

Sam's, however, was really something to see in action. The muscles tightened across his back and bulged beneath his wet shirt. It rippled and swelled into hard, huge knots of muscle, and she had a sudden urge to reach out and touch him just to see if muscle and skin could be that solid.

She dug into the deep pocket of her dress and felt around for some more berries. She'd eaten them all. She judged his distance. He was only a little bit ahead of her now, so she ran over to another orchid bush, plucked off as many handfuls of fruit as she dared, then hurried back to follow him again.

About ten minutes later he stopped and offered her some water. She drank it this time, then handed him back the canteen. He looked at her, an odd expression on his face.

"You haven't been eating more of those berries, have you?"

Now, Lollie had a philosophy, one she'd used with her brothers many times over. If a man asked you a "you haven't" question he really meant "Surely you couldn't be so stupid as to have done such a thing." She figured that when males were being so arrogantly condescending and superior as to ask a question in those words and that tone, they didn't deserve to be told the truth. So she evaded the question.

"You don't think I'd do that, do you?" She brought her hand to her neck to emphasize her horror that he could even suggest such a thing. This technique worked well with her brothers, except Jed. He never asked questions, he just started hollering.

Sam searched for her face a moment longer, as if trying to determine the truth. Then he shook his head, clipped the canteen in place, and told her to follow him.

She did, trotting along behind him, watching his back with rapt attention while she fingered the berries in her pocket. Guilt kept her from eating any, though, at least for the first half hour.

"Are you sure you haven't been eating any more of those berries?"

Lollie swallowed the three in her mouth, then answered his question with one of her own. "Why?"

"Uh, no special reason." He had a strained look; then he coughed a few times, turning his back to her—which of course didn't bother her since she found it so fascinating—and finished filling the canteen from a trickle of fresh water that ran down a rocky hillside.

"How much farther is this camp?"

"Another day. See that small mountain?"

She nodded, although her definition of "small" was obviously different from his.

"Once we get past it we'll be closer. Ready?"

She nodded, smiling with her mouth closed so he couldn't tell she'd eaten two more.

He stared at her for a long minute. That caused her a bit of worry, until she remembered there was no way he could see those berries. They were well on their merry way to her stomach.

She grinned. So did he; then he elbowed past her, holding back a brace of branches for her.

For the next few hours they moved through jungle. They crossed two shallow streams; neither came up past her waist. They crawled through bushes so thick that it took what seemed to be a half hour to move a hundred feet. Lollie didn't mind too much. While Sam was hard at work cutting their path, she managed to pluck plenty of berries.

They came upon another palm and bamboo forest, and Lollie, feeling fortified, asked Sam if she could use the machete.

He came to a dead halt, turned, and gave her one of those "are you crazy" male looks.

"No."

"I don't see why not," she complained, her nose almost buried in his chest, because he'd stopped so suddenly. "I don't have anything else to do, except smell . . . us." She wrinkled her nose at him.

"You're not exactly a peach blossom yourself."

"I said *us!*" She rammed her hands on her hips and glared at him. "You won't let me do anything. I can't talk. I can't sing. I can't even hum! I'm bored and filthy, and I need something to occupy my mind."

Sam swatted a mosquito on his neck. He pulled his hand away and held it out to her. "Here, might be a little snug, but this ought to occupy it just fine."

She narrowed her eyes, giving him her imitation of Madame Devereaux's best glare. He just continued to look pleased with himself.

"You probably think I can't do it, don't you?"

He crossed his arms, not answering her at all.

"Well, for your information, I have been watching you

118

wield that knife for days. Hack and crack, hack and crack. Anyone can do that, including me." She waited to see if he'd accept her challenge.

He handed her the knife, donning a sly smile of inflated male arrogance, and he walked over to lean against a tree, acting as if he had a long, long wait.

She'd show him how long. She hacked at the thick palms. The knife didn't even cut them. Staring at the blade for a curious moment, she tried to figure out what she'd done wrong. She swung again. The fronds bent but didn't break, didn't crack, and didn't fall to the ground as they had for Sam.

"Anyone can do it, huh?"

She stiffened at his baiting, but didn't give him the satisfaction of turning around. Instead she grabbed the palm in one hand, gripped the knife firmly in the other, and hacked until she finally managed to saw the frond from the palm tree.

It took about five minutes.

"Nice work, Lollipop. At this rate we should reach the camp in . . . let's see . . . late August?"

She glared up at him, blowing a hank of tangled wet hair out of her eyes. That did it! She turned back to face the palms, gripping the knife in her right hand, just as he did. Then she raised it as high as she could. One huge deep breath and then she closed her eyes and ripped the knife down and around in a half circle, just like Sam had, but she threw her whole body weight into swinging that machete.

She whirled with it.

It slipped from her hand.

Her eyes flew open.

"Shit!"

Still stunned, she gaped at Sam, then followed his gaze, up, up, up. . . .

Like a soaring eagle the knife sailed through the air, then descended. Sam barreled past her, thrashing through the brush in the direction of their only machete. Lollie followed as fast as she could.

By the time she broke into a small clearing, Sam was standing as still as a hickory tree on a summer day. His neck, however, was a purplish red, and his fists clenched over and over at his sides. He looked up. So did she.

There, wedged into a cluster of green coconuts, was the knife. The tree was a good thirty feet high.

Slowly he turned. "Anyone can do that," he mimicked through a mean smile that made him look as if he wanted to tear trees apart, limb by limb. He stepped toward her.

"It looked so easy," she whispered, stepping back. "It really did."

"You do realize that's our only machete, don't you?" He took another step.

She nodded, unable to decide if maybe she should turn and run. She opted for an apology. "I'm sorry."

She looked at the other two knives that hung from his belt. They were smaller; one was not much bigger than a carving knife. "Couldn't you use one of those?" She pointed toward them.

He took a deep, labored breath. "They won't cut through jungle or bamboo." He paused, meaningfully. "They will cut through your clothes, though, and this one"—his hand rested on the smaller sheath—"will cut a white southern throat easily enough."

"It's not all my fault. You let me have it, remember?"

"I'll let you have it, all right." He took two more menacing steps toward her.

Too late she realized that trying to split the blame was not a good thing to do, especially with a frustrated man who still had two knives.

"I ought to make you climb up there and get that knife."

Lollie looked up at the tree, way, way up. Her stomach lurched. Suddenly her head felt light and she raised her hand to her forehead. "I don't feel very well."

He started counting again, then muttered something about "all those berries."

Chicken gizzards! He knew. She had been so sure about sneaking them, always making sure his back was turned and he was busy hacking away before she'd eaten them. There had been those two times he'd turned around while she was still chewing, but she'd swallowed so quickly.

Oh, well, she'd been found out, so she might as well use the fruit to her advantage. She delved into her pocket and held out a handful of berries. "Since you figured it out, here, have some."

"I'm not that stupid." He shrugged out of the pack and put it and the rifle against another tree. "Stay by these and don't move!" With that pronouncement he strode to the coconut palm and pulled off his boots.

"Are you really gonna climb all the way up there?"

He unsheathed the small knife. "How the hell else am I going to get the machete?"

"Maybe it would fall down if you threw something at it."

"You're too heavy."

She'd have loved to throw her shoes at him again, but one more glance at the knife told her she'd thrown enough things for a while.

He placed the knife between his teeth and straddled the tree, pulling himself up the scarred gray palm bark like a logger shimmying up a Carolina pine.

She watched him, her breath slowing as he moved higher and higher up the tree. Its base was sturdy and thick, but the higher Sam got, the thinner the trunk was. His movements slowed. Every time he pulled himself upward, the tree would bend, a little more and a little more, until it was arched like a rainbow. Within a few minutes he reached the coconuts. He wrapped one arm around the trunk and tried to grab the knife. His arms weren't long enough. He looked down, and Lollie could almost hear him swear.

He seemed to do a lot of swearing. An occasional "damn" slipped from her lately, often preceding the word "Yankee." That was pretty mild compared to the language her brothers used when they didn't know she was around. Actually, she'd learned some real humdingers, but she would never use them. Ladies didn't swear. Lord knew she had reason enough to swear. Besides which being a lady in this jungle had its drawbacks, and if the truth were told, Lollie had always hated all those silly rules.

A coconut thudded to the ground like a falling rock, drawing her attention back to Sam. She could see him pull the small knife from his teeth. Hanging on with one arm, he leaned out and sawed at some more coconuts, each one dropping like the last.

Sunlight broke through the clouds and beamed through the ceiling of treetops. She shaded her eyes with her hand. Sam still couldn't reach the machete.

"Lollie! Can you hear me?"

"Yes!"

"I'm going to cut this whole bunch, so stay back. The knife's going to come down with them!"

"Okay!" she shouted, then turned to stand in safety behind a banyan tree. She stopped when she thought she heard him say something else, something about he'd be damned if he'd lose the money now, after earning every last dime. It didn't make sense to her, so she figured the machete must have had something to do with his job at the camp. She moved around behind the tree.

A moment of silence hung in the air, and then the coconuts pounded to the ground louder than horses' hooves, the machete falling out to lie a couple of inches from the mound of green coconuts.

Lollie figured it was safe, so she walked toward the knife, but her eyes were still on Sam, who slid down the trunk in a quick minute.

"You got it!" She smiled.

He just gave her one of those male looks that said "of course I got it." He walked past her, picked up the machete, and examined it with a practiced eye.

"Is it okay?"

He checked the edge, then grunted. "It's fine."

She breathed a quick but very quiet sigh of relief.

He turned and kicked a coconut away from the bunch, then hunkered down beside it. He raised the knife and slammed it downward, cleaving the coconut in two. He handed her half. "Here drink this. We might as well not waste it."

Lollie took the green, bowllike shell and looked inside. Though the outside was bright green, another hard brown hairy shell lay within. Inside that was a rim of white nut meat. A small amount of milky, sweet-smelling liquid pooled inside. She watched Sam lift his half to his mouth and drink. Slowly she did the same.

Her dulled taste buds almost exploded. The liquid was strong with the flavor of coconut, a delicacy she'd had only in small flakes on special desserts or in rare holiday maca-roons. It was as wonderful as those berries and she drank some more, until she could feel the heat of Sam's gaze. She lowered the shell from her mouth, licking the juice she could feel clinging to her upper lip. He looked away, dig-ging his small knife into the white meat inside the shell.

He must still be mad at me, she thought, drinking down more of the juice and watching him cut some coconut.

As if drawn by her stare he looked up. He stared for a long moment, then looked at the coconut and jabbed the knife into the shell.

She winced.

He withdrew the knife. A hunk of coconut meat was poised on its sharp end, and he handed it to her. "Here. Taste this."

She plucked it off the knife tip and took a small bite. It was tougher than an apple, but not nearly as bad as the jerky, and the flavor was smooth and rich and exotic. She smiled at Sam and bit off some more.

He stared at her for a long, puzzling time, during which the air got thicker and steamier. Then he quickly tossed his coconut into the bushes, straightened, and strode over to where the pack and rifle were, his stiff back to her.

"I'm sorry about the machete."

He slung on the pack and rifle and grunted as he turned. "Forget it."

She finished the coconut and gave the shell a look of

longing. "Can we take the rest of the coconuts with us? They really taste fine." She watched him hopefully.

"I'm not going to lug those coconuts, and the pack, and the rifle, and you through this jungle."

"I didn't ask you to. I'll carry them."

His snort of laughter hit her like a slap in the face, which made her all that much more determined to show him she could do it.

"I can carry them . . . well, not all of them, but that small bunch couldn't be too heavy. I can strap them to my back, the way you do with that pack. Besides, we'll be using them up along the way."

He gave her a long, thoughtful look, then walked over to the bunch of coconuts and lifted them by the thick green stem, testing their weight. He withdrew the machete and sliced two more off, then put them back down. He removed the pack and knelt down, opening it and pulling out some rope.

After a few minutes' work, he had a rope sling attached to the nuts, and he stood, holding them out to her. "They're all yours."

She grinned and joined him.

"Turn around."

She did, and he slid the rope slings up her arms until they were secure over her shoulders.

"Turn," he ordered.

She did.

"Now pull your arms back so your elbows touch the coconuts."

She did. Now her shoulders were arched back, her chest out. She waited for his next command.

Nothing happened.

She looked at him. His gaze was on her chest. It roved slowly upward until he was looking her in the eyes.

After a minute he smiled then asked, "Is that too heavy?"

"No." She moved her shoulders a bit, and he shook the ropes. It wasn't too heavy, and even if it had been, she wouldn't have cared, because the flavor of that juice still lingered in her mouth and she wanted more.

"You're sure? The more you walk the heavier that's going to feel."

"I know," she assured him. "I'm fine. If it gets too heavy I'll tell you, all right?"

"Just remember, I'm not carrying it."

She heaved a sigh. "Fine."

"I just want it clear from the start. Okay?"

"Okay." She watched him pick up the pack and rifle, and they moved on, Lollie feeling right proud.

Her pockets were filled with berries, and those wonderful coconuts were tied to her back. The journey couldn't be so bad now.

Besides the freshness and flavor of their new food, Lollie finally had something to do, something she didn't have to depend on Sam for. So off she went, marching along behind him, her stomach full and her thirst quenched, coconuts bobbing on her small, straight back, and her eyes focused on Sam and all that intriguing, massive muscle.

11

Sam couldn't believe it. The Lollipop was holding her own. No whining, no humming, and the biggest surprise, no stumbling. Of course he'd slowed down some, knowing that the camp was now within a day's walk, and there'd been no sign of the Spanish—another surprise.

He glanced back over his shoulder. She was fairly close behind, paying attention to where she walked, the reason she wasn't keeling over every five minutes like a felled oak.

Instead of staring up, ogling her surroundings, as she had before, she now watched the ground, stepping over vines and weaving her way through thick bushes with her shorter skirt pulled tightly around her so it wouldn't catch.

Turning to look ahead of them, he checked the grade of the trail. For the last few minutes they'd been walking up a slight rise, and a few hundred yards ahead stood a jagged, rocky hill. The trail cut up and through the steep face, weaving its way to the top, where lush leafy vines fell like green curtains over the edge of the rock rim. To the right, a small waterfall, one of many that cascaded from the tall granite plateaus of the high jungle, rushed down the slick rock surface, which was tinted a deep, dark purple-gray that made the froth of the water appear whiter and the rich green of the plants even more vibrant, alive.

He watched Lollie make her way up the grade, slower, from the extra weight of the coconuts. If they rested here, they could eat one of the nuts, making her load lighter. Part of him wanted to take them from her, but something about her attitude stopped him. She seemed pleased to have a job to do, something for which she was responsible. He didn't want to take that away from her, partly because it seemed so important to her and partly because it kept her manageable, and—there was a God— quiet.

"We'll rest here." He leaned his rifle against a tree, unhooked his knife, and crouched down, waiting for her to drop her coconut load. She did, then sagged down against a tree and hugged her knees to her chest. Sam cut off a coconut and split it open. They drank the milk, and then he carved out the meat and handed her a huge hunk.

"We have to go over that hill ahead," he said between bites of his own. "It'll be pretty steep climbing. You might want to lighten your load."

"You mean leave my coconuts here?" She stared at him as if he'd suggested she cut off her hands.

"Last time I looked, that was the only load you carried." The sarcasm was automatic with him, but he managed to bite back the rest of his thought—that lopping off her head wouldn't relieve the load at all. It didn't seem necessary now to cut her down as he had before. The last few hours had been tolerable, and they were making some time, even if it wasn't as good as he'd have done alone.

She eyed the five remaining coconuts as if they were her treasured pets. "They were getting a little heavy, but we just ate one, so that means the load will be lighter." She smiled and he could see the wheels turn slowly. "I don't suppose you would—"

"No." He stood, ready to move on before she was foolish enough to ask him to carry the damn things.

"I didn't think so." She sighed loudly, then got up and shouldered the coconuts again.

"We're not that far from camp. You don't need those. If it's too much for you, leave them here."

Her face grew determined. "That's not the point. Toting these coconuts is my job, and I intend to do it."

"Have it your own way, then." Sam turned and closed the hundred-foot gap between them and the hillside trail. She stayed right behind him, and for the next hour they climbed, trudging up the steep dirt sections of the trail and crawling carefully over the walls of rock that often blocked their progress.

She lagged behind him now, and he turned in time to see her swipe at the back of her hair. She gave her hand a puzzled look, shook her head a second, and waited. Apparently nothing happened, because she shrugged and met his gaze.

"I thought I felt something." She turned around. "Do you see anything?"

He inspected her back. "Nothing there. Not even a mosquito." He turned back and stepped on a high, jagged rock ledge that ran along the sharp face of the hill, forming a bridge between the end of the trail and where it started again some hundred fifty yards away.

He removed his pack and held out a hand. "Come on, I'll need to help you over this section." He pulled her up beside him onto the narrow shelf of rock. Squatting over the pack, he drew out a hank of rope and tied one end of it around his waist. He turned to Lollie.

"I need to loop the other end of this rope around you. It's about an eighty-foot drop to the ground below." He nodded toward the ledge and knotted the rope while she peered over his shoulder, her face suddenly pale and unsure. "There you go."

He stood; she still surveyed the cliff.

"Don't look down."

She shifted her makeshift pack of coconuts and gave him a pale and apprehensive look.

"Just leave the coconuts, Lollipop."

She shook her head, but didn't stop gaping at the drop.

"If you look down, you'll get dizzy, and that'll get us both in trouble. Understand?"

"Okay." She raised her eyes to his and grabbed a tight hold of his hand.

It took almost five eternal minutes to get three-quarters of the way across the ledge. The whole time, Sam kept talking to her as if he were easing a spooked horse, his voice firm, quiet, and as reassuring as he could make it.

"Stay against the side, Lollie," he said, moving farther ahead of her on the narrowest section of the ledge. "It's narrower here—"

She gasped.

He could have kicked himself for telling her it was narrow and probably scaring her senseless—he mentally amended that.

"It's okay." He turned to ease her mind . . . and froze.

"Don't move," he ordered, hoping to God that she wouldn't.

A huge black tarantula crept along the coconuts onto her left shoulder.

Sam could see her wary eyes slowly move to the left.

"Whatever you do, don't move!"

Her mouth fell open.

She'd seen it.

Her eyes grew wide with horror.

He could see the scream coming. "Don't—"

"Aaaaaaaak!"

He moved toward her.

She jumped up and down, as if running in place, flinging and flailing her arms over her head and hair, screaming. Lord, but was she screaming.

The spider flew through the air in a black furry ball, as did the coconuts.

He reached out to grab her waving arms.

The edge of the ledge cracked, and over she went, still rotating her arms faster than a weather vane in a Chicago gale wind.

Sam arched back, bending his knees to absorb the jolt he knew was coming. He grasped the rope in a tight grip. At any second he'd feel the force of her weight dangling off the ledge.

The rope jerked hard, cutting into his waist, but he held tight. His shoulders absorbed the shock. An instant later the rope skidded through his hands so fast it seared his palms. He squeezed tighter, ignoring the burn, gripping the rope until finally it stopped.

Her screaming didn't.

Sam took a deep breath and began to wrap the rope around his fists.

Suddenly it slipped again in small, sharp movements.

"Stop screaming! And hold the hell still!" he yelled, then added under his breath, "You twit."

He pulled up the rope, hand over burning hand. He could feel it when she stilled, and he continued to draw her upward. Her sobs whimpered up as he pulled over and over until he finally dragged her up and over the side of the ledge.

"Oh, Gawd, oh, Gawd," she moaned, grabbing his hands. "G-get-m-me off h-here."

He shoved her back against the rock.

"D-d-did you s-s-see th-that awful th-thing?" She could

barely wheeze out the words she shook so, hiccuping to get her breath.

He sank to his knees, the rope still held loosely in his hands. He didn't know whether to hit her or hold her. She took the decision out of his hands by rolling toward him, then crawling right into his arms and wrapping her own around his neck in a clinging grip. He could feel her shake. Their hearts beat a rapid tattoo, his from exertion and danger, hers from terror and tears.

"It was awful, and black, and hairy," she muttered into his chest, her breath warm, her arms still clasped around his neck. She still shook. Very slowly he started to place his hands on her small heaving back. She burrowed into him as if trying to find solace, clinging, her chest plastered against his.

He stopped in mid-motion. He shouldn't touch her. He didn't want to touch her. He couldn't touch her. There was no way he would touch her. His hands clenched, then opened and started to close the two-inch gap to her back, lower and lower . . .

She pushed away, wiping her eyes and swallowing hard.

His mouth was a little dry. He looked down at her, shook some sense into his rattled head, and asked, "Are you all right?"

She sniffed and nodded.

"Good. Now I can wring your fool neck."

She stared at him for a long, sorrowful moment, then burst into tears, crying—caterwauling—for all she was worth.

Sam winced, completely convinced that if he died and went to hell, it would be full of crying, screaming, whining women.

"I lost the coconuts!" she said in a wail.

Because of the sorrowful way she cried, he couldn't bring himself to give her any more trouble. There was shame and defeat in her Southern voice, as if she carried Pandora's guilt, spilling plague and pestilence on the earth instead of dropping a few spider-infested coconuts.

130

Of course now that he thought about the way the tarantula had flown through the air, Sam guessed she did spill
pestilence, and her whining had definitely plagued him. He
almost smiled at his thoughts, but watched her for a
moment instead, deciding that just letting her cry it out
would be best for her, though not for his ears.

She was an odd little pain in the ass. His first impression
had been of a pampered little rich girl. Now he wondered
about that. Besides the helplessness and trouble that
seemed to be Lollie LaRue—he shook his head, still unable
to get over that name—there was something he'd picked
up about her, loneliness and insecurity, things he'd have
thought money and prestige made up for.

Loneliness wasn't foreign to Sam, only now he liked
being alone. He was in control of his life and he liked it
that way. He chose his friends carefully and could count
them on one hand. Trust was a hard thing for him to give.
He forced most people to earn it, and he was so hard on
them that they usually gave up.

On Quincy Street your friends were only that as long as
you could keep a little fear in them. Otherwise they'd stab
you in the back. They had to to survive. He'd heard this
jungle referred to as the kind of place where only the fittest
survived. The jungles he'd been in, the fights, the small
wars, were nothing compared to the war he had fought to
live to adulthood.

Yes, he knew about survival. He could remember feeling
as if every time someone looked at him they saw "poor
white bastard trash" tattooed across his forehead. It had
taken years to knock that particular chip off his shoulder,
and he wondered now as he looked at the Lollipop if maybe
some of that chip wasn't still there.

Her blubbering tapered off, and he gave her another
minute. "Are you through?"

She took that moment to look at him. Even he couldn't
laugh at her when she looked as if she didn't have a soul
in the world. Sam didn't understand her. She wasn't logical. In fact, her mind worked with a quirky illogic that he'd

never encountered before. He wondered briefly if that was what it was about this harebrained woman that threw his timing off.

Well, whatever it was he didn't have time to analyze it. He needed to get rid of her once and for all; then everything would be nice and normal.

"We don't need those coconuts," he reassured her, hoping that would get her over this little show.

"I needed them. They were my responsibility."

Shaking his head in disgust, he stood, grabbed her small shuddering shoulders, and lifted her up. She sniveled some more, looked around her, then up at him. "I hate spiders."

"Lollipop, come here."

She stepped closer, and he put his hands on her shoulders and turned her so she could see down the other side of the ledge. He pointed down below. "Look."

She craned her neck so she could peer down the hill. "It's just another river." She wiped her eyes.

"No," he said. "It's a freshwater pool. See the waterfalls?" He could feel her nod. The woman was senseless. "Want a bath?"

She spun around, her hands clutching his filthy shirtfront like a shameless beggar. "A bath?" She sounded ready to swoon.

He smiled and peeled her grappling hands from his shirt so he could get the pack and rifle. "Come on." He grabbed her hand and took her down the rocky path that led to the pool. "Let's go get you that bath."

Lollie stood under the falling water, rubbing the large oily leaves Sam told her worked like soap over her filthy skin. She scrubbed her shoulder especially well, washing away the creepy feeling left behind by the huge spider. With each swipe of the large leaf more of the dirt and grime and mud washed away in the cascading water. This was heaven.

She glanced around at the slate gray rock of the small

ledge on which she stood. It was solid and almost completely surrounded her except for one small open area where the water fell. She'd been leery at first, worried that Sam could see her. She had asked him how she could be sure of her privacy.

He'd told her he had better things to do than look at her. When she balked, he'd taken her over to another grotto just like this one. Both had been carved by nature into the rock hillside on opposite ends of the clear silvery pool.

A ridged wall of rock separated the two areas so that in order for him to see her, he'd have to climb onto the rocks where he'd be in plain sight of her. She was safe from prying male eyes. And she wanted to be clean so badly she was willing to trust him. She'd probably have trusted the devil himself if it meant getting clean.

The water felt so good. She let it rush through her long hair, basking in the way it poured over her scalp like gentle, cleansing fingers. She wadded the soap leaf in her hand and rubbed it over her hair, getting a bit of a lather that smelled like expensive exotic perfume. Leaning back, she rinsed her hair, twisting and turning this way and that.

A noise pierced the rushing sound of falling water. She spun, covering her privates, both upper and lower, as best she could with her arms and hands. Then she stepped back and peered out, expecting to see Sam Forester standing on the rocks watching her.

No one was there.

How odd, she thought. The noise sounded like a male groan—a loud male groan. Worried now, she stooped down and picked up her undergarments, which she'd washed and wrung out before placing them on a small ledge near the waterfall. She eyed the corset. That was one garmet she intended to leave behind. She stepped into the lace-edged drawers, pulled them up, and tied the waist cord. Soaking wet, they clung to her like a second skin, a sheer second skin. Ramming her arms into the corset cover, she fumbled with the small pearl buttons, every so often peering out at the rock barrier.

Still no one, she thought, stepping into her ragged and torn petticoat. She glanced down. At least most of her was covered, although now she wasn't cinched in. While it felt odd, that corset was one garment she wouldn't miss. A little freedom was nice, but it was even nicer to be clean all over. Well, almost all over. There was still jerky between her teeth.

Maybe she could borrow Sam's small knife to whittle it out. Moving with purpose she crossed the small shallow pool. He had given her the shallow end to, as he put it, keep her from drowning in four feet of water. She reached the rock barrier and realized that she'd forgotten her shoes. She eyed the distance back, then the few rocks she could use as steps. They were slick and smooth, made so by years of flowing water.

Picking up one foot, she looked at the bottom and assessed the damage already done by walking through miles of jungle for four days. She doubted the rocks could be much worse, so she climbed up them. It took only a few moments to reach the crest of the wall. She pulled herself up so she was just able to peek over the rim.

Her breath lodged in her throat like a boulder.

"Oh, my," she whispered.

Sam stood near the north edge of the pool, barely five feet away. His back was partially to her and waist high water lapped at his bare upper body. He was shaving . . . with the machete. He craned his square jaw upward and drew the knife blade across it. Her eyes followed the blade grazing his hair-roughened cheek. A broken piece of mirror sat propped against a rock shelf and he reached out and adjusted it to a better position, turning slightly before once again drawing the machete over his dark beard.

She pushed herself over the rocks a bit farther so she could still see. Then he turned a little and she could just see a bit of his chest and profile. Practically her whole upper torso now leaned over the top of the rocks, but her view was truly fine. His long hair, black as jet, was slicked back from his broad forehead, and water ran from it like small meandering rivers down the dips and ridges of muscle on his back. Turning his chin, he raised his arm to better angle the blade, and the movement made his skin taut. Beneath the solid muscle of his upper chest, she could see the outline of each rib and the almost corrugated tightness of his hard stomach.

Sam Forester was nothing like her brothers.

Her mouth felt dry, so she swallowed and almost coughed, ducking her head back down so she wouldn't give her position away. Very slowly she peered over the rocks again, unable to stop herself. He reached out to adjust the mirror, and she could see his back sparkle as the sunlight caught some water drops that glistened over his skin. Suddenly she needed to feel that skin. It was the strangest thing. Imagine, wanting to touch someone's skin. Frowning, she stared at her itchy palm, feeling as if it were holding thirty pieces of silver.

He finished shaving; she continued peeking. He picked up two of the same type of leaves he'd given her and rubbed them against his chest slowly. She wished he would turn some more so she could see his chest better. He turned and faced the pool. Her mouth slackened and she ducked down, still peering over the rock edge. A crop of black curly hair ran up from his waist—or down from his breastbone. She eyed him a moment longer, trying to figure out which, finally deciding that whatever direction the trail of hair ran didn't matter. It was there, and every time he ran the leaves over it it would spring outward.

He locked his arms straight over his head, stretching. He twisted this way and that. The motion showed every bulge of muscle, every rib, every indentation in a body so fine that Lollie forgot to breathe. He presented his back again and the water in the pool lapped gently at his bare waist. He looked at his jaw in the mirror, rubbed his chin, then with a quick male shrug that said "good enough," he turned and dove under the water.

Quickly Lollie shot up and craned way over the ledge to try to get a good glimpse of him swimming. Her waist was wedged against the rim of rocks, and she stood on tiptoe. His tanned form skimmed just under the surface of the water. He surfaced, then dove again and swam underwater like a trout in the Congaree River—except that a trout didn't have muscular white buttocks that just broke through the water.

Her mouth dropped and she slapped her hands over her eyes. She could hear him splash through the water. Then there was silence. She waited, wanting to peek but a little afraid to. The wanting superseded the fear, and she slowly spread her fingers.

Once again he stood in waist-high water in front of the piece of mirror on the ledge, his back to her. He leaned over and rubbed a tanned finger over his teeth. Which reminded her why she'd come. She drew her tongue over her teeth, remembering that she'd been planning to ask him for the knife. She looked at him again. Now he held the mirror, obviously trying to get a better angle. As he held it up, his back flexed and all thoughts of talking flew right out of her mind.

"Hey, Lollie. Could you move a little more to the right?"

She froze at the sound of his voice. Focusing on his back, she moved her gaze upward. One black leather eye patch and one amused brown eye stared at her from the mirror. His gaze wasn't fixed on her face, but lower. She followed his stare, down, where her corset cover gaped open so far that she could see clear to her waist.

With a gasp she clasped her hands to her chest. A big mistake . . .

Her hands had been the only thing that kept her from falling. She fell forward, right over the wall and head first into the water.

She wiggled her arms while turning over so she could try to stand up. Water burned up her nostrils. His arm clamped around her waist and jerked her up. The first thing she heard was deep male laughter.

She coughed and sputtered against his bare chest, and when her hands rested against the skin she'd wanted to touch, her palms felt warm, no more itch.

"Enjoy yourself, did you?" His voice was threaded with humor.

She could feel a hot blush stain her face. "Put me down."

One brief glance at his face and she read his thoughts. "Not here!" she quickly amended, knowing he was going to drop her back into the deep water.

He grinned down at her, then walked the few steps to her rocks and set her on the top of the rock wall.

Embarrassed, she began to wring out her hair. Then finally, unable to stall any longer, she looked at him, wondering what she could say. There wasn't anything, no excuse to cover up what they both knew: she'd been watching him, and after making a big to-do about her own privacy. It was one of those moments when she wished the earth could swallow her up and spit her out somewhere—anywhere—else.

He'd waded back across the small pool and lounged against rocks near the mirror, crossing his huge arms, a confident male smile on his face as he let his gaze move to her chest. "Nice. Very, very nice."

She like to died! She hugged her chest instead.

"Is there something I can do for you, Miss Lah-Roo? Maybe"—he turned and stretched his arms up in an embarrassingly slow manner, as if posing for a sculptor—"this angle?"

"I came to get your knife," she stated, unable to look him in his amused eye.

"You came to get the knife?"

"Yes."

"Now, why doesn't that make sense?" He looked around at the high rocks surrounding the small pool. "Funny, I don't see any coconut palms. Where do you plan to fling it this time?"

"At your rotten heart, but I doubt the knife could pierce

it," she shot back, knowing she shouldn't have been ogling him, but with his attitude she'd be crazy to admit it.

"Besides," she added, "I came to borrow the small knife." She pointed to where his belt and knives lay next to the rock ledge with the mirror, something else she wanted to borrow, now that she knew he had it. "I'd like the mirror, too, please."

"No, you wouldn't." He waded toward the knife belt.

"What do you mean, no, I wouldn't? I know what I want."

"You don't want the mirror," he said sounding as sure as Moses at the Red Sea. His confidence annoyed her, and she felt as if she were at home being told by five older brothers exactly what she should do, want, and think.

"I am all-fired sick and tired of men telling me what I want."

He grabbed the small knife and turned, giving her a long and amused one-eyed stare. With a male smirk that should have sent warning bells off in her head, he plucked the mirror off the ledge and waded back toward her, stopping when he was a mere foot away. She kept her eyes on his face.

"Here you are, Miss Lah-Roo. Your wish is my command." He held out the piece of mirror and the knife, then gave an exaggerated bow.

She glared down at the top of his black head and gathered the knife and mirror tightly to her chest, swinging her legs around to her side of the wall. She stepped down and heard his laughter echo from behind her. It just made her move all that much faster. With her chin pride-high, she stepped off the rocks, careful not to slip and further embarrass herself. She walked with purpose along the sandy edge of the shallow end of the pool, making her way to the waterfall curtained ledge where she could finally pick the jerky out of her teeth in privacy.

He was still watching her. She could feel it. When she reached the ledge she looked back. Sam leaned over the rock wall, elbows resting on its rim. He gave her a grin and a quick salute and then began that infernal counting—one, two, three—which only made her that much madder.

Ignoring him, she set the things down and climbed up on the ledge, grabbing the knife and mirror and gladly disappearing behind the curtain of water.

"Seven!" he shouted out, obviously making sure she heard him over the falling water.

She sat down and propped the mirror at a good angle.

"Twelve!"

She looked in the mirror . . .

"Fourteen!"

—and screamed.

His voice pierced the little cave. "Found those spots, huh? Only fifteen seconds. Not bad!"

Sam watched, waiting. . . .

Her head poked out from behind the waterfall. "Oh, my Gawd!" Her hands were plastered to her cheeks—the same cheeks that had been covered with bright red spots for a couple of days. "How long have I had these?"

"A while." He smiled. "Are you sure you weren't eating those berries?"

"Why didn't you tell me?"

"I did."

"You did not!"

"I told you not to eat too many of them."

"But you didn't say anything about spots."

"I warned you."

"Not about the spots!"

He shrugged. "A warning's a warning. I didn't feel I had to get into specifics."

She held the mirror up and winced, poking a few of the welts with her finger. "When will they go away?"

"Don't ask me. I've never known anyone who had them."

"They *will* go away, won't they?"

"Probably."

"What do you mean, probably? Don't you know?"

He shrugged again.

"You knew enough to tell me not to eat them!"

"I was warned and not stupid enough to test that warning."

Her head whipped back behind the water and although he couldn't hear her, he was sure he'd just been dubbed a damn Yankee again.

"Hurry along there, Lollipop. Finish what you're doing and get dressed. We need to get moving."

She didn't answer him.

"Did you hear me?" he shouted.

"I heard you!" she returned equally as loud.

He laughed to himself, wading back over to his things, feeling thoroughly entertained. He got out of the water and put on his pants and shirt. He didn't think he'd ever met anyone quite like Lollie LaRue. Harebrained and a little too innocent, gullible and more stubborn than a team of old livery mules, she was a woman on the run in the jungle, far away from home, and so completely out of her element that even Sam couldn't have abandoned her if he'd wanted to, which he didn't. He wanted that ransom and she was still a hostage, but she didn't know that and probably wouldn't find out until after her father ransomed her.

Just yesterday he would have said the past few days hadn't been worth the money, whatever the amount. No man needed a whiny, pigheaded woman when he had miles of jungle, filled with Spanish soldiers and deadly snakes and counterguerrillas, all anxious to kill him. But he was a soldier for hire, had been known to do what he had to do if the price was right. This was no different, since there was money involved here, probably a good amount, too. And he did need some compensation for the past few days.

But now, after today, he saw something different about her. He'd originally pegged her for a rich snob, but he'd been wrong about that. Remembering the way she begged for something to do, then carried those silly coconuts as if they were the United States Treasury. She had an odd sense of pride, an emotion he could understand. What he'd first assumed was arrogance and an inflated sense of self-worth had turned out to be just the opposite. She had no sense of worth. She was a bundle of insecurites.

He strapped his belt on, ramming the end hard through the buckle when he realized that he had suddenly felt the need to analyze her. He didn't want to analyze her because she was trouble, female trouble with a head that was three bullets short of a full round.

He donned the pack, grabbed the rifle, and made his way across the rocks to the Lollipop's side. "Are you ready?"

She stepped onto the ledge, put her shoes, the mirror, and the knife in her pockets, and jumped into the shallow water near the edge of the pool. She held the wet pink skirt of her ragged dress in her fists, like women did when they wanted to keep it dry.

He stifled a laugh and shook his head, waiting while she joined him. She slipped her shoes on and straightened, handing him the mirror and the knife. He put the mirror in the pack and slipped the knife into its sheath.

Her dress was still torn, but cleaner and she'd ripped off more of the lace and used it to tie back her hair, which was drier, lightening to blonde from the dark whiskey color it had been when it was wet. Now it hung, shiny-clean and a lot paler, in a silky-straight hank that fell past her pink-spotted shoulders. Her face, neck, and shoulders were a mass of pink welts. He said his thoughts aloud, "Your dress matches your spots."

She stiffened like a day-old corpse, then drew back her arm, just like she had when she threw his machete to Kingdom Come.

He grabbed her swinging fist and jerked her up against his chest to keep her from throwing another one. "Stop it!"

She glared up at him, her lips drawn into a thin line of anger, her face flushed with that same emotion. He had the sudden urge to wipe the anger off her face. He lowered his head. Her mouth was barely an inch away. He could taste her breath.

A bullet shot past them.

12

Sam hit the ground with Lollie still clasped to his chest. They lay there, on their sides, their hearts throbbing in double time. He adjusted the rifle between them. Ready to fire, he waited for another bullet. None came. The soldier in him knew they were better off if the bullets were still coming. The silence told him that their sniper had moved to a better position.

Glancing to his right, he scanned the area, praying the sniper was Spanish. The Mauser guns they used were notoriously inaccurate. If the sniper was Spanish, they'd have a chance.

The rock wall was about ten feet away, but they were ten open feet. The ledge where the water fell was an equal distance, but he didn't want to be pinned into that grotto. There might be three stone walls of protection with only one way in, but more importantly, there was only one way out—a tactical mistake made by many men—dead men.

The trajectory of the bullet had angled downward, which meant the sniper was on higher ground. He scanned the small area of jungle. They had to try to find some cover. He looked at Lollie. Her drained, spotted face reflected pure fear.

"Listen closely. We'll run for the small patch of jungle behind me."

She started to raise her head, trying to look over his shoulder.

"Don't look at it!" he whispered the harsh order. "You'll give our direction away."

Her head froze mid-motion.

"Now I'm going to roll over and up." He moved the rifle from between them and held it behind her back. "I have to keep the rifle aimed and ready so you're going to have to hold on to my neck when I roll. The second I'm up, you let go and head straight for that bamboo. Understand?"

She nodded and repeated quietly, "Hang on, let go, run."

"Okay. On three we go. One . . ."

Her arms tightened around his neck.

"Two . . ."

He held the rifle poised over her lower back, his finger on the trigger.

"Three!"

He rolled with her, rifle up. A second later they stood. She let go and took off. A round of bullets tore up the sand around them.

Sam returned fire, running after her. Mauser bullets splattered in the sand like hail. Suddenly another sniper crossfired. The shot angled downward, past Sam. He spun and shot up at the ridge trail. A Spaniard fell. Peripherally, he saw another replace him.

Three more shots and he hit the bamboo, watching Lollie's pink dress move ahead. Five steps and he'd caught up with her, passed her. He grabbed her hand and pulled her along, running in time with his heartbeat.

He jumped the bushes, hauling her with him. She fell; he jerked her up, never once breaking speed. He cut north, running uphill to throw them off.

The air grew heavy. We'll get to the river, he thought, dragging her through palm after low palm to only an occasional whimper.

A wall of bamboo met them. Sam swore. The crack of a machete would draw the Spaniards like flies to the stockyards. He stopped, catching Lollie as she barreled into him.

"Quiet!" He gripped her heaving shoulders to steady

her. "We'll move through the bamboo slowly, quietly. If I cut the bamboo they'll hear us."

She nodded. He took her hand and wormed into the wooden forest, snaking through, stepping over the hemp grass that grew thick as spring hay around the tall green bamboo. No light broke the sea of green. It was slow going, but it was quiet. On and on it went in a seemingly never-ending field that felt like a prison but might easily become a coffin.

Jungle color broke through the light green bamboo ahead. The bamboo ended only a few short feet away. He still held his breath, not knowing what lay beyond or who waited. He tried to see ahead, but it was like looking across a cell through prison bars. He couldn't get the full picture.

He stopped. There was a clearing, surrounded by orchids and canopied by jade vines hanging from giant banyans arced like tunnels above them. He looked left, then right.

"Run!" He pulled Lollie behind him.

Louder than cannon fire, swarms of birds burst from the high black crowns of the trees. Their screeches pierced the air above, higher pitched than rifle shot, and their flapping wings sounded louder than a thousand flags in the wind. The blue sky turned black from the scattering of frightened jungle doves. A shout of Spanish blasted from behind them.

"Son of a bitch!"

"Oh, my Gawd!"

They ran. Two minutes later a river stopped them, a wide, deep, flowing river, which Lollie couldn't swim.

He spun, hooked the rifle over her back and squatted, his back to her. "Lock your arms around my neck, your legs around my waist, and don't let go, even underwater!"

"But—"

"Do it!"

The second he felt her limbs gripping him, Sam dove in and swam to the middle, where he let the current carry them both downstream. A quick glance over his shoulder told him the rifle was still strapped to her back.

"You okay?"

Her arms tightened on his neck. "Yes."

"Good, then will you stop choking me?" he rasped, breathing with relief when the pressure against his Adam's apple slackened.

"Sorry," she whispered.

They moved down the river in silence, Sam working to keep them in the center of the river while he studied the jungle around them. The river twisted and turned, narrowing to only twenty feet wide, and he tried to judge the distance, mentally calculating whether it would be better to go by river or on foot.

He never had the chance to make that decision.

They drifted around a bend, right into Spanish crossfire. Bullets hit the water.

"Take a breath!" Sam shouted, and feeling her chest expand with a deep breath, he dove for the river bottom, the only place safe from the shower of bullets.

He swam along the bottom, turning east toward the riverbank that had been the highest. He hoped it still was, but he couldn't tell, the river was so murky. His lungs burned from the pressure of holding his breath. Her hands tightened to fists around him.

He could take another minute of pressure. She couldn't. He had to surface. He moved up, counting on fate, as he had a hundred times before. If it was still on his side, they would be close enough to the bank and hidden from the Spanish. He looked up and back as they floated toward the surface. A few bullets pierced the water behind them.

Then he saw it—the shadow of a small boat, above them. He stroked toward the bank side. Then, still underwater, he pulled her struggling hands from his neck and turned so he faced her. He grabbed her cheeks in his palms. Her eyes shot open. He tilted her head back, mouth and nose up. They broke the surface, a scarce few inches from the boat. She gasped for air.

His right hand still gripped her neck and head, his left hand pressed against her lips. "Shhh."

He nodded at the boat, scant inches from their bobbing heads.

The sound of gunfire now came from behind them. Carefully he backed away a few inches to see into the boat. It was empty, its bowline sagging in the reeds along the bank. He turned back to Lollie, who now breathed fine and still held his shoulders. He looped her arms around his neck. "I'm going to turn and swim through those reeds. You hang on, okay?"

She gave him her wide-eyed nod.

He moved as silently as he could, keeping only their heads above the waterline. He followed the frayed rope through the tall cattails to a spot where thick mangroves edged the river and provided cover.

As he edged toward the high bank he could see the rock anchoring the rope. He looked around. No one was nearby. He moved into the dark draping branches of the mangroves. Grabbing Lollie's hands, he turned within the loop of her arms so they were face to face. He released her hands and held her waist while he kicked to tread water for them both.

"Grab that branch." He nodded toward a thick branch by their heads.

She locked her hands over the branch.

"Good. Can you hang on here for a few minutes?"

She nodded. "Where're you going?"

"Back to get the boat. I'll bring it into the trees, and then we should be able to take it downstream. You stay here. Don't move. Don't do anything but stay hidden and hang on. Got it?"

"Yes," she whispered, eyeing the thick trees around her.

Sam moved toward the bank, where the rope disappeared in the thick reeds and muddy water. He pulled out the small knife and cut the ragged rope, taking the end with him as he swam back toward the boat.

The crossfire still pinged, though not as many shots sounded. Sam plunged deep, surfacing in the reeds on the exposed side of the river. He could see the flash of rifle fire. There looked to be five men hidden in the trees and bushes on the opposite bank. He could hear their shouts. They still barraged the river, hoping to hit something, but one of the soldiers shouted an order to move downstream. Sam couldn't wait.

He slowly edged the boat toward the reeds, hoping the soldiers wouldn't notice the movement. It took a long, tension-filled minute to get the bow of the boat into the reeds. A few minutes more and then he pulled the boat as fast as he could through the water and toward the mangroves, knowing they had only seconds before someone might notice that the boat was gone.

He made it to the mangroves, shoving the boat under the branches, right beside Lollie.

"Get in! Quick!" He lifted her, practically throwing her into the boat. Then he pushed himself up and into its shell, pulling the rifle off her shoulder. He shook the water from the barrel. "You okay?"

"Uh-huh." She cowered in a small heap near the oars, which were lying on the floor in a few inches of muddy water, and she swatted the mosquitoes away from her face.

He turned, kneeling in the bow of the rowboat, grabbing branch after mangrove branch, as he pulled the boat through the cover of the trees and downriver. The trees became so dense that it seemed like midnight instead of the middle of the day. The deeper into the trees they traveled, the thicker the mosquitoes grew, flicking and darting in the air as thick as winter snowflakes.

He heard her mutter and he looked back over his shoulder. She sat there, a dismayed frown on her spotted face, raking her nails up and down her welted arms so hard that she must have taken off a couple layers of skin. He turned back and pulled them farther through the trees, thankful that the mosquitoes kept her busy.

The sound of running boots thudded from along the bank. Sam stopped instantly. The soldiers were near, too near. He turned, at the very same instant she slapped her bug-bitten arm so loud they could have heard it in Manila.

A Spaniard shouted. Bullets ripped through the trees around them.

He grabbed the branches, jerking them as hard as he could. The boat shot out of the trees onto the river. The bullets kept coming.

"Row!" he shouted, returning rifle fire from the bow of the boat.

"How?" she shouted back.

He ducked down, grabbed the oars, and slammed them into her hands. "Stick them in the water and row, dammit!" He fired again.

Soldiers ran along both banks, shouting and shooting. The boat drifted into the slow river current.

Bullets splattered all around them. One grazed Sam's shoulder. He winced, but kept shooting. The boat lurched and he could hear Lollie banging the oars behind him. Soldiers waded toward them.

Sam hit two and kept yelling, "Row! Row!"

She did row—with one oar, in a perfect circle.

"Shit!" Sam dropped the rifle, dodging the shot, shoved her down, and sat over her, his legs pinning her squirming body to the floor of the boat. He grabbed the oars, hunched over, and ripped them through the water with every ounce of his strength.

The boat caught the current. Spanish shouts echoed from behind them, so did the gunfire. But the boat picked up speed, lurching downriver and out of range.

He stopped rowing, the current now speeding the boat through the water. His aching arms resting on the oars, he closed his eyes and let his head drop back. He waited for the energy to pass, for his blood to slow, for the rest of his muscles to relax. The female form beneath him moved, muttering under her breath—the very breath that he could easily have squeezed from her white throat, and enjoyed every second of it.

"Let me up!"

Sam counted, then prayed; neither worked. His fingers still itched to close around her neck. Even an idiot could row a goddamn boat.

At that exact moment her pink bottom bucked into his calves. He glared down at it. It took every ounce of his control to keep from ramming his bootheel into that wiggling pink butt. He shifted his legs and she popped up like a blond weasel between them, her spotty face a little too indignant for his current mood.

"There's no air down there!" she said, swiping at the wet hair that hung in her face.

"Grab the oars."

"Why?" She looked around at the wide section of the river where the current had slowed. "Aren't we safe now?"

"You're not." He gave her a lethal smile that had nothing to do with humor. "Now, row."

"Why do I have to row? You're the man. Can't you do it?"

He raised the rifle and pointed it right at her.

Her mouth dropped open.

"You can learn to row or I can shoot you. The choice is yours."

"I—"

He leaned toward her very slowly, making sure the cock on the rifle clicked. "I said *row.*"

She looked at the oars, then at him, at the gun, then back at him. His look must have convinced her how close he was to losing his last bit of control because she grabbed one of them and dragged it through the water. Just like before, the boat spun in a circle.

"One oar in each hand," he gritted.

She placed a hand on each oar handle.

"Pull them both back toward you."

The left one cut through the water. The right one slipped up, sending a stream of water on Sam.

He sat there, counting. He reached thirty-two before he swiped the water from his good eye and stared at her, drops of water still dripping from his nose.

She shrugged. "It slipped."

"There isn't enough money in the world . . ." he mumbled.

"What money?"

"Never mind."

"Oh, look! The boat's moving on its own now." She smiled as the boat picked up a faster current and cut downstream. "Now I won't have to row." She turned and gave him an innocent smile. "I must have an angel on my shoulder!"

Yeah, and I've got a boulder around my neck, named Lollie LaRue.

He watched the bank, then checked the position of the sun and the mountains beyond, trying to get his bearings. He figured that they'd go another few miles and then move to the shore. They would only be a few hours from Bonifacio's camp.

An odd whimpering sound pierced his thoughts. He turned back to see what was wrong. She watched the river around her, her skin suddenly drained and pale. The small boat rocked against a crosscurrent, and she sank back against the side, a moan of grievous pain escaping her lips. Her head lolled there for a moment and she raised her hand to her blotchy forehead, which suddenly beaded with sweat.

She groaned, "I don't feel right well. . . ."

It was almost nightfall when they reached the rim of the hillside. Lollie stopped, trying to catch her wind. She'd been weak ever since she'd took sick in the boat. Sam hadn't said much, had never again mentioned rowing, but the few words he had spoken were too blue for her to repeat.

"We'll stop here," he said, dropping the rifle to the black rocky ground that covered the hilltop trail. He fiddled with something so she gazed down at the valley below them. Deep green squares of land, like a multitude of giant steps, layered the hillsides that surrounded a lush tropical valley below them. The square fields were flooded with murky brown water from irrigation ditches that dissected them, and only a small amount of bright green foliage stuck out of the water around an occasional scattering of large brown rocks.

"What are those?" she asked Sam.

"Rice terraces." He handed her the canteen.

They had rice fields back home, but they didn't drop down hillsides like these and they weren't so lush a green. She moved her gaze from the nearest rice fields just below her to the whole panorama. It was a breathtaking sight, the deep valley, the bright green hills surrounding it and the huge blue-black mountains rising so high in the distance that they touched the pink edges of the dark twilight clouds.

A rustling sound drew her attention to the thick, tall trees behind her. She didn't see anything at first, and then a large bird flew to the branch of a neighboring tree. The bird had the most unusual colors she'd ever seen, so colorful and bright that Lollie's breath caught at the sight of it. Its head was bright red, its body a pure deep turquoise blue, and the feathers had a sheen that caught the pale pink light of the setting sun.

"Sam," she whispered.

He looked up from whatever he was doing, an annoyed expression on his face.

"What's that?" She pointed at it.

"A tree." He turned back to his work.

She stared at the top of his head. "I meant on that branch there."

He gave it a cursory glance. "A bird."

"I know it's a bird! I meant what kind of bird?"

"How the hell should I know?" He never even bothered to look at her, just continued to scoop up some fallen leaves and twigs.

She gave up and watched the bird. After a minute she took a drink and went to hand Sam back the canteen, trying really hard not to dump it on his hard head. She stared at that head while she contemplated just what the repercussions of such an action would be.

He was on bended knee, banging a rock against his knife.

She decided she wasn't quite that brave, so instead, she peered over his shoulder. "What're you doing?"

He didn't answer her, but lowered his head and blew at the ground. Suddenly smoke curled upward, and when he drew back, she could see a small fire burning near the knife blade. She wondered how he'd done that.

He stood and slid the knife into its sheath.

She looked at the small fire burning near his boots, and he bent and dipped a banyan-branch torch into the fire. Her thoughts flew right out her mouth. "What'd you do, swear at it and it caught fire?"

He stared down at her. "Hell, Miss Pain-in-the-ass Lah-Roo, maybe I goddamn did."

She closed her eyes and took a deep breath. The man couldn't even speak to her civilly. Her eyes flew open, glaring at him, as frustration boiled up so much inside of her that she opened her mouth to give him a piece of her mind.

Unfortunately at the same time she stomped one agitated foot. The ground beneath her crumbled. Like Jill after Jack, Lollie went tumbling down the hillside. Water splattered in her face and mud gushed all around her. Prickly rice stems snagged on her arms and shoulders as she rolled like a ball right into the center of a muddy, flooded rice field. One of the rocks stopped her.

Stunned silly, she sat there a moment, then scooped the mud from her eyes and face. The first thing she heard was Sam's laughter, drifting down from the hilltop above her. He howled with all the tenor of a jackass.

"Hey there, Lollipop! Did your shoe slip again?" He laughed and laughed, obviously completely certain he was wit itself.

She scowled up at him, standing on that hilltop silhouetted by the pink evening sky. Her scowl fell away. There was no wind, so his long black hair hung free to his shoulders, shoulders that spread as wide as wagon hitches and narrowed to where his fists rested on the thick leather of his belt. The stance was all male arrogance, like a king on his high throne, lording over his subjects. The last bit of sunlight broke through a few clouds, shining through the superior spread of his long legs, the same legs that were as hard as rocks when they pinned her to the floor of the boat. With his black eye patch he looked like a pirate . . . wenching.

Where did that thought come from?

Well, she thought, wherever it came from she didn't like it, and she didn't like him. Her hand closed over a big clod of mud and she slowly lifted it from the water. She stared at it for a long time. His snort of laughter spurred her on. She wound back and threw it at him as hard as she could, and missed by a good yard.

He laughed louder. " 'Bout three feet more to the left!"

She was so mad she threw another handful, and missed again.

He cupped his hands around his obnoxious mouth and shouted, "You might try it with your eyes open!"

She clenched her fists, wanting to pelt him with the entire mud field but was not about to give him any more entertainment. She never threw anything with her eyes open because it made her dizzy. She sat a little straighter, deciding words were more potent than mud balls. "If Abraham's son had been like you, Sam Forester, it wouldn't have been a sacrifice!"

"If Christ'd had you along, he wouldn't have needed a cross to become a martyr."

"I really think you're a vile man."

He crossed his arms. "Did you know that leeches breed in rice fields?"

She scrambled up, turning and trying to pull herself up on the rock—the furry rock, which suddenly moved. "Oh, my Gawd!"

A huge, brown bovine head with two long curved horns emerged from the water. She didn't know if she should run or scream.

She screamed.

The animal blinked its brown eyes, threw its huge head up, and bawled so loud even Lollie shut up. Suddenly three more "rocks" wallowed upright and moseyed toward her. It only took about three seconds for Lollie to hit the hillside and start clawing her way up the damp ground, only to slide back down, whimpering.

An arm like a tree trunk wrapped itself around her waist, hauled her back up the hill, and deposited her on the trail. She stood there shaking for a moment, trying to catch her breath.

"What are those things?"

"Carabao."

She frowned.

"Water buffalo." He wiped his muddy hands on his pants, then looked up, smirking. "They wouldn't have hurt you"—he bent and picked up the rifle—"unless they rolled."

She stood there looking at those huge beasts and remembering that Harrison had some prized bulls that weighed in at over a thousand pounds. Those water buffalo were almost twice the size of Harrison's bulls. She grimaced.

"Any leeches?" Sam asked.

Her breath caught in her throat, and she jerked her dress up to examine her legs. Nothing clung to them but a small bit of muddy water.

Sam whistled.

Her head shot up to find him ogling her legs. She dropped her skirt and narrowed her eyes at him.

His lazy smile told her there were no leeches.

She glanced back at the water buffalo, which also had no leeches and she shook her head, disgusted with her own gullibility and a little angry at Sam for making her feel so foolish. He did that all the time.

"Come on, Lollipop. Get the lead out!"

She tore her gaze away from the water buffalo and noticed that Sam was already well ahead of her. She scurried to catch up. It was getting really dark and soon their only light would be from the torch he carried.

She was also hungry again. She stopped, pressing a hand to her face and rubbing. She was searching for spots. Her skin was still dry. She couldn't bring herself to eat any more of the berries, no matter how good they were. She scanned the surroundings and smiled when her eyes lit on just the thing. Bananas would be just fine.

Glancing in Sam's direction she could still see the torch. It would only take a minute or so to catch up. She ran over to a banana tree and grasped the leaves to try to reach the green bananas above her. She jumped up and batted a bunch of them until finally it clunked to the ground. She pulled some off and stuck them into her pockets. Then she straightened and looked up, right into a smudged black face with huge green eyes and a grin more lethal than Sam's.

13

Sam heard her scream and stopped. *Now what?*

She screamed again, louder.

He shook his head. The dead must be awake.

He turned back and jogged down the trail, slowing when he heard the muffled sound of Lollie's voice and what sounded like a struggle. Slipping the rifle off his shoulder, he looked through a screen of tall oleanders into the small clearing. Five men dressed in dark clothing stood in the clearing, their faces camouflaged with dirt. The tallest man had his hand over Lollie's mouth and struggled to hold on to her. The others appeared stunned, with glazed faces and no doubt echoing ears, something Sam could relate to.

The tall man swore and jerked his hand away. She'd bitten him.

Her face had that look Sam knew so well, and her next scream rose like hot air to the tops of the trees.

It took two of the other men to subdue her. The Lollipop had learned to fight.

Sam lolled against the trunk of a coco palm, crossing his arms and watching her nail one man in the shin while she tried to bite another. He had to hand it to her. She put up a good fight. He watched a minute longer, then asked, "Losing your touch with the ladies, Cassidy?"

The tall man stopped hitting the heel of his unbitten hand against his ear and glanced up at Sam, surprise on his face. "I think I'm deaf, Sam." He shook his head, then frowned at his hand for a moment. "She's no lady. She's pair of lungs with teeth," he paused, looked at her, then added, "and spots."

She glared at his friend, Jim Cassidy, then at him, and she struggled against the two men who still held her, kicking her legs out.

Jim watched her struggle. "Nice legs, though."

She ceased struggling and her face flushed bright red. Sam let his gaze rest on her chest. "I wouldn't know. She showed me other parts."

She gasped so loud you could hear it in spite of the man's hand on her mouth.

Sam bit back a grin. Without a bit of remorse, he let her squirm, then said, "Actually, she's Eulalie Grace LaRue, but I get to call her by her nickname—Lollie."

A snort of laughter sounded from Jim's direction, a reaction Sam had expected. "Yes, she's Lollie LaRue of the *Belleview* LaRues."

She muttered again. Sam assumed she was still correcting him.

He smiled and added some coal to the fire. "Of South Carolina. Owners of Hick Home, Cowhand Industries, and Peachtree Farms." He could hear her muffled outrage and bit back a smile.

Jim stared at him for an unsure moment.

"Daughter of Ambassador LaRue," Sam added, watching recognition hit his friend's black-smudged face.

"How the hell did you get tangled up with her?" Jim leaned on his rifle and eyed Lollie.

"Compliments of Colonel Luna."

Jim stilled, his gaze going back and forth between them. "What are you going to do with her?"

Sam raised his left hand and rubbed his thumb back and forth across his fingers in the time-honored sign of a money payoff.

Jim's eyes lit up with the same look of larceny that had bonded the two of them almost from their first meeting, and he smiled. "How much?"

"Probably not enough for what I've put up with for the last few days." Sam glanced at Lollie, who had suddenly stilled. He watched her closely. Her look changed from fear to betrayal. He'd have bet a year's salary that she wasn't smart enough to catch on. He was wrong, and turned away from those wounded blue eyes, which held such a look of betrayed innocence that he felt something he hadn't felt in years—guilt.

He shrugged it off and looked at Jim. "I'll have to talk to Andrés."

Jim nodded, now eyeing Lollie with new interest, an interest that wasn't only larcenous. It was lascivious, too.

Sam had the sudden urge to draw Jim's attention away from her. "What are you doing this far from camp?"

"The Spanish have been moving deeper and deeper into the interior. They garrisoned off Santa Christina last week."

That news set Sam back. Santa Christina was less than fifteen miles away and a good-sized interior town. Many of Bonifacio's men had come from that town and others nearby. If the Spanish had taken it over, that meant they'd infiltrated even deeper into guerrilla territory, which also meant it wouldn't be long before they did something to get the guerrilla forces out into open combat. The Spanish

157

worked that way, cordoning off a town, gathering its people, and torturing enough innocent villagers to get the word spread from town to town. It was a surefire way to draw out the hotheaded rebels and wipe out the resistance completely. "Have the guns arrived yet?"

Jim shook his head and adjusted the ever-present bow and quiver of arrows slung across his back. His friend would use the rifle for its speed, but Sam knew he preferred the deadly silence and accuracy of a bow and arrow.

Sam took in Jim's black clothes, the hair slicked back with oil, and his ash-smudged face. "On a scavenger run?"

Jim grinned, his white teeth shiny against his dirty face. "Rumor has it the Spanish just got a brand-new supply of dynamite." He nodded at his men. "We thought we might relieve them of that particular burden."

Sam laughed. His friend was known as the camp scrounger, able to steal almost anything from deep within the enemy camp. Last November, when they'd arrived in the island camp, Jim had found the abundance of sweet potatoes inspiration for stealing the local alcalde's turkeys just so they could have an old-fashioned American Thanksgiving dinner.

"I guess I'd better get back to camp and get rid of my own burden." He looked pointedly at Lollie, whose eyes shot cool fire at him. Sam ignored her and nodded at the two Filipino rebels who had subdued her. "Mind if I take Garcia and Montez?"

"Go ahead. From the ringing in my ears and the teeth marks in my hand I'd say you need them more than I do." Jim smiled. "There are only two hundred Spanish in the town. They're the lesser evil."

Lollie tried to kick one of the laughing soldiers and missed. She would have fallen if they hadn't had a death grip on her.

Jim put his fingers to his mouth and whistled. The tree branches rustled, and leaves drifted down the high branches above. A black mynah bird with a red head swooped down from the tree, hovered over them for a moment, then landed on Jim's shoulder. He pulled something out of his shirt pocket and gave it to the bird.

Sam groaned. "The black pigeon from hell."

The bird squawked, bobbed its head a couple of times while it plodded slowly across Jim's shoulder, then flapped twice and screamed, "Raaaaape! Ha-ha-ha-ha-ha-hah!"

Lollie's eyes almost popped right out of her head.

"Easy there, Medusa," Jim soothed the mynah with a few strokes. "You keep goading her, Sam, and she'll go after your good eye."

He laughed. "That bird knows I'd roast her on a spit if she came within three feet of me. Maybe we should cook her this Thanksgiving."

"Sam's full of it! Watch where you step!" Medusa called, weaving her head melodically with each word.

He really hated that bird.

Jim grinned at him then gave the bird another treat. "You keep threatening to cook her. Puts her on the defensive. Remember," he reached up to stroke the bird, which cooed and cocked its head, "females respond better to strokes and compliments."

"Jim's my hero," Medusa said, rubbing her head against her master's ear. She straightened, pulling a shiny black wing toward her chest, and squawked, "Sam's not."

"Well, on that note, we're off." Jim gave Sam a quick, mocking salute, then leered at Lollie and disappeared into the bushes with his men and that obnoxious bird.

Sam glanced at Lollie. She never took those eyes off him, even though she was held by two rebel soldiers. She struggled and mumbled against one soldier's hand. Sam tried to ignore her and all the noise she was making.

It didn't work. He could feel the accusation in those eyes, and he didn't like it, or himself.

"Gag her," he ordered, his tone so sharp it could have cut ice. He turned away and picked up his rifle. *"Tayo na!"* he shouted over his shoulder. "Let's go."

And he didn't look back again.

* * *

Lollie got in two more kicks and another bite before the soldier slammed the door. She ran to it and pounded on the splintered wood. It rattled but didn't budge.

That damn Yankee. She wished it had been his shin she'd kicked and his hand she'd bitten, only she'd have done it harder. He'd planned to hold her for ransom the whole time, and just when she'd started to think—because of the way he kept rescuing her—that maybe he wasn't so bad after all. Little had she known it was because he wanted to get his own ransom payoff.

He wasn't bad. He was horrible.

She'd foolishly thought he would send for her father. All he'd wanted was money. He wanted to sell her. Her only worth seemed to be the sum of the ransom she'd bring, just because she was Ambassador LaRue's daughter. To men like Colonel Luna and Sam Forester she had value only because of her name. She wondered of what value she was to her father, and prayed that he valued her in his heart. Still, it was hard to imagine being loved by a parent who hadn't been around for most of her life.

As a dreamy-eyed young girl she'd thought her father a brave, courageous man who'd sacrificed a life with his daughter for a life devoted to his country. She'd dreamed of their reunion as one where he told her how he'd longed to see her grow up and how he had wanted to be there for all the important events in a little girl's life, but he couldn't. His duty was to so many more people than just one girl. He couldn't, in good conscience, be that selfish.

Now, alone inside the dark little shed, she wondered if that dream would ever come true. She looked around the dank room, her eyes finally adjusting to the dark. Stacked ceiling high were crates and boxes and barrels. She stepped toward them and stumbled on something. She glanced down and saw it was some sort of long metal tool. She thought she heard her brother call it a birdstick. She nudged it out of the way with her foot, went over to a barrel, and dusted off the top before she sat down.

It was quiet, so quiet. She looked around the dark room,

feeling a little scared and very much alone. She wondered how long they'd keep her in here, and the horrifying thought crossed her mind that she might be in here for days. It was suddenly as if she were three years old again and stuck inside that dark well. The air tasted the same— dank and dead. The only light in the well had been through the small opening. The only light in this room was a little bit that cracked through a small opening between the door and its jamb. All she could see was the padlock.

The urge came over her to scream the roof down. She took a deep breath instead.

Something scurried in the corner behind the crate. She jerked her feet up, hugging her knees while she scanned the floor. Chills ran down her arms and she shivered, imagining all the things that could be in here with her . . . for days . . . alone . . . while once again, she waited.

Sam stared at the guerrilla leader as if he couldn't believe what he'd heard, and he couldn't. "What in the hell do you mean you don't want her? She's worth a bloody fortune in ransom, Andrés!"

"I do not care how many silver pesos the girl is worth. One thing she is not worth is the trouble a ransom demand would bring upon our movement." Andrés Bonifacio, leader of the Katipunan insurrectionist rebels, stopped pacing in agitation behind his desk and looked Sam in the eye. "You have made a mistake, my friend. Your government will have my head if we hold her for ransom. Her father will see to that. We have got too much trouble with the Spanish right in our backyard, as you say. I need any U.S. support I can get. It is worth more than the ransom could ever be. Ambassador LaRue has too much influence. I cannot take the chance of losing U.S. backing. Too many Filipinos have fought hard and for too long to lose it for some quick thousands."

Sam watched the rebel leader pace. Any hope of his bonus died faster than a candle in the wind. He had the sudden urge to punch something. He rammed his fists into his pockets. "What are we going to do with her?"

"Not we." Bonifacio gave him a pointed look. "You."

Sam stood there for a stunned moment, then started to back away, his hands out in front of him. "Oh, no. Not me. I've been stuck with her for days. Let some of the men take her back. I don't want anything to do with her."

"You brought her here. You will take her back."

"And if I refuse?" Sam suddenly felt as if he were trapped by artillery fire.

Bonifacio's face changed, his anger now showing clearly. "Then you will not get paid for anything." He slammed his fist down on the table. "*Madre Dios,* Sam! What were you thinking? I need the American support. If I send her back with my men it will look as if I took her, not Aguinaldo." He began to pace again as he spoke, "No, you might not want to, but you have to take her back. You are American and you will convince them that I had nothing to do with this."

"Let Cassidy do it. He's as much an American as I am."

"No." He held up a hand and looked at Sam as if he'd lost his head. "The girl would never make it there . . . untouched. You know that as well as I. Put a woman within a meter of him and she will be under him in ten minutes. No. You will take her back." He paused a moment, then looked Sam in the eye. "She *is* unharmed?"

"Yeah. I'm not that stupid." Sam clenched his hands inside his pockets and stared out the window, not seeing the night but instead remembering two accusing blue eyes.

He didn't like that, or the idea that he was going to have to travel with her again. He'd miscalculated. Andrés was right, but that didn't make the whole thing any easier to swallow, nor did the desire to punch something fade.

There was no bonus—something that would have made his rare bout of guilt a bit easier to live with—and the fact that he'd put up with her for free didn't please the mercenary in him at all. Also at stake here was his soldier's pride, which was bruised from the bad judgment that had almost jeopardized his job. He'd never done that before.

The clincher was that he was stuck with Lollie LaRue,

ordered to take her back to her daddy, a job that he didn't relish and that would be more difficult because she knew, since he'd revealed, in his conversation with Cassidy, what his plan had been all along. That was the biggest screw up of all.

He turned around and leaned against the wall with a nonchalance he was far from feeling. "We've got a little problem."

"What?"

"She knows."

"Knows what?"

"That I'd planned to get paid for her."

Bonifacio swore, then mumbled, *"Estúpido."*

"You're right, it was stupid on my part, but I'll tell you, one day with that woman could turn Machiavelli into a moron."

The room was silent. Sam rubbed his forehead in thought. He needed to find a way to undo his mistake. He thought for a moment longer, recalling his conversation with Jim. She knew he was going to hold her for ransom.

No, he amended that. All she knew was that he would get paid. He pushed against the wall and walked to his commander's desk, placing a hand on either end and leaning over to convince Andrés of the idea. "She only knows I planned to get money when I brought her here. It's possible that we could convince her that she misunderstood."

"We?"

"I'll need your help. We have to make her think that we planned all along to return her to her father safely, with no ransom. But I'll need your help. We need to make her think the money I spoke of was my reward for saving her." Sam paused, suddenly aware of something he might have forgotten. "You don't suppose a reward has been offered already, do you? Or maybe you could persaude her father to pay one."

One look into his commander's eyes told Sam he wouldn't get a red cent. The Chicago street kid in him had to give it a try. He shrugged. "Forget I asked that."

"Always the mercenary, eh, my friend?" Bonifacio gave a quick laugh, then sat down at the desk. "Do whatever you have to do to convince her. I will send a message to her father, telling him we have found her and she is safe and that you, a trusted American will be bringing her back. I will leave the arrangements open in case the ambassador wants to meet you. I do not want him or anyone else to know where we are. The guns are due any day. We cannot miss that shipment." He looked up at Sam. "I will tell her we were concerned only for her safety, and I will help convince her of the reward story, but until we hear from her father, she is your responsibility. I have too much to do with the Spanish so near."

Damn, he had his orders. He was stuck with her.

"Where is she?" Bonifacio asked.

"I had her locked in that shed by the supply hut," Sam answered distractedly.

A loud knock pounded on the door of the bungalow. The door opened, and a soldier entered. His shoulders went ramrod straight, and he saluted Bonifacio, then Sam. "The woman has escaped."

It took them only ten minutes to find her.

It took five men almost half an hour to cut her out of the barbed-wire barrier in one piece. With only torchlight to work by, the job was that much more difficult. Sam flipped his pocket watch closed and slipped it back into his shirt pocket. He bent, retrieved the torch he had stuck in the ground, and straightened, holding it up higher so the men could see in the dark. He rested a booted foot on the sand-bags piled five high on the jungle side of the camp's perimeter and moved the torch closer, watching the extraction of Lollie LaRue.

She must have tried to crawl through the spiraled loops that were used as protection against invading forces. When they'd found her she was trapped like a ragged pink worm in a cocoon of barbed wire. It looked to Sam as if almost every sharp barb was caught on or wrapped in her dress or her hair, and what wasn't caught was tangled like fishing line about her feet and hands. In one of those hands was a crowbar.

One look at her and he knew, absolutely, there was no way on this earth he was going to travel through the jungle with her again, no way at all. If he had to take her back, he'd do it on the mountain road where he could stick her in a cart pulled by a carabao and ride with her to Manila, or wherever that daddy of hers wanted to meet them. Sam didn't care if they had to dress like peasants, natives, the Spanish, whatever, but he was *not* going into the jungle with her again. No way.

The men finished cutting her out, and one of them pried the crowbar out of her hand—something for which Sam was especially grateful. He had a hunch that she'd have swung it at him the first chance she got.

They pulled her to her wobbly feet, grinning and talking in their own native Tagalog. She shook her head and looked at them for a moment, her face confused and a little frightened. The soldiers still grinned at her, and Sam could see the relief ease her stiff shoulders. Of course she had no idea what they were laughing at. They'd called her *lasing paru-paro*, a drunken butterfly.

One look at her and anyone could see the name was appropriate. Pieces of wire jutted out from her messy blond hair like insect antennae. Her skirt was caught in long ropes of wire that poked out from her clothing, and the fabric draped outward like drooping pink wings. His first urge was to tell her how she looked, but he knew anything he said would be so soaked with sarcasm that she'd get mad. Then they'd never convince her that she was not going to be ransomed, but instead taken back to her daddy.

She tried to take a step and wobbled again. He moved toward her and reached out to steady her. She jerked her arm out of his grasp and gave him a scathing look. "Don't you touch me!"

He and Andrés exchanged looks. Covertly, Andrés

pointed to his chest, indicating he should give it a try. Sam watched.

Andrés stepped forward, giving Eulalie a gallant little bow, one in which his hat actually swept the ground. "Miss LaRue, I am Andrés Bonifacio." He straightened and smiled at her. "I am so sorry you were . . . were inconvenienced by our primitive surroundings." He waved a hand at the log fences, ditches, sandbags, and barbed wire that surrounded them for as far as one could see in only the torchlight.

She shook her skirts with an indignant snap, and a few pieces of wire bounced onto the ground while others recoiled outward, then sprang back like broken guitar strings. "Well, I should think so. Of course I suppose you need all this . . . this prison fence to keep your hostages." She waved her hand around, and it caught on a piece of wire, pulling her hair. She winced and jerked it out of her hair, frowning at the blond wad of hair that hung from the wire.

Andrés stiffened. "Hostages? I do not understand." He looked from Lollie back to Sam, his face shocked.

Good work, Bonifacio. A little exaggerated for my taste, but still good work. Sam smiled.

She tossed the wire over her shoulder. "Just because I'm a woman doesn't mean you have to treat me as if I'm stupid. I heard him." She glared at Sam, raising an accusing finger and waving it around his face.

He never took his gaze from hers, but smiled. "What was that?"

Her jaw jutted out like a mule just before it kicks. "You told your friend that you intended to get paid for me, and when he asked how much, you said it was up to you." She turned her accusing finger on Bonifacio.

Andrés laughed and shook his head as if this whole thing was some great joke. Sam joined him. Her shoulders went back, and her chin went up in pure indignation. She wanted to hit them. Sam could read it in her icy eyes.

"There has been a big mistake, Miss LaRue. Sam was

talking about his reward for bringing you to the safety of this camp." Andrés smiled.

She eyed both men with the same wary look that Little Red Riding Hood must have worn when she looked at the wolf in her grandmother's bed. Sam and Andrés exchanged a scheming look.

"We are very close with the United States government," Andrés told her. "I have already sent a note to your father telling him that you are safe, thanks to Sam, and that he will be bringing you back to Manila as soon as we can ensure your safe return."

She was very quiet, then tore her gaze away from his commander and looked at Sam.

He smiled as innocently as a one-eyed mercenary could.

She watched him, then crossed her barb-scraped arms and said, "How do I know that?"

She was learning. Not bad, he thought, watching her with a glimmer of respect.

Andrés lifted his hands in a helpless gesture. "I cannot prove that I sent the note."

"Can you prove that you have ties with my government?" She raised her chin a notch.

Two good questions, Sam thought. Amazing.

"Ah, now, that I can prove." Andrés picked up a torch and placed it near the sandbag wall. "See this?" He pointed to some writing on the bag.

Lollie walked over and looked. Sam knew it said "U.S. Army issue, property of the United States of America." He had bought them from a supply officer out of the Presidio in San Francisco, a man who, for the right price, would supply him with anything that belonged to the army. However, she wouldn't know that.

She read the print and straightened, still watching both men as if she could determine the truth from their faces.

Andrés slid his jacket off, hunkered down near the torch, and turned the coat inside out. "Look, read this."

She leaned over and read aloud, " 'Property of the United States Army.' "

He slapped his knife and sheath down next to it, pointing to the words stamped into the leather sheath.

" 'Property of the United States Army,' " she repeated.

"Gomez! Come here." Andrés called the man over. "Hold out those wire cutters so she can see them."

She leaned over and read, " 'Property of the United States Army.' "

"Do you still doubt we are backed by the U.S.?" Bonifacio asked.

She gave him a full smile and sighed—a good windy one—with relief, then slapped a hand on her chest. "I can't tell you how relieved I am. This whole thing has been such a trial." She gave Sam a pointed look.

Bonifacio shot him a look of warning. "Sam has some . . . some rough edges, Miss LaRue, but he is a fine soldier, a man you can trust with your life. I would always feel safe with him at my flank. I am sure he only did what he had to to keep you both alive."

She made a choked noise of disbelief, which irritated the hell out of Sam. His hands itched.

"Miss LaRue, Sam will be escorting you back to your family just as soon as I can make the arrangements."

"I'd prefer someone else, please," she said, just as if she were ordering a meal.

"Unfortunately, that is not possible. He is the most qualified. He is an American, like you, and is the best man for the job. I am afraid you two will just have to tolerate each other. I have many men, but none I would trust as much as him."

Sam gave her a gloating smile.

"Also, he has volunteered."

His smile faded. *Volunteered, my ass*. He gave his commander a look that said as much and received another warning look.

Lollie still stood there. Then she sighed. "I guess we have no choice." She picked a piece of wire off her dress. "You could apologize. You weren't very nice to me, you know."

He would not apologize. "I saved your pampered southern butt."

"That's what I mean!" Nose and chin up, she turned to his commander, presenting Sam with her stiff back. "He also called me a pain in the . . . well, you know."

"Ass. You were a pain in the ass," Sam repeated, ignoring his commander. "And you still are."

"Quiet! Both of you!" Bonifacio shouted.

"But—" Lollie and Sam spoke at the same time.

"Not one word." Bonifacio held up his hands, then shook his head. "I think you two have just been through too much together the last few days. I changed my mind." He looked at Sam. "Maybe a little time apart would help."

"Thank you, God," Sam mumbled just loud enough for them to hear.

She gasped and turned toward him, glaring like a bulldog.

His commander pinned him with a look that said Sam had pushed too far. After a long silence he said, "On second thought, maybe you should settle this together." His look dared Sam to comment.

He didn't; he cursed his sharp tongue instead. This woman drove him to do the stupidest things.

Bonifacio gave her a quick bow. "I must get back. Our cause is in jeopardy, and I will be very busy. I have placed you in Sam's competent care. Remember, you both made it here in one piece. I am sure you will be able to resolve your differences over the next few days." He looked at her. "It is the best for your welfare. I will talk to you, Miss LaRue, as soon as we hear from your father." He gave Sam a curt nod, turned, and disappeared into the dark camp.

169

14

Lollie pulled the thread taut, bit it in two, and placed the needle and thread on the table next to her cot. She held the black pants up. The waist looked much smaller. Standing, she pulled the pants on over the new underwear she'd been given—men's underwear in a small size.

The drawers and the sleeveless undershirt were made of cotton—new and U.S. government issued. As small as they were, they were still too big for her. The shirt gaped under her arms, and the drawers stayed up only because of the drawstring at the waist. She slid the long sleeves of the stiff black canvas shirt on, and they fell over her hands as if weighted. She rolled the sleeves up, not an easy task, since the other cuff kept falling down and getting in her way.

Finally she managed to get the sleeves to stay up near her elbows. The roll of sleeve was so tight it pinched her skin, but at least they were out of the way. She shoved the long shirttails into the pants and pushed the pants buttons through the holes.

The pants were a little tight, but that was much better than before. She looked over her shoulder to see how they fit. She ran her hands down the side seams, which were now thicker where she'd folded them over and sewed them together, using the only sewing technique she'd mastered at school—the embroidery locking stitch. She just hoped they'd hold.

It felt odd, wearing pants instead of the heavy petticoats and dresses she'd always worn, and even different from the

170

skimpy, ragged dress she'd worn through the jungle. She glanced down at her legs, outlined by the pants. The fabric was especially tight across her fanny and hipbones. Maybe they fit a bit too well. She supposed she could rip out a seam and redo it, but she really didn't feel like it, since sewing had never been her favorite pastime. She had mastered only embroidery—her initials, flowers, and such.

She wondered why certain duties were always associated with women, ladies in particular. Madame Devereaux had been so strict about what a lady did and didn't do. In Lollie's mind, very few of the do's were fun. Dancing was something she liked, but ladies had to wait around for the men to deign to ask them. That was another stupid rule no doubt invented by the superior males in history. It rated down there on the sense scale with that ladylike-appetite business—stupid, really stupid.

Another entertainment was riding, although she'd been denied access to the more spirited horses by her brother Harrison, who thought she was helpless. He'd have looked helpless, too, if he'd been forced to ride almost sideways on a slippery leather saddle, one knee hooked around the sidesaddle pommel. How anyone could be expected to stay on a horse in that position was beyond her. And she never had managed to stay on even once.

It galled her that men seemed to feel that their sole purpose on this earth was to tell women what to do, then save them from the consequences. Seemed like a futile exercise.

But it was a man's world, ruled and run by men, at least her world always had been. It consisted of five brothers who relished telling her what to do and then did whatever they pleased. A father who never bothered with her and still wasn't rushing to meet his daughter. Now she was stuck in a camp full of men, soldiers, and one Yankee in particular who had strong opinions, the social graces of a mule, and the tact and finesse of a cannon blast.

Sam was an odd man. Hardheaded. She thought of his refusal to apologize. Rude. He called her some awful things. Yet there was something about him that intrigued her. She wondered if maybe it was just the differences in their lives, if maybe she was drawn to Sam Forester because she'd never known anyone quite like him.

The few men she'd known socially were gentlemen of the South, male perfection from the tops of their well-groomed heads to the toes of their polished boots. They had manners, grace, and a finely bred handsomeness. Sam was handsome, in a rough way. In her mind she pictured his face as it had been the first time she'd really looked at him in that alley. Some bell had chimed deep inside her, as if warning her away. It had frightened her at the time. Now it intrigued her, for with all of their fine manners and perfectly groomed good looks none—not even one—of the men back home had ever made her swimmy-headed.

Sam did.

He had a powerful lot of pride, maybe even more than a Charlestonian, which was probably way too much for any one person. She thought of the time she'd tried to give him her food. That pride had been there in full force.

His talk was gruff, purposely so, and he swore enough to meet the devil tomorrow face to face. He was a little mysterious and very dangerous. She wondered if the slums had done that to him or if it was caused by something else—his eye, maybe? Sam Forester was no gentleman, and yet . . . there was something. As much as he shouted to the world that she was a burden to him, he'd never abandoned her, not once. She sighed, wondering what that meant and telling herself not to read too much into it.

Placing her chin on her hand, she surveyed the small room for the hundredth time. It was barren. The wooden floor was made of some rough, almost splintery wood. The walls were painted, but the color, if it could be called a color, was flat gray. There were two wooden chairs, one of carved oak with only one arm and a wobbling leg, the other painted a deep green. Imagine painting anything on this island green. As if there wasn't enough green here already.

But the color was tolerable; the holes in the caned seat

were not. She'd made the mistake of sitting in that chair when Sam dragged her to this room and tossed some bedding on the bed, along with the clean clothes. She had been intent on watching him stomp around the room like one of those water buffalo, and she'd flopped into the closest chair to be more comfortable while he vented his anger. Her fanny had sunk straight to the rungs, her knees pinned against her chest. She couldn't have moved if someone had lit a fire under her. Swearing the room blue, he had yanked her out.

Embarrassed at the memory, she plopped down on the hard cot and stared at the thick red socks lying next to a pair of leather boots with a ton of eyelets and laces. The brown leather was rock-hard and uncreased, so she figured they were brand-new, although as hard as they were, she doubted anyone, even the soldier for whom they were intended, could ever wear a crease in them. Obviously they were men's boots, but they looked small enough to fit her and she wondered where he'd gotten them.

With a quick shrug of who knows and who cares, she pulled on the socks and slipped into the boots, then tied them and stood to test the fit. She walked forward, the heavy boots pounding like horses' hooves on the wooden floor.

For the next few minutes she tromped around the small room, trying to get used to walking in the heavy shoes. Satisfied she could walk without keeling over, she decided to explore the camp, unable to take the confinement any longer. Quick as a blink she'd walked to the door, opened it, and stepped outside, just as Jim Cassidy walked around the corner less than three feet from her. At least she assumed it was Jim Cassidy since that big black bird was perched on his shoulder.

The man was very tall, not as muscular as Sam, and his hair wasn't slicked back as it had been before. It was a deep dark blond, with light streaks at the top and gray at his temples. He had very dark brows, which made his blond hair look even lighter. His face was tanned and angular, and without the ash smeared on it, he was absolutely the handsomest man Lollie had ever seen. She just stood there gawking.

"Halt, Jim! Hen at three o'clock!" The bird flapped its wings twice and peered around its master's shoulder to pin her with its curious yellow eyes.

Jim stopped. "Well, well, the carnivore."

Lollie felt her face flush.

"Broken any eardrums lately?" he said, smiling while he gave her a look she could pour on pancakes.

She ignored his words, because something else had her attention—his eyes. She had the strangest feeling that this man's green eyes could see right through her clothes. He prowled toward her. She backed up until her backside smacked against the doorframe.

He stepped closer. "You look a little lost." He placed one hand on the doorjamb and leaned his head down until it was barely two inches from hers. His eyes never blinked, never fluttered, just seemed to scorch her. He had long, thick, dark eyelashes and light green eyes that held a hard, earthy knowledge that she had no wish to know. This man was canned fire.

After a few seconds that seemed like hot hours, he whispered, "How about I help you *find* yourself. I'll even let you"—he cupped her chin in his hand and stroked it with his thumb slowly—"bite."

"Oh, my Gawd!" She ducked under his arm and looked frantically around, then yelled as loud as she could, "Saaaam!"

The bird squawked and flew to the eave of the hut, screeching. "Raaaape! Ha-ha-ha-ha-hah!"

At the same time Jim straightened. "Damn woman! Where'd you learn to yell like that?" He shook his head as if to stop the ringing.

Sam rounded the corner at a full run.

Lollie flew into his chest, wrapping her arms around him like a wisteria on wrought iron.

"What the hell's going on here?"

"Huh?" Jim shook his head.

"Sam's here! He's full of it! Get a shovel!" the bird cried from its perch above them.

Three more men ran around the corner. Two held machetes and another a huge, wide-barreled gun. Lollie took a deep breath and looked at the three men. The one with the huge gun pointed it right at her. She gasped and practically climbed onto Sam, looking up at him while she tried to speak. "I . . . he . . . we . . ." and she burst into tears.

"Shit! Cassidy, you ass."

"What'd you say?" Jim frowned as if in pain.

"Sam's an ass! Sam's an ass!"

"I'm going to kill that bird," Sam muttered. "Stop crying, Lollie. He's not going to hurt you."

She cried even harder, unable to stop herself until Sam finally put his hard arms around her. Her tears tapered to small sniffles almost the second she felt the warmth of his arms and his hand gently rubbing her back. He had the most comforting chest.

"This one's off limits."

"I can't hear you. What'd you say?" Jim blinked.

"Keep away from her!" Sam shouted so loud Lollie jumped. Then she turned within the circle of his arms and looked at Jim.

He looked at them, his gaze going from her to Sam. "Ah, I see." He gave Lollie an annoyed stare. "I can't hear, but I see. It's real plain."

"Just what the hell do you see?" Sam's bellow echoed above her.

"It's all right, Sammy old boy. I won't trespass on your property." He grinned.

"Sam's bought the farm!" crowed the bird, and Jim snorted with laughter.

Lollie looked up at Sam at the same instant he looked at her, his face a mask of pure horror. His arms left her so fast it was as if her skin had turned to fire. He stepped back two strides, putting plenty of distance between them. She was instantly cold.

"I don't want her, Cassidy. I'm stuck with her until I can get her back to her daddy, unharmed." He looked at her as if she were quicksand and then turned his angry gaze toward his friend.

Her heart sank. She felt humiliated that he could be so public about his lack of regard for her, and she was hurt that once again a man didn't want her around. She swallowed to fight back the burn of her silly tears.

"So hands off. That's an order." Sam nodded at the huge-barreled gun that the one soldier held. "The guns are here. I need your help."

Nobody was looking at her, so Lollie quickly wiped her eyes, took a deep cleansing breath, and looked up. One of the soldiers—Gomez, she thought his name was—smiled at her and nodded as if to say it was okay. Then he and the other soldier turned and left. She felt better. Sam might not like her, but his men did.

Jim pushed away from the wall of the wooden bungalow and whistled. The bird paced back and forth, squawking, but it didn't leave its perch. "Come on, Medusa." Jim held out his arm.

It flapped its wings and paced again, still not leaving the eave.

"What's the matter with you?" He stared at the bird, then reached into his shirt pocket and held out a nut.

The bird ignored it, screeched, whistled once, then flew from the eave right onto Lollie's head.

She stood as still as a hickory tree. Her eyes widened as she whispered, "Does she bite?"

"Only me," Sam said, his gaze aimed toward the top of her head.

"Can someone get her off?" Lollie whispered, feeling the bird shift its weight from one foot to the other.

Jim walked over to the bird. "Come on, you. Let's go help Sam."

"Awk! Help Sam! He's full of it! Get him a shovel!"

Medusa stepped off her head, and Lollie exhaled with relief. Then the bird hopped from Jim's arm right back onto Lollie's shoulder. She froze, trying to see out of the corner of her eye. The bird shifted, then hummed a little purring sound and stretched its neck out to peer at her. "Who's that?"

She looked at Sam, at Jim, and finally at the bird. "I'm Eulalie Grace LaRue."

"Awwww. Pretty Eulalie Grace LaRue." The bird ducked her head and nuzzled Lollie's jaw.

Surprised, she laughed. "And what's your name?"

"I'm Medusa. I'm a mynah. Sam's an ass."

Lollie giggled and looked up at Sam. He wasn't happy, which made her giggle more because a grown man could look so irritated with a little bird.

He turned to Jim. "Leave that damn bird with her. Neither of them knows when to shut up. Now let's go." He spun around and stalked away.

Jim shrugged and started to follow him. He glanced in Sam's direction, then quickly back at her. "Later," he said in a voice much too loud for secrecy.

"Like hell!" Sam shouted over his shoulder. Jim frowned, hit his ear a couple of times, and followed him, laughing very loud.

Lollie watched them go, then turned to look at the mynah. "Well, now I have some company."

"Company halt!" Medusa shouted in a deep voice.

"I see I'll have to work on your vocabulary." She turned and walked back to the bungalow. "Now, Medusa, say 'Yan-kee. . . .' "

15

The knife blade sliced through the air. Sam jumped back, dodging its sharp edge. He crouched again, his own knife poised, ready. Others fought around him. He could hear the dull thud of men falling to the ground, the victors' shouts, the exhaled breath of the fallen. He ignored the sounds, instead taking in air slowly, with purpose, controlled. He and his adversary moved in a circle, two instruments of war, combatants with instincts sharp, eyes locked in battle, ready to move with deadly accuracy at the mere blink of the other's eye.

Sam saw it coming. It was always in the eyes. The man shot forward, his knife poised like a bayonet in front of his body. Sam grabbed his wrist and rammed the man's arm and knife upward, his own arm slid in a death pin on the man's throat. Sam squeezed.

Barely ten feet away, a blond head—an empty blond head—poked out from the bushes. It plunged back down, leaving the bush rattling loud enough to be heard above the exercise.

Sam released the rebel. "Take a rest. And, Gomez . . ."

The soldier picked up his knife and shoved it back in its sheath.

". . . Next time don't blink."

The rebel nodded and left the small dirt arena they used to train the men in armed combat. Sam turned back toward the bushes and waited. It didn't take long.

The adjacent bushes shook, branches cracked, a gasp cut through the air. Shaking his head, he moved over to the

178

perimeter, leaning in the comfortable shade of a lowland pine. Lollie was behind a wall of giant croton bushes, tiptoeing in those hard militia boots, something he would have bet a month's pay was impossible. Since she was on tiptoe, he assumed that her intention was furtive silence. He exhaled in disgust. She muttered the whole way.

She moved toward him, pausing to poke her head out of the bushes every so often. Less than five feet from him she stopped again, bending around the bush, butt up, so she could look between the branches. Her blond hair was tied back with a piece of jute rope and hung down her back. He could still see the light blond streaks that blended with the color of the rest of her hair, a dark blond that was the color of Old Crow, his favorite drink.

In the dark rebel clothing Jim'd scrounged up for her, she looked different, less lah-dee-dah LaRuish. She shifted her weight, drawing his gaze to her round rump and the tight black pants that covered it and her legs. His mind flashed with the thought that whoever had invented the skirt ought to be shot.

"Where is he?" she murmured, breaking his concentration and calling his attention away from her butt and back to her head, which shifted from one opening to another.

A lazy smile touched Sam's lips, and he pushed away from the tree. "Looking for me?"

She gasped and shot upright.

He watched her turn and gape at him, and her wide eyes darted left, then right, a sign she was looking for something to say. Finally he gave up, deciding he would be a grandfather by the time she spoke up. "What do you want?"

She rammed her shoulders back and stuck up her chin.
Jesus, what now?

"I'd like something to do."

"Look, I told you before. This is a war camp. We're training soldiers to fight for their freedom and their lives. It's not some social club."

"Where's Mr. Bonifacio? He's in charge. I think he'll give me something to do."

"Andrés is in Quezon, meeting with Aguinaldo. He won't be back for a while." He crossed his arms over his chest and added, "So you're stuck with me."

She sighed one of those hurricane winds, then looked around. He could see her trying to think, and the thought crossed his mind that any minute he might smell smoke.

She looked him in the eye. "I'm just asking for something to do. Can't I help with something, anything, please, Sam?"

"Where's the damn bird? I heard she's been keeping you busy."

"Jim took her with him today."

"That must have been interesting. Jim's been complaining that he never sees Medusa anymore. I understand she's taken quite a liking to you." *Birdbrains of a feather.*

"She didn't want to go with him, but I talked her into it."

"I'm sure that did wonders for Jim's ego." The woman had managed to lure Jim's obnoxious bird away, which didn't exactly bother Sam. He could live without that bird chattering constantly. And if it kept this woman busy, then that was fine with him. But now she was bored again. It might be worthwhile to give her something to do just to keep her out of his hair. "What can you do?"

She looked a little lost for an answer, but eager. Then she asked, "What do you need done?"

I need you gone, he thought, distractedly brushing some dust from his pants while he tried to come up with something. He stopped and stared at his dusty pants. Then he smiled, coming up with the perfect solution. "Laundry."

"Laundry?" The eagerness left her face.

"Follow me." He walked right past her, soon hearing the thud of her boots behind him. He crossed the camp to the north side, where ten long wooden bungalows served as the barracks. He rounded a corner, then moved past a stack of barrels and the small pit the men used for recreation. Her boot steps scurried behind him, and suddenly he felt her tug at his arm.

"Sam?"

He stopped. "What?"

"What's that?" She pointed to the dirt pit lined with sandbags.

"The cockpit." He turned to go, but she wrenched back on his arm.

"The what?"

"The men use it in their free hours. For cockfights."

"Cockfights?"

"Yeah, where they put two birds in a pit and let them fight it out while the men bet on which one will win."

"Oh, my Gawd . . ."

"Gambling's big in the islands. It's their way to relax."

Her face looked like she'd just met the devil. "What about the birds?"

"They're treated like prized pets. Bought and sold based on their strength and number of wins. Most of the birds lead better lives than slum children, since the Filipinos take the sport seriously."

"What happens to the birds? Don't they get hurt?"

"The strongest fighters in the sport survive. The others . . ." Sam shrugged.

"Riding is a sport, horse racing is a sport, lawn tennis and crouquet are sports, even that Yankee pastime, baseball, is a sport. Putting two helpless birds in a ring to fight is *not* a sport!"

"Tell that to the men. Now let's go. I've got to get back." He walked away, moving past some supplies crates and around another corner. He heard her gasp and stopped and turned.

She stood staring past the crates. He followed her gaze to the cock pens where eight rough wooden hutches stood in a line, each one containing a fighting cock.

"Oh, you poor birds! I feel so sorry for them." Her voice caught.

He was damned sorry he'd been stupid enough to come this way. He grabbed her arm. "Do you want something to do or not?"

She nodded, but kept looking at the cages as if they were filled with sick babies.

"Come on." He pulled her with him, determined to give her something to keep her busy, and away from him.

Those poor birds. Lollie sighed and stirred the big black pot of boiling clothes. She kept glancing toward the men's barracks, unable to get those cages out of her mind. She'd grown a special fondness for birds in the last few days. Medusa had become almost a constant companion since she'd first lit on Lollie's shoulder. The bird slept on a crude wooden perch Gomez had carved for her, and many times Lollie had crossed to the cook hut with Medusa perched on her head. The men were nice to her, smiling and bringing her little things, peanuts for the bird, pails of fresh water, ripe papayas and mangoes. Everything had been pleasant until she'd seen those birds and realized what the loud distant cheers had been the night before.

She swiped at her sweaty forehead with an arm, an arm sore from stirring, and then she looked at the other five boiling cauldrons. In an attempt to forget the birds, she'd tried to concentrate on what she was doing, stirring cauldrons of brewing clothes like a laundry witch. She'd switched utensils, from the stirring paddle to a long wooden thing Sam called a dolly. It looked like a small stool, but rising out of where the seat would have been if it were a stool—which it wasn't—was a long wooden stick, not unlike the handle of a broom. At the top of the stick were two wooden handles that she was supposed to hold and then twist. The wooden legs that stuck out of the bottom would then mix up the clothes, spinning out the dirt.

She grabbed the dolly. What a silly name. She drew her arm across her forehead, wiping away the sweat and bits of damp hair. A dolly was something you dressed up in pretty clothes and placed on your bed. It was a toy, a plaything. She moved to the next pot and churned the clothes. This was anything but a game. It was hard work. She blew out a tired breath, then glanced toward the men's quarters, picturing for the hundredth time those poor little roosters. They were used for games, too. Cruel games.

It made her angry that they could do something so cruel and call it a sport. She got chills just thinking about it. Of course once again it was a male sport, and men seemed to dictate what was acceptable. But she didn't find cock-fighting acceptable, and she doubted any other woman would, either. The whole thing just didn't seem right, and somone should have done something about it.

She chewed on her lip for an indecisive moment. Dare she? One mental picture of what a cockfight would be like was enough. She dared. The immediate area was deserted, the men occupied elsewhere.

Sam hadn't said anything about how long to cook the clothes. They had been pretty dirty, so the longer they cooked, the cleaner they'd be. It made sense. Yes, perfect sense.

She returned the paddle and dolly to their hooks on the side of the building. Then she checked to see if anyone was around. Still no one. Must be divine intervention, she decided.

With the Lord on her side, she strolled to the corner and peered around, looking over the wide dirt center of the camp. A few soldiers milled about, moving what she assumed were gun crates and supplies. She waited until she was sure their backs were turned, and then she scurried across the compound trying very hard to be quiet. If Sam saw her, he'd know exactly where she was headed. The man had an uncanny knack of showing up when she least expected him.

She made it to the first barracks, leaned her back against the wooden wall so she was well hidden, then peered around the corner. No one walked her way. The men were still busy talking, laughing and working. She gave a silent prayer of thanks.

In a few seconds she stood in front of the cages watching the birds. She moved to the closest cage. A deep brownish red rooster fanned his feathers, gurgling in his long throat and shaking that dangling red thing under his beak. He lifted his feet, shifting his weight just like Medusa. Lolly's mind was made up. She stepped forward and reached for the wooden latch.

"Ouch!" She drew back her hand. The rooster had pecked her. She pressed on the spot of blood and glared. "You ungrateful thing, you."

The bird stared back.

"But then, fighting is all you've ever known, isn't it?"

The rooster cocked its head.

"I understand," she said, looking around for something long enough to spring the latches but still keep her hands from getting pecked bloody.

Spying a stick she retrieved it and went back to the cages. One by one she unlatched the doors.

There was one thing she hadn't considered, and it happened.

They were fighting cocks, and true to their training, they fought, pecking and clucking right out there in the open. Feathers flew and dirt splattered upward, and the most horrendous noise erupted, squawks and clucks and screeches. It was just awful!

They squawked and she panicked. Stick still in hand, she swirled and ran toward the birds.

"Shoo! Shoo, you all!" She jumped up and down, waving the stick, trying to chase the birds into the jungle where they'd be free. Some of them scattered, some flew to the bushes, some disappeared.

It worked!

"Son of a bitch!"

Uh-oh. She froze. It was Sam's voice, she'd have known that swearing anywhere.

16

"Those men'll kill you! And if they don't, goddammit, I just might!" Sam closed the distance between them, intent on hauling Lollie out of there before he had a riot on his hands.

She froze, her face registered surprise, then guilt. Her arms dropped slowly to her sides, the long stick falling to the ground. Feathers and stirring dust were all that was left behind from the renegade cocks, which had scattered like a retreating army into the jungle brush.

His arm shot out with the speed of a striking snake and hooked itself around her waist, lifting her before she could give him any trouble. With her clamped against his hip, he spun around and made for her bungalow.

She made a sound of protest and he squeezed harder. "Shut up!"

He crossed the camp full bore, stormed up the steps, then threw open the door and crossed to the cot, where he dropped her like a sandbag. She screeched, pushed back the long blond hair that had fallen over her face, and looked up at him.

He moved his face closer to hers, and her blue eyes flashed with worry just before she scrambled up the cot until her back hit the wall with a solid thud. Her wary gaze darted left, then right, then left—her direction of flight.

His arm blocked her before she managed to stand. He threw her back down and planted a hand on either side of her, his upper body hovering over her and blocking her from rising more than a foot from the cot. "You stupid, damn little fool. Do you have any idea what you've done?"

She swallowed hard, shook her head. He moved his face even closer. She stared at his face and slowly nodded. "I saved those birds," she whispered, adding with a note of ignorant pride, "Now they're free."

"Great . . . The damn birds are free. Are you proud of yourself?"

Her look was unsure, but after a second she gave a slight nod.

"Feel like you've done something noble, don't you? The birds are free, but these people aren't free. Do you know why those men are here?"

"To fight," she said with all the surety of someone who thought she knew what she was talking about, but didn't.

"Yes, they fight, but not for fun, not because they want to kill, which is what you thought. This isn't a game. They fight for freedom, lay their lives on the line to get what we Americans take for granted. This isn't Belvedere, South Carolina. It's the Philippines, a Spanish colony. The native people have no freedom, no say in the government, nothing. Their native priests are hung and left to rot in the town square. The Spanish Dominican priests steal everything of value from these people in the name of the church. Women and children are made slaves on the tobacco and cocoa plantations."

Her lip began to quiver, but it didn't stop him. He was too damn mad.

"Those men are here learning to fight to save their country. Many of them will never see their families again. They'll die for a chance at that freedom you take for granted, the freedom that allows you to hide so luxuriously from the cruelties in this world.

"The only, and I mean *only*, recreation they had was cockfighting. The sport might not be your idea of recreation, it might be ugly to the eyes of fine, upstanding pedigreed Americans, but this is not, I repeat, *not* the United States. You can't waltz in here and make everyone think like you do, especially when you know nothing about these people.

"Some of those birds were worth over three months' pay to those men. If they win money, they try to smuggle it home to the families they haven't seen in over a year. You've let loose their only relaxation, the only way they had to forget that they might die tomorrow, that they might never see their wives, their mothers, their children.

"They have nothing here. No family. No *daddy*. They live hidden away and threatened daily with discovery by the Spanish or trouble from another rebel army. You know what the Spanish do to rebels?"

She shook her head.

"Sometimes they roast them on a fire. You can hear the men scream, smell their flesh burn. You know what burning human flesh smells like?" He grabbed her shoulders and shook her. "Do you!"

"No," she whispered, tears running down her face.

He didn't care if she cried a bloody river. He wanted to drive home the stupidity of what she'd done.

"If you'd have ever smelled it, you'd never forget it. Sometimes they use other methods of torture, metal needles as long as my arm, jabbed one by one into the victim's feet, and pulled slowly through the other side. Sometimes they only cut off an arm, a leg, a nose, an ear, sometimes all four. Sometimes they cut off other parts. Sometimes they take out an eye."

He let go of her. She fell back on the cot, sobbing out loud now. He didn't care. He just pinned her with a look that masked none of the scorn he felt, because he was tired, damn sick and tired of her stupid mistakes. "So just lie there, Miss Lah-Roo. Lie there and think about those poor birds. I'm thinking about those men and how I'm going to go back out there and try to teach them to fight, so that they can live free. And at night, when they're tired and lonely and wound up tighter than a trigger spring, I'll try to find something to ease that strain. You see, I care more about the people on this hellhole of an island than I do about myself or about some goddamn chickens."

He crossed to the door, opened it and stopped to look back at her. "I don't know where the hell your father is, and now I don't even care who he is. All I care about is that you are gone." He left, slamming the door so hard the walls shook.

It had been a full day since Sam had stormed from the room. Other than two meals and fresh water—which Gomez had brought to her door, knocked, and handed to her without a word, a smile, or even a look at her face— she had seen or heard from no one.

Lollie peered out the narrow window in her bungalow, afraid to go outside, and if fear wasn't enough to keep her put, the shame and hurt she felt from Sam's words were. The sound of boots outside the front door sent her back to the cot.

The door opened and Sam stepped inside, carrying a small box. He was not a happy man. Three soldiers followed him in, their arms loaded with clothing.

"Put them there," he said, indicating the area on the floor in front of him. The men dropped what soon became a mountain of clothing between them.

She'd forgotten about the laundry. With dread, she watched men deposit the clothes, wondering how they felt about her since she'd let their birds go. Not one of them looked at her. They just did as ordered and left.

The door closed behind the last man, and Sam walked toward her. He bent and picked up a shirt from the top of the pile. Without saying one word he held up the shirt by the shoulders and snapped it once in the air. Buttons flew through the air, bouncing like marbles onto the floor.

She grimaced. He picked up a pair of pants, shook them and the buttons fell off too.

"Every shirt, every pair of pants, at least the ones that weren't stuck to the pots, has the same problem." He dropped the clothes. "Forgot about them, did you?"

As he spoke his speech was less controlled, something that worried her. She nodded. "But you dragged me in here and I—"

"I'm surprised you didn't smell them burning," he interrupted. "The rest of the camp did. Hell, the Spanish probably did!" he shouted as he walked toward her, stopping only when he loomed over her.

She tried to keep from flinching. His neck was purple again, a sure sign that something she'd touched had once again turned to mud.

"You will sew every button back onto every piece of clothing in that pile." He dropped the box on the cot. "You wanted something to do. Now you have something to do." He turned, made it to the door in a few long strides, and left the bungalow.

She stared at the closed door for a moment, gave the pile of clothes a quick glance, then opened the box. It contained row after row of black thread and a big tin of pins and needles. She grabbed a basket and bent down to pick up the scattered buttons.

An hour later, the basket was filled with buttons of various sizes and the clothes sat there waiting. She looked at them and frowned, then gave a deep cleansing sigh of resignation. Sam was right about one thing: now she had something to do.

Five hours later she bit off the thread, held up the twenty-seventh shirt, and eyed the buttons. Only three of the eight were the correct size. She frowned. She'd gone through the whole basket but instead of the pants having one set of a certain size, and the shirts another, they must have all been different. She tried to ram an oversized button through the hole. It wouldn't fit, so she did what she had done to the others: she snipped the end of the buttonhole. That solved the problem, at least for the oversize buttons. The ones that were too small were just gonna have to stay that way.

Someone knocked, but before she could rise the door

opened and Jim Cassidy stepped inside, her meal in his hands and Medusa on his shoulder.

"Awwk!" The bird flapped twice and flew from Jim's shoulder to Lollie's head, her favorite place to perch. Medusa bent over and tried to look at her upside down, which made her laugh for the first time in a while. Then the bird began to sing, "Ohhhhh-ohhhhh, way down south in the land of cotton . . ."

"Oh, Medusa, I've missed you," she whispered, holding out her hand while the bird sang to its heart's content. Still singing, and with a clear Southern accent, Medusa stepped onto Lollie's hand. She brought the bird down to eye level.

"I wish you'd teach her something else. I've been listening to that song for two days. That and Madame Devereaux's Rules of Feminine Deportment." Jim crossed the room, the tray still in his hands. "You women don't really believe that stuff, do you? Like don't discuss music when the temperature is over eighty?"

"You have a big mouth, Medusa," she mumbled, stroking the bird a few times. Then she looked at the tray, let the bird hop onto her table perch, and turned so she could take the meal.

"I especially liked 'Don't make acquaintances you will be ashamed of in town.' Sam said you were a snob—a looker, but a snob nonetheless."

She took the tray from him, ignoring the way his eyes roved over her like hands.

He looked at the clothes, then at her. "Got into a little hot water?"

She slammed the tray down and glared at him. "That comment was in poor taste."

"I have no taste, although"—he moved toward her—"I wouldn't mind tasting you." He closed in, backing her up until the backs of her knees hit the side of the cot. "I like snobs."

"Saaaaam!" she screamed as loud as she could.

Jim grunted, shook his head, then said, "He's not here."

"Where is he?" She didn't like the look in Jim's eyes.

"He's in San Fernando, but I'm sure he heard you." He stroked her cheek.

"Stop it!"

"I can't stop, and I don't think you want me to."

She batted his hand away. "Leave me alone!"

Out of the corner of her eye she caught a flash of raven black, swooping out the open window. They'd scared Medusa away, which made her even angrier at Jim. She reached up to shove him away, but he grabbed her hands and began to kiss them while he pulled her forward. She kicked him.

"Damn!" He flinched, and suddenly his seduction wasn't so slow. He pinned her hands against his chest and clamped his arms around her, tight. She wiggled and tried to kick, but he pressed his legs against her until the edge of the cot cut into them.

She opened her mouth to scream. His mouth slammed over hers. She tried to pull away, but he held her head in a one-handed vise grip that wouldn't allow her to move. His tongue tried to force its way past her lips.

An instant later she was free. It happened so fast, she fell back on the cot, her vision catching only the flash of Sam's long black hair whipping by. She scrambled up to the sound of fists hitting flesh and grunts of pain. Sam and Jim rolled around across the floor, fighting—or at least Sam was fighting. He was the only one throwing punches.

"I told you to leave her alone!" Sam grabbed Jim by the collar and hit him so hard he flew out the open door. Sam bolted out after him. Lollie ran to the doorway.

They rolled in the dirt, shouting. A crowd gathered, forming a circle around the two men. Sam arched back to throw a punch and Jim threw an arm up and blocked Sam's flying fist, planted his boot on Sam's chest and shoved him over. "You're crazy! We've never fought over a woman. And what the hell are you doing back?"

"I'm damn glad I came back," Sam growled, shot up in a cloud of dirt, and lunged at him.

191

Jim rolled, then struggled to his feet. "Stop it, buddy. I don't want to have to hit you."

Sam was on his feet, facing his friend. "Hit me! Go ahead and try. Come on, Cassidy, hit me!" His chin shot up and he pointed to it, daring Cassidy to throw the punch. "Come on, come on." He panted, his look lethal while he circled his friend. "Hit me, so I can goddamn kill you!"

"You keep saying you don't want her, you pigheaded bastard!" Cassidy ducked Sam's left fist, but the right connected, knocking him to the ground. He scrambled up and blocked Sam's next punch, then landed one of his own, but it didn't stop Sam, who was on him, hitting him again and again, like a man crazed with the need to smash another human. It was awful.

Lollie ran down the steps. "Stop it! Stop!"

Neither one paid attention, but now Jim was hitting Sam so hard Lollie could hear the crunch of knuckles hitting jaw full force.

She looked out at the soldiers. "Do something! Please! Stop them!" The men just stared at her, didn't blink, didn't move. They turned away and watched their American commanders beat the devil out of each other.

She turned, ran inside, and grabbed the water bucket she used to wash in. With both hands she lugged it out the door, down the steps, moving toward the tumbling, bloody men. Sam must have seen her, because he paused, fists up, and whipped his head around.

She swung the pail back. Jim threw a knockout right into Sam's jaw. She heard Jim's fist connect. Sam sank to the ground, unconscious. She squeezed her eyes shut and threw the water. The bucket went with it, hitting Jim in the head with a loud clunk. A second later he, too, was out cold.

"Oh, dear." She pulled her hands away from her horrified face. The rebel soldiers watched her, their looks as hostile as if she were Judas with her hands full of silver. Some of them mumbled things, and she was glad she didn't understand their language. But she didn't need to. It was clear that they blamed her for the fight between Sam and Jim. The heat of those looks told her as much.

Taking a deep breath, she took a step toward Sam. The soldiers cut her off, moving in a crowd to where the two men lay and forming a wall that left her outside, an outcast. It was the most helpless, feeble feeling she'd ever had, and as she watched them carry their commanders away, that aching feeling just intensified until once again she could see nothing but blurred images of the soldiers' backs.

An empty wooden thread spool rolled across the plank floor. Lollie followed it with her eyes. Medusa was playing with it. Head down and black wings up, she'd butt the spool across the floor singing her newest song, "Amazing Grace." Whenever she hit the "me" in the chorus, she'd turn and roll sideways with the spool.

Lollie crossed to the door, dodging the other spools on the floor.

"Awk! To save a wretch like meeeeeee!" Medusa sent the spool caroming off the table leg.

Slowly Lollie opened the door and peered outside. No one was near, but a small group of rebels stood in the middle of the compound between the cook hut and her bungalow, and another bunch had lined up nearby. Her heart sped up a little.

She'd thought about this, planned it the whole time she'd been sewing those clothes. She knew of no other way to make up for her mistake. She felt around in the pocket of her pants. She had only a few nuts for Medusa, and she needed more. With one deep fortifying breath, she left the refuge of her bungalow and walked toward the cook hut. Each thud of her boots in the dirt matched the heavy thud of her heart.

Conversation tinged with laughter came from the line of soldiers standing about ten feet from her. A couple of men turned toward her and stared. The others still talked and laughed. But that didn't matter because she'd noticed their clothes. The shirts were buttoned, but there were large gaps every so often. One man's collar was a good two inches higher on one side than on the other. She winced and then saw the worst thing.

The sleeves were too short and some of the men's shirttails had pulled out of their waistbands. And the pants were even worse. On some of them, one pant leg was particularly shorter than the other, and every man had a good three inches of leg showing between the hem of his pants and his boot tops.

She'd cooked their clothes so long they must have shrunk. She stopped, talked to herself for a full minute to get her courage up, and started to walk past them. As she did, she tried desperately not to let them see how nervous she was. She neared, and their laughter died. She didn't look at them. The conversation tapered off until there was nothing but the sound of her boots on the ground and her heart pounding in her ears.

She could feel the contempt in their stares. She swallowed, a reaction to the tension of the moment, but she kept walking, her eyes ahead. She refused to look at them, choosing instead to tilt her chin up a bit more than normal and bluff her way past them, an internal litany of "Gawd give me strength" going through her mind.

Southern pride and pure determination were all that kept her from collapsing in a heap right there on the ground. The closer she got to the hut, the more soldiers appeared, all of them looking like an army of misfits in their mangled clothing. Gomez stood on the steps to the hut, and she walked past him. He didn't smile, didn't say anything, just moved aside, but she could feel his eyes on her just before she closed the wooden door of the hut.

Leaning against the closed door, she exhaled the breath she'd held for an eternity and looked around. A couple of men worked in the kitchen. One stood at one of the four ranges, stirring something, and another scooped flour out of one of the barrels that lined one wall of the rectangular room. Both men looked up at her.

"I need some nuts. For Medusa," she said, watching as

one man gave a quick nod toward a back room, then returned to baking his bread. She hurried into the supply room and searched until she found a burlap bag of peanuts in a corner. Scooping out handfuls, she filled her pants pockets, her shirt pockets, and her shirt front with the nuts and then went to the small doorway, peeking at the men to make sure they were busy enough not to see how many she was taking. Not that it really mattered. She hadn't been denied any food since she'd been here, but she didn't want to explain why she was taking so many nuts.

With her arms crossed over her shirtfront, she left, walking briskly past the men outside and heading for her bungalow. The minute she rounded the corner she made a sharp turn and took off toward the men's barracks. She passed the first three and had only one more bungalow to pass before she reached the camp's jungle edge. The last bungalow belonged to Sam and Jim. She paused.

She'd tried to get someone to take her to see Sam, but the men just looked at her as if she intended to hurt him. Their looks were so accusing that she felt guilty, even though she tried to persuade herself that it wasn't really her fault. Although part of her knew that if she hadn't come here, this wouldn't have happened, which was why the men blamed her.

Her mind flashed with the image of Sam standing in the hut, after Colonel Luna'd had him beaten. This time Sam had instigated the brawl, with his friend, lecher though he was, and Sam had done it because he was trying to protect her. For that reason alone she needed to see if he was okay.

Tiptoeing along, with her body brushing the bungalow's wood plank wall, she moved until she was under the first narrow window. It was too high for her to see in so she grabbed the ledge and tried to pull herself up. She didn't have much arm strength and slid back to the ground.

Taking a deep breath, she knotted her fists, bent her knees, and leapt up with all the momentum she could put into her small body. She caught a brief glimpse of a male form on a cot. Then her feet slammed onto the ground with a jarring thud, and a whole slew of peanuts flew out of her shirtfront and scattered on the ground like hail.

She stared at the peanuts in disgust. She'd forgotten about them. She looked up at the window. She couldn't tell who was in the cot. It could have been Sam or Jim. She leapt again, this time holding her shirt closed. She jumped up repeatedly, her boots crunching on the spilled peanuts, but she still couldn't recognize him.

She looked at her bulging shirtfront and pockets, at the nuts all over the ground. Maybe she should go on with her plan first; then she could check on Sam. Then, too, she'd have less of a load. That was what she'd do. She'd come back later. Then maybe he'd be awake and she could hear if he was all right.

She turned and walked, determination in each step, past the sandbag wall, through the gate in the barbed wire— she'd learned her lesson—and into the jungle perimeter. The growth made the area darker, even though in the cleared camp there was plenty of sunlight. She moved into the bushes, rattling them and looking all around for the cocks. She scoured the oleanders, the palm clumps, the fire bushes, moving deeper and deeper into the jungle. She entered a small clearing and looked up at a huge tree, wondering if a bird might be perched on one of the lower branches, even though she knew chickens never flew higher than a rooftop.

Something rustled in the bushes behind her. She turned, ever so slowly. Two tiny yellow beady eyes stared at her from beneath a thick hibiscus bush. She watched the rooster. It twitched its red-wattled head. She tossed a peanut nearby. It had been over a day since she'd turned the birds loose. They had to be hungry. They had to be. The cock stared at the nut. She tossed another, then another. Still nothing. The bird just looked from her to the peanut, over and over.

"I heard chickens weren't very smart," she mumbled, backing up until she was near the tree. She grabbed a handful of nuts and tossed them onto the ground. Then she slid down the tree to sit on the ground. All she needed was one bird, just one, and then she figured she could use it to locate the others. After all, the birds were trained to fight, and she'd use that training to capture them. She had a plan, a good one, that would right the wrong she'd done. She watched the bird. It watched her.

She looked up at the bright afternoon sky. She had hours before it got dark. She smiled, knowing she had something in her favor that the chicken didn't. With pigheaded determination she sat there, doing one thing she'd done all her life, the one thing she was really good at. She waited.

17

It was almost dark outside when Sam looked across the table at Jim. His face was swollen, his lips were cut, and his left eye was black-and-blue. "Does your jaw hurt as much as mine?"

"No, but I don't dare touch this eye. Must be as black as your patch."

Sam looked at his friend. "It is."

Jim grunted, then grabbed a tooth and wiggled it. "This tooth is loose. God, you can throw a punch."

Sam didn't say anything, just stared at the dark bottle of whiskey between them.

After a long silence, Jim poured them another drink and set the bottle down on the table with a hard clunk. Sam looked up.

"Hands off." Jim said. "From now on, I swear, I'll keep my hands off of her."

Sam acknowledged him with a nod, then lifted his glass and swilled down the whiskey. It hit his stomach with the heat of a fireball.

He'd lost control. Sam Forester, a man who prided himself on his wits, hadn't used one bit of thought earlier. He'd just come back from San Fernando, a town where he'd gone to get supplies. He'd done the job himself because he wanted to get away from Lollie, but once on the road he'd made the trip much faster than normal, choosing not to stay in the town but to turn right around and come back.

He'd no sooner fallen down on his cot than that damn bird had flown over to him, squawking its usual nonsense. Damn thing nearly pecked all his hair out before it said something about saving Eulalie. He'd made it as far as her doorway, and then he'd seen red. After that, he didn't remember much until he'd come to. Now what he did remember he didn't like.

He and Jim had been together for years, saved each other's butts time and again. Yet during all those years, fighting whatever war needed them, they'd never fought each other. And now, when it happened, it happened over a woman and, even worse, that woman.

A crunch sounded from outside. Sam glanced at the open window. A blond head flashed into view, then disappeared. He hoped he'd imagined it, that maybe his head was still woozy from the brawl.

The blond head had popped into view for only the length of time it took to blink, but it was enough for him to know she was there. The thud-crunch sounded again. What the hell was she doing now?

He kicked Jim under the table and gave a quick nod toward the window. Jim turned just as the head popped up and down again. *Thud-crunch!* Her muttering whispered through the window. Jim groaned under his breath. Sam rubbed his suddenly throbbing forehead. His life hadn't been normal since that day in Tondo.

Her fingers crawled over the window ledge and he could hear her body bang against the wall. If his life ever depended on her silence, he'd better have his headstone ready.

She must be trying to see in. He thought about it for a moment, listening to her boots scraping for a foothold on the outside wall. He figured that he had two choices: he could go outside, scare the hell out of her, and drag her back to her room, or . . . he could have some fun. He rubbed his sore jaw thoughtfully, then smiled slowly.

Jim looked up. Sam cupped his ear and pointed at the window, indicating she was listening. Jim nodded, a small grin of anticipation hovering on his swollen, split lips.

That crunch sounded again, only now she was walking. *Crunch, crunch, crunch, crunch.*

Sam picked up a deck of cards that sat forgotten on the table. He shuffled. "Well, Cassidy," he said in a voice he knew would carry. "We have to settle who's going to get the woman. No more fighting."

A slow tentative crunch came through the window, then absolute silence.

Jim grinned, suppressed it, and cleared his throat. "You said you didn't want her. I still think I should take her."

"I don't want her." Sam tried to add as much scorn as possible to his voice. "She's trouble. Remember the laundry? We both know she's not exactly the most accurate gun on the target range."

"Ah, that's truth." Jim nodded, picking up where he'd left off. "But then, I've never known brains and beauty to come in one package."

"You think Lollie LaRue is beautiful?" Sam made sure his tone expressed surprise.

"She's got great legs."

"Really? Hmm, I thought her feet were a little too big. She kept tripping over them all the way here."

"You know, now that you mention it, she's knocked-kneed, isn't she?"

"Yeah." Sam watched the window. "She's flat-chested, too. I like a little more . . . substance in my women."

"I'm a firm believer that more than a mouthful is wasted."

"I suppose . . ." Sam counted to a long five, then asked, "What about her nose?"

"It's okay, if you like bulldogs."

A sound like a stifled gasp came from outside. Sam barked with laughter. He couldn't help it. It took him a minute to control his voice. "My taste has always gone toward dark-haired women."

"That's true. I've never known you to go for a blonde. Why's that?"

"I think blondes are . . . dull."

"I like blondes," Jim said.

"You like everything."

"That's not true. Light blue eyes don't do anything for me. Too cold, vacant."

"Yeah, real vacant, sort of like there's no one home." Sam laughed. "And in her case there isn't."

"You know, now that we've talked about it, I don't think I want her after all. You can have her," Jim conceded.

"I don't want her, either. I guess we'll have to draw cards to see who gets stuck with her." Sam shuffled the cards and slapped them on the table. "You go first."

Jim picked a card and held it up to Sam. It was a king. "Oh, no. It's only a three. I guess I'm stuck with her."

"I'll draw, but anyone can beat that. A three. Bad cards, Cassidy." Sam picked up the ace of spades and showed it to Jim, who saluted him. He wished he could draw like this when the game was real. "My unlucky day. Two of hearts. You win and I'm stuck with her. Pour me another drink, will you. A stiff one." Sam picked up the glass and then slammed it on the table, making a big to-do about pushing his chair out. "Well, I guess I'll have to go check on her."

A sudden scurrying echoed from the window—*crunch, crunch, crunch, thud, thud, thud*—as she ran around the building.

Sam hadn't had this much fun in a long time.

Jim shook his head, laughing. "You're right. She is louder than an advancing platoon."

Sam opened the door and stepped outside, still chuckling. "Yeah, it must be those big feet." And he closed the door.

Her door was locked. "Lollie! Let me in!"

"Go away!"

Sam grabbed the knob and rattled the door. "Unlock the damn door."

"I can't. My feet are too big. I'll probably trip on them and break my vacant head!"

He swore, stepped back, and kicked the door above the knob. It crashed opened, banging with enough force to rattle the walls. Her shoulders flinched, but she didn't look up from the cot, where she lay with her head buried on her arms.

He crossed the room, the tap of his boots on the wooden floor being the only sound. He stood over her.

"Lollie, look at me."

"No."

"I said look at me." He stared at the back of her blond head.

"I can't, there's no one home."

"Aw, crap," he mumbled, and looked at her for a long time before he finally sat down on the edge of the cot.

"Watch out for my knock-knees," she said, her voice muffled into the pillow.

"Lollie, Lollie, Lollie," he said, shaking his head. She didn't budge, so he finally grabbed her shoulders and pulled her up. She stared at his chin instead of his eye.

"You're crying." He couldn't believe the tears.

She wiped the back of a hand across her eyes and sniffed.

"Why the hell are you crying?" he barked, letting go of her as if she would explode any second.

"Men hate meeeeee!" She burst into sobs, fell back on the cot, and cried and cried. "The men in the camp hate me because of the cocks and because of that fight you had with Jim. None of you want me around. Men never do.

What's wrong with me? I don't understand," she wailed, talking into the pillow. "I'm not a bad person. I try, I really do, but no one wants me around. No one needs me."

He watched her sob and felt rotten inside. He could be an ass sometimes. Finally he reached out and touched her shoulder. "Stop crying."

She didn't.

"Hey, Lollipop." He poked her in the shoulder. "Stop, please."

She sobbed as if she didn't have a friend in the world.

He poked her again. "You're not so bad."

She sniffed and looked up at him with watery hopeful eyes. "Really?"

"Yeah." He watched her bite her lip thoughtfully. She didn't look so great right now. Her hair was slicked back and tied at the back of her neck, which made her red-rimmed eyes look even bigger. They almost swallowed her small face, which was all blotchy from crying. It was red enough that she looked as if she'd been eating those berries again. Common sense and past experience stopped him from telling her so. He looked around the room instead.

"What do you mean 'not so bad'?" she whispered.

"You're just different, not what we're used to around here. This is a war camp, not some girls' school." He turned back to her.

"I don't try to make people mad," she said, looking at him with the saddest and most sincere little face he'd ever seen. Something in his chest tightened, a feeling he hadn't had in years.

"I never knew I was so ugly. No one ever told me." Her voice cracked, and suddenly she was bawling all over again, each sob filled with hurt and loneliness and something that really got to him—shame. He'd never have thought it possible. Lollie LaRue, whom he'd pegged as a brainless snob, was ashamed because she wasn't good enough.

He was an ass, a real ass.

"Damn," he muttered and without thought pulled her against his chest and held her, letting her cry on his shoulder. "You're not ugly," he said, disgusted with himself for picking on her. He felt like hell.

"I heard you all talking about me," she told his shoulder, her arms slipping around him and holding on as if she needed to be held more than anything.

He looked down at her head wedged against his shoulder and moved his hand from her back, tilting her face up so he could look at her. "We knew you were out there. We said all those things on purpose."

She stared at him for a moment, her eyes searching for the truth in his words. "Why? Did you do it to hurt me on purpose?" Her face said she expected him to say yes.

"Hell no." He felt as if he'd just kicked a puppy. "We were just teasing you. You shouldn't have been out there listening, so we thought it would be funny."

"I was out there because I wanted to see if you were all right . . . after the fight and all. I didn't think anyone would let me see you. The men blame me for the fight."

That got him. She was concerned for him. Hell, nobody except Cassidy had ever given a rat's ass what happened to him. As sure as if she'd rammed her small fist into his gut, guilt got him. It wasn't a good feeling.

She reached up and touched the sore spot on his jaw. "You're bruised."

He watched her eyes, those innocent ice blue eyes, that a few minutes ago had held such hurt. They never left his. Warning bells went off in his head. He didn't care.

In a quick heated instant, he became aware of the soft pressure of her breasts against his chest, her hand against his back. Each breath she took was like a ticking bomb, counting away the seconds until he'd give in to the urge he felt, an urge he knew would mean trouble.

He grabbed her wrist and pulled her hand away from his mouth. The only sound in the room was the slow, apprehensive sound of their breathing. Her eyes didn't leave his until suddenly she flinched and looked at their hands. He followed her gaze to where his hand gripped hers. Her palm was bright red, the skin of her wrist white because he held her wrist so tight. He hadn't even realized he was doing it. He let go fast, then stood, wanting to put distance between them just as fast. He turned to get the hell out of there.

"Sam." She stood and placed a hand on his forearm, which tightened.

"What?"

"Were you gonna kiss me a minute ago?" Her hand was like a brand on his arm.

Get out of here, Sammy old boy. Get out fast.

"Were you?"

He stiffened. "No."

"I just wondered."

His mind flashed with the image of her words—his mouth on hers, his chest on hers, his hips on hers. Thought left him, sense left him, and he grabbed her shoulders and pulled her hard against his chest. At the same instant his mouth closed over hers, his arms slid around her, and one hand spanned the back of her head, holding her mouth where he wanted it. He tongued her mouth deep and hard, over and over, needing to absorb the taste of her.

A small moan of pleasure caught in her throat, and the sound of it burned a path of fire to his groin. He pulled her tighter against him, suddenly driven by the carnal need to press against her, low and hard.

His hand clasped her buttocks, lifting her up with him. He walked her back against the wall, gently pinning her against it with the pressure of his hips. He rubbed against her and almost groaned aloud from the feel of soft against hard. His hands now free, he raked his fingers from her temples to the back of her head, working her long hair from its tie, running his hands through it, holding her small head in his large hands while he took her mouth the way he wanted to take her body.

Then his thumbs grazed her skin. It was so soft, the softest thing he'd ever touched in his hard life. He pulled back and looked down at her dazed blue eyes, flushed skin, and wet mouth.

God, that mouth . . .

She opened it, and he was lost, tasting it again without gentleness, with intense need. She tasted like whiskey. Fine aged whiskey—sweet, biting, addictive.

His hips moved against hers, rotating slowly, pressing deeper when his body demanded it. Her hands moved over his chest in slow circles as if she were absorbing the feel of him. Her small palm paused, then moved to the neck of his shirt. She touched the bare skin there, toyed with the hair.

His hands left her head, grabbed her shirt, and tore it off her shoulders. He pulled back from her wet mouth, bent and licked a path down her neck. She moaned his name. At the sound of it he gently ran his teeth across her collarbone and felt her shiver. A stream of male power rushed through him. This was instinct, wild and untamed, male versus female. It was primitive power, an instinctive need to make a mate react.

Shoving her shirt down farther, almost to her waist, he used it to pin her arms. He slid the loose undershirt down and lifted her up the wall until her breast was on the same level as his mouth. He licked her nipple.

She gasped, clutching his head to pull him away moaning. "No . . ."

So he watched the pink tip of her breast, didn't touch her with his mouth, just watched.

Her breath increased, and her fingers gripped his scalp. He waited.

She pulled his head back to her breast and groaned in surrender. He smiled just before his mouth closed over it, drawing on it, flicking it with his tongue, while his hand closed over her other soft breast. Then he pulled his mouth away. She cried out and gripped his head. He pushed his hips forward, pinning her completely, and he pulled her legs around his waist so he could press the hard heat of him against her. He rubbed upward. Her hands went from his head to his shoulders, gripping.

"Oh, my Gawd," she whispered on a breath.

He smiled, rubbing his mouth, lips, then beard-roughened cheeks across the tender-soft tips of her breasts, all the while moving his hips in the same slow circle of sex, slow, hot long sex. Sex that took eternal hours. Sex where a man could lose himself in a woman so deeply that nothing else would exist.

He wanted to lose himself in her.

That realization stopped him faster than a spray of ice water. He stilled. His heart beat in his chest as if he'd been running. His mouth dried. Keeping his head bent, he placed a hand on either side of her, pressing his damp palms hard against the wall. He counted. *One . . . two . . .*

"Sam?" she whispered.

Four . . . five . . .

"Sam?"

He took a deep breath and pulled back, letting her slide back down the wall. With his hands still pressed to the wall he looked down at her. Her look was puzzled; then she followed his gaze to her naked chest and quickly pulled up her shirt. Embarrassment flooded her face, and he pushed away from the wall before he did something stupid like ramming his fist through it.

Turning away, he raked the fingers of one hand through his hair and tried to think of something to say. When nothing came to mind he said, "I'd better go."

He crossed to the door as fast as he could. The broken lock stopped him. He turned, forced to look at her again. She stood stock still, her white-knuckled hands clutching her shirt closed. All the color was drained from her face, and her eyes were wide and stunned and hurt.

"Put that chair under the doorknob after I leave."

"But—"

"For your own damn good. Shut up and do it!" He closed the door behind him, hard enough to rattle the jamb, but not hard enough to wipe out the horror of what had almost happened.

The real horror was that he wanted it to happen. He, Sam Forester—the bastard kid who had beaten the odds and escaped the slums of Chicago, lived through blazing war on four continents, survived enough barrages of gunfire to make Swiss cheese of most men, even made it through the loss of an eye—had just been brought to his knees by a little blond from South Carolina who was longer on drawl than brains.

He needed a drink, a good strong drink.

After taking his bungalow steps two at a time, he blasted through the door, kicked it closed, and headed for the bottle on the table. He wrenched out the cork, tossed it over his shoulder, and swilled down a few burning gulps. Wiping his mouth with the back of his shaking hand, he walked over to his cot, then reached over and turned down the wick on the kerosene lamp and sat, staring at nothing in the darkness of the room.

He took another drink, wondering if such a hard life could make a man weak-minded enough to fall for a blond twit with the name of a hootchy-kootchy dancer from the Club Paris.

He wondered what the hell was wrong with him. There'd been women in his life. A man couldn't reach thirty-three, having lived as he had, without there having been plenty of women. Not as many as Cassidy, but Sam doubted many men could have had that many women and lived. He'd had his share of experienced women who never asked for more than what he was willing to give—sex, good, hard, long sex.

Jesus Christ. He stared open-mouthed at the opposite wall, having just had an awful thought. She was probably a virgin. A goddamn virgin. He took another drink, coughed, and lay back on the cot with a groan. He was in deep shit. That stupid bird was right. He needed a shovel to dig himself out of this one. But for tonight, he'd use the bottle instead, drowning himself in whiskey until he didn't see those innocent ice blue eyes staring back at him in the dark.

Lollie lay on her cot staring at the dark room. Every so often her pensive gaze would return to the door where that green chair was wedged under the knob. Part of her wished she'd see the doorknob turn, wished Sam would come back, and part of her wished she were home in her room at Hickory House with everything she knew.

What had happened tonight was nothing she'd known before, never. She lay there, alone on her cot, staring at the dark ceiling and remembering Sam's mouth on hers, the way he tasted. To remind herself it had been real, she ran her fingers lightly over her lips. They felt swollen. She licked them, and they stung a little. Like her pride. It, too, was stinging from the way he'd left her, the way he'd looked at her before he ordered her to keep the chair there, as if he were angry with her.

She sighed, remembering how she'd all but asked him to kiss her. She groaned and flung an arm over her eyes. She'd gone and done it again, done something that angered him.

Admittedly she had said something in the hope that he would kiss her. Some evil little devil within her had wanted him to, wanted to test the difference between the one chaste smooch she'd had at fourteen, Jim Cassidy's advance, and Sam.

Sam won.

Never in all her born days had she felt what Sam made her feel. There was that old phrase she'd always heard about a woman who was in love. It was said she acted as if he had hung the moon and the stars. Now she understood.

Her eyes drifted closed at the memory of him touching her, holding her, kissing her, of the hard weight of his chest against hers, his hands spanning her waist, his fingers tunneling through her hair to pull it free and hold her mouth against his. She could still taste him, and if she breathed very deeply, she could still smell the scent of him on her clothes and her skin.

She didn't know that such things could be between men and women. At school she'd heard some talk, and she knew there was something men and women did after marriage. But it had sounded strange, and it was a sin to do that before marriage.

She pulled a blanket up around her, hugging it because she needed to hold something. The thought crossed her mind that maybe what she'd done with Sam was that sin, the privileges that a woman didn't give a man until they were married. She pondered that thought long and hard. Finally she turned onto her side, having come to a sure conclusion. Anything that felt that good couldn't possibly be sinful.

18

Lollie closed the perimeter gate and walked toward the empty hutches. She counted them. Eight. That was what she'd thought. There had been eight birds, and she'd found only five. Also, she needed a way to capture them since all but two were still apprehensive and skittish whenever she fed them. Somehow she'd have to search out those other birds.

She bit back a yawn, then stared at the cages. But not today, she thought. She'd already spent hours out there in the thick jungle, fending off a cloud of mosquitoes while trying to corral those birds. The bugs had swarmed around her like sugar ants to honey, probably because the humidity had increased so. It was hot, wet, and sticky, and so was she, not to mention itchy, dirty, and plumb tired.

Last night had been another night of tossing and turning,

and the sleeplessness was taking its toll. She rolled her shoulders to work out the kinks, the result of sleeping on that cot and staying hunched over to try to coax those wild cocks out from under the bushes. She rammed her rolled shirtsleeves up past her elbows and scratched the bites on her forearms while she headed back toward her bungalow.

By the time she reached the steps her arms and neck were a mass of itchy red bumps that she hoped a wet cloth would soothe. Shoving open the door, she hurried inside and twisted the lock, which Gomez had repaired the day before. It kept sticking, but he hadn't bothered to speak to her, let alone ask her if the lock was okay. She didn't feel up to suffering that glaring silence again. When she had fixed everything and made up to the men for her mistake, then maybe she'd tell them about the lock. Until then she'd keep to herself.

She used both hands to ram the bolt into place, then rubbed her bloodless fingers as she crossed to the water bucket she used for washing. A small oval mirror speckled with age and without a frame hung from the wall on a piece of bent wire. Directly below was a spindly and splintered wooden chest with three broken drawers and a varnish finish that had cracked orange with age. The legs of the chest were mismatched, and the whole thing rocked whenever she placed anything on it.

She lugged the bucket over and set it on top of the chest, which, true to form, wobbled like a drunken duck for a few water-sloshing seconds. She plunged a rag into the water, wrung it out with a few jerky twists, and plastered the damp cloth onto the throbbing welts on her itchy neck.

Ooooh. It was pure heaven. She closed her eyes and stuck her forearms into the water bucket, elbow high, letting the cool water soothe the itching. Relief was almost immediate. She removed her arms, peeled away the rag, and dropped it into the bucket while she fought with the metal buttons on her shirt. They were too big for the button-holes, and it took a good five minutes to unfasten them.

She slid her arms from the sleeves, letting the shirt dangle down behind the waist of her tightly belted pants.

Wrung-out rag in hand, she moved her gaping undershirt aside and ran the rag over her shoulders, neck, and chest, letting the cool water slop all over her upper body. It felt wonderful. Humming, she grabbed the large yellowish ball of greasy soap and scoured it across the cloth. The soap ball slipped from her hands, fell to the floor, and rolled under the table.

Rats! She tossed the rag near the bucket and bent to get the soap, stepping back so she could better see under the chest. Upside down, with her hair grazing the floor, she extended her hand, feeling around for the soap ball. All she could feel was hard, dusty wooden floor. She took one more step back and moved her head closer, squinting while her hand still searched for the soap.

From the corner of her eye, she caught a flash of black speeding by. Her hand froze. Breath held and without moving her head she looked left, then right, then left. Nothing moved. She peered up at Medusa's perch, thinking for a instant that maybe the mynah had flown back inside. The perch stood empty.

"Medusa." She straightened and looked around the room. The bird wasn't there. She frowned, shrugged, and moved toward the chest.

The black flash scurried by again.

Her breath caught. Whatever it was, it was bigger than her hand—the same size as . . .

"Oh, my Gawd! A tarantula!" She flew toward the cot, her booted feet barely touching the floor before she leapt up on the cot, her heart beating in her throat, chills racing down her arms. She fumbled with her shirt, shoving her arms through the sleeves, then hugging herself as she scanned the floor, trying to see the horrid thing, her breath heaving in fear-driven pants that rasped through the room.

She edged up the cot, still scanning the area, waiting, knowing the huge spider was gonna leap onto the cot any minute. Her fanny hit the wall. The deadly black thing crept over the left edge of the cot.

It was stalking her! She whimpered and moved back just as it crawled over the rim of the cot.

Screaming so loud her hair hurt, she took a flying jump off the cot and bounded across the floor. She had to make the door. She had to. Had to!

Her hand hit cool metal of the lock. She twisted it with a hard, panicked yank. It stuck. She fumbled, knowing that at any second the awful thing was gonna jump on her. She knew she'd feel it.

Oh, Gawd!

The lock clicked. She wrenched open the door, catapulted out, and slammed it hard, sagging back against the door, her breath heaving, her heart pounding, tears running like rain down her hot cheeks.

Fighting for control, she let her head drop, rubbing a hand over her face before she opened her eyes and focused on the bottom of the door. A little bit of black appeared from beneath the door.

It was scrunching itself under . . . Oh, my Gawd! She jumped back and the horrid black thing moved out from under the door. Her heart felt like it was stuck in her throat. She screamed until her throat was dry and then bolted forward.

Sam's chest stopped her.

"What the hell's going on?" He staggered back a step, clamping his arms around her, because she'd hit him with such force.

Her feet didn't stop moving until she'd almost climbed up his chest. She tightened her arms around him. "It's another tarantula! Oh, Gawd, oh, Gawd, get it, please, please!" She buried her nose in his neck and squeezed her arms tighter.

He grunted, and she felt him looking over her shoulder before he said, "Where is it?"

"Behind me. It's coming out from under the door." She answered into his neck, unable to bear to look at it again.

She couldn't stop shaking, but her fear had seemed to dissipate the minute she hit Sam's chest.

Suddenly his shoulders and chest began to shake, slowly at first, then growing stronger and harder. If Sam was shaking, the spider must really be huge and awful, she thought, trying to ignore the chills that ran through her.

"Do you see it?" she whispered.

"Yeah."

"It's awful, isn't it?"

"Oh, yeah, biggest one I've ever seen."

"Get rid of it, please."

"I'm not sure I can kill it . . . alone."

"Ohhhh," she moaned in horror, waiting. When he didn't make any move or say anything, she asked, "Can't you shoot it?"

"I doubt it would do any good."

"Try, please try! I can't stand it."

"A gun won't kill it."

"Don't you have any really big bullets?"

His shoulders shook again. "Bullets won't stop this one."

The image his words conjured up, that of a thick, black, leathery-tough skin beneath the spider's plump hairy body, was enough to make her shake all over again. "Is its skin really that thick?"

"No, but your head is."

She tore her face away from his neck and stared into his sardonic face. Peering over her shoulder she looked down. A big black wad of tangled thread lay harmlessly on the wooden porch. Her embarrassed gaze followed the one long black thread that was stuck to the sticky rubber on the sole of her boot.

Medusa must have gotten hold of a full spool of thread. Lollie let go of Sam's neck and slid down his chest, not knowing whether to run inside and slam the door, burst into tears, or shrivel up and die right there.

Worse yet, Jim Cassidy and a group of soldiers stood a

few feet away, apparently being completely entertained by her foolishness.

"You were right. She is flat-chested," Jim said and suddenly a whole round of male laughter filled the air.

She looked down, remembering her undone shirt. It gaped open, her wet undershirt plastered to her chest and protecting nothing from the eyes of the whole male group. She gripped the shirtfront closed in her tight fists and tried not to cry, which was what she wanted to do. Instead she acted as if she still had some dignity left by lifting her chin a notch before she spun around to take her flat chest inside. She got as far as the door, with its jammed lock.

One hand clutching her shirt closed, she twisted the blasted lock as hard as she could. It didn't budge, and she was so frustrated, so near the edge that her tears just burst forth—a final humiliation. She couldn't even make a grand exit. She let her forehead rest against the wood splintered door and cried as quietly as she could.

"Jim, take the men and keep them busy somewhere else." Sam's deep voice came from behind her.

At his words, she cried even harder. Then she could feel him standing behind her. His big hand closed over hers on the doorknob and turned. The stupid door clicked open as if it always worked perfectly. She took a deep breath and tried to pull her hand away, but he held fast. She refused to look at him. She just wasn't that strong, and couldn't bear to see the droll look in his eye. It hurt to be the brunt of a joke, to be laughed at and never taken seriously.

For some strange reason this man could see right inside her, and she felt too wounded to let anyone see that open, vulnerable side of her. It was just too personal to reveal, especially to a man. None of her brothers could understand and they loved her, so she doubted someone like Sam could.

And yet a part of her wanted Sam to take her seriously, to like her. She wanted his respect, and she didn't know why. Maybe she wanted it because she had a strong feeling that respect was something he didn't give often. If Sam

Forester respected a person, then that respect was something to cherish.

She stepped through the open door and he followed her inside. She took a deep breath and the heaving from her quiet tears sounded louder than a scream. He pulled her into his arms. The second she hit his chest she started crying all over again.

"It's not easy out in the real world, is it, Lollipop?" His hands drifted over her back.

"No," she whispered.

They stood there, neither of them speaking, the only sound in the room an occasional sniffle. "I'm so embarrassed."

"Yeah, I know."

"It really looked like a spider," she whispered.

"Yeah." His voice choked a little, and then he took a deep breath. "I don't mean to laugh at you, but it was funny."

She thought about how she must have looked, screaming the place down and running as if she were tearing up the pea patch, all because of a wad of tangled black thread. It was pretty silly, and now, with Sam's arms around her, it wasn't quite so embarrassing. She smiled a little, imagining her eyes filled with horror and reliving the way she'd been jumping all over the room like a frog leaping from lily pad to lily pad.

The inklings of a giggle escaped her lips. "I guess I did look pretty silly."

"Yeah, you did."

She leaned back and looked up at him. "You could play the gentleman and deny it, you know, out of respect for my sensibilities."

His face grew serious, and his gaze moved to her mouth. "Don't ever forget that I'm no gentleman, Lollie, and if I cared about your sensibilities, I wouldn't do this."

His mouth came down on hers so fast she couldn't get a breath, but she didn't care, because his tongue filled her mouth, stroked, and retreated, only to plunge back inside as if unable to stop. It was just as it had been before, and it felt so wonderful she like to died. *Thank Gawd you're no gentleman, Sam Forester.*

She stood on her toes, trying to wrap her arms farther around his neck. He moved his left hand from her waist to the back of her head, held it in his palm, and lifted her completely off the floor as he walked her to the cot. He sat down and pulled her across his lap, kissing all thought from her.

Over and over his mouth ate at hers, and a hand slid inside her open shirt and toyed with the tip of her breast through her wet undershirt. She groaned against his tongue, and he slid the undershirt aside and exposed her breast. In an instant he left her mouth and drew on her breast until half of it was in his open, warm, wet mouth.

His hand pulled her shirts free of her pants and rubbed up over her ribs, her stomach, then stroked lightly around her navel. Her breath caught, and suddenly he filled her mouth again, stroking and retreating, stroking and retreating, until she was all sensation and no thought. His warm palm slid under her waistband, flicking open a button, then two, then three. He untied the drawers and moved lower.

She ached between her legs, ached for something, a pressure, his touch, anything that would quench the liquid fire there. Her mind flashed with the thought that this was wrong, but the minute his fingers scored through her mound of hair and touched between her legs the ache soothed, so she moaned and moaned with the feel of his fingers rubbing and stroking.

Her legs fell open, widening to accommodate his hand, and he answered her unspoken need by palming her, cupping her, pressing until she cried a different kind of tears. His lips moved on hers with hard passion, his tongue rhythmically stroking at the same tempo as his fingers stroked low. His fingertip circled the small, sensitive point of her, over and over, slower and slower.

He stopped. She cried into his mouth. Then he teased

her, barely grazing around her. Then he stopped; she cried; he started again, slower, building and building until she strained against him, spreading her legs and crying into his mouth for something. He stopped again, and she grabbed his shoulders as hard as she could. "Don't stop. Please don't stop again."

Then his finger slipped inside her, stayed there, unmoving while his thumb touched that point again over and over.

"You're hot inside, so, so hot inside." He groaned onto her lips, moving his mouth to her ear while his thumb flickered against that point. Another finger slipped inside.

Her hips began to rise, striving for something hovering above her. She knew if she just moved a little closer . . .

His thumb stopped, but before she could protest he thrust another finger in until three fingers stretched her open. Her hips dropped and her breath deepened. His thumb started again circling, playing, grazing deeper, faster, then slower.

"Please, oh, Sam, please . . ."

"Don't rush it, sweet, slow down," he told her, laying her back on the cot and pulling her pants downward.

She moaned and moved her hips. He crawled over her, unbuttoning his clothes as he moved downward.

"Raaaaape! Ha-ha-ha-ha-ha-hah!" Medusa flapped through the window, lighting on her perch next to the cot.

Both of them froze for a long, silent moment.

"Son of a bitch!" Sam said under his breath, his forehead dropping to her chest. "I'm going to fry that damn bird!"

Lollie lay there, still as could be, except for her breathing, which matched his. Suddenly embarrassed, she squirmed and pulled up her pants, fumbling to try to rebutton them.

"Awk! Fry the damn son of a bitch!"

Sam looked up, glaring. "You're dead meat." He reached across toward Medusa.

"No, Sam!" Lollie released her pants and grabbed his wrist.

"Sam's dead meat! Get a shovel!" Medusa weaved and

bobbed along her perch. Suddenly her voice lowered to a timbre not unlike Sam's. "You're so, so hot inside."

Lollie's mouth fell open, and a slow flush flooded her face. She looked at Sam, expecting to see murder in his face. His neck was bright red, not at all what she expected, especially from a man with a black leather eye patch. She giggled. She couldn't help it. Sam Forester was embarrassed.

He stopped gawking at Medusa and looked at Lollie, who was biting her lip in an attempt to keep from bursting into a fit of giggles.

"Just what's so goddamn funny?" he barked, pushing himself up off the cot and giving her his one-eyed lethal stare. It didn't work this time, because his face still showed his embarrassment.

"You're blushing," she said, scurrying to button her pants.

"Like hell!"

"You sure are."

"Awk! Sam's blushing," Medusa lowered her voice. "So, so hot inside."

One look at Sam, and Lollie threw her body between him and Medusa. "Don't!"

"Move!" He stepped forward.

She stepped back.

The bird flapped its wings, squawked once, and sang, "To save a wretch like meeeeee!" Then she flew out the window.

Sam continued to glare at Lollie, then turned and left the room before she had a chance to say a thing. She stood there, staring at the closed door. He'd left. One moment they'd been intimate, and a few minutes later he was gone. It was as if he'd never kissed her at all, never touched her, almost as if she had dreamed the whole thing.

But she hadn't dreamed it. The faint tingle of his deep touch, the unexplained need, the restlessness she felt seeping through her, and the lingering taste of him were all still there to remind her. And they stayed with her long into the dark and lonely hours of that hot, tropical night.

19

"Here, little bird. Here, chicky-chicky-chicky. Here cocky-locky." Lollie scattered peanuts over the ground, hoping the last bird would appear from somewhere. She'd found all but one of the roosters, and today she'd ventured deeper into the jungle at the northern end of the camp's perimeter.

There were huge gray stone hills shooting up from this end of the camp, and the trees were taller, thicker, and if possible, greener. The sun hadn't quite reached the crest of the sky, but it was already warm enough to evaporate some of the morning dew. Each day had been getting hotter and wetter, and today a small group of full white clouds with gray bottoms heavy from moisture drifted over the jagged gray teeth of the hilltops.

She moved along, backing up the small viny trail, scattering peanuts and calling for the bird. Before she knew it, the growth seemed to be sparser and the ground less flat. She stumbled, straightened, and turned around.

Huge holes about eight feet in diameter dotted the ground, and there was a marked absence of trees. The area looked as though it had been cleared. She looked at the jungle across the clearing.

Maybe the bird was in there. She shoved her hands in her pockets, grabbing handfuls of peanuts and off she went, moving across the clearing.

A loud boom came from somewhere on her right. She stopped as smoke puffed up from behind an enormous dirt trench. Her gaze followed the smoke high up into the sky where a dark square thing shot in a slow arc through the air. She just stood there watching it until she heard the frantic thud of someone running toward her. She turned around just as Sam dove at her, knocking her to the ground, his arms clamped around her while he rolled over and over with her until the crackling of leaves and thick bushes stopped them. Her face was pressed against his chest, and his heavy body completely covered her. She tried to push him off, but he tucked his body even tighter around hers.

The ground exploded all around them, dirt and rocks spewing into the air, then showering down in a huge dirt cloud. They both coughed over and over until the air cleared and the dirt and rocks settled to the ground.

Sam lifted his chest off hers and grasped her shoulders. "Are you all right?" he asked.

She wiped the dirt from her face and eyes. "I think so."

"Good. Now I can kill you myself." He jerked her upright. "You idiot! What the hell were you doing walking into the artillery field?"

She turned away from his glaring eye and looked out at the clearing. "Oh. Is that what that was?"

He swore and grabbed her hand, jerking her toward the center of the camp. "I'm going to lock you in your hut until that note comes. You're trouble. You're just too much trouble, and I'll be damned if you're going to get yourself killed after all the hell I've been through!"

"Sam!" She pulled back on her hand, but his grip only tightened.

"Shut up."

"Please don't lock me up. Please. I'll just die all alone in the room." She started to cry.

He stopped, turned, and glared at her. "Don't start, dammit."

"But if you lock me up I won't be able to fix everything with the men. Please, Sam, I didn't mean to walk into that field."

He let go of her hand and ran his fingers through his hair. "Look, Lollie. I don't have time to watch over you and to do my job. I've got to get these men trained, and you've got to stay out of the way."

"Can't you give me something to do?"

"No. I can't play nursemaid." He grabbed her hand and pulled her toward her bungalow.

Just as they passed the cooking hut a soldier came down the steps. "Commander!"

Sam stopped yanking on her poor arm and barked, "What?"

"Cartillo's hurt. He can't cook the meal."

Sam swore under his breath, then asked, "What happened?"

"He missed with the knife. Verdugo's sewing him up right now."

"I'll send someone over from the field." Sam turned to drag her back to her quarters, but she dug her heels into the ground.

"I'll do it."

"You'll do what?"

"I'll cook."

"No, you won't."

"Sam, please. Let me do it. I need something to do, and it'll give me a chance to make something really nice for the men. To make up for what I did. Please."

"No."

"Why not?"

"Remember the laundry?"

"But that was a mistake. I forgot about it, and it was partly your fault."

"My fault?"

"Yes. You got so mad and dragged me back to the room. I never had a chance to go back to the laundry."

"No."

"But—"

"No." He grabbed her hand and headed for the bungalow.

She argued over and over. She begged over and over.

She finally gave it one last try. "You're afraid to let me cook."

"Sure," he said.

"You are."

"Explain how you came to that brilliant conclusion."

"You're afraid if the men don't dislike me anymore, then they'll like me—"

"Great logic," he interrupted. "If they don't dislike you, they'll like you. Brilliant, absolutely brilliant deduction."

"You don't have to be so nasty about it. I wasn't finished."

"Please." He waved a hand in the air. "Go on." Then he muttered, "I can't wait to hear the rest."

"If they like me, you'll have to admit you like me and you can't take that."

He stared at her silently.

"You can't admit that you like me."

Silence.

"You kissed me, and . . . uh . . . all."

He looked very uncomfortable.

"You did."

He closed his eye, inhaled a long breath and spun around, heading for the cooking hut. A few minutes later Lollie stared at the chicken Sam had slapped into her hand. She frowned. It was dead, and headless. Nineteen more just like it sat on the large table in the cook hut. She held up the dead bird, as far away from her person as she could, and stared at it. She wouldn't have admitted it to Sam, but she had never cooked a meal in her life.

In fact, ever since the time she'd decided to heat up some water for tea and started a little fire, the cook had forbidden her to go near the kitchen at Hickory House. Actually, it hadn't been something she'd resented, since it had scared her silly when all those flames had leapt from the stove and up the walls. The whole thing had all happened so fast and loud, like the blast of an erupting volcano. She'd tossed the match into the wood grate, walked back to get the tea, and *whoosh!* The whole wall was on fire.

She looked at the chicken, its limp neck dangling at a horrid angle. She could do this. She knew she could. She tossed it onto the pile of dead birds and wandered around the cooking area, taking in all the things that were foreign to her.

Huge black pots were stacked in one corner near a row of sacks and barrels. The barrels were labeled, but not in English. She supposed the sacks held staples—flour and sugar and the like—but there was a whole row of canisters on a crooked shelf above the barrels. She moved to the unlabeled canisters and began opening them and examining the contents in search of something familiar. She snapped the lid off the last one and peered inside.

It looked like lard. She stuck a finger in it. It was greasy like lard. It must be lard. Tucking it under an arm she turned and crossed over to the giant black stoves. Four of them lined one wall of the cooking hut. They sat there like giant black volcanic mountains ready to erupt.

She was being silly. She'd begged for this chance and she would do it. Cooking was the perfect chance to make a great meal for the men. Men liked to have a woman cook for them. They thought it was a good job for females. It was just one she knew nothing about.

She was older now than she had been when she set the fire at home. Surely she could handle this. She eyed the stoves. Age had taught her one thing—it would be more prudent to get someone to light them for her.

She stepped outside the bungalow and looked around the camp. Sam stood near the barracks talking to the soldier who'd told him about the cook's injury. She left the stoop and walked toward them. Sam's voice faded and he turned around, took one irritated look at her, and bit out, "Now what?"

"Would you light the stoves for me, please?" She pointed over her shoulder at the cook bungalow.

His gaze followed her finger, and then he took a deep

breath and turned to the soldier. "You go on," he said. "I'll be there in a minute." He walked right past her, opened the door with an impatient jerk, and disappeared inside before Lollie could take a few steps.

She hurried through the doorway just as Sam heaved wood into the fire bins. He bent over one, held a match to it, and asked, "You have cooked before, right?"

"Not really." She couldn't look him in the eye.

"Not really? Why do I feel you're not telling me everything?"

"Oh, I boiled some water for tea once." She waved her hand as if it was nothing.

"And?"

He wasn't fooled.

"This little fire started."

"And?"

"I burned down one wall of the kitchen. But I know I can do this. Besides, you promised."

"Something I'm sure I'll regret," he muttered, then straightened, moved to the next stove, and lit it, too. "How do you want to cook those birds," he asked, "baked or fried?"

She couldn't really decide. "Both."

"Okay. Remove the feathers, cut up the frying chickens, dip the pieces in flour, and fry them in hot lard. Got it?"

She nodded, mentally repeating: remove the feathers, cut the frying chickens, dip in flour and fry in hot lard. That didn't sound too difficult.

"The baked ones go in roasting pans; season them, and cook them in these ovens." He pointed to the large black doors on the front of the ranges. "Do you know anything about stoves?"

"No, but I'm sure I can learn."

He lit the second stove then slammed the oven door closed. "Come here."

She crossed the few feet between them, and he turned, pointing to a black handle. "This is the damper. Push it down to open it if you want to cook on the range top. Push it up to close it for oven cooking." He looked at her.

"Down is open for cooking on top. Up is closed for cooking in the oven." She repeated proudly.

"Right."

He squatted down beside a stove. "See this grate?"

She leaned over his wide shoulder and nodded. "Uh-huh."

"It's the draft. This probably caused your fire at Hick House."

"Hickory House."

"All right, Hickory House. Now pay attention."

"I was. If *you'd* paid attention you wouldn't keep calling it Hick House."

"Do you want to learn this or not?"

"Yes, but that's not fair. If I have to pay attention then you should have paid attention to me when I told you where I live."

"I don't want fairness, I want quiet." He stood up, glaring down at her.

"Well, I just think that you ought to be able to remember—"

"Do me a favor. Don't think, just listen."

She sighed, counted to five, then said, "All right. I'm listening."

"As I said, this is the grate. You turn it so the holes are exposed. The more holes you expose, the hotter the fire. Now, this handle up here"—he stood and pointed to a black handle on the stovepipe—"is the check draft. It lets cool air in so that the oven won't explode. It is very important that you keep this open. Understand?"

"Draft open."

"*Check* draft open."

"Check draft open," she repeated.

He watched her for an unsure minute.

"Sam, please, I want to do this. I know I can do this, really. Just give me a chance."

"Anything to keep you out of the line of fire," he muttered, moving over to the next range and lighting it. He pointed to the black handle. "What's this?"

"The damper," she said proudly.

He looked surprised. "That's right. He pointed to the handle on the stovepipe and gave her a smug look. "What's this?"

"The *check* draft." She smiled. "You thought you'd trick me by switching the order, didn't you?"

"Just making sure you understand." He leaned over to the side grate and opened his mouth to speak.

"You're testing me, aren't you?"

He took a long breath.

"That's the damper," she said, determined to prove to him that she could do this. "Push it down to open so you can cook on the top. Push it up to close it and use the oven. See, *I* pay attention." She smiled, suddenly feeling as if she'd finally held her own against him.

He shrugged and lit the other two stoves. "They're all yours." He turned to leave, but stopped as if he'd forgotten something. "Don't come and get me. Bang on a pan when the meal is ready and we'll come eat it."

She nodded, watching him until he shut the door. She looked around the hut, a little of her bravado fading now that she was all alone.

Well, she thought, time's a-wasting, and she picked up one of the dead birds. Holding it up by its webbed feet she stared at it for a moment. He'd said to remove the feathers. Or was it cut the feathers? She held the bird a bit closer and examined it, mentally reciting his instructions: remove the feathers, cut the fryers. Okay, he'd said "remove."

Now, how did one remove the feathers? She looked around the kitchen for something to use and spotted some shears hanging on the wall. She marched over and took them back to the table. *Cut the feathers*. Holding the chicken's wing between her finger and thumb, she lifted it and cut off the feathers.

An hour or so later, she hummed "Dixie" as she snipped off the last bit of fluff from the twentieth chicken. She plopped the bird onto the pile of others and swiped the floating feathers out of her face. The birds looked a little like porcupines. Those little spiky things must turn into that crispy stuff on the outside, she reasoned.

Now what had Sam said? "Oh, that's right," she said. "The baked ones go into roasting pans in the ovens." Roasting pans . . . hmm. She eyed the wall where all the black cookware hung. Some of the pans were square and big enough for several chickens. Those must be roasting pans, she thought, marching over to pull two of them off the nails that held them on the wall.

She dropped both pans on the range top and gathered the whole chickens. They sure were prickly. They ought to be good and crispy. She stuffed five in one pan until they were tight as could be; then she filled the next pan. She opened the oven door, lugged the pan off the top, rammed it into the oven, and closed the door. She did the same with the other pan.

There! she thought, wiping her hands together. All done!

She turned back to the others, which still had to be cut up. She grabbed a knife from a nearby barrel and began sawing back and forth, trying to cut the bird, but the knife was too dull. She eyed a thick-bladed rectangular knife with a big handle and decided that was what she needed. She plucked it off the barrel, then spread the chicken out as flat as she could on the table. She raised the cleaver as high as she could, and with all the force she could muster she hacked through the bird with a loud *smack-crunch!*

Over and over she hacked at the bird until she had a whole mess of chicken pieces, none of which were recognizable except the neck and feet. She shrugged. Nothing she ate ever looked like the real thing anyway, she reasoned, continuing on with her massacre until half the birds were lacerated into bony, spiky chunks.

With a zip in her step she crossed to the flour barrel, scooped up a bowl of flour, and carried it back over to her table. She set it down and tossed the pieces in the flour, like Sam had said. She repeated the motion until she really got into the spirit of it, tossing the prickly little chicken pieces in the flour. A white cloud billowed upward as she hummed. She placed the last piece on the table and decided cooking was right fun. Then she sneezed, sending a shower of flour and feathers all around her.

She should have gotten rid of the feathers after she'd cut them off. She fanned them away and looked down at her clothes. They were caked white. She tried to brush them off but succeeded only in smearing flour deeper into the cloth and sending the feathers flying through the air like dandelions in March. She gave up and went over to the monstrous stoves.

She took the huge black iron pans, all six of them, off the wall and plunked them down on the stove tops. There was room for two pans on each stove, so she'd have to use three of the four stoves. She retrieved the lard canister and scooped out a spoonful of lard and tried to drop it into the first pan. It stuck to the spoon. She shook it a minute until it loosened and plopped with a sizzle into the pan.

Confidence recharged, she thwacked the lard-filled spoon against the rim of each pan and watched with satisfaction as it sizzled into liquid fat. This was great fun, and not too hard, either. She crossed to the table, scooped up an armful of floured, prickly chicken, then returned to the stoves, and dropped the pieces into the pans. A few minutes later she had all the chicken sizzling on the stoves.

Now what to serve with them? She rummaged through the sacks and barrels until she spotted some rice. That was perfect. She looked back at the chicken, sizzling away, and wiped some sweat from her forehead. This wasn't easy, and the hut was getting really hot.

She filled a bowl with rice and walked over to the stove. She realized she'd have to boil the rice. She pulled a couple of big pots off the wall and placed them on the fourth stove. Then she walked over to the water barrel, ladled water into a bowl, and carried it back to the pot.

Over and over she repeated the motion until sweat poured from her damp head. But the pots were filled. She dumped in the rice, a couple of big bowls full in each pot. By the time she'd finished, the pots were filled almost to the top with rice. She placed the lids on the pots and checked the frying chicken.

Spoon in hand, she went to the first pan and stuck the spoon in to turn the meat. It wouldn't budge. The grease splattered and sputtered, and she dodged it, still trying to jam the spoon under the chicken. Smoke started drifting upward. A distinct burning smell permeated the room.

A quick glance at the other pans told her the ranges were too hot. She moved like lightning between the stoves, trying to pry the burning chicken off the pans. Grease splattered on her arms and shirtfront as she worked.

The sudden hiss of water sizzled from the far stoves. Lollie turned just as the rice bubbled over in a pasty avalanche. The lid crashed to the floor along with a bubbling mass of gooey, watery rice. It spilled onto the stove, sending a cloud of steam upward to mix with the smoking chicken.

She panicked, running back and forth as rice glopped down the front of the hot ovens. Streaks of pasty, lumpy rice began to bake on the oven doors. The ranges were just too hot. She needed to hit the damper to lessen the heat.

Or was it the draft she needed to close?

Oh, rats! She'd forgotten which was which. Calm down, she told herself, trying to ignore the sound of erupting rice. She waved the smoke away and concentrated.

A damper is something that dampens. A draft is air. Smoke billowed out, turning blacker and blacker. Rice sizzled, then plopped and plopped. A drastic situation called for drastic measures. She grabbed a handle in each hand and closed them both.

The blast turned the head of every soldier on the artillery field, including Sam. His first instinct was that they were being attacked, until the half-burned, half-raw prickly chicken landed next to his foot.

"Aw, crap!" He dropped the shell canister he'd been

holding and ran toward the cooking hut, rounding the corner seconds after the blast.

Black smoke billowed up from where the thatched roof used to be, and chicken feathers rained down like snowflakes. The front door hung on a single hinge, and as Sam stepped forward, he tripped on the back door. Barrels had splintered, tin canisters rolled, and one entire side of the building was white with what looked like flour.

"Lollie!" he yelled, stepping over the wreckage and into something slimy and white. "Lollie!" He moved deeper into the shell of the hut, looking all over for her, finding only a five-foot hole in the back wall.

Sam stepped through it and saw her crumpled form barely eight feet away. He rushed over and knelt beside her. Her breath was the shallow breath of the unconscious. "Lollie, answer me. Come on, wake up."

She didn't move. He ran his hands over her, eyeing the way she lay on the ground. Very carefully, he slid his arms under her, picked her up, and strode toward her bungalow. His gaze never left her pale face. She had no color. Her eyelids were closed and white. Soot smudged her cheeks, which were covered with scratches and nicks. A small trickle of blood dripped from her split lip, and her blond hair was singed and black and five inches shorter.

"Is she all right?" Jim came running up, followed by Gomez and the other soldiers.

"I don't know. She's unconscious." Sam walked up the steps of her bungalow. Jim opened the door, and Sam stepped inside and carried her to the cot. "Get me some water and a towel, will you?" He watched the rise and fall of her chest, assuring himself that she was breathing fine. He looked at her face, at her singed hair, and he wanted to kick himself. He should have followed his first instincts and locked her in her hut until he could take her back to her father. He'd never met anyone who could create more havoc than this one irritating little woman.

Jim set the water bucket and a towel by the bed, drawing Sam's attention away from Lollie's drawn face. "Thanks."

He dipped the towel in the bucket and began washing off the soot and dried blood.

"Is there anything I can do?" Jim asked.

"No, just see to the men for me, would you?"

"Sure."

Sam finished cleaning her face, arms, and neck, then he wrung out the towel, folded it, and placed it on her forehead. He had time, lots and lots of time, to just sit there and watch her, plenty of time to castigate himself.

She'd talked him into letting her do something he knew she couldn't handle. Of course there wasn't much this woman *could* handle . . . but then he amended that thought. She had managed to trek through the jungle, even occasionally kept up with him. She hadn't become hysterical except that one time at the bay when she realized that they had missed the ransom exchange.

She did have something that drove her, a spirit within her that contradicted what she should have been, a spoiled, pampered little rich girl who cared only about herself. That was the label he'd first given her, but he'd been wrong. She wasn't a snob and a spoiled brat. She was someone who needed assurance, acceptance, encouragement. She genuinely wanted to be liked, and yet something about her said she didn't expect anyone to.

Why? Why would a girl who had everything—money, family, social connections—have so little self-esteem? Granted, he hadn't done anything to help her, but he knew he wasn't the reason she felt that way. He was, however, the reason she was hurt, lying there so still and making him forget about guerrillas and guns and greed.

What he did feel at this moment was an intense inability to help her, and once again he felt guilty. How she could inspire guilt in him he didn't know, but she managed it when no other person on this earth ever could. He cared. And he didn't much like it, either. He believed that caring about something colored one's judgment, and Sam prided himself on his ability to make decisions objectively.

Yet as he looked at her, he was overcome by such a

strong sense of protectiveness that it almost made him humble. He couldn't remember when he'd felt protective toward something, if he ever had at all. From the first moment she'd stumbled and stabbed her way into his life he'd felt it, even if he could only now admit it.

He had spent his rotten, mercenary life protecting nothing but his own butt, and that was just a game with him. It gave him a thrill to stare death in the face, spit at it, and still come out the winner. But he got no thrill when Lollie was involved. All he got was a feeling of intense fear.

He drew in a deep breath with that realization. His gaze drifted from her to the window, and as he stared outside, watching the sky turn pink with the sunset, the same shade of pink as that frilly dress and the deadly parasol, he wondered if maybe he was the one who needed protection.

20

The door opened.

Lollie dropped the mirror she'd held and looked up. It was Sam, and he carried a couple of long, thick bamboo poles.

"I brought you these," he said, walking over to the cot and looking down at her.

She felt like an ant, staring up at him, and she struggled to sit up a bit taller so there wasn't as much distance between them. If nothing else at least she felt a little bigger.

"How's the ankle?"

"It still hurts when I put any weight on it."

"That's why I brought you these." He held up the poles. "Gomez made them for you. They're crutches."

"Gomez made them?"

He nodded.

"For me?"

"Yes, for you."

"Oh," she said, surprised that any of the men would give a fig about her.

He bent over her and picked up the mirror; then he stared at her for a long moment. She expected to see pity, disgust, or something similar, but his face didn't reveal his thoughts.

She reached up to brush the hair off her cheek and froze the instant her fingers touched the ragged, burned ends of her hair. She let her embarrassed gaze dart to his, expecting to see a cynical smile. It wasn't there. She quickly tucked the ends behind her ear.

He placed the mirror on the table next to Medusa's empty perch and straightened. "Are you going to sit there all day or are you going to try these things?" He held the crutches out for her.

She stared at them for a minute.

"I take it from the way you're frowning that you've never used crutches before."

She shook her head.

He set them down on the bed and held out his hand to her. "Get up."

She grabbed it and stood, careful to put her weight on her good ankle.

He slid his arm around her and pulled her close to his side. Immediately she felt the warmth from his body. She wrapped her right arm around his waist and slid her other hand over his chest, trying to steady herself.

His sharp intake of breath pierced the silence of the small room. He placed a warm palm over her hand and slid it down to his ribs before he bent and picked up the crutches.

"Here." He handed her one. "Put this under your other arm."

She did.

He gripped her upper arm in one hand and slid the other

233

crutch under her arm. "Hold on to these small handles."
He placed her hand around a smaller piece of bamboo that
stuck out about halfway down the thick pole.

"Now lift the crutches and move them forward." His
mouth was so close to her ear that his words brushed over
it. She shivered. To avoid his breath on her ear and the
way it made her feel, she planted the crutches a good foot
ahead of her.

"That's right. . . . Now, put your weight on the handles
and swing yourself forward."

She did.

"It worked!" she said, smiling as she turned back toward
Sam. "Watch." She did it again. "It's easy, isn't it?" Then
she moved back toward him, taking a big step—too big a
step.

The left crutch slipped on the slick wood of the floor,
and she lost her balance. Her crutch clattered to the floor.
Sam caught her.

"Thank you," she said, looking up at him.

He looked at her for the longest time and in the most
uneasy way. He had no smile on his face, and yet his eye
wasn't hard or tinged with that constant wry cynicism it
usually had whenever she did something foolish.

She didn't know if the lack of that cynical look should
worry her or not. He reached up and fingered the ragged
ends of her burned hair.

"I must look awful." She averted her eyes.

He placed a finger under her chin and tilted her face until
she had to meet his gaze. He searched her face—probably
looking at her bruises, she thought. She'd seen her black-
and-blue cheek, scratched face, and puffy lip in the mirror.

"Yeah, you do." His palm opened to cup her cheek, and
his thumb drifted over her swollen lip.

Honest Sam. She should have been offended, but she
wasn't. She was too fascinated by the feel of his thumb.
He began to lower his head slowly, his gaze never leaving
hers. He's going to kiss me, she thought, a surge of pure
joy filling her chest. Her eyelids felt heavy and seemed to

want to drift closed. She willed them to stay open, watching him and waiting for their lips to touch, waiting for that brief whiff of his warm male breath to graze her mouth.

Barely an inch away from a kiss, he suddenly stopped. It happened so fast she blinked. He pulled back, took a deep, relieved breath, and turned to pick up her crutch. He stuck it back under her arm, then turned away again, leaving her with a cool, empty feeling. She took a deep breath, looking away while her mind raced to figure out why he'd stopped. Her gaze lit on the mirror, and she remembered her reflection; then she didn't blame him. She looked worse than Jim had after that fight with Sam.

"I'm sorry about the cooking hut," she said to his back.

He rammed his hands in his pockets. "It needed a new roof anyway."

There was nothing more to say. They both just stood there, silent. He spun around as if he had something important to say. The door banged open, and Jim walked in with Medusa perched on his shoulder.

"Raaaape! Ha-ha-ha-ha-ha-hah!"

Sam's heated gaze met hers. Her mind flashed with the memory of the last time Medusa had screeched that silly phrase. She could feel the flush heat her face and could see the memory on Sam's face, too.

"I'm sorry I ever taught her that," Jim said.

"So am I." Sam's stare never left hers.

The temperature in the room rose quicker than the tide at a full moon. She knew she should look away, but she didn't want to.

"The note's here."

"What note?" Sam asked distractedly, still holding her with a look that made her wish Jim would leave.

"The note from her father. He'll meet you in Santa Cruz in four days."

She looked at Jim, his words finally penetrating her head. She was leaving, going back to her family. The oddest thing happened. Her stomach sank at the idea, the same way it sank whenever she was in a boat. She looked back at Sam, wanting to see his reaction. He had none. That hot tinge of longing was gone, replaced by the cynical look she hated.

"Well, well, I guess Miss Lah-Roo is going home to her daddy." And without another glance her way, Sam turned and left.

"You know a bottle never pulled a man out of a hole."

Sam scowled at Jim. "What the hell is that supposed to mean?"

"It means I know you. You've got trouble."

Sam lifted the bottle to his lips and chugged down a few burning gulps. "Just what is this remarkable revelation you've come to?"

"Woman trouble."

"That woman is trouble all right. In four more days she'll be back with her daddy and out of my hair."

"Then why are you swilling that stuff?"

"I'm celebrating."

"And I'm the angel Gabriel," Jim muttered.

"Since when have you become my keeper?"

"Since you've been acting like you needed one."

Sam slammed one booted foot on the seat of the chair next to him and stared at the opening in the top of the whiskey bottle. "Don't you have somewhere else to go?"

"Nope, unless I slink over to Lollie's room and give her a thrill before she leaves."

Sam's booted foot hit the floor. "You touch her and I swear—" He stopped, realizing he'd given himself away.

"What?" Jim gave him a knowing smile.

"Nothing. Just stay away from her."

Jim whistled something that sounded a lot like the Wedding March.

"Shut up."

Jim did, but smiled as he poured himself a drink, then leaned back in his own chair, silently watching Sam over the rim of his glass. There was a distinct gleam in Cassidy's green eyes, the same gleam the vampire snake had worn when it cornered Sam.

He didn't like it, so he drank from the bottle again; then he wouldn't have to look at Jim.

"Is she really that hot inside?"

Sam spit whiskey a good three feet, coughed, pinned Jim with a one-eyed stare that had brought others to their knees, and said, "I'm going to kill that bird."

Laughing, Jim reached out and clapped him on the back. "Come on, Sam old buddy, where's your sense of humor."

"I lost it the minute you got that mouthy bird."

"Right. You lost it the minute you let that little blond bit with the voice like molasses get to you."

Sam grunted. After a few minutes he said, "Even if what you say were true"—Sam held up a hand when his friend rolled his eyes—"which it's not, it doesn't matter anyway, because tomorrow I'm taking her back to her internationally esteemed daddy."

"This is a side of you I've never seen." Jim reached out and poured himself another.

"What?" Sam barked.

"Jealousy."

"Me? Jealous? Shit . . ."

"You just sounded as if you were jealous. Of her father."

"I've never been jealous of anyone in my life. For one thing, there's never been anything I wanted enough to feel jealous."

"Deny it all you want, but I've still got a black eye to prove it."

"Jealousy is for fools and dreamers." Sam swilled some more whiskey. "They're the only ones who are stupid enough to want something they can never have. I'm neither a fool nor a dreamer. I learned that lesson as a kid."

"I think you want something you think you can't have, and it's that woman."

"You can think whatever you want, but that doesn't mean you're right." Sam lifted the bottle to his lips again. He supposed he'd have to admit that he did want her physically, but then, they'd been forced together since that day in the marketplace, so his reaction to her was just some failing on his part, like that impulse he felt to protect her. There had to be something he could do to overcome that weakness and change that urge. She must be one of those women who could make a man feel things he didn't want to. Some women could do that, although until now he'd never met one. He must be getting old or something. And he wasn't jealous.

The best plan was to take her back where she belonged, and then he'd never have to worry about Lollie LaRue again. The sooner they left, the sooner he could get rid of her and get on with his job here. That was what was important.

He had to finish up here and then go back to the States for a while. Someplace quiet, where he could get his mind and body functioning on a normal level again. Maybe he'd go to San Francisco or maybe the Northwest. Yeah, Seattle might do. It was the farthest U.S. point from South Carolina.

The rumble of thunder woke Lollie. She sat up at the noise. It was either thunder or a large elephant. Whatever it was, the wooden walls almost shook from its noise. With the suddenness of a hurricane wind, and with almost the same force, the bungalow door blew open. A dark form fell across the threshold.

Lollie screamed.

"Shhh!"

"Sam!" she gasped.

His dark form sat up, and though she couldn't see his face she knew he was looking at her. "Christ, you've got to stop screaming, Lollipop." He shook his head. "My ears can't take it."

"What are you doing?"

"Standing up." He got to his knees, then wobbled to his full height, weaving a little.

"I meant what are you doing here? It's late."

"I came to tell you we're leaving tomorrow morning. Early. First thing."

"Already?"

He shut the door and shuffled toward the cot. "What's wrong, Miss Lah-Roo? Don't you want to see your little old daddy?"

"Of course I do. I just thought I'd have more time to get ready."

"We have to take the mountain road. The rainy season will start soon."

"What does the mountain road have to do with the rains?"

"Floods."

"Oh, I see." At least she thought she might see. He wasn't making himself too clear. "Is that all?"

"Yeah." He belched.

"Have you been drinking?"

"Me? Drink? Why would I do that?" He leaned close enough that the fumes brought tears to her eyes.

"You are drunk!"

"Hurrah!" He applauded. "Give this woman a college diploma! Her mind is amazing!" He waved a hand at an imaginary audience in the dark room.

"I think you should leave."

"I knew I smelled smoke."

"Pardon me?"

"Thinking." He fell onto the cot right next to her. "It's hard work, isn't it?"

"Sam! Get off here!"

"Stop thinking, just feel. It's so much easier." His mouth came at her, and she dodged it, turning back just as his face hit the cot.

She tried to scoot out the other side but his arm clamped over her.

"Un-un-unnn." His breath hit her ear. "Thought you'd get away from me, didn't you?" His leg clamped over hers.

"Sam, stop it!" She dodged his face again, but before she could determine his intention his hands clamped on to her breasts.

"You're not flat, Lollie."

239

"Don't!" She tried to pry his hands off her.

"Aren't you going to thank me? I just paid you a compliment. A kiss'll do." His mouth closed over hers.

She turned her head, breaking contact with his seeking mouth. "Don't do this, Sam. Please." Her voice cracked. He scared her, acting like this, liquor on his breath and his hands and mouth willing to take what he wanted.

He stopped and looked down at her, shook his head as if he needed to clear it, then looked at her again, only this time she felt as if he really saw her. He pushed up from the cot and stood there. She thought for a minute he might apologize, but he didn't. He stood there; then he rubbed a hand across his mouth and turned. He staggered to the door and jerked it open. "We're leaving early. Be ready."

She didn't say anything.

"Did you hear me?" he barked, his back to her.

"Yes," she whispered.

"Good." He stepped through the doorway, then stopped again. "One more thing."

"What?"

"I'm not jealous. I've never been jealous. I never will be jealous." And he slammed the door closed.

21

With the bright orange dawn came a scattering of dark clouds, rain-dark clouds, as Sam had been reminding Lollie. He'd been barking orders at her since the moment he'd beaten on the door and told her to get up, bellowing that he didn't have all damn day. He told her again about the mountain road, which probably meant he didn't remember last night. He made more sense this morning. He said the road was safe from the Spanish patrols. It was longer, but it was a safer trek to the town of Santa Cruz, the meeting spot with her father.

She supposed she should have been anxious for that meeting, but much had happened since that day when she'd paced her room waiting for her father. Gone was her pink dress, the one she'd taken such time and trouble to duplicate from the portrait. Gone was the perfectly curled blond hair, and gone were the shoes with the beaded rosettes. Gone also was the girl who'd felt as if that meeting would be the most important event in her life.

She looked down at her clothes, the black canvas shirt, pants, and heavy boots. That girl was gone all right. She looked at her reflection in the mirror and the girl who stared back. She still had blond hair, but it was shorter, barely reaching her shoulders. Her face was battered from the explosion. Her lips were no longer swollen, but the bruises and a faint scratch or two were still detectable. And she hobbled around on a pair bamboo crutches.

This was Eulalie Grace LaRue. Her brothers would just die!

And her father, what would he think?

It didn't really matter what he thought. She was sick and tired of trying to please a father she didn't even know, tired of trying to get respect from the men around her. Her brothers might shelter her, but the truth of the matter was that they just didn't think her able to take care of herself. They didn't respect her. She wondered if men ever thought of women as capable. Somehow she doubted it, and Sam was a fine example of that blatant lack of respect. Falling down drunk on her cot, for Pete's sake.

The one thing she'd decided, lying there in the dark and staring at the door Sam had slammed, was that she would no longer try to be what she thought men wanted. It hadn't done her a bit good up to now. She'd always tried so hard to get approval, yet not one man had ever given it to her.

It seemed that the harder she tried, the more she messed things up.

She'd fought for her brothers' approval and gotten a pat on her little blond head, and she'd been all but locked away in her own little ivory tower. She'd wanted her father's approval, but he'd never bothered to come home long enough to give her a chance to earn it. And she'd spent all that time waiting, only to face disappointment after disappointment. She'd wanted Sam's approval too, but she'd gotten only his scorn.

Well, not anymore. In the dark of that lonely bungalow she'd made a decision. She was going to control some of the things in her life. She was sick and tired of men telling what she needed to do, when she needed to leave, what she was supposed to be. Her future actions might not bring her male approval, but she would feel that she had some control over her own life. Then maybe she wouldn't care what men thought.

Let them wait for her for a change. And the first male to wait for her was Sam.

Gomez had come to get her twice, claiming Sam had demanded that she come now. She hadn't, but instead used the crutches to hobble over to the cot, sat down, laying the crutches across her lap, and she'd then counted to one thousand. It felt so good that she'd gone and done it all over again.

Nine hundred and ninety-eight . . . She smiled, imagining Sam's scowling face as he paced. *Nine hundred and ninety-nine* . . . She licked her index finger and drew an imaginary line in the air. *One thousand . . . and one for me!*

She stood, picked up a small pouch of peanuts from the cot, and tied it to the belt loops on her pants. Then she positioned the crutches and made her way out of the bungalow, slowly moving across the camp toward the men's barracks. She passed the bungalows, went through the gate, and entered the jungle. She still had one more thing to do before she left.

* * *

Sam turned away from Jim and the group of soldiers who were putting a new roof on the cooking hut. Each time a hammer hit a wooden peg or a nail—about once every two seconds—Sam's teeth rang. He walked the hundred yards or so to the cart they'd take up the mountain road. He moved past the spare carabao tied to the back of the cart, and he checked the wheels for the thousandth time. Stopping near the rear axle, he bent over to look at it—a monumental mistake. Pain shot through his head, across his forehead, and into his temples, which throbbed as if the veins inside were pumping rotgut whiskey through it, a whole quart at a time.

He winced and straightened very slowly, just in time to see the woman responsible for his headache. Lollie LaRue hobbled forward on her crutches, smiling prouder than Grant at Appomattox. She had troops, too, eight plump fighting cocks, or at least what used to be fighting cocks, high-stepping along behind her like ducklings with their mama.

The hammering stopped, and the camp dwindled to complete quiet. Squinting against the morning sun, Sam turned toward the men. Slowly, one by one, they came down from the roof, following Jim, who had come to stand beside Sam. Every man there wore the look of someone who'd just been konked over the head.

She stopped a few feet away. Her chin went up, her blue eyes glowed with ignorant pride, and she said, "I brought the men back their birds. See?" She gestured toward the roosters, which had turned like a well-trained regiment and now stood in a line beside her.

Sam heard Jim's snort of laughter, and he frowned, looked down for a moment, then rubbed his hand over his pounding forehead. He was counting. By the time he looked up again, the entire camp had gathered nearby, all of them still wearing that same dumbfounded look.

"Well?" she said in a voice tinged with impatience. "Who belongs to whom?"

He was just about to tell her she belonged in Belleview

when Gomez stepped forward and pointed at the white and black cock in the middle of the line. "That one's mine."

"Claudette?" She turned toward the bird.

Sam groaned. She'd named them.

"She's just the sweetest thing. You know at first she was a real pecker."

Jim barked out a laugh.

She looked at him, frowning. She didn't have a clue as to why Jim had laughed. Sam shook his head.

She rambled on, "She must have bitten my hand three or four times. But she doesn't do that now." She joined Gomez, took something that looked like a peanut from a pouch at her waist, braced herself on one crutch, and bent down. "Here, Claudette . . ."

The bird flapped once, trotted over to her outstretched hand, plucked off the peanut, and ate it. Lollie dug into her pants pocket and held out her hand. "Take these. She just loves those nuts."

The peanuts spilled into Gomez's outstretched hand.

"Now squat down," Lollie instructed. "Go on."

Gomez squatted.

"Now, put your arm out."

He did, and the cock hopped up on it, then waddled up to his shoulder, and perched there, like Medusa.

Lollie turned her chin up and smiled so brightly that Sam felt the urge to squint again.

"Now then, who belongs to Reba?" she asked, pointing to the bantam cock at the end of the line.

Jim leaned close to Sam and out of the corner of his mouth said, "She's given them all women's names."

"So I noticed." Sam watched her talk to each of the owners, explaining the foibles of each cock and how she'd managed to lure them from their hiding places. She rambled on about how she hadn't known how she'd get them to go back to their cages so she'd taught them to follow her by leaving a trail of peanuts.

Each time she said something, Jim made caustic comments under his breath. Sam'd had enough, and he turned around to check the supplies in the cart.

By the time he'd cataloged everything, she'd finished, said good-bye to each of the men, and hobbled over to talk to Jim. Sam walked up just as she thanked Jim for God only knew what.

She turned to Sam and smiled. "I fixed everything with the men."

She'd fixed everything all right. She'd managed to tame a whole group of fighting cocks. He'd have bet if roosters could talk, she'd have taught them to say "please" and "thank you," too. He'd never met anyone like Lollie LaRue, and if luck was on his side, he never would again. There couldn't be two of them in the world; otherwise mankind wouldn't have lasted this long.

He looked at her, dressed in soldiers' clothes, not a stitch of Calhoun pink anywhere on her person, half of her hair burned off, her white skin bruised, and her smile bright. It was hard to believe this was the same woman who'd whined her way through the jungle. Two weeks ago he would have told her exactly how she looked and what a stupid thing she'd done with those birds, but now, with that smile on her bruised face and the joy in her voice, he couldn't tell her.

And he didn't like that.

"Get the lead out. I haven't got all damn day!" He turned and walked toward the front carabao and stood there waiting for her.

She hobbled over to the cart, and he remembered her ankle. Stomping back to her he swung her into his arms and plopped her into the cart, then tossed the crutches up. Without a backward glance, he went back to the carabao.

"I'll be back in a week," he said to Jim and then started to leave.

"Wait!" Lollie called out.

Sam turned, wondering what the hell she'd forgotten now. She'd just spent ten minutes saying good-bye to every single man in the camp.

Jim smiled, then whistled. That stupid mynah bird flapped down from a nearby tree and perched on Lollie's head. "Awk! Sam's here! Get a shovel!"

"All right, I'm ready now," she informed him, reaching up to give the bird a treat.

Sam stood there for a frozen moment.

"What're you waiting for?" She handed the bird another treat, which it took, swallowed, then gave Sam a look that, if possible for a bird, could have been a sly smile. Sam's forehead throbbed; he ground his teeth together. "That bird is not going with us."

"Of course she is. Jim gave her to me."

Fists ready, Sam spun around. He'd kill Jim, wrap his hands around his throat, and strangle the man who used to be his best friend.

The soldiers milled around, watching as the cocks perform the tricks Lollie had taught them. Sam searched the crowd for Jim's blond head. He'd disappeared.

"I thought you were in a hurry," Lollie said.

Sam turned back, his face hot with suppressed anger. She shifted this way and that, situating herself on top of the supplies like the Queen of Sheba.

Sam eyed the bird from hell. "One word, just one word out of that bird and—"

"Sam's an ass! Ha-ha-ha-ha-hah!" Medusa hopped down onto Lollie's shoulder.

"Shhhh! Medusa. Sam's crabby." Lollie turned to the bird and lifted her finger to her lips. "I think he's feeling wretched."

Sam spun around, grabbed the prod, and poked the lead carabao up the dirt road. The cart lurched forward, creaking and rocking as its hand-carved wheels wobbled along.

"Awwwk! To save a wretch like Sam!"

Sam slowly turned around.

"Shhh!" Lollie told the bird, then looked at Sam and shrugged.

He turned back, knew he was scowling, but didn't care.

246

His head hurt. He hunched his shoulders and guided the carabao up the road. Four days, he thought. Only four more days and then she'll be gone. Four days of Lollie LaRue and that damn bird, and then his life would return to normal. There'd be no more trouble, and everything would be all right.

By that afternoon, when the rear carabao plopped its eight-hundred-pound butt into the dirt for the sixth time, Sam was convinced that nothing would ever be right again. They had left the camp with that bird from hell singing and whistling and name-calling. Two hours up the mountain road the front carabao had decided it was tired. It fell to the ground with all the aplomb of a dead elephant.

He tugged on the carabao's harness. The animal didn't budge. He went around to the spare carabao and untied it, planning to switch early. He brought it forward, unharnessed the tired one and prodded it up and back to the rear of the cart, where he tied it to the gate. Once the spare beast was harnessed, Sam prodded it on, only to watch in frustration as it lay down the minute it felt the drag of the load.

After ten minutes of poking, swearing, and tugging on the harness, he managed to get them moving again. Sam held the lead rope, ignored his pounding head, and walked alongside the carabao. Lollie sat in the cart singing with that bird. The road circled around, with turn after turn, some sharper than others. The wheels crunched over the rocks in the road, and the wind suddenly picked up, swirling and drifting as they moved up the mountain. Sam looked west, where huge dark rain clouds crept over the horizon. Rain was all he needed.

The clouds moved slowly, although not nearly as slowly as the carabao. He'd met army mules less stubborn than these beasts. Another turn and the land on either side of the road leveled out, with a tall rain forest on the left and a rice terrace on the right. One look at the murky water in the rice field, and the lead carabao bawled loud enough to shake the ground, then made a sharp right, jerking the lead from Sam's hand in the fastest move the animal had made yet. It trotted, cart and all, away from Sam and over to the sodden rice field for a mud bath.

"Sam! Sam! What's it doing?" Lollie, still in the cart, was up on her knees, shouting at him. He reached the edge of the field just in time to watch the cart wheels disappear into the thick brown mud.

"Dammit to hell!" He waded into the water after them.

"Sam . . ."

"What!"

"The cart's sinking."

"I can see that!" He moved to unhitch the animals before they decided to roll in the mud, which he knew they were prone to do. Once the hitch was undone and the rear carabao untied, Sam breathed a relieved breath and sagged back against the cart.

It sank some more. He squatted almost shoulder high in the muddy water and felt around to see how deep the wheels were stuck. The cart shifted and moved, and a blond head popped over the side to look at him. "What're you doing?"

"Making mud pies." He scowled up at her. "What the hell does it look like I'm doing?"

"I don't know. If I'd known I wouldn't have asked."

"Awk! Sam's here! Get a shovel!"

"Can't you shut that bird up?"

"Shhh, Medusa. Sam's mad."

"Mad Sam! Mad Sam!"

Sam rammed his fist into the silty bottom, pretending it was Medusa's head, and felt around for the wheel rim. It was stuck in about a foot of mud, but the mud was soft and loose, so he had a chance of being able to pull the cart out himself. He jerked his hand out and swished it around in the water, then walked over to the cart. "Climb out and get on my back, and I'll carry you to the road."

She crawled over to the edge of the cart. "Be quiet, Medusa," she warned the bird, still perched on her shoulder. She slid her feet around his waist and fell onto his back, her hands covering his eye and patch.

"I can't see," he said through gritted teeth.

"Sorry." She slid her arms in a death grip around his neck.

He could feel the bird right next to his ear. Then something pulled his hair.

"Medusa! Stop that! You let go of Sam's hair, right now! That's not nice." She turned her head back toward him and said, "Sorry."

"Awwwwk! Sam's not nice!" The bird screeched into his ear.

Sam slogged through the rice field and trudged up the small bank. He stopped at the road. "Get down."

She slid down his back, and Medusa squawked, "Wheeeeeeeee!"

Lollie's sprained ankle hit the ground, and she gasped when it gave way.

He grabbed her arm. "Are you okay?"

She nodded.

"Just sit down here. This'll take a while," he said, holding her arm while she sat down. The bird paced her shoulder. By the time he'd turned to wade back, she was feeding it peanuts, which he hoped would choke it, or at least make it shut up.

He waded back into the water and went to the cart, dug the wagon tongue out of the mud, and slipped the harness over his own shoulders. Three deep breaths and he pulled hard. It moved one blasted inch.

One of the water buffalo picked that moment to roll— toward him. Sam jumped back. The beast bawled, dunked its horned head, and then shot upright, sending a spray of muddy water over him.

"Damn obnoxious beast," he muttered, wiping the mud from his face while he tugged at the cart. It wouldn't budge.

An hour later he had unloaded half the supplies and carried them to the roadside. The cart was then light enough for him to pull it out. By the time he dropped the cart tongue onto the dirt road, his lungs burned, his back and shoulders hurt, and his thighs ached from laboring through the mud. He sagged against the cart and drank from the water canteen.

Lollie lounged against a pile of blankets covered by the canvas wagon tarp. She looked just as comfortable as could be when she looked up at him. Her gaze locked on the canteen.

"Thirsty?" he asked.

"Uh-huh."

He handed her the canteen. "Why didn't you say something?"

"You looked busy."

"Are you hungry, too?"

She nodded.

"We might as well stop here for the night. I'll build a fire." He gathered some wood and pulled a cardboard cylinder of stick matches from his pocket—wet matches. He swore, then strode over to get some dry ones out of the supplies stacked by the cart. It took him five minutes to find them because of the peanut shells scattered all over the tarp and packs. "What the hell are all these peanut shells doing here?"

"Medusa was hungry."

Sam threw a handful of shells on top of the wood and struck the match. A few minutes later the fire was burning and he'd removed two cans of beans and a pot from the cart. He pulled his knife from its sheath and opened the beans. He turned to put the pot on the fire and ran into one of the carabao. It had left the muddy field and now stood right behind him. It shook like a wet dog, spraying water all around it.

Sam swore.

The other water buffalo moved out of the field, too, and stood next to cart, looking for all the world like it was ready to leave again.

Sam looked heavenward and asked, "Why me?"

Lightning cracked across the sky and thunder bellowed after.

It started to rain, torrents and torrents of rain.

"Sam?"

"What now?"

"I can't breathe."

"There is a God."

"I mean it."

"Now what are you doing?"

"I'm lifting up this heavy thing that's suffocating me."

"Dammit to hell! Drop the tarp! You're letting all the water in!"

"I need some air!"

"I need some sleep."

"Snnnnort. Snno-ork-nork."

Sam groaned. "I never knew a bird could snore."

Lollie sniffled.

"Are you crying?"

"Yes." She sniffed again.

"Why?"

"I can't breathe in here."

Sam swore under his breath.

She sniffed again, then felt him rummage around under the canvas.

A deep banging sound hit the side of the cart. "Ouch! Dammit!"

"What happened?"

"Nothing!" he barked at her again.

"You sure are grouchy at night."

"Snnnnort! Snnno-ork-nork."

"Can't that bird at least be quiet at night?"

"Shh. She's asleep. Don't wake her."

"Why not? I didn't think it was possible, but she's less obnoxious when she's awake."

"She knows you don't like her," Lollie said, just as the heavy tarp suddenly lifted upward. "Oh! That's better. What did you do?"

"I used your crutches as tent stakes." He lay back down. "Now will you please go to sleep?"

"Okay," she whispered and lay there, listening to the loud splattering of the rain on the canvas cover. It had been raining for hours. The minute it started it came down in buckets. The fire had sizzled out, and Sam hauled her into the cart and started throwing the supplies in it. She'd had to dodge two canteens and one heavy pack. Then he'd jumped inside and pulled the tarp over them. They'd sat there, eating the beans cold, right out of the cans, with the heavy, musty canvas over them to keep out the rain.

Now Sam's breathing was quiet, even.

She hesitated a minute, then said, "Sam?"

"What!"

"I . . . uh . . . I . . . ."

"Would you spit it out?"

"I need something."

"What?"

"Some privacy."

"Well, so do I, but you're stuck with both that bird and me, so you'll have to live with it."

"That's not what I meant."

Silence.

"I need to . . . you know. Nature is calling."

Sam's muttereing broke another long pause of silence. "I told you not to drink all that water."

"I was thirsty. Those beans were salty."

"Then go ahead. If nature is calling you, go visit it. Just stay nearby." Then he turned over as if he meant to go back to sleep.

"Sam?"

"Now what?"

"I need some paper."

He mumbled some more, but she heard him burrowing through the supplies. Then she heard the sound of paper crinkling.

"Oh, good, you found some!"

"No, I didn't."

"Yes, you did. I heard it."

"That was my map."

"Oh. Well, maybe—"

"No!"

"I just thought—"

"I know what you thought. N-o, no!"

"Could you hurry, please?"

"I'm sorry, Miss Lah-Roo, but there aren't any Sears Roebuck and Company catalogs in the Philippine Islands." He clattered around some more, and then she heard the sound of paper tearing.

"Here." He shoved some thin paper into her hands.

She rubbed it between her fingers. It was awfully thin. "That's not enough."

She could have sworn she heard his teeth grind. Then he rammed some more into her hands. "Thank you." She crawled over to the edge of the cart, then thought of something. "Sam?"

"Yes."

"What if my ankle gives out?"

He sat up, not saying one word. With a vicious rip he pulled back the canvas, jumped to the muddy ground, and held his arms out to her.

She scrambled over and he lifted her out.

"Can you stand?"

She tested her foot. "A little bit."

"What is that supposed to mean? Either you can or not."

"Not really. You see I can put a little weight on it—"

"Lollie!" he shouted, scaring her, his voice was so loud. "What?"

"Can you stand well enough to do what you need to do?"

"I suppose."

"Do it!"

She started to shuffle slowly away from him. "The paper's getting wet."

"Then you'd better hurry."

She moved a little farther away, into the nearby bushes,

and started to do her business. She turned toward the cart, trying to see him through the black rain. "Sam?"

"What?"

"Can you see me?"

"One! Two!"

She hurried and finished, then limped back to Sam. He turned and lifted the tarp, hauled her inside with little gentleness, and jumped in, slapping the tarp back into place.

He scowled at her. "Is there anything else you need?"

"No."

"Good. Then good night!" He lay down and turned away from her.

A few minutes later there was a loud noise. *Crack! Chomp, chomp, chomp!*

Slowly Sam turned toward her. "What the hell is that?"

"Medusa's awake. She's eating."

"What, the cart?"

"Her peanuts."

Sam swore.

Crack! Chomp, chomp, chomp!

"I think her snoring was quieter," he mumbled. "An artillery barrage is quieter than that bird."

After a few minutes Medusa settled down and was snoring again, only more softly. The rain still beat on the tarp and Sam lay next to Lollie, barely a foot away. His breathing was quiet and even. Hers wasn't. She was wet, soaking wet from her trek in the pouring rain, and now she was cold. She huddled down deeper in the supplies, trying to get warm. There were blankets somewhere, but she was too cold to sit up and look for them. Her teeth began to chatter.

"What is that?" Sam barked, making her jump.

"My teeth. I'm wet and cold."

He turned over and gave her his one-eyed stare. "Use a blanket. That's what they're there for."

"I don't know where they are."

He sat up and searched through the cart. A minute later two blankets sailed past her head. She pulled one around her. With a sharp snap she shook out the other one, lay back down, and drew it over her. She looked over at Sam, but all she saw was his broad back. "Thank you."

He grunted.

She stared up at the dark tarp and listened to the patter of the rain. She closed her eyes, willing herself to sleep. A shiver ran through her. She was still so cold. Turning toward Sam, she watched his back move with each breath. She pulled her hand out from beneath the blanket and waved it around his back. His big body radiated nice warm heat.

Very slowly she inched closer, hoping to feel some of the warmth from his body. The closer she got, the warmer it was. Finally, she managed to get close enough so her shoulder just barely grazed his. She stopped, holding her breath and expecting him to whip around and yell at her. He didn't move. She smiled, feeling so nice, all warm and toasty, so she drew the blanket tighter around her, closed her eyes, and finally drifted off to sleep.

Something tickled Sam's nose. He twitched and willed himself back to sleep. His arm held something warm and soft. The distinct feel of a soft female butt wiggled against him. He awoke instantly—every part of him. He peeled open his eye and stared at the top of a blond head. He blew her hair out of his nose, and she stirred, plastering her butt harder against him. She wiggled some more, then muttered something about "so warm."

He sat up, resting his jaw on one hand, and watched her sigh and draw the blanket up around her small chin.

"Good morning," he said, wondering how she'd feel when she realized she was pressed like a canned fish against his body.

"Mornin'" she whispered, eyes closed, still appearing to be half asleep. Soon her face changed from blissful peace to a frown. She squirmed again, trying to get comfortable.

"You have the boniest knee," she complained, wiggling her butt yet never opening her eyes.

"That's not my knee."

Her eyes shot open. She froze, then scooted away from him so fast it almost made him dizzy. She sat in a corner and eyed him as a cornered mouse eyes a cat.

He gave her his biggest Cheshire cat smile.

She turned away, then a few seconds later looked up at the tarp. "It's still raining."

"Yeah."

"What are we gonna do?"

Crack! Chomp, chomp, chomp!

Sam groaned. *It* was awake.

"Awk! Way down South in the land of cotton . . ."

"I'm going to get up, and then I'm going to kill that bird." Sam wrenched back the tarp. It was raining so hard he could barely see five feet up the road. He let the tarp fall back down and turned to Lollie.

She'd just handed the bird another nut.

Crack! Chomp, chomp, chomp!

Sam winced. He couldn't take much more of this, and didn't know how long he could stand listening to that bird eat.

In less than an hour they'd eaten a breakfast of bread and canned peaches, Lollie had had her nature call and he had untied the carabao from the rock he'd used to secure them. Now, with the animals tied and harnessed to the cart, they were ready to leave. Also, the mynah was still alive, something that said a lot about his self-control. But best of all, it had stopped raining.

Sam slogged through the foot-deep mud back to the cart. "Are you all set?"

"Sure am." Lollie sat perched on the supplies, the ever-present bird on her shoulder. For once Medusa was quiet, although she stared at Sam with a look he didn't like.

Sunlight bled through the clouds, breaking them up until they drifted on, leaving only deep blue sky behind. He moved forward and prodded the carabao. It was slow going, the mud making the road all that much harder to traverse. The road wound through a thick section of rain forest, where the tall, dark crowns of the trees blocked out the sun.

Water, muddy and abundant, streamed between the trees, washing small bits of debris past them. It was oddly quiet, no wind, no birds, which was strange, and no scream or hum of insects. There was only the trickle and occasional rush of water, the bawl of carabao, the squishing and squeaking of the cart rolling along the muddy roadway, and the sound of Lollie and that bird singing.

They reached the end of the rain forest, and the road became steeper, winding up the rocky hillside until finally they crossed onto a plateau. Dark blue mountains ringed the horizon, and Mount Mayon, an active volcano, rose up in the east like a she-devil's breast. A deep lake, as clear and blue as a tropical lagoon, sat at the base of that eastern mountain and upward, in the direction of their road, were more mountaintops, ringed dark gray with water-heavy clouds.

More rain was coming. Sam rounded the bend. They were at the bottom of a deep ravine that ran between two mountains. The narrow valley formed here would be a good place to rest and give Lollie a chance to get out of the cart and limp around a bit. He stopped the carabao, which, since their excursion into the rice field, had been pretty manageable. They'd only plopped down twice.

Sam walked over to the cart and held up his hands to help Lollie out. "We'll stop here." He looked around for the bird. "Where's that black bat?"

"What?"

"The bird."

"Oh, she's right there." Lollie pointed to the rear carabao. The mynah sat on the animal's left horn. "She thinks its her perch."

Sam looked at the stupid bird.

"Why won't you call her by her name?" Lollie asked.

"Medusa?" Sam shrugged. "I don't know. I suppose I should. Every time she opens her mouth snakes should coil from her head."

"You can be so mean."

"I don't like birds."

"I can tell."

He set her on the ground, but held her arm. "How's the ankle?"

She shifted, putting weight on it. "Better. It almost feels normal again." She stretched, raising her arms high above her head. "Do you think that I could walk for a bit tomorrow?"

"Why?" He eyed her skeptically. That was all he needed. Lollie LaRue limping up the road. She'd probably be slower than those water buffalo.

"I'm tired of riding," she said, sighing.

"We'll see." Sam turned to check the other animal.

"Oh, good!"

He stopped and turned back to her. "I said, 'we'll see' as in *maybe*, not yes."

"I know. I heard you."

"I just wanted to make sure you understood. I didn't say yes."

"You said 'we'll see'," she said, then turned and walked toward the bushes mumbling, " 'We' means you and I, and *I'll* see that I do."

Sam watched her disappear into the bushes. Off to visit nature again, he thought, for the tenth time at least. *Women.* He shook his head, then turned back.

It was quiet, almost too quiet. Sam stopped and looked around. The carabao twitched, then turned around. Its bawling broke the silence. The other beast began to sidestep. Sam frowned. Both animals stood, completely still, but their ears twitched rapidly. Sam spun around, suddenly uneasy.

"Awwwwwk!" Medusa screamed, then took off, flying high in the air above the bushes, circling and squawking.

A swift sound, just like rolling thunder, echoed down and around him. A small vibration shook the ground.

Sam looked up.

A wall of water came at him.

22

"Lollie! Lollie!" he yelled, racing for the bushes. The deafening rush of water chased him. He dove into the bushes, tackled her, and rolled down a hillside and through the brush. Over and over they tumbled. Rocks jabbed into him. He pulled her closer, held tighter. The roar grew, thundering and thundering. He jerked her up with him, pinned her against a tree, and locked his arms around the trunk.

With the power of a hundred cannons, the flash flood hit, blasting over them. Water burned up his nose, in his mouth, down his throat. Lollie squirmed against him; he held tighter.

The tree bent. It cracked, uprooted, and they shot down the gorge, riding on the spiraling tree, swirling with the pounding water until it swallowed them. They sped under and over, under and over, with no sound around but the water's hellish roar. It swept them down, down, then with a sudden rush the tree shot up like a rocket, bursting through the foam of pounding water and into the air.

"Breathe!" Sam screamed at Lollie's limp body. "Breathe!"

He felt her gasp for air and took his own.

The tree dropped, slamming into the water with a force that almost threw him free. With dizzying speed, the log spun around and around atop the rapids, then jammed against a rock. The impact threw Sam off. His arm locked around Lollie. They went under, sucked down with the tow and tumbling like dice, until the water once again pushed them to the surface.

He lay back, pulling her up onto his body to keep her head above the surface. The current slowed, little by little, until they drifted into a crater where the floodwater pooled. He used one aching arm to swim to the bank and his last bit of strength to pull them up onto solid ground. He coughed up some water, then rolled Lollie over.

She wasn't breathing.

"Breathe! Damn you, breathe!" He pressed her stomach. Nothing.

He flipped her over, straddled her hips and pressed over and over on her back. "Breathe!"

Nothing.

"You stupid bitch! Breathe!" He pressed down, hard.

Water spewed out of her mouth. She coughed again and again.

The sound washed over him like an answered prayer. He sagged back flat on the ground, panting, his arm flung over his eyes, his knees raised, and he rested, unable to believe they had made it.

Yes, they'd made it, but he shook everywhere—his hands, his legs—and not from the thrill, not from the challenge of defying death. He shook from fear—pure white fear—something he hadn't felt in years.

Sam Forester had defied the odds again, played with chance, and made it, but he was scared, damn scared, because Lollie almost didn't. It took every bit of his willpower not to pull her into his arms. And that kind of emotion was not an easy thing for a man like him to acknowledge.

He heard her pant, felt her stir. Both sounds made his own heart slow down with relief. A few minutes later she moved around some more. Then he felt her shadow over him, blocking out the sun. There was a long silence. He waited for her reaction, the words that would thank him for saving her life.

She kicked him in the shin.

"Ouch! Dammit!" He shot upright, an action that brought stars to his head. "What'd you do that for?"

"You called me a stupid bitch!"

"It got you to breathe, didn't it?" He rubbed his leg. "Damn . . . I just spent the last ten minutes holding on to you until my arms are half dead, saving your butt, and you kick me because of some stupid word."

She stood there, silent. Then she sat down next to him. "Thank you, but don't ever call me stupid again."

He looked at her. "All right. Next time we're in a flash flood I'll call you a dumb bitch."

She looked at him as if to make sure he was teasing her. Her expression showed she realized he was teasing. She smiled at him so brightly that he had to turn away. He didn't want that smile to make his guts stir. He didn't want to care. But what he wanted and what he felt were two different things.

After a few minutes she said, "Sam?"

He turned back.

She cocked her head and stared. "You know, your eye doesn't look so bad."

His hand flew up, feeling for the patch. It was gone. *Of course the patch is gone, you idiot. You just went through liquid hell.*

"Why do you wear it?" she asked.

He shrugged and looked away. "For other people mostly. After it happened, people's reaction was . . . Well, let's just say it wasn't like yours."

"It doesn't bother me," she said, and he could hear the smile in her voice. "In fact it looks like you're winking."

Even he had to laugh at that image. He unbuttoned his shirt pocket and took out a pouch, looked at it for a moment, then untied the strings and opened it. He turned it over, spilling the contents into his palm. Then he bent his head down over his palm and slid another patch into place.

She touched his arm, and he looked up.

"You don't have to do that for me."

"Okay." He pulled off the patch.

She gasped. "You've got an eye!"

"Right now I have two eyes. One's glass." He smiled. Her face was priceless. This was one of his favorite tricks— one he had used to his advantage many times before.

"Let me see." She got to her knees and crawled forward, stopping when she was between his raised knees and placing her hands on his chest so she could get a closer look. She examined his face, her nose only a few inches from his. "Well, if that don't take the rag off the bush."

He did laugh then.

She sat back, never taking her eyes off his. "Why don't you wear it?"

"I save it for special occasions. Balls, teas, coming-out parties, like you have in Belleview."

"*Belvedere*, and stop that. Now, tell me why, really."

He shrugged. "I like the patch."

"If you don't use the eye, why do you have it?"

"It was free."

"Free?"

"Compliments of the United States government."

She sat back on her heels and looked at him for a long time. Then, with a tentative note in her voice, she asked, "How'd you lose your eye?"

He slid the patch back on, flipped it up, and bent down. When he straightened, the patch was in place and the glass eye was in his outstretched hand. "Like this." Then he tossed it lightly, put it back in the pouch, and tucked it away.

She looked just as he'd hoped, uncomfortable. He didn't answer her question and he didn't intend to. It was hard for him to talk about, made him feel vulnerable, and that was a side he refused to show any woman. He stood up and looked around.

Black clouds had rolled over the mountain again and were fast coming their way. "We'd better move to higher ground and find something to eat. Those clouds could start another flood. We're not safe this low."

"Sam?"

He stopped and turned. "What?"

262

Her face was suddenly apprehensive. "What happened to the cart and the animals?"

He saw the real question in her eyes. "Medusa flew away, Lollie. I'm sure she's safe. The cart and the carabao?" He shrugged. "I don't know."

"I heard her squawk and saw her flying above me just before you hit me."

"She swooped around higher than the floodwater, so she might have flown back to the camp. It's been her home for months." Sam started walking toward the steep tree-covered hillside. He heard her scurrying to catch up.

"Sam?" She grabbed his arm.

"Yeah?"

"You don't have to wear that patch for me."

"I know. I'm not." He started to walk again.

"Oh." She sounded disappointed. Then he could hear her walking along behind him. A few silent minutes later she said, "You know what?"

"What?"

"I think you like to wear it because it makes you look more sinister. It makes people wary of you. You like that, don't you?"

He never broke stride, but called back over his shoulder, "I guess you're not a dumb bitch after all." And he kept walking, only faster—protection for his shins.

Lollie sat inside the cave and watched the firelight flicker off its rock walls. Sam had found this cave, seemingly anxious to get her settled in before it started to rain again. They'd walked up some tree-covered hillsides, then out of the gorge and into another small valley. He'd used his knife and a stone to build a fire. Then he'd left her alone to get some more food before it started raining again.

She peeled a banana and ate it, her third since he had left to search for wood and food. And a few minutes ago, true to his forecast, it had started to rain. Wondering where Sam was, she craned her neck to look outside. All she saw was sheet after pouring gray sheet of rain.

Shifting a little, she looked around the cave again. She didn't like being in here all alone. The cave had a sinister atmosphere. It was dark and dank-smelling, and when the thunder rumbled from the storm outside, it echoed like drums through the hollows of the cave. White steam, like smoke from the fires of hell, floated along the back of the cave, where a small cauldron of a mineral pool bubbled up from within the dark depths of the mountain.

Sam had told her they were lucky. The cave was high in the mountain, which he'd said was an inactive volcano. Her stomach had dropped at that news. The minute he'd said it was a volcano, she'd had an image of hell, of red-orange fires bursting up from the very place where they had sought refuge. She turned and eyed the steam from the pool, expecting the devil himself to come bubbling up on a bed of lava any minute.

A twig cracked behind her. She whipped around. The black silhouette of a man with a huge horned head stood at the entrance to the cave.

She screamed.

"Dammit to hell, Lollie! It's me, Sam!" He walked into the firelight.

"Awwwwk! Damn Yankee! Sam's in hell! Get a shovel!"

"Medusa!" Lollie stood up as soon as she spotted the bird, wings open, perched on Sam's head.

"Get her off me, would you?" Sam dropped a bag onto the cave floor.

Lollie lifted her arm, and Medusa flapped and hopped onto it, then walked up to her shoulder and nuzzled her ear. She rubbed the bird's head. "I'm so glad you found her."

"I didn't find her. She found me. Swooped down like a bat and pulled half my hair out." He rubbed the top of his head, then muttered, "I should have known that flying back to the camp was too logical. She *is* a female." He looked at them for a moment, then added, "I don't know how she found us."

"Awwwk! I-ah once was lost, but now I'm found, was blind, like Sam, but now I see . . . Awwwk!"

He scowled. "Keep it up, bird, and we'll have roast fowl for dinner." Sam squatted down beside the bag he'd brought inside.

Lollie looked at it and realized it was the canvas tarp from the cart. He peeled it back, and there were a few of their supplies.

"Some of the supplies washed up at the end of the canyon. There're a few cans of peaches, only one can of beans, this pot, a blanket, and here's something you'll be happy about. Your satchel."

He held up the small canvas bag containing her few personal items: soap, comb, and so forth. He tossed it to her.

"I also found this oilcloth bag." He held up the blue drawstring sack. "I'm not sure what's inside. It wasn't something I packed in the cart. Must belong to someone else." He fumbled with the ties. "Maybe we'll get lucky and there'll be something we need inside."

"Sam . . ." Lollie recognized it immediately, even before Sam jerked it open and spilled the contents into his hand.

"Peanuts?" He groaned.

"Jim slipped the bag to me when he gave me Medusa."

Medusa flew down and took a nut, then waddled over to the tarp. *Crack! Chomp! chomp! chomp!*

Sam winced, shook his head as if someone had just punched him, then laid out the other things he'd brought back. "There were some melons and mangoes—there's a whole grove on the other side of the canyon—more bananas, and your personal favorite." He held up a handful of red berries and grinned.

She crossed her arms and gave him a look that said she didn't think that was funny.

"And, my personal favorite, *ubi*." He held up a handful of long brown-skinned roots.

"What are you-bees?" She scowled at them.

"Yams. Sweet potatoes."

Crack! Chomp! chomp! chomp!

"They go great with roast bird." Sam glared at Medusa and tossed the potato in his hand as if weighing it to throw. The bird just ignored him and cracked open another nut.

"What's in the bottles?" Lollie leaned over to try to see them better.

"Nothing important." Sam jerked the tarp over them.

"Those weren't whiskey bottles, were they?" She frowned, then turned back to him. "Did you have whiskey in that cart?"

"For medicinal purposes, and to keep us warm."

"I thought blankets kept a person warm."

"Not this one." Sam held up the blanket and started wringing the water out of it. He laid it on a rock outcropping near the fire and turned back. "You hungry?"

"I ate some bananas. You go ahead." Lollie watched the rain fall outside. It still came down in sheets. Remembering how fast the water had hit them, she asked, "Will we be safe in here?"

"We'll be fine. This is high ground." He went back to unloading the bundle. "The potatoes will take a while to cook. Maybe you'll want something by then." He turned back and began to stack some rocks near the fire.

"What're you doing?" Lollie leaned over his shoulder.

"Heating the rocks to cook the potatoes."

"Oh." She straightened, watching him stack the flat rocks on the fire. She leaned closer to get a better look, and he suddenly stopped, slowly turning to look up at her. She was so close to his head that their noses almost hit when he turned.

She smiled. "Hi."

He looked away and rubbed his frowning forehead for a minute as if trying to think of something.

"Did you forget how to do it?" she asked, wondering why he'd stopped.

"No." His shoulders stiffened for a moment, and she thought she might have heard him counting under his breath, but before she could comment, he'd taken his knife

266

out of his belt and handed it to her. "Would you do me a favor?"

"Surely." She smiled, happy to help him.

"Take this knife and go over there . . . way over there." He pointed toward the small pile of branches he'd gathered earlier.

She looked to where he pointed.

"And cut some of those leafy branches off the wood," he instructed. "If they're left on they'll smoke too much when we burn them."

"Okay." Off she went to the pile of wood. She lifted a branch and sawed the twigs off, one after another. Before too long she had a whole stack of leafy branches, and all of the firewood was leaf-free except a couple of large branches. She could hear Sam at work near the fire, could hear the clunks as he stacked rocks.

She frowned at her hands, all sticky with sap and pitch. She tried to wipe them on her pants, but the stuff just smeared, making her hands even stickier. Even the knife handle had some of the sap on it. Over her shoulder, she gave Sam a guilty glance. It was his knife, after all. But she was just doing her job, so what harm was a little sap? She figured it would come off, somehow. Whistling "Dixie," she picked up the next hunk of wood, a fairly heavy one, and tried to hack off the leafier branches. No luck.

The sap got stickier with the warmth and dampness of her sweaty palm. She wiped her hand on her pants and tried again but couldn't seem to get it right. Finally she pinned the wood between her bent knees, held the knife in both hands, and whacked at the branch.

It worked. She turned the wood and did it again, and the small leafy branch cracked and fell to the cave floor. She finished that piece and picked up the last one, pinning it between her knees, too. After all, why mess with a successful method?

She raised the knife high and hacked downward. She missed and cut a chunk out of the base of the branch. *If*

267

at first you don't succeed . . . She raised the knife high. It flew right out of her hands.

Oh, darn! She turned to look for the knife.

It was in Sam's right shoulder.

Shocked, she stared at him standing less than ten feet away and staring down at the knife protruding from his bleeding shoulder.

"Any bastard stupid enough to give Lollie LaRue a knife deserves to get stabbed," he muttered and slumped to the floor.

"Sam!" She ran to him. "I'm so sorry! So sorry!" She knelt beside him, patting his cheek. "Please, Sam, wake up, please."

She scrambled around and lifted his head into her lap. "Sam? Sam?" She looked at his pale, dry lips, looked at the knife stuck in his bloody shoulder, and started to cry. She had to do something. She tried patting his cheeks again, only harder, then thought of what he would do in this situation. She slapped his cheek lightly. "Wake up, Sam!"

Nothing.

"Sam? Sam?" She popped his cheek again. "Wake up, you damned Yankee!"

He stared up at her.

"Sam! Oh, I'm so sorry and so glad you're awake. What can I do?"

"Pull it out." His voice was raspier than normal.

"The knife?" she whispered, horrified.

He took a shallow breath. "No, all my teeth." He closed his eye. "Of course I mean the knife."

"Now?"

"Before next year would be nice."

"All right, all right." She grabbed the handle. "How do I pull it out?"

"With your hands."

"No, I meant is there anything special I should do?"

"Don't think, whatever you do. I doubt I could take that."

She grabbed the knife, squeezed her eyes shut, and pulled out the knife.

"You can open your eyes now."

She did. Bright blood seeped through the cut in his shirt. Her stomach lurched. Her eyelids grew heavy.

"Don't you faint, dammit."

Her eyes shot open at the sound of his voice. "I won't."

"Get me the whiskey."

"I don't think you should drink right now, Sam."

"Get the goddamn whiskey. Now!"

"Okay, okay." She gently laid his head down, then scrambled over, grabbed the bottle, and hurried back to his side.

"Give me a drink."

She pulled out the cork and lifted the bottle to his lips. He took a few gulps.

"Now pour some on the wound."

She frowned at him.

"Just do it."

She did, and it was all she could do not to drop the bottle when he sucked in a pain-whistled breath. She sat there helplessly watching him take slow, deep breaths.

Then he opened his eye and looked at her. "Lift me up a little."

She raised him up.

"More," he rasped. "So I can see the wound."

She shifted so her body held him up.

"Pull the shirt aside."

She did as he asked.

He looked down and said, "Okay, put me back down." She did.

"Give me some more to drink."

She lifted the bottle, and he chugged down some more whiskey.

"That's better. Get some kind of cloth to press against the wound to slow the bleeding."

Slowly she lifted his head off her lap and gently settled him back on the floor. She rushed over to the blanket, grabbed it, and hurried back. She knelt next to him and pressed a corner of the blanket against his wound. She started crying again.

"Would you stop crying all over me? You're getting me wet." He opened his sleepy eye and gave her a long look, then a bit of a smile. "Don't worry, Lollipop. I've had worse."

"But I didn't mean to do it," she whispered.

"I know. I'm going to sleep now. You press that against it and it'll stop bleeding soon. It should have some stitches, but . . ." His voice tapered off.

She held her breath and watched him for a minute. He was breathing. She breathed a relieved breath and kept the blanket against his shoulder as his words echoed in her mind. *Stitches . . . stitches . . .*

Should she? She lifted the blanket and looked at the wound. The bleeding had slowed and was barely a trickle of red now, but her guilt was flowing full stream. She eased up and went over to her small satchel and pulled out her comb and soap, then felt around until she found the small tin box Sam had given her when she ruined the laundry.

There were plenty of needles inside and one spool of thread left. She snapped the lid closed, set the satchel aside, and returned to Sam's side. She took a deep breath and stared at the wound. She threaded a needle and then sat there looking from it, to him, trying to muster some nerve.

After five soul-searching minutes she touched his face softly. "Sam?"

A small groan escaped his lips.

"Sam? I've got a needle and thread here. I can stitch you up." She patted his cheek again. "Did you hear me? I can sew you up."

"Yeah," he muttered, never opening his eye.

Well, I guess that means it's okay, she reasoned.

She patted the wound again, took a deep breath, and lowered the needle to the slit in his skin. She pinched the skin together. He didn't make a sound. Very carefully, she slid the needle in and out, wincing and grimacing with each stitch. He moaned once, and her stomach roiled a bit. She took a deep breath, then finally told herself to pretend she was in the embroidery class at Madame Devereaux's. That seemed to work. She reached the end of the wound and finished stitching, tying off the thread just as she always had in school.

She sighed and looked at it. The bleeding had stopped, and her interlocking embroidery stitches were holding perfectly. She had done it. She had really done it.

Wiping the sweat from her forehead, she bent and wadded the blanket up to make a pillow for Sam. Then she put the tin back in her satchel, lay down next to him, and watched him sleep. He was a handsome man. His face was hard and strong, even in sleep. His nose was long and noble and masculine, his cheeks and chin shadowed from his beard. They looked as if they'd been dusted with coal. His neck was thick and molded into those wonderful broad shoulders that had carried her over and over, saved her from drowning, held her against that tree as they shot through the violent water, and pinned her to the wall when he'd first kissed her.

It was the strangest thing. She could almost taste him again. She closed her eyes and willed away her thoughts. Her will wasn't working.

She gave up on that and gave in to the luxury of just watching Sam Forester sleep. After a while she was sure he was okay, and she rested her head on her arm and listened to the splatter of the rain, the crackle of the fire, and Medusa's snore, echoing from the woodpile. Soon she slept, too.

Sam stared at his shoulder and couldn't believe what he saw. He counted to ten, very slowly, then did it again. He looked at Lollie, sitting across from him, that bird on her shoulder as usual, only it was quiet for once. He glanced back at his shoulder and stated the obvious, "You sewed it up."

"Sure enough," she said, then asked, "You don't remember me asking you if I should stitch the cut?"

"No."

"I had needles and thread in my satchel. It's a good thing it washed up here, isn't it?" She smiled proudly.

"I'm not sure."

"Why not?"

"Because if you didn't have the needle and thread, I wouldn't have a wound that looked like . . . an 'L.' "

"Oh, that." She gave a wave of her hand. "It was nothing. I just pretended I was at embroidery class. I only learned how to do the 'E,' the 'G,' and the 'L.' The letter 'L' fit the wound the best."

"Uh-huh." Sam nodded, still staring at his brand. He could do one of two things: he could yell or he could ignore it. He found a third solution: he laughed.

She looked at him oddly, then smiled. "I'm glad you like it."

"Lollie, Lollie, Lollie." Sam shook his head. "You are really something."

"What do you mean?"

"Nothing, but I'm glad you didn't have any buttons." He laughed.

"You know, I didn't think about that. . . ." Her face was thoughtful.

His laughter subsided and he looked at her small face, her wide blue eyes, and burned blond hair. There was something about that face that could move him. Not once since that day in Tondo, in all the time they'd been together, not once had he been bored, and that had never happened with a woman before.

In fact he could barely remember any of the other women who'd been in his life, probably because they'd never been around for more than a week or so before he had an itch to get away. He knew one thing for sure: when he was back at his job and she was long gone, he'd never forget these weeks.

He glanced at the L-shaped wound. He had the scar to remind him.

It had rained on and off for the last two days, but Lollie felt just fine. Sam had healed nicely in the five days since she'd stabbed him. If it hadn't been for the rains, they'd have left sooner, but he didn't want to leave until the skies looked clear. His shoulder was stiff, but he hadn't blamed her or been hard on her. In fact they'd had a friendly truce.

During the long hours she'd talked about her brothers; he'd told her some things that had happened to Jim and him. He'd been lots of places—Europe, Africa, China, and always with Jim. She'd opened up one night and told him about her father. He'd looked at her and said, "Tough break."

She'd asked him about his parents. He'd said he hadn't known who his father was, and his mother and stepsisters had died years before. That was the closest she'd gotten to learning anything about his past. She'd never dared to ask about his eye again, although she was curious.

It had been a fine truce. Even his threats against Medusa had stopped somewhat. . . . Well, at least they had dwindled down to maybe three a day, and he issued those only when Medusa called him a name or ate too noisily.

They'd gone out together and gathered more food that morning. He'd taught her how to find the yams and had said he'd show her how to cook them.

It was late in the afternoon and she'd just given Medusa an empty spool to play with when Sam handed her the potatoes. "Go wash these in the pool."

"Oh, okay." She wasn't too sure about that pool. To her it still looked like the river Styx.

"Hurry up, I've almost got these ready," he said, arranging the rocks around their small fire.

She took a deep breath and walked to the pool edge, where she squatted down and tentatively dipped a pototo into the water, which was warmer than bathwater. She scrubbed one potato, set it down, and started in on the next one—two potato. *One potato, two potato, three potato, four . . .*

She scrubbed the potatoes to the tempo of her rhyme, over and over until she had a nice stack of clean yams next to her. She finished the last one. *Seven potato, more!* And she stood up, still moving to the beat of the rhyme. She shuffled her feet, dancing a bit, and her foot hit the stack, sending them rolling all over.

Oh, rats! She chased them, but two rolled into the pool with a plop. A third potato followed. She reached out. It teetered on the edge of the pool

So did she. Her hand closed over the potato. She'd gotten it! The potato hadn't fallen in.

But Lollie did.

Water burned up her nostrils, down her throat, filled her mouth. She struggled and kicked; then her feet hit the bottom. A splash above her sent water swirling around her and suddenly she was shooting upward.

It was Sam. He pulled her up, and her head burst through the surface. She clung to his neck, coughing and choking. His arms were around her, pressing her hand against him. "You okay?"

She nodded and coughed some more. "Your shoulder . . ."

"It's all right." He set her down on the rock edge, hopped up beside her, and pulled her well away from the edge, then sat next to her just staring. She knew he stared because she could feel it, but she was afraid to look up, ashamed to see the scorn in his face. She'd been fooling around, not paying attention, and gone and gotten herself into another fix.

She felt two inches tall and foolish. So, so foolish. It was just too much. She burst into tears, crying for all she was worth. He put his arm around her and held her, letting her cry like a baby against his good shoulder. "I can't even wash potatoes!" she bawled like that water buffalo. "I stabbed you. I can't do anything right! I'm a jinx, just like Jedidiah said."

"Lollie . . ."

"What?" She sniveled into his neck.

"There's no such thing as a jinx. You just don't have any confidence, and if you want to succeed at something you have to concentrate."

She pulled her face from his neck and looked up.

"Tell me something. When you went over there to wash those potatoes, what were you thinking?"

She thought about it for a minute. Before she'd gone to the pool she'd been wary of it. "I thought about the water. I didn't like the pool."

"So you thought you were afraid."

Actually, at the time, she hadn't been thinking at all.

"And what was all that wiggling about?"

She groaned. He'd seen her dancing to that silly rhyme.

"I was singing," she whispered, unable to look up at him and imagining how she must have looked.

"Singing," he repeated.

She could feel his shoulder shake a little.

"Next time I think you might forget about singing and just concentrate on what you're doing."

"Okay," she whispered.

"You know something?"

"What?"

"As important as concentration is, confidence is even more important. Trust me on this one, I know. You've got to be a fighter to make it in this world, Lollipop. That's something you've never had to face, locked away in your little protected world. But remember, you're not back home in Belton—"

"Belvedere."

"Belvedere. You've got to stand up and spit in the eyes of the world and say 'I will make it.' The only reason you keep failing is because you believe you will."

He leaned back, grabbed one of his bottles, and pulled the cork out with his teeth. "Here, take a swig of this."

"Whiskey?" She grimaced.

"False confidence. Here, try it."

275

She put the bottle to her lips and took a tiny sip, then started to pull it away.

"More." He tilted the bottle back, and the whiskey burned into her mouth. She swallowed and gasped, pushing the bottle away from her lips. Her mouth, her throat, and her stomach were on fire.

He watched her, then shoved the bottle at her. "Again."

She took another mouthful and he handed her the cork, then moved down to her feet and started untying her boots.

"What're you doing?"

"Untying your boots."

"Why?"

"So you can take them off."

"Why?"

"Because, Lollipop, you're going to have your first lesson in believing in yourself."

"What're you gonna make me do, walk through the fire?" She knew he wouldn't do that, but some little devil made her first thought just fly right out of her mouth. She took another drink. The stuff wasn't so bad after all. Once she got used to the burn, she realized she liked the bittersweet flavor and the way it warmed her insides.

"No. You're going to learn to swim."

23

Sam stood in the pool waiting for her. "Are you going to come in here or stand there all night."

"Yes, I believe I will—stand here, that is. I've changed my mind." Lollie stood at the rim of the pool, wearing only the cotton knit sleeveless undershirt and half drawers while she looked at the water. She felt as if it would swallow her whole. In fact, water had already done it once to her today. It seemed downright stupid to willingly get in that cauldron of a pool and chance it again. "I'll just see about Medusa." She turned and started to walk to the bird's makeshift perch.

"Snnnort! Snno-ork-nork . . ."

Rats! Medusa was asleep.

"Doesn't sound like she needs you, right now," Sam announced in a wry tone.

She'd run out of excuses.

"You know how I learned to swim?" Sam swam one-armed out into the pool and stopped in the middle, managing somehow to stay above water.

"How?"

"My uncle threw me off the end of a pier in Lake Michigan, then turned around and walked home. Either I swam or I drowned."

"Your own uncle?"

"Yeah. Now, you and I, on the other hand"—his face took on a menacing look—"aren't related." He swam back toward the edge of the pool, where it was shallow and he could stand.

She didn't like the look in his eye, so she backed up a bit.

"Come on, Lollipop. Or I might have to play uncle."

"I'm scared."

"That's okay, be scared. A little fear is good for you, but doubt isn't. Remember how many people learn to swim every day. If everyone else can do it, so can you. Right?"

"I guess."

"Right?" he almost shouted.

"Right!"

"That's better. Now tell me something."

"What?"

"How do people swim?"

"Well, that's a silly question. I don't know how they swim. If I did I wouldn't be scared."

"Let me rephrase that." He leaned his arms on the rock edge and watched her. "What do you see people doing when they swim?"

"Swimming."

"Describe it, Lollie."

"They just swim." She didn't know what he was talking about, and she didn't understand the perturbed look on his face. He looked as if he was counting again.

"Watch me." He swam out into the pool, turned, and swam back. "What did I do? And don't say 'you swam.'"

She thought about it for a minute, then answered, "You kicked your feet and slapped your arms in the water."

"Ah," he muttered, "the bell chimed."

"What does that mean?"

"Never mind. I used my arms and legs, right?" His voice was very slow and patient.

"Right."

"And you have arms and legs, right?" He gave her a strained smile that made his cheek twitch a little.

"Right." She watched him, trying to understand what he was getting at.

"So you can swim, right?"

"Wrong."

"Why the hell not?" he yelled.

"Because I don't know how!" she yelled back.

"And I can't teach you unless you get in this goddamn pool! So move!"

"I'm scared."

He didn't say anything for the longest time. Then he shrugged as if he didn't care. "I guess you are a failure."

She gritted her teeth. Her pride really hated to hear that. It hadn't sounded so bad when she'd been crying and feeling sorry for herself, but hearing it from him . . . well, that wasn't easy to take. She didn't want Sam to think of her as a failure. She sighed, a long one, then sighed again.

He muttered something and started to get out.

"Wait, I'm coming." She walked to the pool and stood

there, getting all swimmy-headed—an appropriate term—just looking down at that dark, steamy water.

"Sit on the edge and let your legs dangle in the water, to get used to it." He moved in front of her and held her hand while she sat down.

Very slowly she inched her feet into the water.

"A little more . . ."

She lowered her feet until her calves were in the pool.

"Good. Now I'm going to put my hands on your waist, and you slide into the water. I won't let you go under, I promise."

His hands closed around her waist and she squeezed her eyes shut as tightly as she could. She immediately clamped a death grip on his bare shoulder.

"Ouch!" he grunted.

"Did I hurt your wound?"

"No, it's fine. Could you loosen your grip a little? Ah, that's better. Lollie?"

"What?"

"Open your eyes."

"Why?"

"So you can see me."

"Why?"

"So you can learn to swim," he said through gritted teeth.

Her eyes flew open, but her hands immediately tightened on his bare skin again, and her legs clamped like a vise around his waist.

"Something tells me you're not feeling very confident."

"Why?"

"Because you're cutting off my blood flow."

"Oh." She loosened her hands and let her legs relax a bit, but kept whipping her head around looking over her shoulders.

"Let's try something else," he suggested. "Put your arms around my neck, tightly. It's okay. I'll hold you with my arm against my hip, and I'll dip down until only our heads are above water. You just let your body hang in the water and get used to the feel of it. Okay?''

She nodded.

"Unclamp your legs, Lollie."

"Oh," She glanced down at their position. She felt better when she had a good hold of him. "Do I have to?"

"Yes."

Slowly she let her legs go limp in the water.

He walked around the pool, near the edge for the longest time, patiently holding her in the water. Soon her body swirled with each motion and she wasn't feeling so tense. It was kind of fun.

She laughed. "This isn't so bad."

"I think you're ready to learn to float. I'm going to put my arms under you, as if I'm lifting you. Okay?"

"Okay."

He slid his large arm around her back, then slid the other one behind her knees. The minute she felt his hard forearm and the prick of hair on the skin behind her knees her stomach dove. She stiffened.

"I'm not going to drop you," he said patiently, misunderstanding her reaction.

She tried to shift her legs so the cotton drawers would protect her skin from his.

"Stop squirming around or you might slip." He shifted his hold a little and lowered her upper body into the water. "I won't drop you, so straighten your legs and let your arms drift out to the sides. . . . That's right. Now put your head back. Loosen your neck; it's too stiff. Pretend you're lying on a soft bed, and let the water support you. My arms will stay right below so you can't sink. Just relax."

She closed her eyes and let the warm water lap softly around her body. It felt heavenly.

He groaned under his breath, and she opened her eyes. He wasn't looking at her face. His gaze was on her body. He must be watching to see if I'm going to sink, she thought, and closed her eyes again. "That feels nice."

"Hmm."

"It's so warm and wet."

He groaned again.

She looked at him. "Are you all right?"

He took a long, deep breath and tore his gaze away from her body. He didn't answer her; he just watched her face. Then he finally said, "I'm going to let my arms fall away. Don't stiffen," he warned, then muttered something about enough things being stiff.

"What?"

"Nothing. Just stay relaxed." He stooped down in the water until his face was level with her body. His arms fell away.

She floated. "I did it! Look, Sam! I'm doing it!"

"Yeah," he said, "I think you are going to do it." He closed his eye and took a deep breath.

"Let me try it by myself."

"Go ahead, but it's not going to be as much fun." He smiled then, as if he knew something she didn't, which worried her.

"Is something wrong?"

"Yeah, but not with you. Don't worry about it. Go ahead. I'll just stand here and . . . uh . . . watch." With the fire in the cave flickering gold behind him he leaned against the side of the pool, his elbows resting on either side of him, and he did watch. She could feel the heat of his gaze every time she drifted by. She mastered kicking so she could float across the entire pool; then she floated back to him, grabbed the side, and smiled up at him. "Okay, I'm ready."

He didn't say a word, just watched her as if he were fighting something. His cheek twitched a good one.

"Aren't you gonna teach me more?"

"Yeah, Lollipop, I think I'm going to teach you a lot more."

"Good. Let's do it now."

He stood there for the longest time. Then he stepped toward her, lifted her straight up in the air, and held her high above him.

"What are you doing?"

His gaze drifted down from her face to her chest, his look heated. She glanced down and liked to died. She could see right through her underwear, see the nubs of her budded breasts, her navel, and the darker shadow of private hair between her legs. She gasped, "Oh, my Gawd . . ."

He pulled her open mouth down to his and kissed her hard, as if the drive to do so was beyond his control. His large hand spanned her head, held it so his mouth could eat at hers, his tongue filled her mouth and made her want to touch it with her own. He groaned when she did.

He pulled his mouth away and moved to her ear. "You taste like whiskey—fine aged whiskey."

"Oh . . . Sam."

Then his mouth was on her again, drinking her flavor. He slid her down his body in slow inches until all she could do was cling to his neck. His body felt so good against hers. It made her insides weak and made her never want to let go.

His hand still held her head to his hungry mouth, but his other hand skimmed a chilling path down to her hips, over her fanny; then he pressed her against him, moving his hips with hers, slowly. She caught his rhythm and moved her hips in answer. His hand roved upward again, gripped her undershirt, and suddenly jerked it off her right shoulder, shoving it down until it was under her breast. He pulled away from her mouth and looked down. She followed his gaze. Her breast was pressed against the thick curly hair on his chest. He moaned, and the sound floated over her like a teasing hand.

He lifted her above him so his mouth could draw on that breast. Her head fell back, and she reveled in the rough sensation of his tongue flicking her hard nipple. Just when she thought she would scream with the need for something more—a harder touch, something—he opened his mouth wide and sucked so hard that half her breast entered his warm pulling mouth and grazed against his teeth. She moaned until his tongue filled her mouth again, swirling and retreating, only to flick over her lips and teeth in a slow tease.

His hand touched her breast rubbing the tip between his forefinger and thumb, then palming her. He tore the other side of the shirt down, and both of his hands closed over her bottom, pulling her hard against the tight male knot beneath his own underwear. He pushed up against her, the same place he'd touched and fingered and dipped into, the same place he'd said was so hot. And it was. It felt on fire, deep deep fire. She clasped her ankles around him, not from fear of falling into the water but to try to move against him. Something deep inside her needed that friction, wanted it, wanted to rub against him to ease the spiraling heat for a brief moment.

He laid her back on the edge of the pool and started to pull off her clothes. She grabbed his wrist and looked at him, unsure. His gaze never left hers, but he let go of the wad of clothes at her waist and let his fingers trail down to her cloth-covered thighs, stroking her, yet never touching her center. He rubbed both palms from the insides of her knees upward, slowly, stopping at the hollows of her upper thighs. He ran his fingers across the wet cotton, never touching her aching center, teasing. His gaze never left hers. She felt as if he watched every moan escape her dry lips, and she moaned every time he brushed against her. He seemed to watch every reaction on her face, and he stroked ever more slowly.

His right hand drifted to her waist and fingered the ties, then slowly pulled them free. He pulled off her shirt and drawers and flung them on the rocks behind her. He touched her then, with one slow finger. She cried it felt so good.

He pressed his hot callused palm against her and cupped her, then pressed and cupped again, until finally he slid his finger into her. Tears streamed from her eyes over her temples. His thumb circled and flicked the point of her over and over, and another finger stretched inside, and then he moved them in and out until she rose higher and higher.

He leaned over her, his face just inches from hers. His fingers kept on moving, faster and faster. His lips brushed hers, catching her quick breaths.

"Come on, sweet. Come now," he whispered, and his fingers pushed in and his thumb pressed down.

Lollie screamed into his mouth, her body pulsing in thick throbs of the most exquisite death.

She shook in his arms, arms she never wanted to leave. He pushed up out of the pool, pulled off his own drawers, and crawled up her body, his arms holding his weight off her. His lips barely touched hers.

"More," he whispered. Then he kissed her, long, hot, and stroking. He lifted his body to her side and turned her toward him. His hand drifted over her breast, to tease each rib, her stomach, her belly, and down to comb through her mound of hair. Then he stopped and lifted her hand and rubbed it over his chest, pressed it hard against his own nipple, which hardened like hers had done. Then he released her hand and let his drift over her ribs. She followed his lead.

His hand moved down to that place of fire. Her hand scored through his body hair lower and lower, until it brushed a hardness. She pulled back. He groaned and grabbed her hand, placed it on him, and pressed.

"Do it," he whispered, his hand covering hers and making it grip him. He moaned. "That's it. Hold me. More . . . more."

She reached down with her other hand and closed both over him and still could not hold all. He shifted, moving his hips so her hands slid up and down him.

His own hand moved back to her center, delving inside again and starting the friction all over. It happened faster, longer, and harder this time.

He moaned and pulled her hands away from him, then got to his knees, pulling her up with him. He sat back on his heels and pulled her head forward for a deep kiss.

"Inside. I want to be inside you." He lifted her so her

legs went around his waist, her burning center resting against his.

Now she understood, but she didn't want to think, she wanted to feel. Her whole body was so finely alert to him that just a brush of his body hair sent strange hot chills over her. Her mouth met his, an answer to his plea.

"Yes, inside me," she breathed into his mouth just before his tongue filled it. His hands grabbed her hips and slid her back and forth over his length.

He tilted her back so the very tip of him entered her, as his fingers had. Then he touched her center with his thumb over and over, brushing and pushing and rubbing until she tried to pull him closer with her legs.

Just as she throbbed with that exquisite pulsing, he drove up. Something tore within her, a sharp pain, but the pleasure kept coming over and over, so strong that only thick pressure remained.

He pushed upward, and her eyes shot open to look at him. He watched her with a look so intense, so binding, that tears ran freely down her cheeks. He bent his head and drew on each breast over and over, all the while sliding up and pulling back, so slowly. The ecstasy built again, higher and higher, and she pulsed around him.

He stilled, breathing with forced slowness. "Don't move," he whispered.

She didn't. She stayed still in his arms, feeling him absorb her heart and soul, feeling the warmth of his body, the warmth of the fire behind her on her back.

He was still inside her, full and hard, when the fire finally flickered out.

She lay drained against his chest; the only thing holding her up was his arm. He slid one arm under her left knee and raised it.

"More." Then he started again, hard and fast for long, deep minutes. She couldn't believe it was happening again, quicker and faster, and suddenly he was thrusting in rapid tempo. The harder and faster he pushed, the deeper her pleasure spiraled until he dropped her leg, held her hips in his gripping hands, and ground up. She did it again, throbbed and pulsed with such strength that she was dizzy with it. He moaned and she felt him pulse within her just before she blacked out.

Sam stared down at Lollie, asleep in his arms. She thought herself a failure. He laughed at the irony. He'd found something she excelled at. The virgin, the little southern virgin who could talk longer than she could think, had just taken a part of him.

He leaned up on one elbow and watched her sleep. There wasn't anything different about this woman. He'd had women who were prettier, women who had known all the tricks to make a man feel the most intense pleasure, hot pleasure that burned at that moment but eventually died out like that fire.

But not with her. With her he didn't want to leave. With her he wanted to start all over again, to stay inside her until he died. Then he'd never need heaven.

The idea was enough to bring a giant to his knees, and it scared the bloody hell out him. He was no giant. He was a slum kid, a professional soldier, a man who had done things he could never tell her about. They weren't pretty. They weren't things she'd understand. Her world was too different from his.

They were too different, like fire and wood, water and salt, one would consume the other until one of them was lost, gone completely. He had a hunch that he would be the one who was consumed.

He looked at her sleeping so soundly, and something inside him said it would be worth it. But his mind, his logical mind, said it wouldn't. Lollie LaRue and Sam Forester had no future, and it was up to him to make sure they both remembered that.

JILL BARNETT

24

Lollie awoke with the taste of Sam on her lips. She sighed, wanting to open her eyes to see him but not wanting her dreams to end. And wonderful dreams they were, too. Dreams of a husband who whispered "More" against her lips, a houseful of children, laughing children with hair as black as Sam's and the Calhoun family's light blue eyes.

She stirred under the blanket, her body aching in places she didn't know she had. But it was a new ache, a wonderful ache, one that proved last night was no dream. They had experienced something she'd never known existed, and she wanted to go on experiencing it for the rest of her born days.

It was truly amazing what a few weeks could do, and how much one could change. She would never have thought her view of Sam could change so. The roughness, rudeness, and danger she'd found so disagreeable at first were now things that intrigued her, even drew her to him. She'd discovered a strength in his roughness. What she first thought was rudeness was in reality a hard honesty. The dangerous side of Sam Forester turned out to be not something fearful, but a strong sense of valor.

Somehow, somewhere along the way, she'd fallen for Sam. And right now she wanted to see him, have him hold her like he did last night and kiss her, because when Sam kissed her she felt as if the sun had risen inside her.

Sighing, she opened her eyes. He wasn't next to her. She turned over and spotted him sitting near the entrance to the cave. He was in the same position he'd been in when they were prisoners in Luna's camp, his back braced against the rock wall, knees up, arms resting on them, hands dangling between. He watched the rain, and then, as if he sensed her, he turned.

"Mornin'." She smiled, pulled the blanket around her and got up, padding barefooted over to where he sat. She stood there, waiting for him to say something.

He didn't.

A sense of uneasiness swept over her. She stepped closer to him and sat down, tucking the blanket under her arms. He still didn't say anything, so she placed her hand on his arm and slowly trailed her fingers up the length of it.

His gaze turned to her trailing hand, and he watched it for the longest time. Finally his hand covered hers and she felt better, for about two seconds. She realized his hand hadn't covered hers out of affection, like it had so many times the night before. It had covered hers only to stop the movement of her fingers.

"Don't," he said with no gentleness in the word. His tone was an order, coldly given.

"Sam? I thought we . . ."

He pinned her with that one-eyed stare.

"I mean you and I . . . Why are you acting like this?"

"Like what?"

"Like last night didn't happen."

"What about it?"

She stared at him, stunned silent.

"Expecting rings and roses? Sorry there, Lollipop, that's not me."

His words registered. Her chest suddenly ached, as if something inside had just broken.

"Don't go naming the kids. It was just good sex, probably spurred by our circumstances, being stuck together like we've been."

The sun had just fallen from her bright sky. She tried to breathe; it was a struggle. Her throat closed and the back of her eyes burned. She felt helpless against all the things that welled within her. She loved him, but he didn't love her back.

"Oh . . ." she whispered, backing away from him, unable to bear being close to him. Shame swelled over her, humiliating shame. She turned away, crying, but so devastated that her tears were silent. She had never cried such silent tears, but she had never lost her heart before, and now that she had, it was to a man who didn't care. But how could he care? Sam Forester had no heart.

The sunlight broke through the clouds just long enough for Lollie to make her decision. It had stopped raining hours ago, and now the sun was shining—she peered up at the cloudy sky—sort of, and she wasn't about to endure any more of Sam than she'd had to. They'd spent eternal silent hours confined to the cave. The only break had been an occasional comment from Medusa or the sound of her eating peanuts.

It had taken a while for Lollie's hurt to change to anger. Now she was good and angry, not because Sam didn't love her, although that fact still hurt, but because he'd treated her without respect for her feelings—just like her brothers and her father. And some little part of her wanted to hurt him back. She just couldn't help that feeling. She needed to fight back.

The fighting would start now.

She knew how the bird affected Sam, so after a while she and Medusa had sung their repertoire of songs. Every time the bird had sung a chorus Lollie had given her a nut and taken great pleasure in watching Sam wince and grimace at Medusa's loud munching. After a good half hour of *crack! chomp! chomp! chomp!* Sam had stood, twitched at the noise, and said something about getting some wood while the rain had let up. Then he'd left.

She intended to do the same, but she wouldn't come back. He'd said something about spitting in the eyes of the world. Well, she'd do that to him. If he didn't want her, fine. After hurting her, using her, she didn't think Sam Forester was worth the trouble it would take to spit.

She picked up the bundle beside her and walked over to Medusa. "Come on, hop up. We're going for a little walk."

Medusa hopped up on her shoulder, settled down, and began to whistle "Dixie." She went to the entrance to the cave, where she stood and looked down. It had been steep climbing when they'd found the cave, but now, since the rains, the mountainside had eroded even more, and from her angle it looked very steep.

"Spit at the world, Lollie," she told herself. Then she squared her shoulders, gave Medusa a nut, and walked along the edge of the hillside, working her way toward a tree that stood on the right side of the entrance.

Sam had worked his way up the muddy hill, his arms loaded with firewood. He'd made a decision, something that had been one hell of a lot easier without the accompaniment of that obnoxious bird. He would talk to Lollie, explain that they had no future. He figured he could live with that. It was honest. What he couldn't live with was the look of shame and hurt she tried to hide from him so proudly. Somehow she'd gotten to him. Somehow that little southern woman had a damn hard grip on him, and he'd never have thought that possible.

They were so different. She had family, respect, social standing, wealth. He had money; his earnings over the last ten years had been substantial enough that when he wished to stop working, he could. Nothing had ever made him think he wanted to stop what he was doing. He'd always imagined that any other way of life would be boring. Of course he'd never known anything but fighting—fighting his way out of the slums and fighting for profit and excitement.

Lollie's life couldn't have been more different from his. She didn't have to fight for anything. Everything was given to her, just because of who she was and who her family was. That kind of acceptance wasn't something he could understand or respect. In fact, he still wasn't quite sure what it was about her that got to him. But something did, and whatever it was, it touched a place he didn't want touched.

Time would make it easier for her, and once she was back home where she belonged, she'd eventually forget him. But he doubted if he'd ever forget her face and the way it had changed from joy to confusion to devastation. He did know that the sooner he put an end to this, the better it would be for both of them. But that didn't make the doing of it any more palatable.

What he wanted was to do the same thing he'd done last night—hold her, kiss her, lose himself in her until nothing else mattered but her. To do so would be crazy, sort of like continuing to walk the wrong way once you realized you were lost. Sam knew one thing for sure: a part of him was lost.

Life could deal a man the strangest hands. Who'd have thought it possible? Lollie LaRue and him, Sam Forester— unbelievable. Jesus Christ, was he sunk.

He shook his head, resigned to the inevitable, and he climbed up to the cave and dropped the armful of wood. He straightened and scanned the cave. He couldn't see Lollie. He stepped deeper inside and looked in the dark corners.

Nothing.

An uneasy feeling coiled inside him. He ran to edge of the pool. Nothing. Then he realized the bird was gone. That stupid damn woman had left, alone.

"Aw crap," he muttered, running to the cave entrance and slowly scanned the densely treed area below. His trained eye covered every inch of the panorama. He didn't see a sign of her. He squatted down and looked for signs of her trail in the soft mud hillside. Her boot prints went along the east side, and he followed them until he reached the first tree.

There he found two peanut shells and smiled. This wouldn't be so difficult after all. The two of them were leaving a trail that could be found by a blind man—or a one-eyed soldier.

"Shh!" Lollie said to Medusa as she listened to the sounds of the jungle. She could have sworn she'd heard someone. She peered out from behind a plump, vine-tied tree trunk just as a small molelike animal moved past. It had beady little eyes that reminded her of that awful Colonel Luna.

She looked up at the thick forest surrounding her and again felt uneasy. She listened a little longer to all the sounds, the dark sounds—hums and whistles and screeches. Some of the birds in the crowns of the trees sounded just like humans, dying humans. The deeper she traveled, the scarier the noises became, and the darker the forest. She glanced upward. The clouds had completely swallowed any patches of blue sky, and she thought she heard the rumble of thunder in the distance.

"Awk! I wish I was in Dixie. Hurrah! Hurrah!"

"So do I Medusa, so do I." She looked around the dark, thick rain forest with it tall ominous trees, vines that looked like snakes hanging all around her, and the noise, the horrible noise. "You know what? It was really stupid to take off all alone."

"Awk! Stupid bitch!" Medusa's voice had lowered into a perfect imitation of Sam's muttering.

"Did Sam call me that again?"

"Awk! Damn Yankee!"

She smiled. The bird had that right. "It would serve him right if I went back and gave him enough trouble to make him never forget what he did. In fact . . ." She turned and looked at Medusa. "You know what? We should have never left. He's the one who's acted like . . . well, like Sam. Right, Medusa?"

"Awk! I'm Medusa. I'm a mynah! Sam's an ass!"

"I won't argue that point," Lollie mumbled, her head churning with the bud of a new idea, a much better one and a much safer one. "Since he's the problem, why should we leave the cave? This was a dumb idea." She paused and shook a warning finger at the bird. "But don't you tell him I said that. I'd die before I'd admit to Sam that I'd lived up to his expectations."

She handed Medusa another peanut, a bribe. "We're going back. He might not love me, but he's not gonna forget me. I'll make sure of that." She turned and marched back the way she'd come.

Ten minutes later, as she made her way through the edge of the basin forest, it began to rain again. She looked up at the mountain and could see the dark entrance to the cave. If she cut across to the right, she could get there without having to climb that steep hillside. From the bottom she could see that the other side was less treacherous.

"Come on, Medusa, we're going back a quicker way." She turned off her old trail just as the first drops of rain splattered to the basin floor.

The rain came down in sheets, sending any evidence of Lollie's trail running down the hillside. Sam pushed off from the tree where he'd stopped to try to determine her direction. She'd been traveling southeast, so he had continued that way even after the rain washed her tracks away.

He cupped his hands around his mouth. "Lollie! Lollie!" He waited, but the only reply was the thrumming of the rain and a distant rumble of thunder. He whistled the shrill signal Jim used to call the bird. Nothing.

This was all his fault. He'd been pretty hard on her, and he'd meant to be, but he'd had no idea she would do something like this. Although now that he thought about it, he realized he should have figured as much. It was just the kind of stupid thing she'd do, especially after the stupid thing he'd done.

If she was hurt, or worse, he'd never forgive himself. He sagged against a tree, respite from the torrents of water raining down from the sky. He cupped his hands again and called her name.

No answer.

He moved on, the mud so deep now that it came almost to his knees. Rivers of water flowed around the trees, dragging vines and plants and ground debris with them, but worse yet, he'd seen a vampire snake slithering against the tow of the water. Rains like this could wash every deadly reptile and insect right into her, and she'd never know what hit her.

"Lollie! Lollie!" he called, stumbling in the mud and dragging himself up again.

Lightning cracked across the almost black sky, and it rained so hard he could barely see three feet in front of him. His foot hit some loose mud, and the hillside gave way. He slid down, his body flowing on a stream of mud and water. He grabbed a tree and pulled himself out of the flow, then up, where he watched the water run around him.

The most incredible feeling of despair welled inside him. He had to find her.

A hour later he pulled himself up and out of the water again. The basin floor was a lake, the surrounding hillsides little more than rivers, carrying monsoon rains into the valley below. But worse yet, it was dark. He looked back over his shoulder, knowing he couldn't see her, couldn't find her in this rain. He crawled up the hill, making his way back to the cave. Maybe he could light a fire and signal her somehow. Maybe she'd see it and come back.

He felt so damned helpless. Never in his entire life had he felt so powerless, completely unable to do anything but wait. He wanted to punch something. He wanted some sense of control. He had none.

He moved to the trees alongside the cave. The ground gave way, and he slid back down the hillside. He lay in the muddy mire and looked up. The hillside was even steeper than before, almost straight up, and the rain still came down so hard that he could see only halfway up the hill. He swiped his hair from his face and grabbed a long exposed root. He pulled himself up, hand over hand, slipping only when one of the tree roots broke. He climbed onto the bed of roots near the base of the tree. The woody roots weren't as slick as the mud, and he could get his footing. He slid both arms around the tree and pulled his body up and over until he was safely on the sheltered side of the trunk. He stood there, catching his breath before he moved on to the next tangle of roots and slowly worked his way up the hillside.

He reached the tree nearest the cave and crawled toward the entrance. The rain slackened a bit, and he could see the glow from the fire within. Lightning cracked, thunder boomed, and a huge muddy section of the hillside slid over him. He held on and finally dragged himself up to the cave. He lay there with his muddy head on his aching arms, panting from the struggle to pull against the weight of the mud.

"No, no. Listen closely. It's 'Look away, look away, look away, *Dixie*land.' "

Sam's head shot up at the sound of Lollie's voice. She sat in the warm, dry, mudless circle of the fire teaching that goddamn song to a group of Igorot natives. She munched on something. He wiped the mud from his nose. It smelled like meat—cooked meat. Something they hadn't had since they'd left the camp.

She tossed a bone over her shoulder and reached out. One of the men gave her a beaming smile of worship, then cut off a slice from the huge hunk of cooked meat that was spitted over the fire. She sat there like a queen before her subjects, eating the meat and chatting away with those men who couldn't understand a word she said.

All this time his mind had been filled with the horrors of what could have happened to her. He'd been scared she was hurt or worse. But she'd been back here all the time. Safe, dry, warm, and having a great old time eating and singing.

He crawled onto his knees, mud dripping from his head and his patch string, leaves stuck to his cheeks. He couldn't speak. His hands began to itch with the sudden need to squeeze something—her throat would be nice for starters.

She must have sensed his presence, because she turned and glanced at him.

"Oh, hi, Sam." She turned her attention back to the native men while distractedly handing the bird a piece of banana.

Red. He saw nothing but red. His shout of pure rage echoed through the cave, and he heard it, but it was as if it wasn't him. He dove at her, his hands reaching for her.

In an instant he was flat on the ground, natives all over him like fruit flies on papaya.

"Let me at her! Let me at her!" He struggled to break their hold, madder than hell. "You stupid bitch! I've been searching this whole goddamn valley for you! For two hours! For two frigging hours!" He pulled, trying to break free of the natives' hold.

Her face had been startled at first, then a little frightened, and now it looked angry. The damn woman looked bloody angry.

"I told you not to call me that." She glared at him.

He glared back. "I'll call you any damn thing I want, especially when the phrase fits!" He struggled again, then shouted at the men who held him, "Let me go, dammit!"

They turned toward Lollie, looking for her to tell them what to do. He couldn't believe it.

"Let me go!" he spouted off in Tagalog.

They ignored him and turned to her again, chanting, calling her a golden princess.

He gave her a look that could almost singe off the rest of that blond hair. "Tell them to let me go."

She glanced at her fingernail and made a fuss about cleaning it. He wasn't fooled one bit.

"Lollie," he said, gritting his teeth.

She glanced up at him. "Why should I?"

"Because if you don't, when I get loose—which I can promise you I will—you'll wish you had."

"I think not."

"Tell them, now!"

"Uh-uh." She shook her head.

The natives looked from him to her. He glared at them and they muttered something. The only word he made out was "madman." That was the problem. His anger showed. He needed to reason with her. Well, he thought, "persuade" was a better term, since reasoning with her would be like trying to fight a war with a squirt gun. "Tell them to let me go and I won't do anything."

"I think you're still mad."

"Okay, you're right. I am still mad."

"Then telling them to let you go wouldn't be very smart, would it?"

He was silent.

"Now, as I see it, when someone's action isn't very smart, some people call them stupid, don't they, Sam?"

"Dammit, Lollie!"

"If I tell them to let you go, then I'd be acting stupid, wouldn't I?"

"I'm warning you. I will get loose."

She gave a little wave of her hand. "Fine. I'm willing to take that chance. I wouldn't want to do anything *stupid*." She smiled and fluttered her eyelashes.

He chose not to speak. Nothing short of thrashing her would do at that moment. While they bound his hands and feet, he sat there, relishing the mental image of just what he'd do to her when he got free. They moved him to a dark corner, four of the men forming a guard wall between Lollie and him.

She picked up something and then sauntered toward him. One of the men touched her arm, pointed at Sam, and shook his head as if to warn her away. "I'll be fine," she said, and strolled over to stand next to Sam, watching and gloating. "Hungry?" she asked with a smirk.

When he didn't answer, she plopped down next to him and held up a hunk of meat. "It's some kind of bird. Turkey, I think. One of the natives kept gobbling when he handed it to me. Want some?"

"Untie me."

"I think you're still mad."

"I'm more hungry than I am angry. Untie me. I won't do anything," he lied.

She rested her chin on her other hand and looked thoughtful. "Hmm. I don't think so. I'll feed you." She smiled and held the meat in front of his mouth.

This was war. He never looked away from her smug face. He just bit into the meat, hard, tearing it from the bone and slowly chewing. He'd fight this battle in his own way. He took another bite of the meat.

"Good, huh?"

He chewed and swallowed.

She smiled, having no idea what was coming. He'd wipe that smile right off her smug little southern face.

"More," he whispered, then opened his mouth and waited.

Her eyes grew wide. Then she flushed, looking at him uneasily. She'd remembered. She held the meat up again. He tore off more, still never breaking his gaze. He chewed as slowly as he could, then swallowed. He let his gaze drift downward and rest on her breasts.

"More."

She held the meat again. He bit again, but his stare was purposely hot and directed right at her chest. She squirmed. He hid his smile. "More."

She fed him and he let his gaze drift back to hers. Her face was still flushed, getting more so each time he said it, and her mouth was open just enough to tell him he'd made his point. He leaned his head back against the rock and raked her body with the hottest look he could give. "Yeah, it's real good. The best thing I've had in my mouth since last night."

She gasped and scooted back, and he thought for a moment she might hit him with the turkey leg.

One for you, Sammy old boy. He didn't gloat, externally anyway.

Then she leaned forward, holding out the meat for him to take another bite. She had to lean farther than before, and he had a perfect view down the front of her shirt.

Automatically he opened his mouth, his concentration having just moved to the scenery.

"Sam . . ." Her voice was soft, but he really wasn't listening. He opened his mouth to bite off the meat.

"Stick this in your mouth." She let go of the turkey leg, leaving it stuck in his mouth. She stood, and without another glance she walked away.

Sam coughed and pushed the meat out of his mouth with his tongue, swearing the whole time. Then he scowled at her retreating back. Her head was high, her shoulders back, and she walked with all the swagger of a winning general. Lollie LaRue could fight after all.

Sam's scowl changed to a small smile of admiration.

One for Lollie.

25

A ring of bluish mountains surrounded the small group of people winding their way across a jagged lava bed. Lollie lounged against the back of the sedan chair the native men had fashioned for her comfort. She leaned down from her seat supported on the shoulders of four of the men and gestured to one of the natives. "You can take off the gag." She pointed to Sam and then to her own mouth. The native stopped Sam with a spear in his face and took off the gag she'd tied on him.

"Sam?"

He spit a few times, then scowled at her.

"Where do you think we're going?"

"How the hell should I know? I'm not a damn mind reader," Sam barked back at her just before he stumbled on the rock bed. He'd been having a rough time of it, from what she could tell. His hands were still bound behind him, something that made his rock crossing more difficult. For some odd little devil of a reason that made her smile.

"Do you think you keep stumbling because your feet are too big?" She gave him an innocent smile before adding, "You should watch where you're going Sam. You're gonna hurt yourself."

"I can't watch where I'm going *and* answer stupid questions." He traversed the large rocks and rain-slick stones, and she could see he had trouble keeping his balance. Of course the two spears at his back could have had something to do with it, too. It served him right for calling her questions stupid again.

"What's wrong, Sam? Having a bad day? Isn't your gun . . ." She raised a finger to her lips in concentration. "Ah, yes, now I remember the phrase. Isn't your gun the most accurate on the target range?"

He mumbled something about showing her just how accurate his gun was.

"What was that? I didn't quite hear you."

He scowled at her and almost fell.

"You're having all kinds of trouble, aren't you? Does your head hurt? Do you think maybe there's no one home today?" she inquired as politely as she could without laughing out loud. This was really fun.

"Keep it up!"

"Here, Medusa. Have a nut." She gave the bird a peanut.

Crack! Chomp! chomp! chomp!

Smiling like the cat who had just eaten the canary, she leaned back in her comfortable sedan chair and watched Sam's shoulders jerk with each loud crunch.

By afternoon they reached the native village after traveling over mountain trails so steep that Lollie had held her breath when she looked down. Sam hadn't seemed bothered by the height, but when she'd fed Medusa, the chomping sound had echoed loudly as they moved through the tall mountains. It had sounded as if the mountaintops were cracking away.

They reached a deep gorge, and the natives set down the chair and helped her up. Medusa squawked and flew from her shoulder. She turned, her gaze following Medusa as she flew to a tree on the opposite side. Past the gorge was a village of nipa huts built on bamboo stilts that balanced the huts about six feet off the ground. The huts varied in size and seemed to be scattered randomly throughout the village. Their ages varied, from the bright greenish color of new nipa palm to the grayed brown of weathered palm.

Playing in the center of the village was a group of children, and women worked at everything from washing clothing and hanging it on the branches of wide acacia trees to cooking and basket weaving. Smoke from cook fires billowed up here and there, and a large bamboo-fenced area, not unlike a corral, housed carabao that wallowed in the muddy center.

Her native guides stood talking to their leader. At least she assumed he was the leader since he gave most of the orders. She'd determined through hand gestures and one-word speeches that his name was Mojala. He was the one who'd gobbled and scratched the ground like a turkey when she frowned at the meat he'd given her. Between the two of them, they managed to understand each other fairly well.

Sam had tried to get the natives to side with him, but he'd had no luck, to her delight. He'd let go with a few heated outbursts at first, most of them colorful descriptions of his retribution. She'd gagged him, and he'd continued shouting against the gag until he lapsed into stubborn, brooding silence.

Lollie tried not to gloat, an effort that took a great deal of willpower. Instead, she eyed the narrow bamboo bridge that spanned the deep gorge surrounding the village. The gorge reminded her of a castle moat and appeared to supply the same type of protection.

"Lallooee."

She turned at the sound of Mojala's voice. He pointed

301

at the bridge and nodded. He wanted her to cross it. The bridge was little more than a rickety gangplank of gaping bamboo poles strung on hemp, and it swayed like a cradle in the wind that whistled through the gorge.

She frowned and pointed at the bridge. "Cross that?"

Mojala nodded with grinning vigor.

The bridge looked . . . challenging.

"What's wrong, Lollipop, afraid of a little hundred-foot drop"—Sam paused with meaning—"straight down?"

She looked from the bridge to the rock-jutted riverbed at the bottom of the gorge. She didn't want to cross it.

Sam laughed, then whistled, imitating the sound of something falling, and ended by saying "Splat!"

She glared at him, not appreciating his sick humor. He grinned back, leaving no doubt in her mind that he enjoyed her reaction.

Less than a week ago, she wouldn't have crossed the bridge. She'd have sat her fanny down and refused to do it. But not now. The Lollie LaRue who had waited for the world to come to her existed no more, at least not if the new Lollie could help it. Her pride was at stake here.

Armed with more determination than courage, she started walking toward the bridge. Mojala grabbed her elbow, stopping her. He shook his head and held up a finger. She assumed he meant for her to wait. He pointed to her boots. She looked down, then up at him. He pointed to his bare feet: she was supposed to take her boots off.

Sam's snort of laughter set her teeth on edge. She ignored him and sat down to untie her boots. She glanced up just as the two natives guarding Sam untied him, then gestured for him to sit down and remove his boots, too. She undid the second lace and then suddenly remembered the guerrilla hut.

"Wait!" She shot up like a bedspring and ran over to Sam just as he was starting to pull off a boot. She grabbed his right boot and pulled with all her might.

"Dammit, Lollie, let go!" Sam tried to jerk his foot back and kick her off him, but she clung to it and fell to the ground, struggling to get it off. Before he could grab her, the natives pressed spears to his neck and chest, holding him still.

The boot popped off his foot, and she scooted back, reached inside, and removed the knife he kept hidden there. She held it up, letting it dangle between her forefinger and thumb. "Thought I'd forgotten, didn't you?"

Sam glared fire at her. "That was our only means of escape, you stupid—"

She aimed the knife at him and warned, "Don't say it."

She could hear his teeth grind.

"Why would we need to escape?" she said. "You told me yourself they're treating me like a princess. If we want to leave I'll order them to let us leave." She sat back down and pulled off a boot, then a sock.

"Some of the tribes here in the north are headhunters."

She froze, halfway through pulling off her other boot. Her head whipped around, and she looked at Sam to see if he looked like he was fooling.

He wasn't. He looked dead serious.

She looked at Mojala, not that it did much good, since she had no idea what a headhunter looked like. The natives, who had been so nice to her until now, grinned and pointed to the bridge. She turned back to Sam. "I don't believe you."

He shrugged. "It's too late now anyway."

She stood up and dusted off her fanny, ignoring him. One of the natives took her boots for her and started across the bridge. It rocked and swayed with his weight, but that didn't seem to faze him. He'd tied her boots together and slung them over his tattooed shoulder, then grabbed the bamboo poles that served as handrails—wobbly handrails, since they were strung with hemp to the two thicker bamboo poles that served as footrails. The man walked with his feet turned out so his toes could curl over the bamboo, and he waddled across the bridge as if wasn't moving at all.

Now it was her turn. She took a deep breath and stepped

onto the foot poles. The bridge moved a little but not too badly. She duck-waddled about halfway across before a gust of wind whipped through the gorge, making the bridge sway like a hammock in a gale.

Lollie did what she did better than anything in the world. She screamed.

The sound echoed through the gorge, up the walls, and into the sky. The natives jumped back, mumbling and pointing and shaking their heads. Villagers ran and scurried to see why the entire heavens were screaming. Some shouted that their gods must be very angry, for never had they heard such a sound.

The bridge wiggled and rocked so she couldn't move. Her scream echoed back from the gorge below as if to say "Look down at me." But she knew if she looked down she'd fall.

Just when she thought she might give in to the dizzying sway of the bridge, Sam was at her back. "Don't look down. Lean back against my chest and take some deep breaths. I won't let you fall."

The second her head touched his shoulder a calmness washed over her. It was Sam the hero, there to save her again, even after she'd tormented him.

"Very slowly slide your foot back until you can lift it and stand on my foot. Understand?"

"Yes," she whispered, already succeeding in getting her left foot on his. The wind set the bridge to rocking. It took longer to get her right foot on his, but she finally did. The minute they'd started to rock Sam had whispered near her ear that it was all right. She believed him.

"Now place your hands on mine, hold my wrist if you'll feel better, and I'm going to walk us both the rest of the way. All right?"

She nodded.

He moved so smoothly she hardly felt the rocking of the bridge, and by the time she'd expelled her breath they were safely on the other side, on firm ground.

"Sam. Thank you." She slipped her arms around his

neck and held on tight until she stopped shaking inside. His hands brushed slowly over her back, calming her and just letting her rest within the haven of his arms. She could hear the muttering of the natives surrounding them, but she didn't care. She just wanted him to hold her.

Finally she pulled back and looked up at him. His face searched hers, and she felt as if he were trying to make sure she was okay. Suddenly the need to kiss him was so strong that she started to move toward his mouth. She could see the same urge in his own gaze. He lowered his head.

A spear suddenly jabbed between them. Mojala stood there frowning at Sam and giving him some angry order. She assumed he was telling Sam to let her go. He waved the spear in front of their noses, so they had to let go of each other, but not before she heard Sam swear under his breath. They both stepped back.

The minute there was space between them a horde of native girls swarmed around Sam like orphans around a Christmas tree. They oohed and aahed and ran their hands all over him as if to see if he was real.

Lollie ignored the men who were fingering her singed blond hair and stroking her hands. She watched with horror as the girls giggled and laughed and stroked Sam. She wanted to grab handfuls of their hip-long black glossy hair and snatch them bald. She shook off the native man who was trying to kiss her left foot and started to walk over and extract Sam from that group of females when she was stopped cold by the sound of his laughter.

She looked right at his preening face and decided *he* was one she should snatch bald. He'd slid his arms around two of the girls—naturally the prettiest ones—and he smiled at them as they laid their heads against his shoulders. He liked it. Those women were fawning all over him, and he lapped it up like cream.

She was so upset she could have spit, and he must have sensed her stare because his laughing gaze met hers. She scowled. He shrugged with such forced innocence that it took every ounce of her pride and willpower to stand there instead of ripping through the crowd. Of course she wasn't sure whom she'd rather rip apart, the native women or Sam.

Someone touched her arm, and she assumed it was one of the native men, so she turned around, intending to lap up the natives' fawning, like Sam had, a little sauce for the goose. An old woman with hair whiter than a cotton bud stood beside her. Her face had all the wrinkles of time and age, and yet her small black eyes showed a childlike twinkle that said, "I'm not dead yet." She was stocky and solid, with a bosom from shoulder to waist and the shortest legs Lollie had ever seen. The woman was all knees and only tall enough to reach Lollie's shoulder.

"Come 'ere, ducks," she said in what Lollie thought might be some sort of English accent.

"You speak English!" She could have hugged the little woman.

"Not 'xactly. Them's there what would argue that what I speaks ain't English at all, ducks. Now come along 'ere. I 'aven't got all day, you know." The woman spun around and marched down the dirt path toward the village.

Lollie hurried along behind the woman. "I guess that means you aren't headhunters."

"Not bloody likely," she shot back over an aged-slumped shoulder.

"You're native, aren't you?" Lollie asked, recognizing that the woman had all the native features including three tattooed designs on her arms and neck.

"Me 'usband were from London. A bloody fine man 'e was, too, me 'Arry. 'E was a sailor on the *Victoria Crown*, finest bloody ship to sail the seas. I lived there for five years, I did. Till 'im 'n' me came back 'ere. The fever was what took 'im. That was in 'ninety."

"I'm sorry."

The woman stopped and spun around like a top, hands planted on her sturdy hips. "Why? You never met the man. That's what you ought to be sorry 'bout."

306

Lollie stood there a little dumbfounded, then tried to explain, "Well, I wish I had met him . . . uh, I mean, I'm sorry you are all alone now. You know, sorry he's gone."

"I ain't all alone. Got fifteen young ones and thirty-eight children what call me Granny. Ain't bloody likely I'd be alone, what with them to trip over. Blimey, every time I turn around, one of em's tugging 'n' yanking on me like a bloody duchess wit the bellpull."

Lollie laughed. Then realized she didn't even know the woman's name. "I'm Eulalie Grace LaRue, and you can call me Lollie. What's your name?"

The woman stopped and slowly turned around. "Yer name is Lollie LaRue?"

She nodded.

The woman's black eyes raked her from head to toe. "You should 'ave shot the bloomin' fool that named you fer a hootchy-kootchy dancer." She shook her head, then answered, "Me name's Oktu'bre, but call me Oku."

"Where are we going, Oku?"

"To meet the bloomin' king."

"Oh." Lollie stopped cold. "The king?"

" 'Course the king. Who's you think ran the bloody village, a carabao? Not to worry yer 'ead 'bout it. 'E's just like any other man—farts 'n' belches the village down when 'e 'as a bloody bellyache."

And speaking of men, Lollie remembered Sam. She turned around in time to see him being pulled along behind her by his horde of women. She whipped her head back around so he wouldn't see her looking at him. She didn't want to give him the satisfaction.

Oku led her to a large circle to the left of the village. A group of natives stood in a ring, children staring in awe and the women whispering. The loud clash of a large gong split the air, and suddenly the natives parted, revealing a small three-walled hut with a stone bench. On the bench sat a native man, obviously the king.

Smoke streamed upward from a small black pipe he held in his red-stained teeth. A long black braid hung over a shoulder, and his entire torso was tattooed. Four necklaces of betel nut and crystal and lapis hung around his neck, and a cluster of red rooster feathers dangled from his long black braid. At his side a young boy stood fanning him with palm fronds. On his other side stood two guards, both with spears and long bolo knives.

As she approached, the king stood, and the sunlight caught a bit of shiny metal on his thigh. The man had the sharpest, most lethal-looking knife she'd ever seen strapped to his leg. In his hand was a small wooden disk stained a deep red. He whipped his hand up, and she jumped a little, but then realized that he'd thrown the disk.

Spinning, the disk slid down a string attached to his finger, and when it reached the end of the string it rolled right back up again. She'd never seen anything like it. The disk slid up and down the string as if by magic command. He gave the string a quick snap, and the disk flew back up into his hand. Her gaze moved upward. He stared at her, then took the pipe from his mouth and stuck the pipe stem in a dark scarred slit in his cheek.

Lollie knew she was staring open-mouthed, but she figured anyone would be surprised to see a man stick a smoking pipe through a slit in his cheek. He hadn't even bothered to put it out, and now a small stream of white smoke drifted up from beside his dark ear.

Oku elbowed her, gesturing that Lollie should walk up to him. She took a deep breath and started toward him. Sam walked quickly by her, heading straight for the man. Lollie walked faster, churning her elbows. She didn't want him to get there first.

Her bare foot hit a stone, and she hopped the last few feet, ignoring Sam's snort of laughter. She stood before the king, barefoot, dressed in men's clothing, her hair singed, but her pride intact. She held out her hand. "It's nice to meet you."

The king looked at her hand, then held out the hand with the disk. "Yo-yo," he said.

She frowned, then repeated, "Yo-yo."

"Yo-yo." He nodded and smiled with those strange red teeth. Then he stared at her face and very slowly walked around her, pausing every so often to pat her hair, her shoulder, even her behind, which almost brought a squeal from her.

"Maybe they're not headhunters . . . just cannibals," Sam whispered out of the corner of his mouth.

At that exact moment Medusa flew overhead and soared downward to land on Lollie's head. Then she hopped onto her shoulder. "I'm Medusa. I'm a mynah. Sam's an ass."

The natives started mumbling and pointing at Medusa, their expressions awed. Mojala said something to the king, and while they spoke Sam leaned down. "Maybe they'll add that bird to the pot for flavoring. It's salty enough."

"They are not cannibals, Sam. Oku told me. You're just trying to scare me."

"Isn't she one of them?"

Lollie nodded, handing Medusa a nut.

"And you believe her, huh?" Sam had a disbelieving look on his face.

She glared at him. The king had walked his full circle and now stood in front of them speaking to the villagers. She didn't understand a word he said, but she understood the really foul word Sam muttered. She gasped and looked at him, but the king grabbed her in a big bear hug that lifted her clean off the ground. He carried her for a moment, then set her down, and in a flash, Oku was at her side.

"What's going on?" she asked the woman over the shouts of the native crowd.

"The king has just adopted you as his daughter. He calls you the golden princess."

"Me?" She pointed to her chest in surprise, then caught Sam's look and couldn't help but grin. "I'm a princess," she told him, her nose a little higher in the air. "Royalty, not dinner."

"Probably the royal dinner," he said out of the corner of his mouth, and he made the mistake of leaning toward her. "Ouch!" He stepped back. "Damn bird almost bit me."

She ignored Sam and handed Medusa a treat. "Here, Medusa, eat the nut, not Sam."

Crack! Chomp! Chomp! Chomp!

Sam turned his back to her and flinched at the noise. She opted for a glimpse of the king, her new father. He'd pulled the pipe from his cheek, and he puffed on it while he listened to the native girls talk to him. She stretched to try to figure out what they were talking about.

"Come along 'ere." Oku all but yanked Lollie's arm out of its socket, then dragged her away from the group.

"What's going to happen to Sam?"

Oku stopped and looked at her. They both looked back at Sam. The girls had flocked around him again, touching him, giggling. One of them, a beautiful girl who was taller than the others, placed a ring of flowers on his head. He was grinning like a fool.

Lollie had a sudden urge to walk over and rip him away from all those petting female hands. She didn't, though. What Sam did was no concern of hers. She stuck her chin up and turned around. Oku watched her, and she squirmed a little under the woman's scrutiny. She had a sudden feeling that the older woman could read every thought in her head and her heart.

Sam watched Lollie leave with the old woman. The golden princess. Now they were in real trouble. The people of this tribe weren't headhunters—he'd known that—but they weren't overly friendly, either, especially to foreigners, thanks to the Spanish. They seemed friendly to Lollie, but only the women were pleasant to him. That Mojala fellow was talking to the king, but Sam couldn't hear what they said. The way the man kept talking and then scowling at Sam, he figured something was up, something not in his favor.

He glanced in Lollie's direction. They were separated, and that was not a good thing, especially if they need to get out of there fast. The golden princess, he mentally repeated, rubbing his stubbled chin. The tribe was superstitious. That could work in his favor. His hand drifted to his shirt pocket, and he felt for the bulge of his pouch. It was still there and probably just the thing to get them out of this mess. He gave the pocket a quick pat, his insurance. Sam had the perfect plan.

Lollie followed Oku up a bamboo ladder and onto a porch that ran around the outside of a hut. From the low eaves hung baskets filled with mangoes, papayas, bananas, breadfruit, and more. The baskets on the end held chickens, complete with nests.

She shoved open a bamboo and thatch door, and Lollie followed her inside, never expecting what she found. The interior of the dark hut was dimly lit with a lamp made from a large, oval seashell with a hemp wick. Oku moved from lamp to lamp, lighting five more just like it until the dark hut was as bright as morning. Lollie slowly turned, staring in amazement at the things inside, things she'd never have expected to see in a native hut.

Victorian clutter covered every bamboo wall of the hut. Giant brass urns as big as Oku herself, filled with sea-colored peacock feathers, stood like plumed guards near the door. A huge English oak sideboard with three beveled mirrors ran a good ten feet down the left wall and atop its polished surface were silver serving pieces, including tureens and a full tea service. They sat polished and gleaming in resplendence in the crude hut.

A rosewood sofa and chair upholstered in deep rose tapestry sat nearby, and a marble-topped spindle table held a painted dolphin lamp with a mushroom bubble shade in red glass that had multicolored prisms dangling from its rim. Six-inch gold fringe hung from a crimson table scarf that covered another square table on which were arranged at least twenty clocks.

Lollie walked over to them. There was a brass steeple clock, a French carriage clock with pictures of Napoleon painted on its sides, a clock of metal shaped like a cannon with the clock face serving as a cannon's wheel, and numerous German porcelain clocks of various sizes. Every clock on the table was set for a different time. Suddenly the most unusual clock began to chime, playing "Greensleeves" while its top moved. The piece itself was shaped like a black enamel cylinder with gold leaf and mother-of-pearl inlays. Its top was brass, finely wrought, and in the center was a golden brass sun. Revolving slowly around the sun was a replica of the earth, and as the top moved, a small moon also revolved around the earth. It was the most delightful thing she'd ever seen. That clock finished, and another started playing "Auld Lang Syne."

"These are wonderful," Lollie said.

Oku smiled and joined her. As one clock finished, another would start, and they watched them all perform. When the last clock gonged, Oku took Lollie's hand and led her past a huge draped bed to a painted screen. She folded it back, and there was the most wonderful thing Lollie had seen in weeks.

"A bathtub!" Lollie turned toward the older woman, ready to beg. She'd have killed for bath.

"You going to stand 'ere gawking like Ben Ben or are you going to take off them bloody rags?"

It took Lollie twenty seconds to strip, two hours to soak and bathe and cool down, half an hour to dress in the native garments Oku gave her, and five seconds to find out that Sam was going to die.

26

Sam's perfect plan had failed. He tried to jerk his wrists free of the thick hemp ropes. No luck. He strained his feet, too, trying to loosen the ankle bindings, but they were as tight as the ones that bound his hands around the bamboo pole behind him.

He glanced at the group of native guards huddled on his right. Mojala stood in the middle, bragging and holding up Sam's glass eye. It had worked before, when he'd been in Africa. He'd managed to convince some Matabele tribal warriors that he was a god by removing his eye and tossing it around like a ball. It didn't work this time.

That damn Mojala had started ranting and raving, and the next thing Sam knew he was dragged from the king's hut, tied to this bamboo pole, and his eye was in Mojala's thieving hands.

"Sam!" Lollie ran toward him. "Oh, Sam!" She slammed into him, driving the wind from his lungs. Her arms clamped like a vise around him, and she babbled into his chest. "They're gonna kill you!"

"I gathered that much from the contraption they're building over there."

Lollie leaned around him and looked at a group of men who were building what Sam figured to be a catapult of some sort.

"Looks like they're going to fling me out over the gorge. It's a long drop." He whistled again as he'd done when he wanted to irk her earlier, at the bridge. He'd never thought he'd be the splat.

She stepped back. "How can you joke about this? It's not funny!"

"Yeah, but I'll die laughing." He tried for a wry smile, but wasn't sure he'd succeeded when he saw her face. She looked as if she was about to cry. Her head was down, and she took little quivering breaths. He could tell she was having a hard time.

"I was just thinkin' . . ."

Yes, he thought, that would give her a hard time.

"It's my fault you're here." She looked up at him. "I've been a lot of trouble to you for these last weeks, haven't I?"

"I haven't been bored." He smiled a little, looking at her bowed head.

"I wish . . ." She stopped and raised her head, her expression suddenly changed from defeat to something more . . . inspirational.

He could almost smell the smoke.

She scanned the village, then looked at the king's throne. "Where's the king?"

"Your new daddy?"

"Seriously, Sam, where is he?"

"In that big hut over there." Sam nodded at it.

"I'll be right back," she said and started for the hut, but she stopped suddenly, then turned back and came close to him. She placed her hand on his chest and looked up at him, an almost pained expression of pure determination on her small face. "You're not gonna die." Then she spun around, stuck her chin up high enough to drown if it rained, and marched toward the king's hut like a conquering general.

Sam watched her head for the hut. She intended to save him by speaking her mind—no doubt a short talk. He struggled and pulled at his wrist bindings. They didn't give. He looked at the catapult and came to one conclusion: he *was* going to die.

Lollie took one deep breath and marched into the king's hut. It was huge and long and filled with people. The king sat in a large woven chair decorated with red feathers and shells and the like. The moment they realized she was there the noise subsided, and the natives who stood between her and the king parted.

Trying to act as if she wasn't the least bit intimidated, she walked toward him. He watched her every step, and when she stopped in front of him he sat there, waiting.

"Yo-yo," she said, figuring she should at least greet him like before.

He looked at her, then reached over to the table next to him and grabbed that wooden disk. He held it in his open palm and nodded. "Yo-yo."

There was a ruckus behind her, and she could feel someone else's presence. Oku stood next to her.

"What in the bloody 'ell do you think yer doing?"

"Saving Sam," she whispered.

" 'Ow?"

"I'm not exactly sure, but please tell the king that Sam's not evil."

Oku spoke, but before she finished, Mojala moved to the king and said something. Then he held out his hand and showed something to the king.

"Sam's eye!" Lollie turned to Oku. "He's got Sam's eye."

Oku gave her a look that said she thought Lollie was crazy.

"His glass eye," she explained. "Get it back."

Oku spoke, and Mojala argued. The king just sat there.

Lollie elbowed Oku in the ribs. "Forget about the eye for now. Tell them they can't hurt Sam. He's my friend."

Oku spoke, and gasps filled the room. Then everyone began to whisper. Mojala looked mad enough to spit spears. The king raised his hand, and the room quieted.

Lollie had an uneasy feeling. "Do they always act so excited?"

"You want to save 'im, don't you?"

She nodded.

"I told 'em 'e was . . . uh . . . a little more than a friend."

"That's all right. Anything to save him."

"Anything?"

She nodded again.

"I told 'em you wanted to share a bloomin' blanket."

Lollie looked at her a moment. "That's all right. I'd share a blanket with him, or anything else I had. I owe him my life."

"Lord luv a duck! I told 'em you wanted 'im for a mate. You know, like a bloody 'usband."

"Oh, my Gawd . . ." Then Lollie thought about it, after a moment smiled a devious little smile of success. "That's okay, Oku. You did what you had to." She tried not to look too happy.

Oku shrugged, but before Lollie could say anything, the king's daughters had knelt at their father's knees and were all talking at once.

"What's happening?" Lollie whispered to Oku.

"Them's what want 'im, too."

The king stood, and the room was again silent. He made some kind of announcement, touching each daughter's head. Then he walked to Lollie and touched hers. The people cheered, and many of them left.

"Oku? What's going on? Did I get him?"

"Not 'xactly."

"What do you mean, not exactly?"

"You 'ave to win 'im."

"Win him? How?"

"Games."

Games?

"Go thank 'im." Oku nodded toward the king, who looked at Lollie expectantly.

"How do I say thank you?"

"*Salamat.*"

Lollie walked up to the king and bowed her head. "Sallee-mot," she said, then raised her head, only to be greeted by a red-toothed smile. She decided to ensure her thanks and whispered, "Yo-yo." And then she backed away.

He frowned at her and raised the wooden disk, letting it slid down the string again. "Yo-yo," he said with a nod.

Oku grabbed Lollie's arm and pulled her out of the hut, telling her the games would start at noon, only an hour away.

For the past hour Sam had been rubbing the ropes against a joint on the bamboo pole. It had taken him only a few minutes to decide that leaving his fate in the hands of Lollie LaRue was the equivalent of committing suicide. He knew the only way for him to get free was to do it himself. It was then that he'd discovered the rough spot on the joint of the pole. He'd pulled the hemp rope as taut as he could and slowly, with hard force, rubbed it over and over the spot. Slowly but surely the rough threads of hemp gave way.

He felt another thread give way and smiled. It wouldn't take much longer.

The villagers milled around and soon began to form lines, leaving a wide open path in front of him. Some of the men who'd been with Mojala used bamboo poles to mark off sections in the dirt. He slowed his rubbing until he was sure what he was doing was undetectable, and he watched them, trying to determine what the circles and lines were for.

Five carabao were led to the far end of what Sam now realized was an arena. The king and his entourage walked through the crowd to the beat of the village gong. In the entourage were the king's five daughters, and pulling up the rear was the sixth, the golden princess herself, Lollie LaRue.

Still dressed in the native wraps of brightly striped cloth, she spoke to that Oku woman as they walked along. As if beckoned, she looked at Sam, her face worried. She left the line and walked over to him.

317

"I only have a moment," she whispered. "But don't worry, Sam, I'm gonna save you."

"What is going on?" He nodded at the dirt arena.

"Some kind of tournament. I have to win each event and then you'll be free, sort of."

"What do you mean, 'sort of'?"

"I have to go; Oku's waving me over." She hurried away, but stopped and turned. "Don't worry, Sam. I know I can do it. I'm not gonna fail." Her chin went up, and her face was so serious, so determined, that he almost laughed, but another small part of him—a foolish part of him—believed her. It didn't matter now, though, because at that moment he managed to break the ropes. All he needed was a distraction and a chance to grab Lollie.

Sam waited for the right moment.

Ten minutes later Lollie's bottom smacked down hard on the ridged back of her galloping carabao. She gripped the rope around the beast's horns, locked her feet under its neck, and held on for dear life as she thundered past the others. She didn't dare look at Sam or at Oku, who had been her prodder—the person who slapped the animal at the start of the race.

The animal's hooves pounded, and her small body jolted up and down, but she held the rope so tightly that she didn't think a crowbar could have pried it away. In the distance she could hear the cheers of the villagers, but her animal bounded by them so fast she couldn't see anything but a blur of color. Lordy, but these beasts could run when they wanted to.

A roar echoed around her, and the animal suddenly skidded to a stop so fast she almost flew over the horns. When she could focus again, she shook her head to clear it. In a wink two natives pulled her off, and she was on solid ground before the other animals had lumbered over the line. The last daughter across the line, a young girl who looked to be only fifteen, was eliminated. According to

Oku, the subsequent games would be the same—one contestant eliminated per event.

"Not bloody bad. You stayed on!" Oku said, running up to Lollie, who still swayed a little, and hugging her.

Lollie pushed her hair from her face. "I never knew they could lope like that."

Oku mumbled something.

"What?" Lollie asked.

"Nothing." Oku stuck her hand in her pocket and looked away.

"I won, didn't I?" Lollie hugged Oku again.

The old woman grinned. "You bloody did." Then she patted Lollie on the back.

"Ouch!" Lollie jumped back, then turned and grabbed Oku's hand. She turned it over and there was a long, sharp needle poking out from the woman's palm. The needle was attached to a string around her finger. Lollie frowned at her.

Oku closed her fist and hid it behind her back. "It got the bloody beast running, now, didn't it?"

"Did you cheat?"

"No. I bloomin' prodded, just like I was supposed to." Oku's face took on a stubborn look.

Lollie glanced over at Sam. He looked surprised. She smiled, tilted her head a notch higher, and gave him a wave that said "I did it!" He didn't have to know about the needle, especially since this was a matter of life and death, his.

There were three more games. In the one called *pindutan*, or hand-squeezing, Lollie came in second but managed to stay in the running. The oldest daughter, Mari, squeezed so hard she almost broke Lollie's fingers. Mari was the prettiest of the king's natural daughters, and she really wanted Sam. That awareness alone gave Lollie the stamina to hold out.

It also enabled her to win the next contest, something called San Juan, a game of mud-throwing. She wanted to hit the other woman with mud so badly that she kept her eyes open and, remembering Sam's advice, she aimed three feet to the left. Lollie hit her every time.

After being allowed to clean up—Oku had been right there with water and cloths and encouragement for Lollie—they were seated for *buwal paré,* the second to the last game. She'd been worried about this one, not having any idea what it was, and knowing that the two remaining daughters had experience on their side. She sat there and remembered all the times Sam had rescued her, telling herself that now it was her turn to help him and that she could do this, whatever it was, no matter how difficult.

The king strolled over and dropped a handful of sticks on the tabletop. Lollie smiled. Her chances of winning had just increased tenfold. The game was the native equivalent of pickup sticks, something she'd played for long, lonely hours in the Hickory House nursery. It was one of the few games a child could play alone.

She won that event, too.

Three down, one more to go.

Mari and Lollie stood waiting. This would be the last game. Oku came forward to explain to Lollie what she had to do. The old woman had a small box in her hand. She handed it to her with the explanation. Lollie opened the box. It was all she could do not to drop the box and scream. She slammed the lid shut. The box held a cockroach, which she had to race by making noises and tickling its underside to make it scuttle forward.

"Oku, I can't do this," she whispered.

"Then Mari will get Sam," Oku said matter-of-factly.

Lollie followed Oku's gaze to where the last daughter stood. She was absolutely the most beautiful girl Lollie had ever seen. She had straight hair that swayed down to the backs of her knees and shone like black jet. Lollie touched the ragged ends of her burned hair and sighed. Mari was tall and slim, and she had a bigger bosom. The conversation between Jim and Sam flashed through her mind. She promptly marched over to the starting line.

The two women knelt at their places, holding the boxes

with the bugs. Lollie looked up at Sam. He was talking to Oku and his shaking his head. She wondered if they were talking about her.

Sam probably believed she couldn't do it. Her mind flashed with the image of the rice bowl sitting on his angry head, and she had to admit he had good reason, a baptism by rice so to speak. But that had been weeks before. That Lollie LaRue was gone, she hoped.

She took the lid off the box and scowled at the thing. It was brown and black and just as ugly as sin. A native stood nearby with a spear. When the spear dropped, the race would start. Lollie looked at Mari, who fingered her bug, stroking it as if it were treasured pet.

Lollie's stomach tightened, and chills raced down her arms. The cockroaches were just awful.

The spear dropped. Mari tickled her bug and whistled and coaxed it along. Lollie took a deep breath, squeezed her eyes shut and touched the cockroach's underside. It scurried over her finger.

She screamed loud enough to crack heaven. Her bug flew right past Mari's.

Lollie's shriek finally faded into a groan. Her shaking stopped. She opened her eyes to see her brown and black bug crawling in the dirt a good three feet past the finish line. She'd won again, and she'd saved Sam.

The natives closed in, carrying her along with the crowd. She laughed and smiled. She was so excited. She'd done it! Pushing and digging her way through the natives, she worked her way toward him, shouting his name, "Sam! Sam!"

She reached the end of the crowd and squeezed through, a proud smile on her face.

Sam was gone.

27

Lollie looked at Oku, who practically dragged her down some steep, primitive steps that had been cut into the gorge. "Where are you taking me?"

"Awk! Quiet! You bloomin' little pecker!" Medusa was perched on Oku's head.

"Shh, Medusa!" Lollie glared at Oku's back. "I see she's picked up a new voice."

"Keep that bloody pigeon quiet. We're almost there." Oku yanked even harder on Lollie's hand as they ran down what must have been a thousand steps. "Mojala's got them all worked up. You bloody need to get out now."

Lollie followed Oku down the rocky steps, looking toward the bottom of the gorge. Soon she could see the river below, coming closer and closer, and a small rock landing, and a native boat.

Sam stood on the rock landing, pacing. He glanced up and stopped. "Get the lead out!"

"Awk! Sam's here. Get a shovel fer the bloomin' little pecker!"

"Goddamn bird," Sam muttered.

Lollie tried to stop, but Oku dragged her across the flat granite rock. Before she could blink, Sam had lifted her into the boat.

"It took you long enough. And couldn't you leave the damn bird behind?" Sam said, scowling at her before he turned and unhooked a rope that moored the boat.

" 'Ere." Oku leaned over and handed Sam something. "Better keep yer prized possessions a little closer to yer 'eart. Don't gamble with what you don't want to lose, if you get me drift.''

Oku had given Sam back his glass eye. He put it in the pouch. "Thanks." He turned and gave Lollie a long, odd look, then grabbed the oar. "I get it, old woman."

He scowled at Lollie. "Will you sit the hell down so we can get out of here?" He turned back to do something.

Lollie stood there, stunned and wondering what right he had to be angry. She should be angry after going through all those awful games to save him, when all the time he'd been able to escape. And he hadn't even seen her win the last one. She shivered, still feeling that horrid bug. Then she thought about his face—angry, trying to intimidate her, all bossy male arrogance.

He turned around.

She punched him in the jaw, hard.

"Dammit to hell!"

The boat wobbled and tipped, and both Sam and Lollie fell into the water. She started to move her arms the way Sam had taught her, but he grabbed her clothes and pulled her over to the landing. He hauled her onto the rock ledge, none too gently, and flipped the boat over.

"Get in . . . now." He was mad.

Well, she wasn't too happy with him, either. She stuck her nose up and stepped into the boat.

"Sit down!" He shook the water from his head and got in, too. He glared at her. She glared right back.

" 'Ave yer bloody fight later. Go!" Oku shouted, then pointed up to where a large number of natives with torches were running down the steps.

Lollie took Medusa from Oku and sat, but gave Sam her most scathing look.

He shoved off.

She turned to the old woman, wanting to thank her, to say something, but not good-bye. "Will you be all right?" She pointed at the approaching natives.

Oku grinned and waved them on. "Them won't 'urt me." She laughed. "I'm the bloomin' king's mother!" She blew

323

Lollie a kiss and waved as the boat caught the current and drifted downstream.

Half an hour later, Medusa was perched on the rim of the drifting boat, singing "Britannia Rules the Waves." Sam and Lollie sat at opposite ends of the boat, each trying to outglare the other. Lollie felt she was winning.

Sam lolled against the bow of the boat, his arms hooked over the rim of the bow, his long legs stretched out in front of him, and his boots resting on the small plank seat in the center of the wooden boat. He reached up and rubbed his dark, stubbly jaw and eyed her.

"I hope it hurts." She stuck her nose up and looked away.

"Why the hell are you so mad?"

"Because I saved you!"

"So."

She slowly turned back to face him. "So? So? Your backside isn't throbbing from riding one of those . . . those horned cows. You didn't have your hand crushed by some love-struck native girl. You didn't have mud flung at you and natives yelling at you. You damn Yankee, you! You didn't have to tickle a horrid cockroach!" She shivered.

"Are you through?" He hadn't moved, hadn't flinched, just sat there, grinning.

"No! I hate you, Sam. I really do."

"Then why did you save me?" He looked as if he was really enjoying this, which made her even madder.

"Because I thought *you* needed saving for a change!"

"I suppose I did."

"No, you didn't, you damn Yankee. I fought for you and you'd already gotten free by the time I'd won."

"Awk! Damn Yankee!"

"Shhh! Quiet, Medusa." She frowned. "How did you get free?"

"I rubbed the ropes against the bamboo until they tore through."

"You didn't think I could do it, did you? I was trying to hard, concentrating just like you said, fighting the way you'd told me to, and all the while you didn't think I could do it."

"Now, Lollie—"

"Don't you 'now Lollie' me, you ... you—" She stopped, her attention caught by a distant sound. She peered over his shoulder. "Sam?"

"Hmm?"

"Is that a waterfall we're heading for?"

He shot upright, his head whipping around. "Oh, shit!" He grabbed an oar and rammed it into the water, trying to take the boat out of the current. "Grab the other oar and try to slow the boat down!"

She stuck the oar in the water. The current was so strong it took every ounce of strength to hold the oar straight. The water pushed and pulled, and the boat would start to slow, then suddenly pick up speed. Every time that happened Sam swore.

The river was long and rushing faster and faster, the roar of falling water grew louder and a massive waterfall, as wide as the native village, lay in the distance. The boat rocked and reeled—the same motions that always made her sick. This time she was too scared to be sick.

Sam's oar broke with a piercing crack. He swore, threw it in the river, and grabbed her oar. A few seconds later it broke, too. He just stared at the falls.

"Sam?"

"What?"

"Are we gonna die?"

He turned back, sat down, and looked at her. The boat picked up speed. "I can't get us out of this one, Lollipop."

She looked at Medusa and held out her hand for the bird to step onto. "You sweet bird . . ."

Sam snorted.

She ignored him and lifted the mynah bird high. "Go! Fly back to Jim, Medusa." She tossed the bird up, and it flew up, higher and higher. Then it circled and flew off into the trees.

Lollie looked at Sam for a long moment. They were

gonna die, and he sat there, opposite her, no sign of emotion on his hard, handsome face. She wondered what he was thinking. "Sam?"

"What?"

"I love you."

He closed his eye and looked down briefly.

"I'm sorry I hit you."

"Lollie . . . I—"

The current grew so strong the boat whipped ahead.

"You what?" She held the sides of the boat.

He took a deep, resolved breath. "I was wrong. It wasn't just good sex. I only said that to stop the whole thing before it went too far. We're too different, you and I. I'm a mongrel, a slum mongrel. You're show stock."

"I don't care, Sam. I love you."

The boat dipped and swirled. His hands gripped the rim of the boat until his knuckles were white. His gaze never left her face. "Yeah. Me, too."

She looked at him. "Do you mean it?"

The boat spun again, and she held on tighter, needing to hear his answer.

"Yeah."

"Oh, Sam. I needed you."

He laughed in that sardonic way of his. "You sure did. I've never met anyone who needed saving as much as you." He paused, looked at the water for an uncomfortable moment, and admitted, "I *was* jealous."

"Good." She smiled. Then her smile faded as she remembered something she'd wanted so badly. "I dreamed of having your children, Sam."

"Aw crap, Lollie, I told you I'm not a hero in a romance novel. I can't say that stuff to you."

"I love you, Sam!" She had to shout over the roar of the water.

He didn't say anything.

"Say something, please! We're gonna die!" she screamed at him.

He took a deep breath and yelled, "I lost my eye when I was a prisoner during a rebellion in Angola. I was twenty-five years old, and I'd been sent by the army to Angola to fight. I got caught. They tortured me to get the whereabouts of a rebel leader who was being protected by the United States. I wouldn't tell them. They took out an eye before anyone could get me out. No one knew the U.S. was involved. Jim got me out, against orders." He didn't look at her.

"I still love you, Sam!"

"Dammit . . ." He sounded angry. With a deep breath of resignation he looked at her. "I'd have given you those kids."

"What?"

"I said I'd have given you those kids!" He moved closer to her and touched her cheek.

"I wanted you to love me again," she admited, "like that night in the cave."

He gave her a slow, lazy smile. "I wanted to . . . more."

"Oh, Sam." She covered his hand with her own. "I wanted your face be the last one I saw every night, and I wanted to wake up every morning in your arms."

"Come here," he yelled, opening his arms.

She dove into them. "You're my hero."

"You're . . . aw, crap," he muttered.

"What?"

He looked down at her. "I almost said, 'You're my heart.' "

"Am I?"

"Yeah."

She tore her gaze from his and looked toward the falls, only twenty feet away.

"Come closer, Lollipop." He put his hand behind her head and pulled her up until she was just a kiss away. "If I'm going to die, I'll do it with at least part of me where I want it to be."

He kissed her, hard, and they soared over the falls.

* * *

She was cold, so, so cold. Sam's arms were no longer around her, protecting her. A heat swelled over her, a hot beating heat that burned over her back, her shoulders. Something heavy, maybe the weight of death, pressed against her, over and over.

"Breathe, dammit! Breathe!"

She could hear Sam, far, far away.

"Fight! Dammit! You fought for me before! Fight for me now! Breathe!"

Breathe. She had to breathe. . . .

Someone turned her over. The heat was on her front now. Something pressed hard, pushing on her belly. Then Sam was near.

"Breathe, you stupid bitch, breathe!" His breath hit her lips. She could taste him. Sam . . . her Sam.

She coughed and choked, water pouring out of her mouth as if her chest were emptying. Someone flipped her over as she coughed. Sand stuck to her wet face. She turned her head.

She heard Sam's voice. "There is a God."

She took long slow breaths of air. Every muscle felt dead, drained. Her eyes were still closed, but the darkness was gone. Her eyelids seemed to lighten. The heat that had beaten against her was sun. She could feel it now, burning down on her. She could feel her wet clothes, feel the fabric, the sand beneath her, Sam's presence kneeling next to her.

"I told you not to call me that, you damn Yankee," she said, her voice little more than a rasp.

"It worked, didn't it?" His voice gave away his smile.

She drummed up the energy to roll over. The sun flared in her eyes. She groaned and flung her arm over them, not caring about the sand that stuck to her. She could feel the grit of it against her closed eyelids.

She was just glad she could feel at all. "Are we alive?"

"Last time I looked."

"Hmm." She took a couple of deep breaths and tried to sit up. Her whole head throbbed. She slapped a hand against her left temple and groaned.

Sam's hands steadied her. "Easy. I've got you."

She peeled open her eyes. The first thing she saw was Sam's one-eyed face.

His expression told her exactly how he felt about her for that one brief instant. Then the harsh, cynical curtain came down again. He released her and looked around the sandy bank.

It all happened so fast she wasn't sure she'd really seen it. All the things he'd admitted came back to her. She looked at him. His back was to her, but his neck was red, bright red, like it had been that time in her bungalow, the time Medusa repeated his words. Sam was embarrassed.

A pang of pure joy shot through her, and she smiled, resisting the urge to hum a victory tune. She really should let him off the hook. But she remembered the cockroach race. She counted to one thousand, then said, "I love you, Sam."

Silence.

"You damn Yankee . . ."

He turned around slowly, looked into her eyes. "Me, too."

"Say it."

"I just did."

"No, you didn't. You said 'me too.' "

"Same thing."

"No, it's not. Say it, or I'll—"

"What? Sock me in the jaw again?"

"That reminds me . . ." She hauled off and rammed her fist into his hard stomach.

"God . . . damn." He scowled at her, rubbing his stomach. "What the hell did you do that for?"

"Don't ever call me a stupid bitch again." She dusted the sand off her fist and turned it this way and that.

"Okay. I promise. I won't ever call you that again." He grabbed her by the shoulders. "Now shut up!" And he kissed her hard.

She clung to him, moving her hands over him again and again.

"Sweet Jesus, Lollie." He tore at her clothes.

She tore at his, touching his skin over and over. His hands cupped her face and he shoved her down in the sand, his body covering hers while he gripped her head and thrust his tongue deep into her mouth.

She gripped his wet hair in both hands and pulled his head away. "Love me now, Sam. Please."

He'd ripped her shirt off before she had his shirt over a shoulder. He touched her over and over, until she writhed against his hand.

"Please."

He undid his pants, shoving them down and kneeling between her legs all in one swift motion. He entered her, long, slow, and hard.

He groaned, then muttered, "A hot . . . hot heaven." He gripped her thighs and pulled her up against him. Then he slipped his arm behind her lower back, holding her up over his splayed knees while he moved in grinding circles against her, inside her. "Come with me, sweet." His free hand held her head so their kiss was unbroken. His hips never once broke the beat, over and over, even when she throbbed around him for the third time. Then suddenly he moved faster, deeper, wrapped his arms around her, and gripped her buttocks.

"Sweet Jesus!" He thrust hard and fell back in the sand with her atop him.

She had no idea how long they lay there, how long it took to still their breathing. She sighed and rubbed her cheek against his chest. "I love you, Sam."

He didn't say anything, so she crossed her arms on his chest and rested her chin in them, watching him.

A few long moments later he lifted his head and looked at her.

She grinned.

"All right." He dropped his head back down on the sand and yelled, "I love you, dammit!" He reached out again and pulled her head up toward his for a kiss.

She put her hands on his chest and shoved back away from his mouth. "Why?"

"What the hell do you mean, why?"

"Why do you love me?"

"Because God has a sense of humor." And his mouth closed over hers.

28

One week later, and over two weeks late, they rode into Santa Cruz in the back of a chicken wagon. Two days after going over the falls, they had made their way to an interior road and run into Jim Cassidy and the other guerrillas. Lollie had been reunited with Medusa, much to her delight and Sam's displeasure.

Jim filled them in on all that had happened in the last two weeks, and it had been a lot. Aguinaldo and Bonifacio had come to an agreement and had combined their insurrectionist forces. The Spanish had destroyed two more rural towns and managed to strain their relations with the U.S. even further. Two days after Sam and Lollie had left the camp, the revolution had begun, starting in interior towns and spreading outward toward Cavite and Manila. The guerrilla base was now Santa Cruz, the largest interior city in the northern provinces, and Lollie's father was believed to be there still, meeting with the rebel commanders.

The cart rambled over the cobbled street on the outskirts of the town. Chickens cackled and squawked, and Medusa joined in. She'd been mimicking them for the last four days. Lollie plucked a feather from Sam's head and smiled. He looked like an Indian, with chicken feathers sticking out of his eye-patch string.

"If I ever see another bird . . . another feather . . . hear one more squawk . . ." Sam muttered after watching Medusa carry on with the caged chickens.

"Now, Sam, if it wasn't for this cart we'd still be on foot."

He gave her his best grumpy look and waved away some floating feathers. He'd grown progressively grouchier the closer they gotten to the town, and for the past hour he'd done nothing but scowl.

She wondered if maybe Sam was upset because he'd missed fighting with the others. It was his life. She contemplated that for a few minutes, then decided that wasn't what was wrong. He hadn't been anxious to leave with Jim.

Picking off an occasional chicken feather, Lollie glanced down at her clothes and wondered what her father would think when he saw her. She was a far cry from the girl who'd worn the pink frills and a cameo and had paced the floor in her room, waiting. Her hair hung in ragged ends despite the combs she'd gotten from the same native woman who'd given her the clothes. Her shirt was a blousy sheer white cotton that was two sizes too big and showed the men's underwear she wore underneath. The skirt was full and long—dragged on the ground, in fact—and it was made of a green and red striped cotton fabric. On her feet she wore flat embroidered slippers, and her toes stuck out of the ragged, tattered ends.

Her face had colored from the sun, and Sam told her she had freckles. She was horrified, immediately picturing her brother Harrison's hounds, with their freckled noses, heads, and backs. Sam had laughed at her and told her he could only see the freckles when he was just a kiss away.

The cart rumbled to a stop in front of a tall adobe building. Sam hopped out and helped her down. He held her for a moment longer than necessary, the released her waist. She stumbled, her legs being asleep from sitting in one position too long. Never breaking eye contact, he asked, "You okay?"

She smiled and nodded, then turned back to the cart. "Medusa!"

Sam muttered something.

The bird hopped down from the chicken cages and perched on her shoulder. Lollie turned to the bird and said, "Now, you behave, and be quiet. We're gonna go meet my daddy."

"Awk! Quiet! Ya bloomin' little pecker!" The bird's voice changed to a distant drawl. "Damn Yankee! Awk! I'm Medusa. I'm a mynah. Sam's an ass."

"Don't you think we should leave that bird somewhere else?" Sam asked. "Like the nearest butcher."

She ignored them both and turned to look at the building. There were five sets of heavy doors. "What one do we go in?"

"He's your daddy. You decide." He crossed his arms and gave her a cold look.

"I know why you're acting like this."

"Like what?"

"As if you'd like to pick a fight with the world."

He grunted.

"You're nervous."

"I've never been nervous a day in my sordid life."

"I know, and you never get jealous, either." She grabbed his arm and pulled him toward the closest doors. They walked inside.

"This can't be my daughter." The tall gray-haired man turned imperiously to the Filipino man who stood at the door holding Medusa and gave him a look that would have fried an egg. The poor man's reaction was to stand stone-still.

"My God," her father went on. "She's dressed like a filthy peasant, her hair looks like a rat's nest, and her skin is almost . . . brown."

333

The Filipino man gave Lollie a look of pity before he left with Medusa, closing the door in his wake.

Her father turned back to her and raked her with a disdainful look. "Thank God your mother isn't alive to see you."

Lollie closed her eyes to block the tears she felt rise. They were tears of shame, of humiliation, of hurt. She wanted a mother and father who loved her and were proud of her. She took a deep breath and looked at the man who was her father, that revered scion of the LaRue family. Her brothers stood behind him, having come to the Philippines after her kidnapping. Now they all were there—the LaRue men. And she stood across from them like a naughty child.

But Sam stood behind her and held her hand. He was there for her. Sam Forester was always there for her, and right now she loved him even more for it. Her father started to pace in front of her, and she gripped Sam's hand a little tighter.

Her father stopped in front of her and looked down. "You've caused enough trouble, something you've been good at since you were small, if your brothers' letters were anything to go by. In the last few weeks, you've kept me waiting hours at that bay and now over two weeks here. Well, girl, what do you have to say for yourself?"

She'd kept *him* waiting? She thought about that for a moment. My God, she thought, I've waited for some sign of acceptance and love from this man for seventeen years. She didn't even realize that she'd clamped a death grip on Sam's hand until he squeezed it—for encouragement. She squeezed it back—in thanks.

A couple of deep breaths and she looked up at her father. "I've kept you waiting?" she said, then repeated it louder and louder until she shouted, "I've kept *you* waiting! You pompous old man!" She could feel her tears rise again and spill this time, but she couldn't help it.

She took another step closer to the man who had conceived her, yet never had given her a lick of his time. "I'll tell you about waiting, Father dear. Waiting isn't a few hours or a few weeks; it's seventeen years. For seventeen years I waited for you to come home, waited for some sign of love from you, my own father. You never came, never had the time, or was it that you never cared to give me the time?"

"Now see here, young woman—"

"No! You see here." She rammed a finger against his chest. "I'm your daughter. I'm Eulalie Grace LaRue, the same girl who spent all those years trying to be what I thought you wanted. A lady. Well, I'm not a lady. I'm a person, with feelings, a mind, and a heart. And I'm a good person, with a lot of love to give someone. Too bad you never came around to find that out, isn't it?"

"Lollie . . . Ladies don't—" Jeffrey warned.

Lollie turned to her eldest brother. "Ladies don't what? Argue? Swear? Talk? Eat? Think? Who made up those stupid rules anyway, Jeffrey? Aren't ladies allowed to be human? Well, if they're not, I'm glad I'm no lady!"

The sound of someone clapping sent the room into silence. It was Sam. Lollie turned and smiled at him. "Thank you."

Sam looked at the men in her family. "She's right. She's no lady; she's a woman."

"Who's that?" Jedidiah asked.

"Sam Forester," she answered, turning back to her father. "And if it wasn't for him I wouldn't be here. A real father would be thankful I was alive. What kind of man are you, anyway? What kind of man abandons his child?"

"I didn't abandon you," he scoffed. "You had your brothers and the servants, who obviously didn't teach you respect."

"Respect is earned."

"And how do *you* earn respect? By running all over the country in rags?" He turned toward her brothers. "Look what you've created. My God—"

"I think you mean *thank* God. At least I know my brothers tried. They cared enough to be there." She waved a hand at her brothers, standing behind her father. "I also know they love me, in their own way, but you—you don't know anything about love. I don't understand you. You have these ideals you live by. You won't take the trolleys in Manila because of the mistreated horses. But what about the daughter you never gave a fig for? You care more about those sick trolley horses than you care about your own flesh and blood. How sad." She stepped back against Sam.

Her father gave her a cold look, icier than her own eyes. "I've always found horses to be of more value than women."

She took a long, deep breath to help control her hurt.

Her father turned his disdain toward Sam. "Who are you?"

Sam assumed that position of nonchalance, the one that he'd used with Colonel Luna. "I'm Forester, from the slums of Chicago."

"You're that American mercenary, the man who kills for a price." Her father looked at him as if being in the same room with Sam was offensive.

Lollie shook with anger. "Why, you aren't even half the man Sam is."

Sam's arm slid around her.

Her father looked pointedly at Sam's arm, then at her. "You whore."

Sam stiffened. "One more comment like that and my price won't matter. I'll tear out your throat."

Her father turned and walked to the door. Her brothers parted as he walked by. He grabbed the door, opened it and turned around. "She's not worth the trouble. Nothing like what I expected. You boys raised this . . . You handle it. I don't have a daughter." He left and closed the door behind him.

"That dirty bastard," Sam muttered, his hand tightening so hard on her shoulders that she flinched. He released her shoulder and rubbed it slightly while he glanced down at her. "Sorry."

She cried then, and Sam pulled her into the haven of his

arms. She cried hard, not out of hurt, not out of loss, but mostly for all those wasted dreams. The time she had spent trying hard to be something special to someone who didn't want her. She cried for the parents she'd never had. She cried for the child she'd been, Eulalie LaRue, who'd never had her questions answered, who never known a parent's love.

She pulled back from Sam's chest. Her brothers were there, looking as they always did when she cried, uncomfortable and helpless. But they loved her. She knew that they loved her and had tried.

Jeffrey rubbed his forehead, something he always did when he had to tell her something unpleasant. "We tried to protect you, Lollie. All those years. He's a hard man."

"He's stone, pitiable stone," she said. "I understand now that you all tried to protect me. I think you tried to protect me from everything."

She turned to Jedidiah, the brother who so reminded her of Sam. "Especially you, Jed. I didn't understand until now why you didn't want me to come to the Philippines. You don't really think I'm a jinx, do you?"

He looked embarrassed and seemed to accept that emotion about as well as Sam did. "No, you're not a jinx," he groused. "Just trouble, and I've got the scars to prove it." Then he actually smiled.

"I'd bet a month's pay he hasn't got an L-shaped scar on his chest," Sam muttered.

She hugged each of them, one by one. When she reached Jeffrey he said, "Come on, little sister, we'll take you home now."

"No! Sam . . ." She turned away from her brother and ran back to Sam just as the little Filipino man opened the door. Medusa flew inside and landed on Lollie's head, like she always did.

Her brothers stood stunned, staring at the bird.

She smiled. "This is Medusa."

"Awk! I'm Medusa! I'm a mynah! Sam's an ass!"

Her brothers laughed.

337

Sam didn't.

"Awk!" Medusa's voice lowered to Sam's timbre. "You taste like whiskey, fine, aged whiskey." Her voice changed again to one that was breathy and female. "Oh . . . Sam."

Lollie's brothers stopped laughing.

"Awk! Come on, sweet. Come now. I want inside you."

There was a ponderous moment of silence, and five sets of Calhoun blue eyes turned from the bird to Sam, then to Lollie, then back to Sam.

Lollie felt Sam stiffen and heard him mutter, "I thought Medusa was asleep."

She looked at her brothers. "Now, Jed . . ."

Jedidiah threw the first punch.

Lollie threw the second.

Wedding bells rang from the Church of the Blessed Virgin the next morning. The curious filed into the adobe church and quietly sat in dark mahogany pews to watch the ceremony. The priest, in gold and white vestments, blessed the union, ignoring the squawking black bird with the dirty mouth, the battered, bruised faces on the bride's brothers, who stood in a human wall around the couple. He ignored the cut lips, the black eyes, the occasional wince. He also turned the other way when the plain gold wedding band wouldn't fit over the bride's bruised and swollen knuckles.

He did his job in the eyes of God, and he blessed the union. The instant the blessing was over the bridegroom, a tall, blacked-haired devil with a sinister patch on one eye and shiner on the other, grabbed the bride and kissed her, and not the length it took to give the Benediction, but as long as the Liturgy, the Apostles Creed, and the Eucharistic Prayer all combined. When the groom pulled away, not a soul inside those thick walls doubted his willingness to wed her.

They walked down the aisle, this motley group that bore all the markings yet none of the actions of a shotgun marriage. The bride and groom were too happy. No one could doubt that. The priest watched them leave and, shaking his head at life's little oddities, turned back to the altar, and suddenly froze.

Deep booming laughter echoed in the rafters of the church. God was laughing.

And God kept on laughing, for over the next ten years he gave Sam and Lollie Forester six little girls, all of them with hair as black as jet and light blue eyes the color of alpine ice. Each little girl had said her first word when she was ten months old and hadn't stopped talking since.

Samantha, the oldest, had her father's strong, square jaw, determined nature, and stamina. She could out-run, out-think, and to her father's secret pride, out-fight any boy in the neighborhood. Anna moved as slow as a Southern drawl, yearned to be a great actress, and always wore pink. Priscilla loved animals and had a menagerie of pets that kept the house in turmoil—two dogs, a cat, a parakeet, four hamsters, three goldfish, sixteen guppies, two turtles, three frogs, and her favorite pet, a twelve-year-old, peanut-eating, snoring mynah bird named Medusa who tattled on her sisters.

Abigail was known for her mild temperament. She needed that sweet nature since not a week went past that she didn't trip, slip, or break something. Most recently, she'd managed to get stuck in the dumb waiter, in between floors. It'd taken Sam a hour to get her out. Jessamine was the little chatterer. She fired questions like a repeating rifle fired bullets, but she'd learned to add numbers this Christmas and she was only four. Sam had taught her to add up the burnt batches of her mother's Christmas cookies.

Last, but certainly not the least, nor the quietest, was Lily, the baby. She was the screamer. All of McLean Virginia knew when Lillian Grace Forester was awake. Her father had been known to swear he had heard her from his office as a government military advisor at the capitol.

But on Christmas night, 1904, it was fairly quiet.

Sam picked up the magazine that lay on his favorite

leather chair and sat down, dropping the magazine onto the table beside him. He leaned back and rolled his stiff shoulders, then locked his hands behind his head and stared at the flickering candles—thirty for every foot—on the huge Christmas tree. He wondered why women, of any age, had to have the biggest tree on the face of the Earth. In fact, the most quiet moment in the last week had been when he'd suggested getting a smaller tree and setting it on table. Six pairs of ice blue eyes had turned and stared at him as if he had just blasphemed.

The giant fir tree stood ten feet tall, anchored in a heavy stone crock he'd filled with sand and water. Lollie had argued with him for fifteen minutes over whether or not the tree was straight. He eyed it for a moment. It still leaned a little too much to the left.

It was decorated with sparkling, three-dimensional paper animals and scenes imported from Germany that his wife called Dresdens. There were striped candy sticks tied with Calhoun pink ribbons, lacy fans, and twinkling blown glass icicles. Hanging in gilded cages were musical birds that sang whenever someone would wind the aggravating little suckers.

Sam patted his pocket. He had the winding key.

Glass fairy-tale figurines and angels hung among the gold and silver crinkled wire and shiny paper cornucopias that he and Lollie had filled with sweets and were now empty. Crowning the tree top was a huge porcelain angel and here and there, among the laden branches of the tree, dangled a burned gingerbread man.

Late last night, locked behind the huge sliding doors of the parlor after they'd laid out the gifts, filled the stockings, and lit the candles, he'd made long hot love to his wife by the light of that tree. Over the years, the kid from Quincy Street had learned to love Christmas.

He looked at Lollie, who sat on the floor playing jacks with their daughters. She hadn't changed much. She'd filled out a little from the births of their children, but only in the chest, which was fine with him. Her whiskey-colored hair puffed out around her head and topped in a lopsided knot that always looked as if the whole thing might tumble down at any minute. It reminded him of bedrooms, crumpled sheets, tousled hair, soft white skin and a husky Southern drawl . . .

Sam moved his gaze to safer territory—Matilda, their housekeeper, or as he liked to refer to her—his Lollie-keeper. She was fifty years old, built as square as his new Pierce Great Arrow touring car, and ran the household with the command of the Kaiser. She sat at the piano, playing Christmas carols while Medusa sang "O Holy Night" off key. Soon the girls stopped playing and joined Matilda by the piano. Lollie got up and came over and sat on the arm of his chair. He slipped his arm around her.

After a few comfortable minutes, he glanced at the table next to his chair, looking for his pipe and hoping that Jessie hadn't put soap in it again. He picked up the magazine but something in it caught his eye. It was the latest issue of *The Ladies Home Journal* and an article illustrated with bows and flowers and other frilly female stuff stared back at him. It was entitled, "The True Spirit of Christmas," and Sam began to read:

Children are God's own angels, sent by Him to brighten our world, and what we do for these messengers from the sky, especially at that time of year which belongs to them, will come back to us threefold, like bread cast upon the waters.

He looked at his family—his bread cast upon the waters. His daughters stood there, all dressed in white linen and lace with Christmas red sashes, singing like a group of motley angels. Samantha had a shiner and Annie had a giant Calhoun pink bow in her hair despite the fact that it clashed with the red on her dress. Prissy had that everpresent cat slung over her shoulder, a hamster in her pocket, and the parakeet on her head; Abby had her finger stuck in a candle-

JILL BARNETT

stick, but managed to yank it out before he could get up, and Jessie was singing louder than Medusa except when she'd interrupt to ask Matilda who invented Christmas carols. Lily was upstairs, sound asleep. She had just turned ten months old and said her first word today. But Sam smiled, anyway. The word had been "Daddy."

He turned his gaze to his beautiful wife, dressed in velvet and lace with her whiskey-colored hair piled on top of her head in a knot that looked as if it was going to tumble down any minute. Her love had given him those children and her harebrained ways had captured his heart. If their children were his angels, then she was his heaven.

A lazy, comfortable smile cut across his jaw.

Sam Forester lived for this.

Dear Reader,

I suppose I can breathe a relieved sigh—weaker than one of Lollie's—because you've finished *Just a Kiss Away*. You've met Sam and Lollie. I hope you had a good time.

Of course, there's always the chance that you're reading the last page first—I do that—and if you are, then I'd better make this compelling so you'll want to read the whole story. But what can I tell you? We're strangers, you and I, who meet only through the pages of a book. Should I tell you about my life? Nope. You'd put the book back, after you woke up.

I'm thinking . . . Can you smell the smoke? Let's see, maybe I should tell you what I want in a book, what's important to me. Well, here goes . . .

I adore the past. Of course, my husband would tell you that I adore the past because I've never done anything on time, and my father would add that my birth was the only time I ever arrived early. With men like that in my life—witty devils—it's little wonder I believe that love and laughter go hand in hand.

But on to romance . . . I want to read about people who do all those screwball things we do when we're in love, characters you can laugh at and with, and who seem so real that you feel someone you know is on the page looking out at you. Add to that a taste of the past, tales rich in the flavor of a bygone era, when people loved hard and fought for what they wanted. A book should make you laugh at the antics of an animal, smell the bite of cinnamon in a hot apple pie, hear the joy in a song of the past, and feel a character's heart ache.

Those are the stories I want to tell. Then maybe you'll open the book and drift into the pages, forget about today and experience the delights of yesterday, and maybe you'll smile; that is . . . if I can just get that next book in on time.

All my best,

Jill Barnett

P.O. Box 785
Pleasanton, CA 94566

The Duchess
Jude Deveraux

Claire Willoughby, a beautiful young American heiress, had been trained her whole life for one thing— to be an English duchess. But when she travels to Scotland to visit her fiance, Harry Montgomery, the duke of McArran, she finds out his family is more than she'd bargained for. Fascinated by his peculiar family, Claire is most intrigued by Trevelyan Montgomery, Harry's mysterious brilliant cousin who she finds living secretly in an unused part of the estate. As she spends more and more time with the magnetic Trevelyan, Claire finds herself drawn to him against her will, yearning to know everything about him. But if Trevelyan's secret is discovered life at Bramley will never be the same.

AVAILABLE IN HARDCOVER FROM POCKET BOOKS